# LOVE SUCKS

Ken Shakin

# Love Sucks

First published 1997 by GMP Publishers Ltd,
P O Box 247, Swaffham, Norfolk PE37 8PA, England



A CIP catalogue record for this book is available
from the British Library

ISBN 0 85449 254 2

Distributed in Europe by Central Books,
99 Wallis Rd, London E9 5LN

Distributed in North America by InBook/LPC Group,
1436 West Randolph, Chicago, IL 60607

Distributed in Australia by Bulldog Books,
P O Box 300, Beaconsfield, NSW 2014

Printed and bound in the EU by The Cromwell Press,
Melksham, Wilts, England

*Life is short; nature is hostile; man is ridiculous.*
– W. Somerset Maugham

# Preface

You hear it said often enough. Times have changed. Well they have and they haven't. Most of these stories take place in the late 80's and early 90's. As the political climate in New York has changed so has the sex scene. Here and there I make note of that. But this book is not meant as a cruising guide. There are enough of them and they're usually out-of-date by the time they make it to the bookstore. So if you happen by some of the haunts mentioned in this book, don't be surprised to find them boarded up or patrolled by those brave men in blue. In which case you'll find the party down the block, picking up where it left off. Trends come and go, but sex and politics in the naked city continue to write the same old story. In New Yawk tawk, that's: "Shit happens." What you hear in trendy conversation these days about sex and drugs and crime and poverty all on the decline only goes to show how truly insensitive and unaware the media generation is. Whatever fashion dictates, human experience continues to follow suit with human needs. Though Mr Right may tell his friends he would never do nasty things like *that,* the nasty continues to happen and any attempts by the powers-that-be to clean it up are just sweeping it under the rug.

My roving eye and ear are such that the material in this volume, as free-range reportage, walks the thin line between journalism and fiction. The perspective is certainly my own. And I can't vouch for the accuracy of hearsay. Of course the names have been changed (to protect the guilty). All except my own. Some of the facts are altered as well. Finally, I think it needs to be said that in writing these accounts my intent was in no way to trivialize the health risks of anonymous sex, drinking or drug abuse. Read this book at your own risk.

# The Anonymous Dog

She doesn't know his name. But she talks to him whenever she sees him in the elevator. Always smiling and friendly. A sweet little hairy man. Wouldn't hurt a fly. The dog is almost bigger than him. A big frisky smooth black muscular dog. My anonymous friend – let's call her Barbie – lives in the same building as the little man and will sometimes run into him and the dog in the elevator on their way out for a walk in Riverside Park. Sometimes she sees him coming back from the park, but late at night and without the dog. Then he often has a big man with him.

He works as a waiter in one of the diners on Broadway. A sweet little man. Ugly in a way, but very friendly. Barbie likes him. She loves the dog. Such a big handsome dog. A huge head, but a tiny clipped tail. And not that she's looking so closely, but you can't help but notice... the dog has an immense schlong. Bobbing up and down as he runs around the elevator like a trapped animal. He *is* a trapped animal. Until the door opens and he lunges out dragging his little master by the leash. A dog like that is meant to run wild, free. Fortunately the building is right off of the river so it's just a dash down the hill into the landscaped wild. It's doggy paradise down there. Dogs of every size, color and shape running for their bones, sniffing each other, biting and licking and whatever else dogs do. And a big dog like that one must tear up the place. Barbie wonders how the little man survives it. He looks like he can't quite handle such a big dog. It could be dangerous.

Sure enough the little man in the elevator has a series of accidents. She sees him once with a broken arm. Another time his face black and blue. She figures he must be having some pretty rough walks with the dog. Then one night at three in the morning he buzzes her from downstairs. In a whisper he tells her that he got mugged and doesn't have his keys. She buzzes him in, wondering how he knew her name. She must have mentioned it. There's a certain paranoia associated with living in New York. He comes up to her apartment and rings the bell. She unlocks her series of locks but leaves the chain hooked because although she can see him through the peephole there might be someone standing next to him out of sight with a gun. I told you, New York is a paranoid place. When she opens the door he's alone, but he's missing his pants and he looks like he got punched in the face. They stole his pants along with his wallet and keys. Can he call the 24-hour locksmith from her phone. Waiting for the locksmith they talk about how dangerous the neighborhood is getting. Picture it. The little man standing there in his underwear in Barbie's kitchen telling her how he was just going for a stroll in the park... Barbie is shocked. She would never! She doesn't even go there during the day. It's dangerous. A woman got raped in Central Park in broad daylight. The little man says he likes breathing the night air off the Hudson.

The next time she sees him in the elevator he's with one of those big black men. Barbie would insist she is not a racist. Some of her best friends are of African or Latino descent. But when she sees a big black man in the elevator – if he's not dressed in a business suit, carrying a brief case, with a *New York Times* tucked under his arm – she gets a little nervous. She's wondering why she keeps seeing the little man with these big black men, and such mean, rough ones. She calls me and I tell her a bit harshly that anyone can see it's perfectly obvious that he's picking them up in the park and paying them to do him. No! Are the big black men half his age? Yes. Well that pretty much says it, but I hate to generalize because you just never know. People are people, and it's idiotic to assume things based on their size, color, shape and clothes. For every black man who might slit your throat there are many more who might save your life. For every little hairy man with bruises on his face who brings home young machos late at night there's a dog who's rough in bed. Let's not jump to conclusions.

The next time she sees him he's with the dog. Full of smiles and compliments. He tells her how much he loves her dress. Where *did* you get that. It's lovely. She's a little shy, suddenly. The attention of men makes Barbie blush. She's a shy girl, even when she's wearing a red silk dress cut short enough that you can see her panties. The dog is in the usual good spirits. Sniffing around. She doesn't mind when he sniffs her crotch. Barbie loves animals and she knows that they don't mean anything by it. It's just their sense of smell.

But the next time she sees the little hairy man he's with a big black man again. The sight startles her because she is just coming out of the elevator on the ground floor as they are coming in. The little man apologizes for startling her and she's reassured for the moment. But she has a bad feeling. She leaves the building and hops into a lurching cab, wondering how people can put themselves in such dangerous positions.

So she phones me. Barbie wants to know – just curious – what exactly goes on in Riverside Park at night. Well not as much as Central Park, but there is quite a little party going on. Along the promenade they walk up and down glancing at each other. The view, as she must know, can be quite spectacular, overlooking the broad depth and length of the great river. Men look out over the sea smoking a cigarette. Or they look straight down to the cove underneath the promenade to see who's down there. Much of the action is in picking up hustlers on the promenade and either taking them home or doing it in the bushes. I have the feeling that the little hairy man prefers to take them home. Really? She seems shocked that such things could go on right under her nose. In *her* building, where she bought *her* co-op. Welcome to the real world, Barbie.

Riverside Park is known especially for its dangerous action. It's a good place to pick up trouble. I'm sure that is exactly what the little man is up to. She listens in silence to what I have to say. But she finds it unbelievable. Why do these men do these things? She seems to have no idea that I am sometimes one of these men, although she knows that I have sex with men. She knows that her friend Ken... is gay. I think she accepts homosexuality like she does black men. As long as they don't look like black men, they're okay. As long as the homos don't actually do it with each other. It's a precarious balance in her mind between tolerance and disgust. In any case she can't at all fathom men doing it in the park. Why would a man risk his life to have sex with another man, a perfect stranger? For the same reason you do, honey. It's just not as easy when you're a little hairy man. She takes offense. She does not seduce men. You don't have to, your body does it for you. Our conversation ends rather abruptly. I often shock her with my candid remarks and just as often she hangs up on me. A long pause. And then bang. The line is dead. I put the phone down, a smirk forming under my nose. I know I'll hear from her again. She always calls back for more.

Six months go by and she calls to say that I was right. One night sirens woke her up. She looked out the window and saw the ambulance. And the bloody mess on the stretcher being hauled away. She could barely recognize him in all that blood. She recognized the dog. Barking away, fearful for his beloved master. Barbie put on her nightgown and went down to see what she could do. She ended up taking the dog back with her to her apartment and kept him there until the little man got out of the hospital. The story is one for a children's book if you could leave out the part about the hustler. Call him the bogeyman. The bogeyman stabbed the nice little man something like ten times, took the money and ran, leaving him for dead. He would certainly have bled to death right there on the floor if not for his faithful companion, man's best friend, who licked his face over and over again until he woke up enough to drag himself to the phone. The dog even got the phone off the table because the little man was too weak to get off the floor.

"Isn't that an incredible story?" she asks. Touching, actually. She thinks I'm being nasty. She hangs up but months later calls back to tell me that the little hairy man finally came home from the hospital and whatta ya know she's seeing him in the elevator again with those big black men. Like nothing ever happened. "Can you believe?"

I can believe.

"You would think after all that he would stay home and play with the dog and never go near that park again."

You would.

They never catch the bogeyman. No name, no description except *big black man.* Just another anonymous black man in a city of anonymous men. Barbie will never understand certain things about bogeymen and men in general, even the ones she dates. The way men are with each other. The things they do, with their penises, with their knives. Why did the black man have to try to kill him when he could have just taken the money? Barbie wants to know. Maybe he's had a really shitty life. She admits to me that she's afraid of men. They can be awfully aggressive. And unpredictable. You can't tell just by looking at them what they might do in certain circumstances. Or what they might be up to in their private lives. This sweet little man doing such unlikely things. She thought she knew him, in a way. Always so friendly in the elevator. It just goes to show that you never really know someone unless you really know them. The little guy is as much a stranger to her as the big black men are to him. Not quite anonymous, but then again, after all that she still doesn't know the man's name. She did find out the dog's name though, when he stayed with her, because it was written on his name tag. *Blacky.*

# Mr. Right

In the city of millions there are a million different possibilities for everything. A million different ways to survive. A million different hairdos. A million life stories. A million desires. Certainly every person is different. Every fingerprint unique. Every face one of a kind. But as soon as you start lumping them together it comes down to a few basic choices.

Eliot is your average Gay White Male. An ad in the personals would read: "GWM 28 5'10" 155 brown hair brown eyes. Into movies, restaurants, cycling and working out. Average guy. Looking for same." How many would fit that description. Yet how difficult it can be to make a match.

Eliot enjoys many things in his average GWM life. But all of them are held in place by one singular reason for being – his search for Mr Right. Plenty of compromising along the way, but in the back of his mind there is a one and only waiting for him, somewhere over the rainbow, in a bar or a backroom. Or in a shoe store.

Eliot goes shopping. He has a sick day coming to him and decides to take the day off, use the opportunity to avoid the weekend crowds and look for a new pair of shoes, which he really needs. No quick venture in a city housing untold millions of shoes. Eliot tells himself he's not going to make a big deal out of it. Shouldn't be too difficult to find one suitable pair. The day starts out relaxed enough. He wakes up late and has a slow breakfast. The coffee gets him gabbing so he wastes no time in picking up the phone and calling yours truly to fill me in on everything that happened to him the previous day from sleep to sleep in minute detail, especially the dirty parts. An hour later he hangs up feeling energized, ready for his shopping adventure. Another day. Another million possibilities. Let's make it easy. Just pick up something quick, right here in the neighborhood.

There are certainly plenty of shoes in the stores on the Upper West Side. But which one is right for Eliot? Walking down Columbus Avenue in the cool sunlight of the afternoon he knows instinctively that there is nothing there for him. Some of those stores are just for show. You go in, the staff looks the other way. You look around. All left shoes so you don't steal anything. All in small sizes. When you ask the salesman if he has bigger sizes he pulls on his earring, sucks his teeth and tells you in a way that suggests it's difficult for him to form words: "Whatever's on the shelf." Bitch.

Eliot goes from store to store, shoe to shoe. Always something wrong. This one too wide, this one too narrow. The buckle is all wrong. The heel too high. Maybe I should get a boot. Too cloney. Beige gets dirty. Black too S&M. Who needs a steel toe? Way too heavy. My poor feet. How about wearing sneakers? The ones that are made to look like shoes. Too suburban. He works himself into such a dither that running across the street he trips on his shoelaces and skids on the pavement. A car swerves around him. He picks himself up. No blood, but bad scrapes. Fucking shoes! The laces are fucked. The shoes are shit. I have the money to buy ten new pairs. Why can't I buy one?

In one of the chicest stores on the block Eliot finds himself out of place among the fabulous and the fabulous shoes. As they walk through the door somewhere in the continuum fabulous words are floating around: "Ready for my close-up, Mr DeMille." It's not a shoe store. It's the Museum of Modern Shoes. He stands there gawking at the shoes on display like they're gonna start dancing, thinking these shoes are too...? Too too. That's right. Nice shoes but too... too eccentric. No, not eccentric. Too too. Too fabulous for words. I want shoes. Just plain old black shoes. But special in a way. And just the right proportions. Can't be too long and pointy. They have to look butch. Not Euro-faggy.

But the next thing he knows he's cabbing it to 5th Avenue. One Italian shoe store after another. Eliot clops along in his broken old shoes thinking if he doesn't get a new pair today he'll jump off the Brooklyn Bridge. He's been putting this off for months. Today is the day. Just pick one.

But all the shoes on 5th Avenue look too conservative or chic or a combination. For the wealthy businessman. Blah! I hate this part of town, he tells the traffic light. For all those snooty people who think they are so fabulous just for being New Yorkers. Too many French restaurants. Well la di da. A bunch of tacky lawyers from New Jersey pretending they're oh so European. He jumps out into the street, the traffic flying by. Hand in the air. TAXI!

It's a short ride west. Maybe he can find what he wants in the department stores. The cabdriver looks like a terrorist, head dress and all. He drives that thing like they're in a holy war. Eliot grabs on to the seat for dear life. At each light the brakes slam the car to a halt. The man seems hostile. Speechless. When they stop in front of Macy's Eliot puts the money in the slot in the bullet-proof divider. The man smiles and says in the peepiest voice: "Tankyou sir."

Herald Square is scary. A few million people seem to be coming and going from Macy's, or crossing the street to A&S. Eliot dreads the thought of a department store. Too many people. Too many distractions on the way to getting what you want. On the way to the escalator he finds himself browsing through ties and choked by perfume. How do these women work here every day? Their lungs must smell real nice. It takes a while to find the shoe department. Too many floors with too many departments. Clothes, furniture, electronics. Anything and everything that a person could spend money on. The shoe department is spread out, full of people browsing, over-worked salesmen. And the same shoes as everywhere else. Fuck.

He walks back out into the madness. The streets are lined with stores selling everything and more than the department stores. More of everything and more exacting in their specialty. Computers. Food. Or just software. Just chocolate. Videos. Leather. Pens. Are there enough people to buy all of it? Too much of everything, but always coming down to a few basic choices. So many shoes in this city but where's the right one for Eliot?

When in doubt try Bloomingdale's. The cabdriver gets stuck in cross-street traffic. A weird New York guy who likes to talk. About nothing. "You know what da problem wit dis city is? I'll tell ya what da problem wit dis city is. Too many people. Ya see what um sayin'? You got ya native New Yawkas like me," taking his hands off the wheel to count on his grubby fingers. "Ya got all kinds. Ya got ya Irish, Italians, Jews, an' whateva. Then ya got ya nigs and spics. Too many a dem, if ya know what I mean. But now you got all a dese fuckin' people from all ova da fuckin' world comin' to New Yawk cause it's so shitty wheah deah comin' from. Asians, Africans, da Arab mothafuckas blowin' up buildin's. You see what um sayin'? It's like crazy. You know what I think? I'll tell ya what I think. Send em all back weah dey come from. Ya know why? I'll tell ya why..." The man is still talking after Eliot slams the door. Hate needs no audience. It screams out unheard in the roar of the city. Loving souls trampled by the machine until they start screaming too. The frenzy sucks you up and spits you out like an unstoppable tornado. And all you can do is run.

If almost calm when he started out his shopping day, by now Eliot is dashing through the crowds bumping into people right and left. The great escape. But there's nowhere to hide in Bloomingdale's. Through the revolving door. Past the perfume cloud. Those sweet ladies spraying the air. Up the escalator. Too far. Down the escalator.

Same shoes as Macy's. A little more expensive. On his way out he spends half an hour nervously browsing through a stack of men's shirts on sale. All funny colors or patterns. But the price is right. But who cares. They're ugly. I don't want them. What am I doing here? I don't need shirts. I came here to get shoes!

He has to take a deep breath to calm down enough to decide where to go next. He runs out into the street. A man with no legs wheels by on a skateboard. Eliot tries to concentrate. Okay, so it's true. There are only so many styles made and basically all the stores carry the same stuff. I have to choose. But wait. What about the Village. That's where the funky stuff is. Maybe I can find something not too funky, but not too conservative.

The cabdriver on the way downtown is an impeccably dressed black man, a silent type doing his job as impeccably as he can, driving with such ease and care that it's impressive. The cab itself is impeccably perfect, fresh off the showroom floor. Does he own the car? Because it feels like you're sitting in his living room. Neater than neat. The upholstery red corduroy. Soft soul music on. A white Virgin Mary hanging from the rear-view mirror, watching over the driver. Eliot relaxes for the moment. But then there's traffic and soon they're not moving. Two drag queens walk by weaving through the cars. The driver mutters: "Fucking faggots. Get AIDS and die." Eliot puts the money in the slot, throws open the door and runs from the temple of love.

The subway isn't that bad. At least there's no traffic. The crowd squeezes into the train, but it won't last long. Only a few stops. Except then the train stops just before 14th Street. For no apparent reason. The smell of body odor is extreme. Someone's sweaty arm is pressing against Eliot's sweaty arm. The lights go out. Dim emergency lighting remains. The door between the cars opens. A man with one crutch pushes his way in, stops right next to Eliot and the sweaty arm and starts blowing on a soprano saxophone. The lights go on. Eliot can see that the man has one eye and scabs all over his face. But the crutch is a con. The man is standing fine without it. And who needs crutches with a face like that. "Please help the homeless. God bless you. Please help the homeless. God bless you..." The man makes a path through the crowd with his crutch. He spits out the words fast and without conviction. No one gives him a dime. Some kids start laughing. The train finally moves and when the doors open the crowd literally pours out.

Eighth Street is one long row of shoe stores all selling the same shoes. He walks east through the crowds, in and out of each shop until he gets to Broadway. Onward down through the increasing crowds, in and out of every other store, the further he goes the more stores he skips. When he reaches Chinatown he realizes that most of the stores are closing. The shopping day is over. His feet ache. He looks down at his old shoes. If there's one thing you need in a place like this, it's a good pair of walking shoes. He tries to imagine looking at shoes again tomorrow. But where would he look? He's been to just about every store in the city and they all have the same stuff.

A homeless man walks by barefoot, his feet a dirty mess of sores and cuts. The point rings true. Eliot realizes how silly he's been acting. Go into the nearest store and buy any fucking shoe within reason. If nothing else you'll have something to wear until you find something better. You can't wear these old shit things for one more step. You can drop them in the garbage on the way out of the store and make some homeless guy's day.

So he marches into the nearest shop which happens to be an Army Navy Store. He picks the second shoe he sees, a standard police issue. Black and shiny. It's cheap enough he could buy two and throw them out the next day. He feels relieved to have come to some decision. He feels light-headed with the decision. I'm a relaxed person, he seems to be saying. I just pick any old thing and buy it.

They don't have it in his size. His eyes fall back into his head. He's going to faint. But then she suggests that maybe the display model is his size. He can buy that one if they can find the other shoe. He looks up. Prayerful. The Virgin answers his prayers. They don't fit perfectly, but he's thrilled to have bought anything at all, his blood literally pumped from the success. If he could barely walk before, now he struts out of the store with conviction in spite of the ache in his toes where the hard leather bends and jabs his foot. She warned him it would take a little while to work in. The shoes or his feet? One of them has to give. Fuck it. He's alive and well and living in the city of endless possibilities. At the nearest garbage he drops his old shoes feeling like a new man.

Time for a drink. 2-4-1 with the afterwork special. It's been a long hard day's work. Shopping *is* work. On his way to the bars he can't help but look at his new shoes. They're a bit cloddy. But that's the style. He feels cute. Like wearing daddy's shoes. He can't help but notice everyone else's shoes. How true that there are only these certain styles of shoes and as soon as someone walks by you see their shoes and you immediately think: Oh, those. Because you've seen those very shoes in the stores. Then maybe you look at the person and the shoes sort of go with the personality or with what you can tell by a moment's glance and that seems to say it all. Eliot notices a homeless man rummaging through the garbage, finding what looks like an old shoe and dumping it in favor of half a cheese sandwich. Further down the street old shoes are on display on the sidewalk along with old clothing, old magazines, and a broken toaster. Who buys this shit? But there they are, a crowd of browsers staring at the garbage. Like they're in Tiffany's.

At one point he has to decide whether to go east or west. What am I in the mood for? The East Side bars, or the West Side bars. This one or that one. He decides to start with the West. The East is a later scene. Walking back along 8th Street he looks in each window to spot his new shoes to see if he got the best price. At one point he walks into a pole with such force that he almost falls over. He recovers, feeling stupid, and walks on.

He stands in the video bar with lights flashing and music thumping all around him, men cruising or chatting with friends and all he can think about is his shoes. He bumps into a friend he used to know and they strike up a limp conversation. About this and that and how it's all too this and too that. When the conversation becomes too jaded for words they join in with a little group Eliot doesn't know. Their conversation is giddy, but just as jaded and dull. Everyone trying to be so funny. Screaming over the music. Eliot wants to leave, but he's too lazy to make the effort. He finds himself studying shoes. Everyone's shoes. The one has such nice cowboy boots. Maybe he should buy cowboy boots. They don't look very comfortable.

Tired as he is he doesn't go home. Drink leads to drink. Bar leads to bar. Hours later he's standing in the basement of a haunt that should have gone out of business a decade ago but just won't quit, wondering why he ever comes here. The atmosphere is comical. Leftovers from the 70's. Something cruisy about the place though. Some butch guys, mostly black and Puerto Rican. A guy with a shaved head cruises him. Too weird. Another guy, dark with a hairy chest. Too hairy. A very handsome black guy asks him if he wants to dance. "I don't dance." The guy walks away. He realizes his voice sounded too arrogant. He didn't mean it. But really he can't dance. No point in making a fool out of yourself. A Chinese guy asks him if he wants to get it on. He doesn't even respond. A fat guy winks at him. He's beginning to feel like there are only so many kinds of guys out there. You have a choice, but only from this or that. If you closed your eyes and imagined the man of your dreams an image would come to you, but of someone who doesn't exist. You can only get hints of it. In the end you have to settle for one or the other or stay alone. Maybe this is why he hasn't had many boyfriends in spite of the fact that it's clear that he is much admired. He's not full of himself, but he feels like no one is quite good enough for him. Good enough for his fantasy. The Chinese guy returns to tell him that he's not Chinese, he's Vietnamese and that there are 70 million people in Vietnam and that someday the world will be Asian. So now do you want to get it on?

Hours later and he's still standing. In yet another bar, back in the East Village. More of the same, but dressed sloppy. Again he finds himself looking at their shoes. From bar to bar, a slice of pizza in between, he searches for the right one. Not to settle down with forever, just someone to get it on with for the night. He ends up in a backroom. The DJ is playing house and disco. For Eliot at this point the beat is a lullaby. He actually falls asleep standing. Standing in his new shoes waiting for Mr Right to come along. On and on the beat goes on all night long, this song and that song running into each other all sounding the same. A Plutonian would hear no difference between disco and a march. Same four beats. Can you tell the difference between Chinese and Japanese music?

Eliot at the end of the night. It's so late it's early. They mill around breathing the stale air looking from one to another for the right one or at least an acceptable one. All the styles and sizes are there. Each has a look you swear you've seen before. Some types you would do it with, others you wouldn't. The lighting is bad enough that you never really know. You can't see the details. Only the look. Eliot opens his eyes one more time, straining to see what he wants to see. Along comes the average-looking guy. Mr Medium. Medium height, medium weight. Short hair, not too short. Young, not too young. Jeans, teeshirt, leather jacket. GWM 5'10"155. And he's wearing Eliot's shoes. The same police issue that's walking all over Manhattan. Your kind of guy. He looks at you. You look at his shoes. The next thing you know you're rubbing cocks. You even kiss. So it's not love. Not the one and only Mr Right. But there is something passionate there. You grab his cock. It feels nice and strong. Thick. He grabs yours. You feel one with him. You look down and you can't help looking at the two pairs of shoes pointing at each other, almost identical, yours new and his already worn in. So it took an awfully long time to meet him and you can barely stand up anymore and after all that it will all be over in a few minutes. But it was worth it, because when you come he comes and you both feel like for that moment you belong to each other. It doesn't matter whether he's the right one. He fits. Well enough that you hardly notice and you don't even mind when he comes on your brand new shoes.

## The Hole

At a cocktail party recently I had a long conversation with a New York businessman of the usual type, the anonymous man in suit and tie. It has been said that in New York people will tell you the most intimate details of their life within five minutes of meeting you and will then five minutes later walk by like they don't know you. This man told me the most salacious things when I swear I think we never exchanged names. I enjoyed our conversation, though he did most of the talking, bragging about this and that. His business, his money, his house, and his penis. I'm a good listener. I let people make fools of themselves. And who of us isn't a fool underneath all the lame attempts to put ourselves off as fabulous worldly sophisticated all-knowing but not conceited beings. My grandmother used to say: "If you don't open your mouth nobody will know how stupid you are." She was a woman of few words herself.

I usually don't drink champagne when I'm drinking heavily because I find that even the best bubbly gives me the worst hangover before I get a chance to sleep it off. I must have had something like a dozen glasses of decidedly mediocre stuff during the course of my conversation with this man so that halfway through I was already getting a headache. The main thrust of his monologue was himself and at a certain point it focused on one small part of his rather large body, his giant cock. It soon dominated the conversation. Somewhere during the first few glasses he informed me with some pride that it's a good foot long, no exaggeration. "When guys say they got nine inches it's usually an exaggeration," he says with precision. "Go around with a tape measure and you'll see that the male anatomy is largely overrated."

One way to find out.

"In fact any mortician will tell you that as a general rule six inches is big, depending on where you're measuring from. My twelve inches is for real. I don't want to sound conceited or anything... but it's not easy having a piece like that."

Don't hate me because I'm hung? I look at the man. He is quite tall and big all around. Not fat, but not tight either. I look at his hands, his feet. His shoes are enormous. His hands remind me of those Picassos where the fingers look like clutzy stubs. I decide that his thing must be a giant clutzy stub. Long and incredibly wide.

"It's thick too," he says, reading my mind.

Is that a problem?

"In a way it is. I mean I don't want to sound conceited or anything... but my dick is a source of fascination to a lot of people."

Men? Women? Dwarfs? Since when is it a problem to have an awesome penis?

"It *is* a problem. Just because they're in awe of it doesn't mean they can satisfy it. As a general rule, women don't appreciate my dick. It's a fallacy of men's imaginations that women want a big one. You try to fuck them with it and they scream that you're hurting them. You try to stick it in their mouth but they really don't know how to suck. You push it down their throats and they gag."

I swallow the last of my drink. Perfect timing. The waiter goes by with a tray and I grab two more. For myself.

"The truth is, men suck cock like they really know what they're doing. They love to suck. And it shows. You shove it down their throats and they can't get enough. You pull it out and they stick their tongue out begging for more. Just like dogs."

Ruff ruff.

"I guess the problem is I like to fuck," he says.

Is that a problem?

"I mean really fuck. Only the pros can take what I got. A few full-blooded women. But nobody can take it, and I mean take it up the ass, like a gay man who's really into it. Hard to find. Believe it or not a lot of gay guys, even screaming queens, do not get fucked. Maybe they dream about it, I don't know. But when it comes down to it they can't take it. Especially when it's a foot long."

Maybe you need to go easy on them at first. Sort of work it in slowly.

"Well in any case, there's still the problem of sight unseen. It's one thing if their butt is smooth and fleshy but when it's hard and hairy I can't look at it."

Don't look.

"You gotta look to stick it in. And then the image sticks. I can't get it out of my head."

Hm. I grab a shrimp cocktail off a passing tray. It looks kind of strange in the bright red sauce. I eat it anyway, to soak up some of the alcohol. The piano player is mindlessly playing *My Way*. In the thick of a room full of conversations we must look like we're talking about the stock market.

"I'm not saying I don't get some satisfaction. It's just not as much as I want it. It's not easy to find the right hole. First, a hole that I find presentable. Then a hole that can take what I got. And not to mention, a hole that doesn't insist that I use a rubber."

You don't use a condom?

"I know that sounds like some kind of sin these days. But from my perspective I'm not doing anything wrong. I'm not risking my own health because everyone knows, in spite of what they say, that you can't get it from giving it. And furthermore the ones who take it are safe with me because... I've been tested and I know for a fact that I don't have HIV."

Not yet.

"It just doesn't feel good to put one of those things on. They never fit."

Extra extra large?

"Forget it. The rubber ruins it for me. I refuse. If they want it, they have to take it like it is."

That seems to say it all. Take it or leave it. I grab an hors d'oeuvre off a passing tray. I look at it to see what it is. One of those tiny hot dogs stuck in a bready hole. I have a new understanding about why they call them *pigs in blankets*. I munch away on the sleeping hog trying not to think about what it is I'm really sticking in my mouth. It certainly tastes good. And isn't that the main thing? I look at the man. Big man, big ego. Big dick, small brain. He's still talking about his big dick with occasional references to the holes he sticks it in. I have to ask. Where do you find these holes?

"To tell you the truth, I've discovered that the best way to get what I want is to go to the public men's room. That's right, you probably had no idea that sex goes on in those places."

Really????

"That's right. You'd be amazed how much sex goes on in men's rooms all over the country. I do a lot of traveling on business. You know, some of these toilets are even – how can I put it – *equipped* for it. They have holes in the partitions. You can stick your dick in the holes. And believe it or not, the guy in the next stall sucks your dick. Even sticks it up his ass. And for me it's great because I don't have to see the person. I can let my imagination run wild. And nine times out of ten when I stick it in the hole there's some anxious hole on the other side raring to go, ready to please, and more than able to satisfy."

You mean you've just now discovered the glory hole?

"Is that what they call them? I wouldn't know. I'm not gay."

## Men at Play

On my way to the park I step over a construction site. The sign proudly warns: MEN AT WORK. Where? Where? I look around. There they are, big beefy smelly men whistling at a young woman dressed impeccably in New York drop-dead style. Short skirt, high heels. Skeletal body in loose fitting tight clothes. And a tight face under three inches of makeup. The men are impressed. Enough to scream after her: "Hey baby, you know you want it." She doesn't so much as flinch. Her heels pound the concrete of Columbus Avenue. Her walk suggests that the only way she would give them what they claim she wants is if they bludgeoned her. Their tone suggests that they would if they were drunk enough.

I seek relief from the ever-increasing population swarming around the avenues. I will hold my breath until I am safely surrounded by greenery. I can see down the grid to Central Park, an oasis that draws from all sides. After work on a nice fall day, they come from all directions to get their bit of relief only to create more traffic. They come on foot, on rollerskates, on bicycles and skateboards. They run or speed-walk, rollerskate with baby in stroller, or cross-country ski with doggy on a leash. Some, like me, just stroll. Alone.

I pass the Dakota and John Lennon's ghost and cross the corner of 72nd Street looking too many ways because there are so many ways to get run over. The pedestrians plow through the vehicles, a wave in an ocean. They don't have the right of way, but they have the power, fragile as it is. In New York you just have to be bitchy enough and you'll get your way. Maybe. I stroll down through the frantic pedestrian traffic in Strawberry Fields, past the memorial. Imagine all the people giving peace a chance. A few dead roses mark the spot where peace and hope are remembered as dead ideals. I almost get run over by a rollerblader but I make it down the hill, dashing across the main loop through the runners and cyclers to near safety at the edge of the pond. Walking by the stagnant water I know that I will breathe a sigh of relief as soon as I make it to my destination.

Night is already descending on the park as I head for the little footbridge which leads to the area commonly but mistakenly known as the *Rambles.* In fact there has only ever been one Ramble. New *Yawkas* have a way of adding s's where they will. To go with the funny vowels and flavored consonants. Sheep Meadow is often called Sheep's Meadow. If you hang out in the *shtreets* enough you might hear the word *mens,* without the apostrophe. Anyways, the extra s suits the Ramble, this part of the park so appropriately named. A maze of rambling paths and vegetation. A last refuge from the madness, shared by a melting pot of obsessed birdwatchers and obsessed men lurking, waiting for sex. A place where at least when the light goes and the people go with it, there is a sense of peace. The birdwatchers go home and the men come out to play. With the fear of prowling the darkest parts of the park comes the tranquillity of a place where only certain men would dare to visit. The later it gets, the more ominous and the more tranquil. It's a compromise. But in a city where one can rarely claim to be fifty feet away from the next being, the peace of this refuge is worth the risk. The serenity and the mystery are undeniable. As I cross the little footbridge I am overwhelmed by the reflection of the skyline on the dark still waters. The city looms in the close distance. Glass and steel mountains beyond the valley. You can hear the roar echoing around the park. Otherwise you're safe, in a way, alone with your anonymous fantasy in the company of anonymous men.

They don't exactly come for the fresh air, but that's not to say that they don't delight in the soft breezes and green smells, the quiet rustling of leaves. Sometimes mistaken for scampering rats. In the darkness rats blend in with squirrels, as do the bushes with the men. A paradise of illusion. Central Park in the dark. Landscaped for the nature yearnings of cityslickers. And who would want to see the details when the illusion is so alluring. The men come to indulge their senses. The relief from noise and commotion allows for the release of inhibitions. The darkness is their cover. Where else can they find their dark earthy fantasies? Manly obsessions of strength, submission, domination, and yes, love, incredible as that may seem. Hate too. All to be found somewhere in the shadows. If you can find it.

As I enter the maze of paths I begin to see the sentries. Anonymous men posted here and there military style. They position themselves in relation to each other so that they can get in on whatever starts happening. It seems prescribed, but it's not. The order is based on a strict code, unspoken but understood. I take my place among four men who have captured a small hill. They wait in numb silence for one to make the first move, like soldiers in a hopeless battle. Finally one exits behind a bush and I follow. Up further to the next hill, a high point in the rambling rambles. I get a panorama view but I can't see much close at hand. I almost trip and fall on my face stepping over a downed tree. When I walk by the dark figure I can see that the guy is jerking himself off. I join in. He's no matinee idol. A nondescript young man. Real, and that's the main thing. Flesh and blood, and semen. I jerk him off in a matter of minutes, content to just watch. For now. When he comes it shoots out straight in front of him. No need to run to the bathroom. He lets out a pagan cry. I have the feeling this orgasm was building for a long time. A minute later without a single word spoken I'm walking down the hill just as the others are climbing up to get in on what they missed. The rule of cruising the park if not of cruising in general is whatever you do, get it while it's hot. If you wait a moment it may be gone before you can make your move.

I light up a joint. I often bring a beer with me. Sometimes there is even music. Then the Ramble is turned into an open-air bar. A gay bar, but more manly and more diverse. Men of all types, all ages, all tastes and preferences, all races and nationalities congregating out of common desire. Call it need, obsession, or fetish. Call it what you like. Either way they come and wander, meander and walk in circles. They stop and linger behind a tree, penis in hand. Or they stand still and smoke in the calm and let the mind do the wandering. Getting high I think I see a naked man in a thicket of bushes. His body is far from beautiful. He bends over. His asshole an exhibit for the passerby, the two white mounds shining in the moonlight. He moans in expectation. He can almost feel it. The touch of a hand on his skin. The penetration into his body. Pierce me, his asshole says to the night. I'm yours. Take me. Fill me, great phallic god. Open me up so I can be free at last.

But no one stops to take advantage of the opportunity. I walk on, quickening my pace to get away from what I don't want to see. I look up at the dark shapes of the treetops against the black blue sky. I pee on the side of the road. No need to find a private spot. The night protects us here in this foreboding place. We need safety from the bustle of people. We risk our lives for that.

Just then from the other side of the Ramble a red light swirls around above the trees. I hear cars. Not the usual distant ones from the surrounding city. These sound awfully close. I zip up my pants.

The next thing I know the cars are coming towards me. The lights are shining in my face. I stand on the side of the road. It's the police. Little three-wheeled vehicles patrolling the Ramble. I heard about this. Since the Republican mayor got in office security in the park has been beefed up. The good Catholic sending patrols into the infamous gay cruising ground. They approach me from the safety of their vehicles. The lights shining in my face seem to be saying: Go home. Run. Hide. I wonder whether they're trying to scare me away or protect me. This is Central Park after all. Either way I feel like a criminal.

I decide to check out the small peninsula which forms a dead end jutting out into the pond. There's no road there for the police. It's the most dense cruising spot and maybe I'll find some action there. As I approach I can see the self-appointed sentries. Homeboys guarding their turf. I feel safer with them around than with the police. I breathe the cool moisture in the air. I walk along the water's edge. It's the long way but definitely the scenic route. Midtown looms in the distance under a full moon. The air is fresh with the smell of autumn. The trees give off a seductive smell, their sap almost ready to be raped. The pond is as still as a toilet. A strayed row boat stuck in the mud and slime. The water must be green, but in the cover of night, everything – the water, the trees, the air – takes on a mysterious hue, dark and rich and infinite in depth. As I walk along in this dream all around me the rats scurry. I know they're there. I can hear them. Must be thousands. Millions. Every once in a while one big fat one, big as a rabbit, flies across the path right in front of me daring me to stop him. Rats, our long lost cousins, living the good life. Playing their own horny games. Scrounging for food, trying their damnedest to survive in the jungle. Better at it than we. Perhaps one day our heirs. Imagine the great megalopolis as ghost town with rats crawling over the jewels to get at the garbage.

I continue my quest. Walking the gauntlet. More sentries at each junction along the path. Others nestle in the thick of it, waiting to be spotted. The brush used to be thicker but they cut a lot of it down in the 80's. It's still private enough, or not, depending on what you're into. As I walk down the main path I look into the darkness of the little paths that serve as arteries leading to the water's edge. I peek around, but stay on the main path. Each time an anonymous man comes from the other direction we strain to see each other in the darkness. I stop for a moment to watch the procession. And out of nowhere the music comes. A string quartet playing, of all things, *Here Comes The Bride.* At first I think I'm imagining this. It's the dope and my evil humor conspiring against me. Then I realize where it's coming from. Across the water is the Boathouse Cafe. A wedding in progress, a religious ceremony, catered, with no idea of what's going on only a few steps away (if you could walk on water). And here come the brides. Anonymous ladies-in-waiting. Big brawny ones with smelly dicks looking for some hot action on their wedding night.

I walk on, smiling, curious that no one else seems to be catching the unintentional satire. They're all serious as hell about their cruising. At the tip of the peninsula an orgy is in progress. A few cocksuckers kneeling in the middle of six or seven guys. Others wanking on the outskirts of the circle. And from the distance more, yours truly among them, stand and watch. This is some kind of sport. A team sport where anyone can join. No rules, but no confrontation. Some sort of perfect anarchy that works out of an unwritten code of conduct. If you don't want someone to touch you, you can simply move on to the next. No problems with date rape here.

Then I here the cars coming. And when I turn around I see the red lights. A helicopter flies over, but I'm sure it has nothing to do with the police patrol. Just a coincidence. But all together it creates a feeling of siege. We are under attack. I stand there ready for the confrontation. I'm an old 70's radical. In spirit, anyway. I *like* the confrontation. Come and tell me that I can't stand there in the park and whip my dick out. Tell me there's a fucking law against that!

My comrades are not as brave. Maybe it's a generational thing. And maybe the foreigners know from experience that you do not stand up to police. I stick my ground but the rest of them, I swear almost every last one of them, scurry off like rats. The sentries run like rabbits. The orgy ends abruptly. Flies pulled up as hardons are painfully stuffed away. They all run off leaving one lone cocksucker on his knees, his tongue still hanging out. I walk back along the path in the direction of the swirling red lights, head on, facing my enemy. As the lights approach the men lingering along the path scurry off down the little paths to the water's edge. I hold my ground. We're trapped here. Might as well stand and fight.

As I march onward I realize that the little cars are still too big to make it down the path. They wait at the entrance while, believe it or not, cops with flashlights do the leg work and continue down the path. They pass me shining the flashlight in my face. I'm not intimidated. I let out a pig snort and tell him to get that fucking thing out of my face. The cop stops. Looks at me. I have the feeling that if I were black he'd beat me up and then arrest me for resisting arrest. He's pissed though. "The park is closing. Ya betta get outa heah." I'm still not intimidated. I ask him if he's going to arrest me for playing with my peepee? Now he's really pissed. "If I catch anyone doin' anything um takin' them in." He goes on his way in search of sexual criminals. A female cop follows him. I tell her she needs more makeup. She tries to ignore me. She walks down one of the little paths shining her flashlight into the thick of it like she's looking for something. I follow in pursuit of her. Did you lose your dildo, honey? I call after her, but get no response. She's only doing her job. Right?

At the entrance to the peninsula the patrols are parked. I brave the white lights shining directly into my face. The party's over. Men are coming out of the bushes spilling out into the paths that lead out of the park. I know they'll linger for a few hours. There's always somewhere to hide. I walk by the patrol. A fat cop sits behind the wheel. I tell him he'll never get laid sitting in there. He tries to ignore me but I can see in his flinch that his first reaction was to hit me over the head with his billy club. He controls himself, and grunts. This was not an assignment he wanted.

I walk and walk. There's plenty of cruising going on everywhere. Just like when they try to kick the homeless out of one street, they inevitably end up on another. If I dashed into the bushes the rats would run but there are plenty of places for them to hide. I walk by the wooden gazebo towards the west side. A few homeless guys are spending the night. A small fire in the hibachi. Hot dogs on the grill. There must be a law against having a barbecue in the park. There are certainly laws about living in the park. Like the laws about having sex in the park, difficult to enforce.

On my way out a bush calls to me. "Hey." The voice is hushed. No thanks. I'm going home. I walk on through those rambling rambles until I get to the bridge. I'm ready to leave this naked utopia and venture back into the real world when from under the bridge I hear slurpy love sounds. On second thought, maybe I'll stay a while. I try to peer over. I can't see much, so I walk around the bridge down to the water's edge. Two men kissing. Just kissing, but maybe with cocks out, clutched in the shadows. The moonlight cuts through their kiss. An absurdly romantic scene.

I walk on. I decide to leave them to their private fantasy, under the bridge, hidden from the city. I'll let them break the law in peace.

# Center Stage

Murray called the other day. "You remember Andy. He's coming to town."

Roll out the red carpet. I remember Andy. A big handsome blonde guy from out West. Back in the 70's he came to New York to become a star. Andy and Murray met at some workshop and became roommates in a horrible crappy apartment on Houston Street. Half the windows boarded up. Roaches crawling out of the shower head. The usual misery that goes into the making of a star. To make a long story short, Andy didn't last very long in showbiz. He got real, studied some computer thing early on in the computer revolution and got a well-paying job back West. It was meant to be. Big, handsome, and blond as he is, there are so many wannabes of that description you could fill a showroom on every block. Never mind all the big, handsome browns (who dye their hair blond in a last attempt at stardom). To say nothing for the short, ugly ones too. And isn't that the irony of it all. Sometimes, it's the short ugly ones who get the careers. Because they want it so bad. And they stick with it. Murray, who is short, fat and bald would simply not quit. He kept up his quest for stardom, stayed in the city in that same old crappy apartment, where he still lives, and eked out a career in showbiz. Which it is, in a way. Murray "does" puppets. Professionally. I guess that makes him a puppeteer, but he's in the actor's union. Though most of his work is off the books. Entertaining rich little East Side brats at their extravagant birthday parties. A career in showbiz. Murray takes it in stride. He's full of snappy anecdotes. Like the time the kids, five-year olds, didn't like the show and made the most of the evening by ripping apart the puppets. The lady of the house didn't want to pay for the damages. She told Murray that the kids were just expressing themselves. And let's face it, when on stage – especially center stage – one must be prepared for the tomatoes as well as the applause. That's... showbiz.

Murray is a vivacious character. In expectation of Andy's arrival he's practically foaming at the mouth. I think he was always a bit sweet on the guy. I wouldn't be surprised if he made a few attempts at seduction back when they were roomies. I never heard about it if he did. That's the funny thing about Murray. He's a real big talker. A nonstop gossip. A filthy vulgar little man. But about himself, he's actually quite reserved. He'll tell you the most intimate details of people's lives, people you hardly know, like they were characters in a novel. Or soap opera stars. But never does he mention his own personal sufferings. He'll tell you about his puppets, even when they're torn to shreds, but he won't confess his own aches and pains. Not even a bad headache. The show must go on. Most curious of all, the man will tell you about everyone's sex life but his own, as though he were still a virgin. He'll give you blow-by-blow details of what everyone did at the sex club with the subtle omission of himself from the picture. Just into the voyeurism? Just along for the ride?

The scoop on Andy, broadcast before he even got off the plane, was that he'd been living all this time in suburban bliss. The job, the house, and the husband. They even raised dogs. The whole thing as corny as can be. Until... the husband died. No, not of AIDS. Bone cancer did him in. A painful, merciless death. Andy almost died from the mental torment of having to watch. Such is life, like the stage. Unpredictable. Thrilling at its best. Horrible at its worst. Oh well. The body laid to rest. Peace, finally. Andy was recovering from it all, relieved, but thoroughly saddened. Getting home from work each day there is nothing to do but walk around from room to room through a whole house full of memories. Or sit on the couch, alone, and cry through a sitcom. Dinner alone. Breakfast alone. And in between, the lonely sleep. No one to talk to, to hold and touch, or just to have there with you. He certainly lived alone before marriage, but that was long ago. Now the change was a shock. Friends told him to go take a vacation. See the world. Meet new people. Not to marry. Just go play around. And where better to see the world and play around than the biggest amusement park on the planet. Fun City, USA. The sleaziest place on earth. Sometimes called the biggest toilet in the world. That city of broken dreams that keeps them coming no matter what. And coming back for more.

Andy sees the skyline looming in his dreams. But he's not just dreaming about sexual adventures. Midlife is coming on and Andy thinks about returning to the stage. A comeback. Yeah, he's gonna take that trip to New York. Check out the theater scene. Visit his roomie from way back when, good ole Murray. See how life is for the working actor. Take a trip down memory lane. How about spending a week in the same apartment you lived in a decade ago. The same bed, because Murray has kept it there on the wall across from his own as a sort of shrine, a leftover from the days when he couldn't afford the whole dump for himself. Murray has come a long way, hasn't he. Andy's bed is now the sofa/guest bed. Well they won't be spending much time in bed, anyway. They'll be out and about all day and night. Murray is, as usual, "between gigs." And Andy has plenty of money to blow. Murray wastes no time in planning an itinerary of shopping by day, and night life all through the night into the next morning. Restaurants. Plenty of shows. All the ones he's been dying to see but couldn't afford. Oh, and there are bawdy plans. A tour of the latest sex haunts will fill up the latenight slots. Things have changed since the late 70's in that world. Andy was never the one for it. But times have changed for Andy, too. He's no spring chicken anymore. And what better after a decade of marriage than some refreshing anonymous sleaze.

Murray gives me a daily account. Andy sleeps late each day in the week, I suppose from the nonstop activity. But Murray is up with the birds, seeming not to sleep at all. He's a ball of energy. A short fat ball that talks. From the privacy of the bathroom he tells me about each meaningless item they buy, each succulent morsel they eat. A synopsis of each show and an indepth critique of the performances, the music, the book, the lyrics, the sets and costumes. It saves me the trouble of seeing the tacky shit for myself. I'm not one for the theater scene. At least not that Broadway shtick. It's all so shticky. Or shtickish, as I've actually heard said. Kitsch nonsense overstated. Each line delivered like the gospel according to Ethel Merman. Broadway, for my tastes, sums up everything that is fabulously offensive about this city and its inhabitants. If you can make it here you can make it anywhere. For that they truly think they are the most worldy people on earth. And even if you don't agree, you will soon enough because they're gonna shove it down your throat. With bigger-than-life smiles plastered on their faces. The sheer aggression of their shtick is the main point. Ethel Merman, as the story goes, pushed her way through the chorus line and belted it out in that taxihorn voice of hers. There was no stopping her. She was the one for the part. And she got it. And if she hadn't she would have done what so many do when they don't get the part: sing on the street. Manhattan, a small island inhabited by too many singers. They sing walking down the street. It's easy. You wait till someone passes by, which doesn't take very long. Then open your mouth, and sing. Preferably as loud as you can to be heard above the din of taxihorns and singers.

Okay, it's a matter of taste. If Murray and Andy can't get enough of song and dance and endless shtickiness, I can accept that. What I find difficult to imagine is Andy getting into it. He always seemed to me to be such a reserved midwestern type. Murray fills me in on the latest in Andy's complex psyche. The classic New Yawka, Murray has an opinion on everything and a detailed psychoanalysis of everyone. From the toilet seat, he relates Andy's fear of intimacy. "He's uptight. Shy. Very very shy. The boy's gotta loosen up. Faw his own good."

I wonder how a guy like Andy ever thought about going on stage himself. You have to have something of the performer – talent, ego, or balls. Or you have to be just really crass and insensitive like Murray to get up in front of an audience, even just a roomful of precocious toddlers, and let it out. Perform.

"He misses the stage. You can see it in his face when he watches them performing on stage."

With Murray watching him watch them the whole time. How annoying.

"Those beautiful blue eyes get all glowy when the curtain comes up. It's what ya call a vye-carious experience." Two words. The first pronounced like the bread. "At the enda the show he gets all teary-eyed. Can't stop applauding. But just as soon as the house lights come up he crawls right back inta himself and he's a mummy. So uptight. The boy's gotta loosen up. It's not healthy ta be like that. Ya know, they say a lotta these cancers come from bein' uptight. You can even fight them by loosening up."

Murray Freud. Keep him away from my deathbed. The last thing I want when I'm screaming in pain is to have someone tell me that it's all about attitude.

Murray feels for the guy. He wants to bring him out of his shell. Over dinner they have long talks about Andy's problems, the death of his lover, his midlife crisis, his lost youth and missed career in show-biz. Ludicrous as it sounds Andy wonders if he could pick up where he left off. Murray says, sure. Why the fuck not. There are always character roles. Coming from the biggest character of them all that should be taken as a compliment. Andy barely notices Murray's lunacy. His gaze is focused on a spot far off in the rainbow, somewhere over the Jersey shore. In dinner theater. Just a dream. The long-awaited comeback. An actor is always an actor. He's nothing without his stage.

When Andy gets tired of dreaming and reminiscing and listening to Murray analyze him, they both join in to analyze the shows they saw. Every detail and nuance criticized. The themes. The interplay of characters. The tension. Murray repeats some of this nonsense to me. "I really felt the tension," he tells me regarding a play they saw. "Skillful. Drama at its finest. Riveting. Absolutely riveting. A terse weave of all the elements." Whatever the hell that means. I skillfully move the conversation back to Andy's sexual tension. Murray sighs. "I try to bring him out of his shell. We even visited the sex shops and bought a few grownup toys for the child. But you wouldn't believe what a time I'm having getting him to go cruisin'. He won't go to the sex clubs. All night we spend in these stupid clone bars. He fits right in, but ya know how it is. Even when yaw big and beautiful, and he's as hunky as ever, hasn't changed a bit, in fact bigger and manlier than he usta be. Even when yaw all that, ya could stand around those clone bars until the ceiling caves in and no one will even brush by ya. They're all so uptight!"

The week goes by. More of the same. A nonstop shuttle from stores to restaurants to theaters to bars. They take it all in from sushi to hot dogs, the opera and the drag reviews. They barhop the singalong haunts. Andy gets teary-eyed singing full voice in a room full of singing strangers, all men belting out women-against-the-world torch songs. Murray watches him from the side thinking this boy needs a stage. And he needs some dick. But no time to dwell. They're off to the next singalong. And the next. And a poetry reading. And dinner at an African place where you sit on the floor and eat with your hands. They check out the comedy clubs. Cheer up. Life's so seriously ridiculous it's not worth crying over. They even check out some avant-garde theater downtown. My favorite avant-garde theater story. Talk about seriously ridiculous. It's some play about... well it's hard to say what it's about but it got good reviews. A man walks out on a stage with nothing but a chain hanging from the ceiling. He starts climbing up. No song and dance. No jokes. No bigger-than-life smiles. No music. No words even. No costumes. No sets, except the chain. To add to the excitement, the night Murray and Andy see it something unexpected happens. The chain breaks. The man falls to the stage, center stage, where he lies on his back writhing and screaming in agony. The audience is held to their seats. I suppose by the tension. A vye-carious experience. Until another man comes walking out and says, there's been an accident. You'll all have to leave. Murray tells me that they really weren't sure if it had been an accident or just part of the play until the man came out and told them to leave and even then they weren't quite sure. Drama at its finest. Riveting. Absolutely riveting.

By the end of the week Andy has seen it all but not seen quite enough because out-of-the-blue he suggests that Murray take him to some sex club. Murray is in shock, though he knew in his heart, New Yawka that he is, that if he just kept at it, he'd get what he wanted. To show Andy the wild side and bring him out of his shell. Andy even admits to having tried his hand at anonymous sex once or twice in the past. There's plenty of cruising going on in nowheresville. Just a bit more low-key. The problem he has with anonymous sex is he hates, really hates, when people watch. He hates to be watched, to be stared at, even when they just walk by. He hates to have people watch him with lust in their eyes. I can't imagine what he's doing with Murray. He must like it in some way. There I go, now. Ken Freud. But after all, he wanted to be an actor. Had his moment on the stage. How do you get up on stage if you can't bare to be watched? Strange. But there it is. He tells Murray that it makes him uncomfortable to be in the big city, much as he's having a great time, because the people are always checking you out, rudely staring at you until you stare back and they look the other way. Since he won't look back, they just keep staring and he feels positively followed around by eyes. Murray tells him he's paranoid. He's been living out there in nowheresville too long. He's... uptight. What he needs is to loosen up. Get some dick action. Anonymous fucking. No games. No stand and model. The only S&M is when they pull out the whips. And don't worry about who's watching. No one cares. No one gives a shit. It's too dark down there in those dungeons to see anything anyway. It'll be just you and the one you love.

The doors open early, but no one gets there till late. The ticket man sits in his booth. Another night of the longest running show on Broadway. An extended run for the never-ending revival. For Andy it's opening night. An actor must treat every night like opening night if he is to perform with full gusto. The cast has the jitters. They're milling around nervously when Murray and Andy creep down into the basement. There's a platform. A stage. But no one has hopped up there yet. The audience has a watchful eye on the empty stage. There are chairs along the walls but few sit. All anyone can do at this point is pace. And pace.

Murray is talking away. He recognizes half the men and fills in Andy on their sexual tendencies and their hangups. "That one in the corner likes to get slapped. I see her every Saturday night and by the time they're ringing the church bells Sunday morning she's gettin' good and slapped. Her tushy gets so hot you could fry an egg on it."

I can picture Andy edging away. But Murray is unstoppable. The show must go on.

"Don't be like that. Yaw uptight. Loosen up. Look at that queen over theah. Now she's loose. She's so loose she needs a bra. I seen her on all fours too many times. Sagging around like an old cow. Too old and too tired to be milked. Put her to pasture already. She's so loose the shit's slippin' out. Oh look, it's Cookie. I know her. We did dinner theater together. *Guys and Dolls* in South Jersey." Murray runs over to chat with this man named Cookie. I've met him a few times. A black muscle man with the most incredible pectorals. Nothing loose there. Muscle breasts. Another one of those. He dances and sings pretty well but hasn't quite reached stardom. Far from it. I fear he'll do dinner theater until he drops. Right into someone's salad bowl.

By the time Murray chases Cookie away Andy is not to be found. Lost in some dark corner somewhere. Murray calls out: "Oh, Andy? Yoohoo. Where are you honey? Maybe he's in the toilet." Murray goes upstairs, runs into Cookie again. They talk. Cookie, I imagine, figured it wasn't going to be his night for anonymity. Not with Murray around. Might as well enjoy the show. The two frustrated actors talk about this and that. The theater scene (Murray has seen them all in one week) and the scene in the basement. Cookie, it turns out, has the hots for Murray's "farm boy." He's no farm boy, honey. More like another frustrated actor. Murray supplies the life story. They both agree that the dear boy is uptight. He needs to loosen up. Maybe he should take some movement classes. Bio-energetics did wonders for Cookie's pent-up anger. Murray is at a loss. What to do with that boy. He's so uptight. He needs to loosen up. And where *did* he disappear to. They decide to go have a look around and find him. Maybe Cookie can get through to him.

When they get downstairs, to their surprise and delight, they find Andy back on stage where he belongs, performing for admiring fans. On the little platform he's getting fucked up the ass by a man who is actually quite homely, the face of a snail, the body skinny and strangely proportioned but with a dick the size of a baseball bat. There are always parts for them. Character roles. The man is fucking Andy with abandon, pushing that enormous thing all the way in and pulling it all the way out, this while the rest of them watch. Andy's worst nightmare and there ain't a goddam thing he can do about it. A crowd has formed. The audience is brazen enough to actually pull the chairs up to the stage and gather around for the performance. It's a tour de force worth the admission price. Both performers are giving it their all, losing all inhibitions to the demands of the script. Andy looks stunning. And the homely guy with the baseball bat was made for the part. The lighting is subtly done. Not too bright, not too dark. And the sets – a bit too minimalist but the script and the performers are good enough to carry the show. Drama at its finest. Tragedy, in a way, if you judge by the serious, painful expressions on their faces. The tension is riveting. Absolutely riveting. To sum up: a terse weave of all the elements. No songs needed. Just a little background thumping to lend rhythm to the drama. The audience is held, gripped by the intensity of conflict. The fucker and fuckee tied together in a bond of love and hate. At the climax the tension explodes, right there on the stage. Andy comes in buckets and lets out a heaving groan. Murray and Cookie and the rest groan a little too. What you call a vye-carious experience. At that point there is only one thing left to do. When it's good, it's good, and it deserves a triumphant round of applause. So the whole room of dreary monsters put their hands together and clap, clap, clap.

Andy is not amused. He's feeling pretty ridiculous standing there on stage with his dick dripping on the front row, bent over with that baseball bat being precariously yanked out of his asshole. He crawls back into his shell, pulls up his pants, without wiping, and hisses at the unwanted audience.

A drunken heckler in the front row hisses right back and says: "You loved it, bitch."

Andy in a post-orgasm rage says what many performers would sometimes like to say out of their ambivalence towards their fans and their own part in the dialogue between performer and audience. He says it gritting his teeth. It's from the gut. He means it. "I hate you. I hate you all, you disgusting pigs."

They boo. And that, my friends, ends once and for all any dreams this one frustrated actor had of really going back on stage. For the hasbeen that never was, a comeback was not to be.

↘↖↗↙

## Love Sucks

Young and impetuous: "It does. It sucks."

Old and patient: "In what way? Be more specific."

"It sucks. That's the only way to say it. Love sucks."

The boy is at that age where everything sucks except what needs to get sucked. The man subtly patronizes him, mostly just listening to the endless list of things that suck. Here and there he asks a pointed question. The man is much older. I'd say he's old, except he's in surprisingly good shape for his age. A calm distinguished gentleman who must be in his sixties? But with a full head of white hair and a denim shirt and cowboy boots he looks actually quite cool. Hot. He puffs on a long pipe and exudes his confidence by not even once trying to put the boy in his place. I would like to slap the little bugger, the ungrateful brat who thinks that everything sucks but takes for granted that he's being served in style an overpriced hamburger cooked by immigrants who couldn't afford the rent in the corner of the basement where they cooked it. Not that he should be grateful. But it's just rather annoying to listen to him put everything down when he seems to be living a decidedly upscale, posh Manhattan life. The clothes say it all. The Charivari baseball cap. The boy will soon enough be a man, but I wish in the meantime he would shutup about it. I'm sitting at the next table trying to decide which burger to order, trying to tune out their conversation. But I can't.

"This burger sucks."

"What about it don't you like?"

Really. This is too much. I study the grandiloquent menu feeling like the burgers are from Charivari too. La Burger in fifty flavors. The waiter comes over. He stands before me with the most incredibly bored expression on his face and says with a smile: "Hi, I'm Frederick. I'll be your waiter this evening. Would you like something from the bar?"

Yeah. The bartender. I order a coke. I'm trying not to drink. Today. For the whole day since the morning. They say it's good for the liver to give it a day off now and then. Frederick slides away and I continue to stare at the menu pretending to read it.

"It sucks."

I can only wonder at the origin of such an idiom.

"It sucks."

One more time.

"It sucks."

What? The burger? It's all-beef. Sounds harmless enough. I can only wonder at the origin of what I'm about to stick in my mouth.

"I don't know why it sucks."

Neither do I. I can't listen to this anymore.

"It just does. Cause like when I see these fags in the bars – "

Now I'm listening.

" – like when I see these guys like acting like girls um like: God, I don't ever want to be like that."

Give yourself time, honey. Soon enough you'll be standing around the piano, drunk, lip-syncing *Somewhere Over The Rainbow*.

"They're all so queeny."

The man pulls out his pipe and nods in a gesture of warm understanding. Maybe he's a professor who takes an interest in the personal lives of his students. Maybe he's a shrink. He talks like one. "Are they *all* so queeny? Aren't there any that you like?"

The boy pushes his burger around the plate with his fork, resting his mopey head on the other hand. "Yeah, well there's always like a few guys who I think are like cute."

"So then they aren't *all* so queeny."

"No, I guess not."

The man is impressive. He must be a shrink. Dr Gay. Specializing in victims of coming out.

"Do you talk to the guys you find cute?"

The boy lets out a heavy sigh. "No."

"Why not?"

"Because. It sucks."

Oh shit. There we go again. I'm ready to butt in and tell the little brat what really sucks when the waiter comes back with the coke. "Will you be ready to order now?"

What kind of a question is that? I look at Frederick thinking that if the boy hangs out in those bars for twenty years he'll turn into this. If niceness could kill they'd make this guy commander-in-chief. I know, he's had a shitty life. The job makes him talk that way. The boy won't turn into him because the boy has a bank account with an annual interest more than Frederick will earn till the day he dies. I stare back at the menu. A complete list of the day's slaughter. We all draw the line somewhere. Even the most kindhearted allow for some savagery. Save the whale. Save the mink. But you never hear, save the cow.

Frederick clears his throat.

Oh, gimme a cheeseburger.

"The *jumbo au gratin*?"

Yeah. With fries.

"Pommes frites?"

Yeah. With a bottle of ketchup.

"We only serve our own homemade *catsup*."

You say tomato, I say who gives a fuck.

"Would you like it mild, medium, or... hot?"

Hot.

"Thank you for your order."

Don't mention it. He takes that gay face off to the kitchen. Life's a bitch. Me, him, and everyone who works for it and pays for it. I hate to say it, but it rings true. It sucks.

"It like sucks."

More than plain old sucks.

"You can't talk to anyone in the bars cause like it's not cool to just like go up to some guy and say hi. I mean like that would like really suck."

Your turn, doctor. Talk your way out of that one. The world can be an awfully obnoxious place. Especially this city. It's not easy for a baby gay out there. Trying to play it cool. Trying to be manly and not show his emotions and then walk up to his man fantasy and tell him he wants to suck him off without actually saying it. Go ahead, give him your words of wisdom.

"Have you *tried* just saying hi?" When in doubt, ask a question.

"No."

"Well if you did, you might meet some nice guys, make some friends." Or he might get his first taste of rejection and reality when his man fantasy sucks his teeth and sashays away.

"Yeah but the guys who are like real guys, not fags... they're like totally unapproachable. Everybody wants them. And like no one goes up to them."

"They must be lonely if no one talks to them."

The catsup arrives with pomp and circumstance. "Would you like to try our homemade Cajun relish as well?"

No, just some mayo, honey.

"It sucks. I mean like I even went to one of those like sex parties with a friend. I mean like I wasn't gonna go there alone. And like it was like really weird. It like sucked. In the front it was just as sucky as the bars with like all these guys standing around and then like in the back where it was like so dark you couldn't see anything they were all like..."

Yes?

"...like I dunno. It was like in some vampire movie. With these like sucking noises everywhere."

Sex parties suck too. My burger arrives without fanfare, but heads turn. What a burger. I've never seen a burger like that. And I must admit the service is quick. I thank Frederick warmly. He apologizes. "I'm sorry but we don't seem to have any mayonnaise. I could bring you the *creamy chunky blue cheese dressing*. I'm pretty sure they make it with mayonnaise."

That's all right. The burger's cheesy enough. I'll cream on it myself. I would. It's such a magnificent burger it's turning me on.

"It sucks. I don't wanna like grow up to be a gay vampire."

"Then don't." Said with conviction from an attractive, masculine but not macho, sensitive heterosexual man.

"But like some of my friends, they were like cool until they like started sleeping around, and then like suddenly they're like acting like sex monsters. Like they need more and more flesh to survive. Or blood, like some kind of gay vampires. It sucks."

I toss a wad of red sauce on that monstrous burger, stick my face in it and suck. Yum. I feel like a monster. A hungry, thirsty vampire. I'm not that much older than the boy, but already I'm his worst nightmare. The one he's afraid of turning into. The one who finally corners him in the sex party and gives him his first suck turning him then forever into a sucker himself.

"It sucks. I wish I was straight."

Now we're getting somewhere. The good doctor smiles knowingly. "You think it's easier for straight people?"

Nothing like yet another question to confuse the patient into finally getting cured against his will. Nothing like experience to make the boy grow up. He doesn't answer the question except to say once more that it sucks. Love sucks and so everything sucks. Poor baby gay. The point is he has no experience in anything but the frustration of young lust to know anything about anything. But the older wiser man does.

"Look at me and your mother. I thought we were a perfect couple. Everybody did. Then I met the most wonderful man in the world and look at us. We're a perfect gay couple. That doesn't change the fact that your mother is a wonderful woman. But people change. Their desires change. It's an ongoing process as you discover yourself. It doesn't end with puberty or marriage or old age. And there are many frustrations along the way. Too many. That's life. And love. It sucks. But it doesn't suck. It depends how you look at it. In any case... it's all we have."

↘↖↗↙

## Alone Together

Another old song about being together, alone. The correct order. A romantic picture. But then there's the other side of the coin.

He stands by himself. Alone in a room full of men. Still among the many walking around in circles. Standing in the dark with his pants down. Wanger in hand. Whackin' off in the breeze of a fan blowing smoke and sweat in his face. A lame attempt at clearing the air. There he is in this den of iniquity known the world over as the backroom. Dirty, dingy, stinking. For the anonymous man, nothing makes him happier than standing there in the muck breathing the shit in the air. You can keep your pricey hi-tech clubs. A dark smelly room is all he needs.

It's amazing how one can get used to just about anything. As long as there's a good reason for getting used to it. One makes the best out of a bad situation. Prison must certainly be pretty horrible. I have no firsthand knowledge of it. But a friend who had that misfortune told me that once you're in, and you stop trying to fight it, you get accustomed to it. You make good use of the gym. Or you read a lot. In solitary confinement you think a lot. Standing in the dark muck of the darkest muckiest backroom in New York the anonymous man does a lot of thinking. He thinks about how shitty it is. He thinks about how horny he is in it. He thinks about how he likes the grossness of it. Rather, he's grown to like it. To the point where he loves it. Can't live without it. It turns him on. The smell of men. The smell of smoke and sweat and cum and dirt. Yes. Grime is a turnon. He can remember how the first time he went to a backroom he found it disgusting. He still does. Disgusting but hot. And he can remember how as a child he was the neatest, cleanest little boy on the block. Endlessly made fun of because he looked like mommy's best boy. The shirt buttoned up to the top. The hair combed neatly. Clean teeth because oral hygiene is so important. Clean hands and clean thoughts. That's the main thing. Make mommy proud. Stand tall in church and sing praise to poor dead Jesus wilting on his cross because you love him because he loves you because you're good and clean and the fact that he's naked and bloody is beside the point. Nobody sees that because their thoughts are too clean. About virginity and wholesomeness. He can remember believing all of it, and cherishing his cleanliness like his mother's love.

Until he started growing up before her very eyes and suddenly all he wanted to do was get dirty. Really dirty. Suck dick. Eat ass. Have his face shoved into a toilet. Drink piss. Lick dirty shit-stinking boots. Suddenly mommy's best boy who always washed behind the ears and held in farts until his ears turned red became a man and in the process was transformed into a human chair. Sit on my mouth. Please. All are welcome. My face seats five.

The anonymous man sighs. He really does some of his best thinking in these places. Pensive recollections to bring him up-to-date. His mother. His boyfriend. His time away from them. The neat, the clean, and the dirt in between. Analyzing where he fits into it. Who am I in this world created around me? Free association, just standing there with his pants down, getting into the common vibe of men being dirty. Being themselves. With no mommy and no boyfriend to see what they're up to. He often waits for a while like that before getting into the heat of it, just thinking about this and that, enjoying the ambience. When he first came to these places he found himself playing the same bar games of hard-to-get and tag. This childish following each other around. The sheer monotony of all these men walking around in circles is enough to drive you crazy. It may explain some of the irrational behavior. You follow him. He follows you. You start getting it on. He stops in the middle. Then he's getting it on with someone else so you think: Okay he wasn't into me. But the next thing you know he wants you to join. Then you do. And then he pulls up his pants again and leaves. Or the ones who only suck or who only get sucked or the ones who don't like to be kissed. There are even ones who don't like to be touched. They can only do the touching. Every sort of human idiosyncracy is brought out in the silent maneuverings of the backroom. After years of it he finally learned not to take any of it personally. He also learned not to chase after anyone. Ever. And that the best way to get off was to do just that. Don't wait for the right one to come along. Just do it, like the commercial says. With the whole room if you want. No one is watching. No one cares. The more the merrier. Hotter too. All the dicks and assholes you want. And all the dirty smelly cummy shitty grime this side of a toilet bowl.

There he is, out for the night, late enough on Saturday night that it's Sunday morning. There he is in his church of sleaze, with his pants down, staff in hand. Hiding in the darkness. Unseen. Not waiting for anybody or anything. Just happily enjoying the feeling that he's among friends. Maybe not friends, exactly. But among his people. Fellow believers. In the great melting pot most people stick to their own. They have their neighborhoods, their ghettos, and they have their meeting points where they come from all over to share in common interests. To assert their identity in the familiarity of their tribe. So maybe he doesn't know anyone's name. He never even talks to anyone. He doesn't know anything about them. He can barely see them. But he knows them. Because he knows that like him they have come to share in this sordid realm. To become one in the muck, away from the gaze of loved ones. To share bodily fluids in silence with only groans as mother tongue. To be loved anonymously. The spirit is the main thing. No talking. No lights. Just the music of sex. Alone together they hide in the warmth of their shadows.

He's off to the side. Quietly minding his own business. You can't see much anyhow. This place is the darkest dingiest of them all. Come out, come out, wherever you are. In the darkest corner of the darkest spot the epicenter is created. That's where they all end up in a mad free-for-all. A hellish huddle where anonymity reaches new heights. Nameless body parts instead of people. Not for the fainthearted. He often finds himself down on the floor, squatting, kneeling, sniffing and licking like a dog, getting it, giving it, bathing in it, a happy pig wallowing in the mud. Right now it's still too early. Too much milling around. Looks like the zombies in *Night of the Living Dead*. Soon enough they'll get tired of wandering and someone will get it going in the corner and one by one the rest will join in until they all come piling on top of each other like mad dogs. That's when he gets on his knees and crawls under their legs, through their crotches into the hot and crusty nook.

His mind wanders. He realizes he's hungry. In a few hours, breakfast. Maybe he'll pick up some bagels on his way home. His boyfriend will just be getting up. They'll have a nice breakfast. Strong coffee. Bagels. Cream cheese. The *Times*, with all its lurid stories. Their own sleaze will be left unsaid. No need for confession. All is known in heaven-on-earth, but so little of it spoken. The two of them will sit down together, alone in their clean room, smiling like the happy couple that they are and have remained all these years. As wholesome as two little altar boys. Keeping the dirty stuff outside of the apartment. Their sacred home. Where they live cleanly together, no matter how dirty the lonely world is outside the door. When he walks in after a night of fucking like a dog he has his sweet little puppy to kiss and hold and cuddle, to be with, as one, together alone. Just as soon as he deposits those shitty boots in the hall, strips and tosses all the dirty clothes in the hamper and thoroughly showers and scrubs his defiled body, every crevice down to the last pore.

So goes the life of the anonymous couple. And everything goes along just like that old song meant it to be. Except that now and then they are pulled apart. By fights. Or maybe the fights are just the excuse. An argument erupts and suddenly they're alone again. Together, but distinctly alone.

The fights are always the same. About nothing. Or the dirt. Clean as their small paradise is, the dirt is always there. Hiding. It's an ongoing battle with entropy. Dust and roaches will have their way. An endless supply from the master load of humans and insects. As we all know, Mommy Dearest is not mad at you – she's mad at the dirt. But when she gets mad – at the dirt – look out!

This morning they have their strong coffee and bagels and cream cheese and sections of *New York Times* and round it all off with a good spat. It starts slowly. Quietly. I think we really should be doing the laundry one of these days.

We just did the laundry.

We did the whites and lights, but not the darks and dark darks.

Just throw them all in one load.

Did you have a nice time, last night?

Nice is not the word. But yes, I had some fun.

Well that's nice. Because I had an exhausting evening.

Uh-oh. Here it comes. Calm as the eye of a storm, Mommy Dearest pulls out the white glove. Look at that dust. No one vacuums. The toilet's a mess. The sills and sashes haven't been done in god knows how long.

Fresh from the muck of a backroom, feeling more than clean from his shower and scrub, sitting in the middle of the cleanest room outside a Holiday Inn, the anonymous man listens with a tense smirk, watching the grains of dust in the light, thinking his boyfriend should live in a vacuum. I vacuumed just the other day. You scrubbed the toilet yesterday. The sills and sashes are probably rather dusty, but then what do you expect? The weather's been nice. We leave the windows open. We live in Soot City. It's in the air. If you don't like it, then close the windows. Turn on the air-conditioner.

Mommy Dearest knows better. Vacuuming has to be done at least every other day anyway. Toilets every day. And is it too much to ask to do the sills and sashes once a week?

How about the sills one week, and the sashes the next.

There you go. When you know you're wrong you make a joke out of it. Idiot.

Maybe I'm an idiot but you're insane. I feel like I'm living with my mother sometimes. The place is fucking cleaner than the rooms at the Holiday Inn. It's antiseptic around here. What a relief it is to go cruising. Seems like the only time I don't have to wipe my feet before walking in a room.

Since when are the rooms at the Holiday Inn clean?

Maybe you should consider getting a job there with the cleaning staff. Tidy up the Holiday Inn.

Maybe you should consider staying home one night and helping around here with the cleaning instead of slutting around.

I don't slut around.

Well whatever you call pulling down your pants and spreading your fat asshole for a roomful of men –

I don't spread my asshole (a lie).

Okay, so you eat asshole.

I don't eat asshole (another lie).

Well whatever you do in those shitholes it's filthy and disgusting.

Well maybe if you weren't so busy cleaning the sills and sashes and once in a while spread your asshole I might just stay home.

I haven't cleaned the sills and sashes in weeks!

Pause. Silence. Then comes the punch line.

It's not just that I do all the cleaning around here. It's that I feel alone in it. Like you don't care if we live in a shithole. I'm all alone in keeping our home in order. You don't take an interest in it when it's something we both share.

Because it's something that matters to you. It doesn't matter to me. I like a dirty toilet (he certainly does).

We have nothing in common anymore, if we ever did. You don't care about what matters to me – keeping a home, shopping, and decorating – and I don't care what matters to you – having boring intellectual discussions with those fat-assed friends of yours. Okay, I understand we have our differences. But can't we at least be a team when it comes to keeping the toilet clean since we both use the fucking thing?

I told you once and I'll tell you again: It doesn't matter to me. I like a dirty toilet. And anyway, you're the one who leaves piles of shit everywhere.

That's not shit. That's important stuff. Papers, clothes, and memorabilia. I'm organizing it.

Well maybe you're clean, but you're fucking sloppy. I'm at least neat.

You're neat alright. Just like your valium-popping mom. You're fucking obsessive. Who the hell folds their socks?

Well who the fuck changes their underwear twice a day?

You're a pig. You're fat and disgusting and I... I hate you!

Clean storms out of the room leaving Neat to fold and refold the cumbersome sections of the *New York Times*. Clean vs Neat. Who's the better man? Clean wins by sheer stubborness. With breakfast over by default, Mommy Dearest pulls out the vacuum cleaner for dessert. A clean revenge. It's too much to take. Neat would like to straighten the sheets and lie down for a long nap, but it's not to be. So he tucks in his shirt and picks up the telephone.

He spends a good half hour confessing the night's exploits to his best friend and confidante, a fellow toilet sinner, his "sister," Emile. That's Emily in fagspeak. I know her well. She's got big ears and an even bigger mouth that she uses to blab everyone's gossip all over town (which I then pass on to the world). Emily sucks telephone air through her ooing lips as each intricate maneuver is described in detail for her listening pleasure. The nose in the armpit while the nipples are pulled while the dick goes up the ass and the other dick pulls out of the mouth with the other dick in hand while the other dick pisses and the balls hit the armpit. Dance of the disassembled body parts. Hard to follow. Hard to describe. Especially with the vacuum blasting in the background. Each time that it subsides while Mommy Dearest moves a piece of furniture, a word pronounced too loudly is left hanging in the air. Dick! The voice hushes down to a whisper. Mommy Dearest stomps the button on the vacuum and the roar begins again.

The anonymous man goes to the toilet. Where he belongs. He takes the phone into the bathroom. At last some peace. But his coordination is off. With the phone in one hand he stands before the toilet in flagrant disregard of Mommy Dearest's rules on toilet etiquette. He tries to direct his pee with the free hand, straight down without getting it on the rim, and ends up peeing on his pants. The phone conversation is cut short just as Emily is about to confess her sins. Sorry I can't talk. I have to go to the bathroom. I'll call you later. More lies to cover up the shame. He can tell her about the sex but not that he's been peeing while on the phone and certainly not that he peed on his pants.

A change of pants and back to the kitchen. The vacuum seems louder than ever. He nervously flips through the sections of the *Times* reading the same headlines over and over. He folds and refolds the clumsy paper. In the background the roar of the vacuum penetrates his nerves. He makes war with the newspaper to get it to fold the way he wants it to and finally knocks over a cup of coffee, spilling it, brown and muddy, on the white rug.

The vacuum is turned off. Silence. What happened? There he is on his knees again but this time with a rag in hand trying desperately to rub out that coffee stain from the rug. Mommy Dearest comes running in. My rug! Stop, you're making it worse!

He is. Nothing like rubbing in a brown stain on a white rug. It spreads. And though Mommy Dearest is certainly more angry at the dirt than at him, she gets awfully nasty. You moron. Clutz. Oaf. Fat piece of shit. Look what you did! She yanks the rag out of his helpless hand and attacks the rug with vengeance. The guilty man can only watch from the side. It's something to watch. A televised war. On one side, Mommy Dearest. On the other, the dirt. A Blitzkrieg. A losing battle. The dirt is unbeatable this time. Nothing to do but surrender. Never. Clean will never surrender. So Neat does. He tucks in his shirt and walks out the door to buy a pack of cigarettes. He quit for good last year.

He comes back. The two of them, Clean and Neat, live together all week in a state of tense loneliness. Clean vacuums every single day, but only when Neat is around. He calms his nerves by folding and refolding his wardrobe and smoking in the bathroom with the window open. He doesn't go out cruising. Not that it relates. But a certain guilt overtakes him beckoning him to stay home. And suffer. As long as that coffee stain remains glaring at him from the rug. By the following Saturday night he has to go out. Can't hold it in any longer. He flushes the last cigarette down the toilet and makes an excuse that he made plans to have a late dinner with Emily. Which is true, but it feels like an excuse because the only reason he made the plans was so that he could sneak off to the darkroom after dinner. Maybe he will, maybe he won't. But he can't stay here any longer. Something has to give. It's truly amazing how one can get used to things unbearable. The filth, and the cleanliness, and the silent rage between. But there's a point of no return, at least with the cleanliness. This has gone too far, he tells himself. I'm going out now. I am. And maybe I'll never come back.

Mommy Dearest stays home and... vacuums. From top to bottom. Every last corner. The sills and sashes too, though they need to be gone over by hand after the vacuuming. In the middle of it he gets second thoughts. Who is he punishing anyway? His friend is out on the town and there he is on his hands and knees wiping the microscopic grains of dust off the tops of the footboards. A sadness comes over him. He's scaring away the one he loves. Then obstinate defiance. I don't need him. That fat slob. I'm young and cute still. I can find myself a hot stud. Live alone and fool around on the side, outside the home. Who wants a marriage anyway? Such a burden. Always compromising. Horniness creeps into his loins. Cleaning in his underwear often does that. Maybe it's time for him to slut around too, something he hasn't done in an incredibly long time. Their relationship has been an antidote for the obssesive cruising of his past. To the point that he seems to have become asexual. And liking it that way. Or getting used to it. But there must be something wrong with being that way. It's not healthy to live without sex. He puts it out of his mind. He finishes cleaning. It takes hours and hours. Each task leads to another. The pace quickens into a frenzy of chores, from top to bottom, from one to the next all the way down to finishing it off with the laundry, all seven loads up and down the elevator from the top floor to the basement. Nothing like a New York elevator to add to the agony of an obsessive on the verge of a nervous breakdown. He's a step away from cracking each time the door creaks open and closed when the elevator stops to let on and let off the endless stream of passengers in full costume for their Saturday night on the town, all dolled up for a night out while he stays home doing his laundry. They seem giddy. It irks him and he can only squeeze in a stoic response. He perseveres and in the end he succeeds. He even manages to get that coffee stain off the rug. Or at least you can't see it under the frothy miracle cleaner. A miracle is what's needed to remove the unsightly filth of earthly life from paradise. He stands before it, and focuses in on that insufferable blemish. We can only pray.

It's late now. He showers, scrubs the tub once more while showering, puts on a fresh robe and sits down in front of TV with a sandwich. On a plate. On a napkin. From the couch he can admire the perfect cleanliness of his kingdom, here and there dabbing a missed spot with the napkin in between bites of the sandwich careful not to misplace a crumb off the plate. Then he's back to the kitchen where he discards the napkin and crumbs, washes the plate, dries it and returns it to its perfect place in the freshly-cleaned shelf. He inspects the kitchen. No roaches in sight. He adds a few final touches, washing out the fruit bowl. Cleaning the drain for the third time. He walks away conscious of the dusty trail left behind, trying his best to minimize it by swerving with his feet. Every step seems like yet another chore. He tiptoes around the apartment feeling that each move, each breath is somehow adding to the accumulation of new dirt causing a reflex of yet another chore. Only one thing to do. Leave.

Mommy Dearest changes into her cruising outfit and is transformed into another role. The cute boy. He *is* cute. Without the vacuum and the apron he's a little guy with a tight bod and the face of a boy half his age. The clean life has paid off. No sunken eyes or droopy skin. He feels fit. Ready to be loved. Here I am. Cuteboy. Complete with backwards baseball cap and whiter-than-white jeans.

Now where to go? Those sex clubs are way too filthy. He imagines running into his boyfriend there. The fat pig crawling around, squealing with joy. Disgusting. Too early for those haunts, anyway. How about the Y? Used to go there in the old days. I wonder if they still do it in the Y or if there's some law against masturbation posted on the walls of the showers nowadays. It used to be nice to get all clean in the showers, then have sex and be able to get clean again as soon as it was over. But no, what am I saying, it's hours and hours too late for the Y. Too late for some, too early for others. What's left?

The park. At least it's fresh there. Natural dirt. Grass and dirt. Hours later cuteboy finds himself kneeling in the mud. One loses all sense of reality at the moment of fantasy. Only when it's over does he realize what he's done and what it's done to him. The mud stains on his knees can be bleached out and the cum dripping down his rosy cheeks can be wiped off with a Kleenex (if he had only remembered to bring one) but for the moment there is nothing to do about it. He's a mess. An obvious one. The man who made a mess of him seems to be laughing at him, enjoying the sight of this cute clean boy stained by love or hate or whatever that was. Look at you now. He gets up off his aching knees and reaches for a leaf to wipe himself and succeeds only in making a mess of the leaf. He walks away from the laughing stranger and hobbles away up and over the hill down past all those dirty men, all those laughing strangers. He walks too fast and draws too much attention as he flies by stickily wiping his mouth with the back of his hand. But the knees say it all. No hiding those nasty brown stains on the whiter-than-white jeans. One nasty frustrated queen seizes the opportunity to hatch a joke. "Looks like you been drinkin' from the pond again, girl."

The anonymous man runs out of the park, through the dirty streets, past all the laughing strangers, wearing his shame on his brown knees like shit-colored matching scarlet letters. God, what will the doorman think! The doorman stops him. Catches him. Deah's a note fa you. I tried to give it to you when you was goin' out but you was in such a hurry. What's da rush?

The man must be toying with him. He tries not to notice the laughing face without looking down and attracting attention to his knees. He keeps his eyes on the man's hand as an envelope is offered. The embarrassment of the awkward moment turns those rosy cheeks scarlet. The doorman hands him the envelope with what can only be mockery. Ya *friend* gave dis ta me on his way out.

Thanks. Thanks a million. He rushes for the elevator just as it's closing and misses it. And waits. And waits. And waits as one by one they saunter into the lobby. Everyone in the whole fucking city, dressed in their costumes, still sparkling and perfumed after their Saturday night out, or fresh for Sunday morning. Hard to tell. The conversation is hushed. He faces away from them but he's sure that they are all looking at his brown knees. And commenting. When the elevator comes he rushes for it to be the first one in so that he can hide in the back. The door opens. A woman with a laundry basket. Going down. The door closes. He turns around. They all stare at him. And his knees. He turns around. The second elevator comes. They pile in. Damn. He lives on the top floor. The wait is unendurable. Silence, with only the creaking of the old elevator to cover up the ear-splitting thoughts. Someone keeps sniffing like they can smell the sex on him. He sniffs. Oh no. I must have kneeled in dog shit! More sniffs. The elevator stops on too many floors. Sometimes no one's there. The crowd is tense. Their impatience is breaking at the seams. Yet no one touches, even brushes by each other. A crowd together, alone in their separate bubbles, close as they can get to each other without touching. Never touching. Not one of them speaking a single word. But all of them conscious of each other, scrutinizing each other. If one whispered or even twitched the rest would respond like dominos. Alone together they live fragile lives.

The elevator stops. Someone gets out, but then another gets in and takes it one floor up. It's too much to bear. He holds his breath. He remembers the letter. He opens it and reads it, trying to shield the words from anyone's view.

I'm sorry about everything, it says, but I can't take it anymore.

What does that mean? Did he leave me? But then he would have taken his clothes and his stuff. But then why did he give the note to the doorman? He's not coming back! Oh my god. He's not coming back this time. He was afraid to tell me so he just pretended to go out. He's moved in with that slut Emily and he'll send her to fetch the clothes that I laundered for the slob. Well I won't give them to that bitch. If he wants them he'll have to get them himself. And he better hurry because I'm gonna throw them in the garbage. I'm gonna throw all his shit in the trash where it belongs. After all I did for him, he's gone and left me. I hate him. I hate him so much. I hate him more than I've ever hated anyone. And I won't take him back even when he comes crawling back on his knees. That's it. He left me. And that's it. I'm through with it. I'm alone now. And that's how I want it.

The thought rings loud and clear. He looks up and realizes that the elevator is empty. Only his floor to go. But what's this? The elevator is going down. Oh no! He forgot to press his floor. He lunges for it. Too late. Down, down, down it goes, stopping a hundred times to reveal empty halls where people could wait no longer and ran down the twenty flights instead. Or worse, to receive more sparkling clean costumes with people inside and eyes popping out at the sight of those dirty knees in the elevator. People dressed for church or for Sunday with the relatives. Off to clean friendly worlds where only nice things are said. Down, down, down it goes and each time it stops it's a short eternity waiting for the doors to close again. Hit the button! But he knows from experience that the elevator has a mind of its own. It closes when it wants to and not a moment sooner. On one floor a whole family gets in. There he is in the middle of them, the loneliest man in the world in a crowded elevator. It's packed full again as it descends in freefall through the last stretch until it comes lurching to a stop on the ground floor where they all have to squeeze by the loneliest man in the world to get out of that elevator.

Then it's up again. Hardly any passengers this time. But each one seems to be staring at his knees as they enter wondering what this man with the white pants and muddy knees is doing in the elevator since he doesn't get off with everyone else. Joyriding? Up, up, up and away. The agony prolonged only so much longer. But would have been even longer if he hadn't remembered at the last minute to press his floor just before the last passenger got out. A long sigh. Made it. Almost. He almost runs over one of his neighbors flying down the hall, makes it to the door of his apartment, searches his pockets for the key and realizes it must have fallen out in the mud near the pond. SHIT!!! The price one pays for the slightest bit of pleasure, if that was what is was. He's ready to cry his eyes out. The dirt. The shame. The incredible loneliness. He tells himself he's alone now, but it has a different ring than the last time he said it. It's no longer assertive and independent. It's painful. How he could use a hug. Just now he needs that warm embrace of his friend who has surely left him after the week of torture he put him through. Look what I've done. I scared him away. I brought all this on me and now I'm a dirty mess all alone in this world locked out of my one place of refuge. An abandoned child without love or shelter, thrown out into the world to crawl through the mud to survive.

He falls to his knees, this time in total exhaustion, thinking about how sooner or later we fall to our knees for whatever reason and realize our prayers will not be answered, when he hears the keys dropping out of his shirt pocket just as the door opens and there is his one and only true friend in this lonely world, standing in the doorway, slouching in his pajamas, all clean and fresh like a laundered Teddy Bear, looking just like the big lovable oaf that he is. Mouth open. Not understanding. Nothing to say but the truth: a question that answers that unanswerable question of whether or not we are ever more alone than when we are together.

"Where *were* you?"

## Two Men, One Room

Let's call them Robby and Bobby. Because they're two of a kind. They told me a sweet little anecdote from their cozy life that sums up their relationship in a way. I was having breakfast when the phone rang and I just knew it was someone with a story. A good story. Some friend had a hot night and wanted to relive it by passing it along to me.

Robby and Bobby are the original cozy couple. They live in a one-room apartment, a studio as the landlords so euphemistically put it. One small room that changes from a bedroom into a living room when you turn on the TV and into a kitchen when you plug in the microwave. Two doors lead to the "other rooms" – a bathroom and a closet about the same size. No, it's not a big closet.

But Robby and Bobby are happy as can be. They sleep in the same bed, eat all their meals together (in bed), and even work at the same desk. They run a computer business out of that little room. They do well enough at this business that they could afford a bigger place. But they like the low rent, pre-gentrification rent-stabilized. They like the location and the view, a slit of the Hudson River. Maybe the point is that they like each other, so it doesn't matter. It is to the constant amazement of their friends, especially their single friends, that they have lasted as a relationship so long in that apartment, that anyone could live and work together 24 hours a day in such confined circumstances. But one only has to spend an evening with them to see that they are living proof that space, like freedom, is a relative thing.

They do have two phones, although only one jack so that when they give you a call they literally give you a call together. "Hi, Ken. It's Robby... and Bobby."

I know instantly that a story is coming because when people have something juicy to tell me their voices take on a salacious quality complete with heavy breathing, like they're drooling on the receiver. Even the opening Hi sounds loaded. For that matter, rarely do people call me without having something to confess.

I knew they had been spending time lately with a friend of theirs, a psychologist friend, who needed their help with a computer problem. He was of course paying them for their professional advice. They weren't paying him for his. They never asked for it. He gave it as one gives a friend advice, for their own good. Because you care about them. Not to meddle. To help. The fact that he is a professional only means that his advice should be taken more seriously than any old advice from a friend because as a professional he knows from experience what he's talking about and would never allow himself to project his own psyche onto them.

Dr Helpful does mostly couple therapy in his practice. I met him once. He seemed like a rather eerie fellow. I had the feeling he was chewing his words, tasting his eloquence. He seems to think much of what he has to say and his patients reward him duly for that. He makes quite a lot of money and has written a few books. In passing he mentioned to Robby and Bobby how many of *his* couples suffered needlessly from the strain of spending too much time together or living in too close quarters due to the lack of space in New York. How extraordinary that Robby and Bobby should live in one room. Many of his couples found it necessary to rent a second apartment because their two- or three-room apartments were still too claustrophobic for comfort. He has had to more than a few times split up a couple – for their own good – in order to save their relationship or at least the possibility of a relationship in the future. "The self requires space to function properly," he told them in his very precise, articulate voice. "People are like nations. When boundaries are not clear and borders not wide enough the less dominant nation will either fight to gain more ground or will simply be swallowed up by the more dominant nation."

Robby and Bobby did their best to try to convince Dr Helpful that they were quite happy with the way things were, that they didn't need borders or boundaries. They like living in the same country. They would marry each other if the law would allow it.

"I counsel many married couples. It doesn't matter how close you are. Each is a separate individual and craves the room to grow, even to grow apart if that should happen," he told them in somber tones. "You are like two flowers. Sure you can grow side by side. You can drink the same water and nurture in the same soil. But when there is not enough soil, the roots cannot spread and one inevitably wilts." His hands have a way of demonstrating his meaning. I can picture his hands coming together in a prayerful gesture each time he speaks of togetherness. Growth brings the hands up and the opposite brings them down. What I find most annoying about the man is the way he listens. He will nod his head, almost with impatience as if he knows what you're going to say but it means nothing because he expected you to say that. When you agree with him he will nod with exaggeration as though punctuating your thoughts because you finally *got* it. And then he says: "Good, good," with a smile that suggests: "Yes, now you understand. You're a quick learner." Always his voice sounds dreadfully patronizing, like he's talking to a child. I wouldn't be the least bit surprised to read in the paper one day that they find some little boys chopped up in his basement.

The man is persuasive, though. With each meeting over his computer problems he managed to convince the happy couple that they weren't so happy after all. His soft words needled at their brains, picking at their buried wounds until they responded one evening after he left by having a good fight. Robby and Bobby never fight. They even mentioned that to the good doctor. He smiled but seemed unconvinced. "It is unhealthy for a couple not to fight. That is a sure sign of bottled-up emotions. One has to vent, now and then, in order to be heard." His hands shooing away the vented words. "The important thing is to fight in a constructive manner." Smart bombs. Wars for peace. Well Robby and Bobby had their battle. They said things to each other that they had never said before. Words came out of their mouths that sounded awkward. Have I been holding this in all the time? It doesn't sound like me to say such things, but there it is. I said it. It must be true.

Hard feelings lingered after the fight was over. Robby offered to sleep on the floor since there is only the one bed. A nice gesture in spite of the fact that only a minute before he had complained that he's the one who always ends up compromising. Finally they decided to sleep together but separately. On opposite sides of the bed instead of the usual spooning. The next day they told the good doctor about their fight and he nodded with great exaggeration. Finally they were getting it. "This is only the beginning. You are both now beginning to assert yourselves. As you deal with painful issues it will become more difficult at first, sometimes terrible. But in the end it will be for the better." His advice, free of charge, was that they should try to spend an evening apart. They work all day together. That can't be avoided, for now. It would be a good start to go their separate ways one evening just to see what it's like.

So the next night it was decided that they would go their separate ways. They always see friends as a couple. This night they would each see a different friend. Robby finds himself in the company of Steven, a rather large and expressive man who works at the opera in an administrative position. An obsessive opera buff, he will often carry on a conversation as though singing on stage. His words are almost sung and his gestures are bigger than life. The man needs to have an orchestra behind him at all times to support his grand entrances. He takes Robby to a bar in Chelsea where muscle men bump and grind on the bar in their bathing suits while the bartenders squirt them with seltzer. The place is usually packed with Chelsea guys cloned from a jeans commercial. The atmosphere is exuberant but the faces are anything but. Such vanity never makes for a free and easy social atmosphere. Little Robby stands there quietly listening to bigger-than-life Steven belt out a recitative over the racket. Robby looks up at him feeling himself shrinking within. He feels totally out of place there among the bloated muscles and smug faces. Like a puppy dog in a pack of wolves. In a way all he wants is to be back home with Bobby. He wonders what Bobby is doing just then on his night out with another of their friends, a trashy queen who spends half his life in toilets. He wonders how Steven can come to these video bars night after night, most every night going home alone. He watches Steven's histrionic gestures and feels a sadness for all these lonely New Yorkers who keep busy, have a full life in every way except one: the emptiness within. Their souls are broken. It must be terrible not to have someone who really loves you, who will hold you at night when you're afraid. Someone who you can hold when they're afraid. Someone who can be part of your life in such a way that you feel like it's the two of you holding on to each other in the middle of a cruel and hostile world, empowering each other enough that you can both laugh it off with shared humor.

Steven goes for the high note, concluding for now his endless aria about himself. On to a short recitative about Robby, sotto voce. "What you need, my dear, is to have some fun. This droopy face will not do."

"I'm sorry, but I'm not much of a barfly."

Defensive: "Neither am I, darling. I rarely come here." A lie. "I like the videos, but these men are way too stuck up." Men are pushing through the crowd from all sides. Robby continuously dodging out of the way, but Steven unmovable. Brünnhilde center stage. "You know, my dear. there's a tres chic sex party tonight and I think we should go. It's just what you need. Everyone will be there. The hottest men in New York. But not that *borough crowd.* They have a discretionary policy at the door and that usually keeps the trolls and the hoodlums out. I just don't understand this fascination that so many of my associates have with the underclass. Now mind you I work with many fine men of Afro-American descent. They are of course quite educated and refined. But I do not understand this emulation of fagbashing brutes. If I hear one more rap song, I'll scream." He already is. "And then you see these whiteboys carrying on like a bunch of... of... " looking for the right word, "like a bunch of ghetto riffraff swinging their arms like monkeys."

Robby is feeling more depressed than ever. Steven's words are aggressive and hateful. If Bobby were with them it would be different. They wouldn't be standing in a bar. They would have invited Steven for supper. His words would be taken as comedy, light opera, something bigoted but silly enough that Robby and Bobby could have a good laugh over it in bed. But here in this place alone with nothing to cushion the harsh words except the blasting music, Robby feels physically hurt by the meanness of it all. He wouldn't dare contradict Steven, anymore than he would ask the bartender to turn down the music. So he sulks.

"I'll tell you what I really hate is all these faggots dressing up like Marky Mark. This thing with the baseball caps and baggy clothes and this hoodlum attitude I find absolutely repulsive. I am afraid that we are in dark times, my dear. The age of the lowest common denominator. And I'm just petrified of the thought that the great culture of the western tradition will not be able to withstand these trends. You know, darling, the royal family is not doing well."

Missing the connection: "Which royal family?"

"Why the British Monarchy, of course."

"Oh. But I thought they're like the richest family in England," he timidly suggests.

Steven looks shocked, like someone just hit him over the head. "My dearest Robert, dear oh dear, it's not a question of money."

"No?"

"No, darling. It's a question of allegiance. And of preserving the culture." His accent becoming more British with each noble vow. "You know with all these third world people invading the capitals of Europe I fear that it is inevitably changing the old ways so that Europe will become like America, a barren wasteland of tribal enclaves."

"Why do you live in America, then?"

Shocked: "Darling, you must be kidding. I don't live in America. I live in New York."

"But New York has more foreigners I would think than probably any other city in the world."

"Yes, but you know most of them live in the boroughs."

The back of the bar opens up and out come the muscle men. The crowd screams. Steven screams, his voice projecting above the crowd and the music. Robby shrivels up in his spot. The crowd will not let him be. He has to fight to keep his square foot. He has a headache. He drank too much. The smoke is choking his breath. He wants to go home but he knows he'll have to wait out the muscle parade. He's too short to see much. What he sees doesn't turn him on. What's the big deal about these muscles? They look artificial. A few men reach up to stick dollar bills in the G-strings. The cheapness of it all is depressing. He misses Bobby suddenly. Steven in spite of his high and mighty words is entranced with the show, screaming trashy things at the muscle men: "Let's see that ass, baby!" The bartenders squirt the muscles and the crowd swoons and Robby feels positively stepped on. When it's over Steven, beaming, looks down to see where Robby is hiding, and exclaims: "Wasn't that wonnnnderful! But c'mon, deary, let's get out of here. The show's over. It's time for some real action."

He drags Robby off to the sex party. They have some trouble getting in. Probably it's Robby's mousy stance there in the entrance. But Steven is not to be told that he can't come in. His voice is so overpowering, the door seems to vibrate. The bouncers, wiry queers with too many earrings are no match for Steven's bulldozing words: "Don't be ridiculous, darling. We're going in. Here's the money."

Inside it's even more crowded than the bar, if that's possible. Robby wants nothing more than to go home. The men are all peering at each other. But just as you peer back they look away. Some sort of popularity contest. None of them are so perfect although Robby would have a hard time saying what perfection would be. The men here seem to be trying their hardest to look like Mr America. But after all they are men, like so many men who pass in the street. They have two eyes, a nose, and a mouth. And a body. Walking into the next room Robby sees some of those bodies. Almost naked. Wow. Some are quite impressive. But in a curious way. Robby wonders how they did it. How they got their chests to bulge so.

"Come darling. We'll check our clothes." Steven drags him off to the counter where men are stuffing their clothes into giant hefty bags. It reminds him of homeless men living out of plastic bags. He doesn't want to get naked. He's perking up to the idea of seeing the others naked. But he's too shy to strip himself. Steven won't take no for an answer. "Let's go, deary, take it off, everything except shoes and undies, and stick it in the bag." Robby blushes as he exposes his small frame. It's a well-formed physique although he never works out. He has a swimmer's body from the swimming he did as a kid. When he looks at Steven's body, it's a shock. He realizes he has never seen this body naked before. Steven's bigness is revealed as rolls of fat somewhat hardened by weightlifting. Like a very hard balloon. Hair sprouts from every corner, from the back, from the ankles, the cheeks of his ass. He strips to his jockstrap. It looks strange with his pointy dress shoes. But Steven shows not the slightest embarrassment. He puffs out his chest like he's gonna blow the house down. And a few guys cruise him as he marches into the main room.

Robby meekly follows. They end up in a dark airless space, the one small room where everybody crams in. It's dark enough that Robby has lost track of his immense companion. He keeps looking around to see him, but his eyes are fooled. He thinks he sees him and then it turns out to be a tall curtain. Robby's eyes aren't much good without his glasses and Steven insisted he check them. Finally he gives up looking for Steven and contents himself to lean back against the wall.

Then he starts to get horny. Nothing particular does it. Just the general mood. The freedom of being camouflaged by the absence of light. Like little kids getting rowdy when the lights go out. His dick gets hard. Men brush by in their hungry search. The situation is appalling to him in one way. He cannot imagine coming here ever again. But since he is here now, it's not without some thrill.

A man approaches him after a while. Without a word the man starts to touch Robby's crotch, rubbing his dick through the underwear. The man is bigger than him. It's a change of pace from Bobby and in any case the whole scenario is so new and different that suddenly Robby is beside himself, ready to get down on his knees and blow the guy. But before he can do anything the guy is bending over and about to blow Robby. So Robby reaches for the guy's crotch. Seems like the thing to do. But no sooner does he touch him than the guy pulls away. Robby meekly asks in his concerned way: "What's wrong?" But all the guy can do is suck his teeth, heave a bitchy sigh, and walk away.

Poor Robby is left standing there, feeling mortified. What did I do wrong? No time to dwell on his first failure at backroom sex. Another anonymous man is approaching. This one about the same size, same build as his. Seems like a perfect match. Robby's dick springs up. The man is almost in his face. He can't make out the other face, but it doesn't seem to matter in the faceless crowd. And from what he can see, this is the hottest body in the room. This is the one he really wants to do it with. Better be careful this time not to make the wrong move. But when the face is a few inches from his own he thinks he recognizes it. Oh, how embarrassing to recognize someone you know. His dick starts to shrink again. He squints as hard as he can to see who the hell it is. The round eyes, the pug nose, the silly mouth. Could it be?

"Hey, cutey-pie," Bobby says and the voice brings the face into focus. They can't stop giggling for a while. The others in the room seemed pissed that anyone isn't taking this with extreme seriousness. Robby and Bobby whisper in each other's ears. It's actually no great coincidence that they should meet here because Bobby's companion for the night is a notorious slut and this *is* the happening party for the night. I almost went to that party myself. Generally I don't like to go to places where you're expected to check your clothes. I like to feel that I'm just passing through and if something happens it happens. Spontaneity is my thing. I spent the night cruising the park instead. After hearing about the crowded party I was glad I hadn't gone.

Well, well. What a touching story. It must have been nice to discover each other and be able to put their clothes back on and go home and snuggle up with their Teddy bears.

On the contrary. Since they were both horny they decided that it was a good time to get their rocks off. Their sex life had become rather monotonous and infrequent the last years. The anonymous environment was adding a bit of excitement. So they pretended with the help of a dark corner to have just met and took turns blowing each other pretending to be having anonymous sex. It certainly felt like anonymous sex because neither of them had ever had anonymous sex, hard as that is to believe. Now finally they could discover the thrill, and without cheating. They didn't have to worry about catching anything. They could lose it with no regrets later. And no inhibitions now. Two men, one room, but crowded with other men. There was a certain charge to it that they had never experienced before. The sheer exhibitionism of it. The orgasms were better than ever. Maybe Dr Helpful was helpful after all. This is just what they needed to break up the routine. Not that they would want to give up the routine. They're not jealous of their single friends. After shooting their stuff on the wall the whole scene looked rather silly. They realized that they wanted nothing more than to go home to their little room and cuddle and kiss in their little bed. Which they did. On the way out Bobby called out into the darkness a quiet toodle-loo to Victor, and Robby was shocked indeed when he almost tripped over Steven's massive lump of body squatting on the floor as he blew the baddest-looking negro this side of Brooklyn.

## The Shortest Love Affair

An old friend who recently died told me a story that continues to stick in my mind. I write it as a tribute to him and his very particular sensitivities.

I was visiting him in the hospital. That year his health went up and down. Just when he seemed to be getting better, he got worse overnight and looked ready to die. Then just as quickly he recovered and was released from the hospital only to get something else a few weeks later and be back sick as a dog telling me stories of the good old days from his bed, propped up on pillows, trying not to interrupt the stories with a coughing fit. Mack had HIV before there was such a thing. His blood had been frozen in the 70's as part of a research project on hepatitis. When he got sick they were able to test his blood from a generation earlier. He certainly lived at least 25 years with the virus, most of that unknowingly, and had his share of fun. Those were the days when sex was good for you. Gave you soul. Cured hemorrhoids. Sperm was a cheap source of protein. Of course Mack had his share of the clap, of crabs, warts, worms and amebas, and received the appropriate treatments. But in spite of it all he never could have imagined that sex could kill you.

Mack was a classical pianist, had a doctorate from Juilliard, and till near the end kept up a busy schedule of teaching and performing. Before he got sick he managed to find the time to have sex with as many men as he could. No small task. For two decades he was a part of the gay revolution which exploded as he was coming out and got muffled as he got sick. Times have changed. The realities of cruising have changed. Much remains, although with a dark cloud hanging over it. The scene has changed. Certainly anonymous men are getting it on as much as ever, but under different circumstances. Part of the reason for the emergence of so many private sex parties in New York in the 90's is the death of the bathhouses, closed down by the city in the 80's. Some of the empty spaces left as relics of an era. They should be turned into museums. More than just sex went on there. Men came together to express their identity. To assert their newly found freedom. To live as they could never live in the real world even after gay rights. They were gay utopias, fantasy resorts complete with water sports and top-notch entertainment. Stars found their first audience there. Mack found his first love there.

It lasted less than an hour. Maybe because it was his first it now evokes warmer memories than the long stormy affairs he had later on, the "meaningful relationships" that went on for years and years and inevitably ended with a breakup leaving Mack alone again and wondering what the meaningful relationship meant.

One wouldn't call such a short affair an affair at all. I ask him why he doesn't call it what it was: yet another encounter of anonymous sex. He explains: "It wasn't anonymous. I knew his name." He'd had plenty of anonymous sex by the time he met this guy. This was different.

1975? Something like that. Cold New York winter night. Mack goes out to the *baths,* as they were generically called. Mack strutting around in his towel showing off his young body. He was thin then, but well proportioned. In the 80's he, like everyone else, got into weight-lifting and pumped those lithe muscles into sandbags. But remember, in the 70's it was cool to be skinny and have long hair and sport the unisex look. Mack looked good for the era. And the era looked good for him.

He was walking by the stalls checking out the day's selection, browsing with nothing much on his mind except sex and enjoying the warmth of the overheated space. He insists that it was love at first sight. The guy had something about him. A twinkle in his eye. A young hippie with a great smile. Long hair. From the southwest. That real American accent. And friendly. Smiling, talking. He fucked the guy good and hard but it wasn't just about domination. It was close, warm. They kissed passionately while they came, at the same time, together locked in an embrace. One of those perfect moments when nothing is forced. The timing works because the lovers are in sync.

They talked after. About this and that. The guy wanted to get a job taking people around in those horse-drawn carriages that you see trotting through the park. The guy had grown up in a place where they had lots of horses. He described it as a place of incredible natural beauty. Long rolling plains. Mountains in the distance. Warm dry air. And wild horses, some of which were captured and tamed in the ranches. Mack asked him why he wanted to live in New York if it was so beautiful back where he came from. The guy said it's a beautiful place, but if you're gay you wouldn't want to be caught dead there.

When they parted ways it was not without emotion. They dressed in the locker room, put on their winter coats. Out on the street they embraced one last time, kissed passionately, and said goodbye. Mack turned once in the street and could see the guy running through the cold, his long hair flying straight back in the wind.

I mention to him that he's been referring to the guy as "the guy." If it wasn't anonymous, what was the guy's name?

"He had a name. But I couldn't possibly remember it after all these years. Maybe I never knew his name. But it didn't matter. A name is just a word. What we had was a love affair, however short it was," he says and then begins one of his coughing fits that sounds like his insides are coming out.

I don't press the point. I'm surprised he can get up the energy to talk after the physical ordeal he's been through. Bad enough to be feeling sick to death, but the battery of tests and operations are enough to kill you. Spinal taps. Heart surgeries. Chemotherapy and radiation.

It amazed me that during those last months, weeks, days, Mack could muster up what little strength he had left to keep his mind going, thinking. He refused to turn on the TV in his room and just sit back and quietly turn into a corpse. He certainly had done his share of TV watching before he got sick. But there wasn't a moment to waste now. He spent his hours reading historical works and practicing his French. I mean, why practice French when you know you're going to die? I guess for the same reason you practice French when you're alive.

When the pain became unbearable and he couldn't read or practice French, he would become playfully sadistic with the help, buzzing the nurses, suggesting that they might want to massage his sores. His subtle revenge against a world in denial? From my perspective, painful to watch, as they would give him that service-with-a-smile, listening attentively but suggesting that he might do better to wait for the specialist. Then Mack playing this strange word game, repeating their last words in the same service-with-a-smile voice. Specialist. Specialist. And so on until they shut him up by giving him the long-awaited injection which they previously refused to give him except at the appointed hours. I've never understood that. Are they afraid the dying man will get addicted?

His eyes are drooping now. I think I should leave him so that he can sleep. But he wants to say something else. Some last thoughts. He seems to want to say goodbye to me. To somehow wrap up his short life. He tells me he's glad that he never bothered much about money. He always had enough to get by. A wealthy lawyer friend of his died a few years before about the same time that a rather impoverished actor friend died. The only difference he can think of is that the rich one died in a single room, alone, threatening to sue the doctors and the hospital. The poor one died in a row of beds surrounded by friends.

At a moment of last-minute soul-searching Mack confesses his frustration at how much of his short life was consumed by frustration. Simply not getting what he wanted. Not enough. Maybe he expected too much. But those of us brought up in an America where we were told we could have anything we wanted within reason, wanted it. Desperately. Love, money. Success, the power and the glory. And sex. Because our generation was free, liberated from love and money. Sex so good it's love. Mack got some of everything. But the little bits and the big bits too just aren't enough unless you can have them forever.

I saw Mack that day for the last time. His very last words I shall never forget. They still ring in my ears each morning: "I never realized what it was to live until I found out I was going to die. I'm glad I found out before it's too late."

⬊⬉⬈⬋

## Memorial

He told me it was some of the hottest sex he ever had. He hated himself for it. But he couldn't stop. He fucked one guy after the other. Half of them without a condom. He knew it was wrong. But suddenly everything was wrong. Nothing mattered except fucking. His lover dead and nothing could change that. He felt alive suddenly, like for the longest time he'd been sleepwalking. And that was something worth celebrating.

But he still feels guilty for doing what he did. I tell him it was a natural reaction to the grief. He shakes his head. Somewhere in the back of his eyes is the awful vision that all of us would rather not think about. Although he saw the worst in the hospital and he'll never get that out of his mind, it's something he didn't actually see which disturbs him the most. The body of this person he knew so well put in the ground, just settled in the grave. The lifeless corpse in a wooden box planted in the dirt. What a concept. When did people start planting the dead? That night he tried desperately to put it out of his mind. The picture of this person who had been so alive even when he was sick, now an empty shell, drained, prepared, and buried. He couldn't get the picture out of his thoughts. He would have wanted to run back to the cemetery and dig it up and hold the body, kiss the lips. But there's nothing to kiss. The person is gone. The body is just a body. And what's a body?

The only way he could get it out of his mind was to fuck. A lot of people fuck to forget. Just the timing was all wrong. Tasteless. He tells me I'm the only one he ever told this to. Don't torture yourself over it. You were temporarily insane. No I wasn't. I was horny.

That's right, when all is said and done I'm a horny pig looking to plant my pig seed wherever I can. All the pious words said. The sad people comforted. The family giving me dirty looks like I killed their son. Fuck them. They didn't want me there. I went anyway. Their son hadn't spoken to them in ten years. I was his family. He didn't want a funeral. He certainly didn't want to be buried. He wanted to be cremated. For as long as I knew him he cursed the church and his family for poisoning his mind the first half of his life. If the coffin hadn't been sealed shut he would have jumped out of it and strangled the priest. He didn't believe in all that nonsense. The priest said they weren't crying for the dead, they were crying for themselves. Then why have a funeral for the dead? Leave him be. I didn't want to go to the fucking funeral. But I wanted to be near him. To save him from those phony fucking people who never really knew him. I wanted to say goodbye even though he was already gone. I wanted to hold him. To save him. To be with him. And all I got was a fucking ceremony. Organ music! People standing around with long faces waiting for the drinks to be served. A catered affair!!

Maybe I'm a horny pig but they're hungry pigs. They should have served hors d'oeuvres at the graveyard. My god. The graveyard. One of the largest in the world, a city of graves off the highway on your way out of the city. Convenient. They take the body out of your apartment, stop off at the funeral home, the church, and then dump it on the outskirts of the city without getting off the highway. Next. What a cynical place. City of broken dreams. You live, you die. Always more people to take your place and no one gives a shit because there are so many fucking people and everyone wants their four walls. Cram them into those apartments. Dump them in their coffins. Down into their long-awaited plots. A place on earth, finally. Until they dig it up.

Meanwhile let's make room for a few million more. Stuff them into the buildings. The apartments. The offices. The bars, the restaurants. The sex clubs.

So I crammed myself into the sleaziest place I could find and crammed my dick into as many assholes as I could, fucked all night, planted my seed in as many graves as there are people. You know I never shed a tear at that funeral even though they were burying my baby. It was too ridiculous. Some kind of theater piece. Comedy. They must have thought I was a piece of shit. They were all so tearful, crying for their long lost boy who never was. Crying for themselves, for their image of what a son should be and what he turned into. An AIDS corpse devoured by sin. That's what happens to you when you stick dicks up your asshole. And there I was, the one who stuck it to their little boy. They halfheartedly invited me "back to the house." But I didn't want to spoil the party. I couldn't go back with them to their suburban hole to celebrate the memory, cry over the baby pictures. Get drunk, stuff my face with Swedish meatballs. They didn't want me around anyway. Me, the one who killed their darling son, who turned him into a sissy. Who killed him with my penis. I went straight to the sex club and had my own party with anyone and everyone. I spread the good news. Jesus has come. Up your ass. I didn't feel guilty for giving them a disease I didn't know if I had. Still don't. If they wanted it, they could have it. I didn't feel guilty for fucking every piece of ass I could two hours after my baby was buried in the ground. I swear I didn't feel guilty. I was too drunk. And too happy to be alive! When I got out into the street I felt incredibly relieved. I ran home screaming at the top of my lungs. I was mad with the lust of the living. I'm not dead yet, I told the buildings. The dark windows. The living dead sleeping soundly. Tomorrow is another day. They think. Wake up, you idiots! No time to sleep! I screamed. Don't let them bury you alive!

You didn't know what you were doing, I say into the cold phone, lying on the couch surrounded by my cozy four walls. You were in shock.

No I wasn't. I was temporarily *sane*. I went home. I dropped down into my bed. I saw the other pillow. I held it in my arms, curled up around it and cried myself to sleep.

## Safest Sex

"There is no such thing as safety in this world. Life itself is unsafe," I pronounce with a pompous flick of the wrist. My nervous friend is listening but too nervous to comprehend. He twitches as I speak. My flick causes a wave of tics in his body as though he were afraid I would hit him. My words too make him cringe. Poor guy, rich as he is. How he suffers. Let's call him Mr Angst, since he's German. I like the man. There's something charming about his weirdness and his insights are often quite curious. But he needs to relax. There must be some medication for what ails him. Besides the twitches and tics, he has this annoying habit of staring at your crotch when you speak. I have come to realize that he's not actually looking at your crotch, not on purpose. He means to look you in the eye but is so acutely look-shy that, hard as he tries to control the reflex, his glance will avert downwards as soon as you catch it.

I don't want to make fun of German people. The word *verklemmt* easily comes to mind, but one shouldn't take Mr Angst as representative of any national character. In fact he complains of Germans being unsympathetic, even antagonistic towards his affliction and his generally verklemmt ways and that he prefers to live in America where he is more accepted for his eccentricities. Mr Angst is not incapable of self-reflection. He has talked to me many times about his look-shyness, although his twitchiness remains an unmentioned quirk. He claims that living in New York, he can be himself. People here are not as confrontational. Nicer. I can't imagine this to be true. These superficial generalizations are usually nothing more than a projection. But he insists that America is a much freer place. More open. The people are less verklemmt. Also he hates the weather in Germany.

"I need sun to live," he tells my crotch.

Why don't you move to California? Much sunnier there.

"Are you kidding? Never. Earthquakes, mud slides. To say nothing of race riots and forest fires."

His English is perfect, if a bit awkward. All the words in the right place. Almost without accent. But something in his speech is decidedly verklemmt, as tight as his trembling lips. He seems to pronounce each word separately, one after the other with the slightest gaps in between. We sit in his fab apartment. High up in a modern tower in midtown. Small, but windows on all sides. The view is startling. A glittery panorama of lights and windows, so close you could imagine reaching out and touching them. With a long stick you could probably spear a bagel off a kitchen counter in the next building. Up here you feel like you're sitting in the center of the world in the densest spot. On high, but surrounded. Seeing this nervous creature twitching in the middle of such a frantic setting, I wonder that he doesn't retire to a spacious suburb. I can't help myself, but I want to prod his angst. Why not live somewhere green? Have a garden. With a white picket fence around it. Locked.

"Never. It's dangerous in those places. All alone in a big house. Anyone could come by in the middle of the night and kill you."

A rational mind. I remind him of the infamous dangers of city life.

"I can avoid these."

How.

"I never use the subway. As you can see I live in a doorman building. And I have installed an impenetrable series of locks on my door including that bar." I look over at the hardware shining around the front door. A steel bar sticks in the floor and into a slot in the door. "I have a wonderful air-conditioning/air-filtering system that runs all year."

I didn't realize the air was so dangerous. But I guess it is. And shouldn't you also have bars on the windows? After all, the murderers could conceivably come through the windows.

"Don't laugh. It happens! In my last apartment I was sitting in the living room with a friend when we heard something in the bedroom, figured it was just the roaches, and then later discovered that someone had come through the window and stolen my VCR. That apartment was on the first floor. I had to install window guards after that. The building is supposed to do it. I had to sue them to get the money. But then I moved, anyway. I never felt safe there after that. Always like someone was waiting outside the window. Terrible. That's why I live on the 39th floor now."

Where else but New York can you live on the 39th floor and still look straight across at the people in the next building. My friend's angst is contagious. Couldn't someone string something between the buildings and somehow get across?

He twitches at the possibility, but then shakes his head and waves his finger. "Not possible. Never. You Americans watch too many action movies."

I think I've tortured him enough, even if he tortures himself. He seems shriveled up sitting there in his plush white leather couch. I look around at the stark whiteness of everything. White walls, white ceilings, white wall-to-wall carpeting. Every last piece of furniture, ever last ornament white. The TV is painted white. One red piece of sculpture for an accent. This must be the cleanest apartment in Manhattan. The roaches are white. The only blackness comes from the panorama through the windows, dark blotches between the lights. I notice that there are no curtains. With the other buildings so close, isn't this a bit exhibitionist?

"I have blinds." He points to the tops of the windows where a cover hides the blinds.

With a gun they could shoot you from across.

His head twitches to one side away from the shock of my remark. Then he asserts himself, even tries to look me in the eye, although as soon as I look back he drops his gaze to just below my chin. "Not likely," he tells my Adam's apple. "I'm safe."

Mr Angst serves some snacks. Organically grown vegetables. Soya dip. Free-range chicken morsels. It's nice to know that at least the chickens can run free. Before they're hacked into morsels. I wonder what my friend will do when his time comes. So many of our generation, raised on the culture of eternal youth, are dealing with sobering realities at a relatively early age. Does a month go by that I don't hear of someone my age stricken with cancer or AIDS? I suppose my friend is safe from cancer because the chickens had a good life, but I wonder how he deals with the prospect of sexually transmitted disease. I know for a fact that this man sluts around as much as the next.

"I'm negative."

You sure are, honey.

"I am HIV-negative," he proudly claims.

One test is not definitive.

"I have been tested once a month for the last two years. All negative except for one time. That was a mistake."

Accidents can happen. What about the future. You're asexual these days?

"Certainly not. But I will not engage in any risky behavior and I believe that anyone who does knowing now what we know, anyone who takes those risks should not be surprised when they catch something," he tells my forehead. How daring. His voice is unwavering. Cruel, in a way. The man is humorless. He seems totally unaware that I'm just pulling his leg. At least his neck has stopped twitching for the moment. He bites his lip.

I inform him that there is no such thing as sex without risk if you want to think in those terms. There is no safe sex. Only saf*er*.

"Not true. If you never suck or fuck, on either end, you are safe."

Mutual masturbation must have its risks. Certainly finger fucking is risky. Isn't it? And what about kissing? You can get worms from kissing. What about hepatitis? Salad bars are dangerous.

"I don't eat out."

Crabs? Not life-threatening, but posing a risk nonetheless. Fungus too can be transmitted through mere touch.

"I don't touch." He reaches for his glass of soya milk but pauses trying to figure out if he might be by accident reaching for mine. "Is this yours or mine?"

Yours. I lie. But actually I'm not sure whose is whose. He can have them both. My esophagus is still reeling from the first sip. A shot of bourbon would do the trick. "Tell me. How does one have sex without touching?" I ask with a flick of the finger, flinging perhaps countless millions of microbes in his direction.

He ducks. Then pretends not to by casually leaning forward to replace his glass of bean on the table. He sits back to stretch, craning his small body to the side so that he can face me. He doesn't look comfortable. His position, or my question, has created a chain of tics. His knee is shaking. His left eye blinking as his right eye stares at my armpit. Most horrific is this gruesome habit one sometimes sees. The man is ever so slightly ripping a tiny piece of chapped skin off his lower lip. Yikes. I feel guilty for bringing out the worst in him, although he seems to take a certain pleasure in it because now he's smiling as he prepares to answer my question, ready to unravel this new-age paradox of sex without touching.

"Sex," he declares, "is all in the mind."

The body has something to do with it.

"Not really. The body is just the tool. Sex is in the imagination. A pianist plays with his fingers. Plays on an instrument. But the music comes from his mind."

That still doesn't explain how you can have sex with another person without touching. You mean you only masturbate.

"Of course I masturbate. But that is not to say that I do not have sex with other people."

How?

"As you know I very much enjoy these anonymous situations. I don't need to have intimate relations in order to feel satisfied. Nothing turns me on as much as to be in a place where men come together to have sex. To be around nakedness. To see their penises. To hear them groan. To masturbate and see them masturbate."

You mean you just watch?

"No. I am involved. Only I do not touch, and will not permit anyone to touch me."

I'm about to ask how he manages that, but stop myself. Watching him twist like a pretzel I can see how he avoids being touched. The man is not ugly. He has each hair on his head perfectly in place. The clothes are perfect. The body is small, not muscular, but not out of shape. He's perfectly presentable, but I can imagine that even if he let them no one would touch him. He might jump out of his skin. There is something truly sexless about the man. I stretch my arm around the back of the couch and his shoulder flinches out of the way. How does he get his bit of relief? What haunt does he haunt, twitching the night away?

"I will not go to those places. It is too difficult to prevent being touched when you stand in a room with so many."

The park has lots of space.

"Are you kidding? Never. The park is dangerous. Do you go to the park?"

Who me? Never.

"I do not understand these men who risk their lives in parks and public restrooms. Unbelievably dangerous. I will only go to private establishments. And... only to places which have booths. From inside a booth I can see everything going by. If someone tries to enter, I simply close the door. I have discovered that the only way to really protect yourself is through the use of the booth."

The booth?

"My favorite is the video booth." His excitement is building. He hovers forward on the couch, licking his picked lips and scratching the back of his head. He seems to have calmed down though. No more twitching. Rather tremors. "I must admit I love these video booths. Have you seen them? The ones where you can lift the screen on the side in order to see the man in the next booth. And he, as well, can see you."

I heard about them. Seems rather alienating.

"It's wonderful. You always have control. You can permit the other to see you, or not. And each has the possibility."

Sounds like a perfect world. Divided into booths. Each man king of his booth. Sounds like it must get awfully bitchy in there. Frustrated queens flipping those screens up and down in a dither. And talk about fear of rejection. This is like having doors slammed in your face. How cold. Why not just watch the video if you can't touch?

"The video is artificial. This is real. Another man. Right in front of you." Mr Angst stands up and marches off to the bathroom leaving me on the couch to ponder the possibilities of a see-through utopia. Maybe I should check out these booths for myself.

I guess the important difference between the men in the video and the men in the booth next door is that the men in the video can't look back. Either way you look through a window. You can't touch anyone but yourself. With the screens up you could both press up against the window. Sort of like phonesex, but you get to see instead of hear. Always these barriers. It seems to me that if you're not going to touch you might as well have sex with the fantasy guys in the video and leave the screen down. Or just stay home and cuddle up with the VCR. Unless of course your fetish is pure exhibitionism. I wonder, is the key to the thrill just in being seen?

I look out the window at the building across the way. Hm. I bet he never puts the blinds down.

## Man With a Mission

It's Saturday night. He slept all day. The night is young. But there's no time to waste.

He's off and running. The Saturday night sex addict. Too tired Friday night. Best boy all week long. Work, night school, socializing (but only with up and coming people), working out at the gym, and Wednesday night volunteer work (good for the image). He doesn't drink or smoke during the week. Doesn't even jerk off because it zaps the energy. No time anyway. Up every morning at 5:30 to run a mile before sitting down to his bowl of wheat germ and the morning paper. There isn't a moment from Monday to Friday to turn on the TV. His life is on the move. Kyle lives uptown and works downtown. Phone calls are reserved for the commute. What did man do before the cellular phone was invented?

Kyle starts his Saturday night with the usual barhopping. Kissy kissy with his bar friends. He would never socialize with them outside of the gay scene. Some of them are in business but they couldn't offer him anything except their physical presence in the bar. Kyle hates to stand around alone in a bar. Too vulnerable. He has to have a group around him. The group must look presentable. Nice haircuts. Leather jackets. Jeans. Black shoes. At one point a weird guy comes up to him. Imagine the audacity of someone to think that they can barge into a clique. The guy must be drunk. From New Jersey or something. What a nerd. Kyle ignores the guy. He hears the words, but pretends he doesn't hear them. "Hey man, how's it going?" What a dork. Kyle fluffs the hair at the back of his head as though to say: F uck off. The guy refuses to take the hint. Kyle's friends giggle at what is too ludicrous to bear. The littlest one says: "This is just like absurd."

The creepy guy gawks. He asks politely: "Can I buy you a drink?" Duh.

Kyle turns around, just barely. He looks down at the creepy guy. Nose still up in the air, tongue on the side of his mouth, he says without expression, quietly: "I have one." He holds up his glass, almost smiling, sucks his teeth and turns away.

"Well I could buy you another. Whatta ya drinkin'?"

More giggles. Someone whispers: "Let's walk around." And the whole troop, en masse like a school of nervous penguins, shifts around to the other side of the bar leaving the creepy guy standing there alone like the jerk he is.

A few hours later the same group is transplanted to the bar at the club. *The* club, where everyone who's anyone who's gay or otherwise goes. The truth is, for the really and truly fabulous this place is already passé. The door lets most everyone in. Some just have to wait longer and pay more. Kyle and his fabulous friends paid less with their membership cards. They stand in a circle in the exact same collective pose they had in the last place, the only minor change being their checked coats so that their bodies are looking not quite as beefy without the leather jackets. "I think John Blair throws the most fabulous parties. Don't you think?"

"I think Madonna's here tonight."

"Don't be silly. Madonna never comes here. She goes to Limelight or Sound Factory."

The Madonna experts in their matching outfits, matching hairdos, matching voices. Time to mix it up, girls. Kyle sees another clique that he sometimes hangs out with. He knows some of them from the gym. He excuses himself: "I think I'm gonna walk around." He crosses the dancefloor, cuts through the girating bodies, and swaggers over to the other clique, which is almost identical, but a lot bigger and butcher. In just teeshirts their torsos look stuffed with leather jackets. He stands with them in a row of pectorals trying to fit in, to act more butch than before. If he felt like one of the butchest in the last clique now he feels a bit dwarfed by his gym buddies but eases his insecurity with the thought that they have all the time in the world to pump their bodies whereas he has to make money and maybe their pecs are bigger than his but his bank account is even bigger. And growing. In any case he feels damn good standing with them. Barely a word is uttered. The music is loud when you stand around the dancefloor. Together they look like a bodybuilding team. Kyle feels like a god in this circle of gods, the envy of mortals. He looks back at the other clique. Even though the style is the same, those clones look like a bunch of wimps compared to these. He starts to think he should stay away from those wimps. Bad for his image.

One of the gym buddies, the one standing next to him, grunts something to him. Sure he'd like a beer. He slips his white wine out of sight. The truth is he hates beer. But it's good for the muscles. Something to do with electrolytes. Kyle stands in the muscle line keeping the space for his buddy while he gets them a few brews. He doesn't know the guy too well. They see each other often enough at the gym and nod to each other. But that's it. What's his name: Dan, maybe? When Dan the man comes back with the beers Kyle gets an erection. Taking the beer from him is a sexual act. "Thanks, man," he says, and the bond is sealed. He tugs on his beer bottle. He feels like he's standing with his big strong buddy and all he can think about is how good it's gonna feel to get fucked. He catches himself thinking it because you should never count your chickens before they hatch, especially when it comes to getting laid. But his horniness is overwhelming. When you don't orgasm for a whole week the cum has a way of dribbling out in your pants. He sucks on his beer and then positions it in front of his hardon, pressing lightly thinking about the guy standing next to him. Cock-to-cock, chest-to-chest. All of the gym guys standing there a step above the dancefloor, guy-to-guy, hip-to-hip, muscle-to-muscle. His heart throbs to the beat pounding around him and his dick swells with the confidence that he and his team are the hottest guys in the club and he's one of them. So butch that they don't dance. They just pose with the crowd dancing at their feet.

His maniacal fantasies are interrupted by the realization that someone down on the dancefloor is trying to talk to him. His head tilts down just enough to see with horror that the same creepy guy from the bar is here now standing eye level with his crotch looking up at him saying something. Kyle shakes his head in disbelief. I can't believe this is happening. I'm not going to say a word. This insect better take the hint and fly away before I swat it and put it out of its misery.

But the insect is tenacious. And drunk. He's not going anywhere. Actually talking to Kyle even though Kyle is looking the other way. Until his gym buddy nudges him with his trapezoid and grunts something. He turns around, all ears for his gym buddy. The music is loud. He can smell the guy's strong manly fresh clean smell but he can't hear what he's saying. Scuse me? His gym buddy speaks into his ear in a most intimate gesture. "I think your friend is talkin' to ya."

Shit! Kyle bends down just enough to look the twerp in the eye and mouth the words: FUCK... OFF. But before he can straighten up again his gym buddy grunts the six deadly words: "I think I'm gonna walk around." And before Kyle can call after him – what would he say? – the stud is off and Kyle is left standing there with the creepy guy still at his feet. There is clearly no way to deal with this dweeb except to just walk away. Which he does, in a tither, searching for his wandering gym buddy.

He walks from bar to bar, room to room. He checks out the men's room. A long line to get in. His impatience is getting the best of him. Standing alone anywhere, even on the line to the men's room, is not something he likes to do. The little queens in front of him are arguing about whether or not that *was* Madonna they saw on the dancefloor.

"I'm telling you, that was her!"

"No way. Madonna would have like a bunch of like bodyguards around her."

"You don't think I know what Madonna looks like. I talked to her once."

From in front of them on the line a drippy druggy guy with an earring in his nose turns around to correct them both. With the air of an insider: "She *is* coming. But she's not here yet. I know her manager."

Well la di da. Kyle is just about to throw up when the line shifts forward and he finds himself walking into the men's room. Almost. The line stops at the door. He keeps looking ahead to see if his gym buddy is coming out. Then one of the guys from the other clique comes out of the men's room and stops to say Hi. As much as Kyle had been thinking only a few minutes before that he would stay away from them because they're too wimpy, he finds himself smiling suddenly and phoney as can be, glad to stand with someone while he waits. "Can you be-*lieve* this?"

"I know. They like need more bathrooms."

Like I know." Kyle hates the bitchiness coming out of their voices. It was cool and detached when he spoke to his gym buddy.

The line moves in through the door and he's able to get away from the queeny friend and no sooner does he get in there than he realizes how ridiculous he's acting because even if the stud was in there what would he say to him and how could the stud be in there now when anybody who had been in there would have walked out past him already. But he does have to take a piss by now and he should take the opportunity and suddenly the line moves in quickly and the next thing he knows he's standing in front of a urinal with the little Madonna tarts on one side of him and –

It couldn't be. The creepy guy has followed him in. Must have been standing behind him in the line. As soon as he realizes it's him he turns the other way but he can't leave because he's in the middle of peeing. The creep has the nerve to talk to him while he's peeing: "Hi," he says in this icky nasal voice. Kyle is thoroughly grossed out. He cuts off his stream of piss and shoves his dick back in his pants. The thought of this creep looking at his dick! They're so close he can smell the guy's cheap cologne. Ewww! He rushes past him but not without catching a glimpse in the bright men's room lighting of the pimply face and the loose fleshy body, the hideous tacky clothes and goddamit I didn't mean to look but yes I saw it. His little shrivelled greasy thing. And he was rubbing it while he smiled at me. Ahhhh!!

Leaving the men's room he thinks: This is too, too ridiculous. I mean who goes chasing after a guy when he obviously doesn't want you. Kyle pushes through the crowds of clones with his nose in the air pointing this way and that way in search of his gym buddy. And then it occurs to him where the stud must be. Why didn't I think of it before. The VIP lounge, or whatever the hell they're calling it these days.

The bouncer at the entrance to the VIP lounge is telling two guys that they can't come in without a special invitation when Kyle walks up to the rope. The bouncer looks the other way but he does unfasten the rope, nonchalantly granting admission to Kyle. Everything is such a game. The way Kyle walks up to the rope, the way the guy pretends he doesn't see him but then lets him in. The way those two will never get in no matter how much they bitch. Kyle, feeling like a very important person, runs up the steps, then stops himself. Don't wanna look too anxious. He peers out from the landing at the giant dancefloor down below and straight down at the entrance to the VIP lounge. His eye takes in the bouncer, the two guys, and he should have figured, there he is – the creepy guy – trying to talk his way in. Kyle smiles. The bouncer won't even talk to the insect. When he lets some other people in the creepy guy actually has the nerve to try to walk in with them and the bouncer puts his arm out and bars his entrance. He can't hear what they're saying but he can see that the bouncer is pissed, pointing his finger at the creepy guy, threatening him. The creepy guy with his mouth open. Duh? Kyle laughs. That'll teach the dickbrain a lesson.

Up in the heavenly realm of the VIP lounge the scene is quieter and more subdued. People stand around in small groups looking very important. Here are the gods and goddesses of the club world. Their kingdom is perched above the vast throbbing masses on the dancefloor. Here they are, the truly fabulous. Even the bartender has an air of importance. Kyle enters from below and immediately is infected with the superior attitude floating around in the smoke. His eyes shift from one fabulous face to the next. He tries not to seem obvious about his search for his gym buddy. He feels uncomfortable enough about being there alone. Some faces stare at him like they're thinking: What are you doing here alone? You're not one of us. The laughter plays on his momentary frailty. He's about to lose hope, no gym buddy in sight, when he thinks he recognizes the butch body from behind. Yes! That's him standing in the corner with his back to me. Kyle struts across the room with confidence now but in a second his heart drops through his chest, through the floor, down to earth, and lands on the dancefloor where a million mortals trample on it with their dancing feet. He stops in his path and turns around before he makes a complete fool out of himself. Dan the man, the stud of his dreams, his godly gym buddy who just a few minutes before was talking to him like they would soon be fuck buddies is now talking to a – no it couldn't be, not that – to a *woman*. A real one. Complete with dyed-blonde hair, red lipstick, short skirt and fake boobs sticking straight out like mangoes ripe for picking. She's smiling at him from ear to ear, her head tilted up, showering him with such fake adulation. She's playing it for all it's worth. Her expression says: Really? I didn't know that. You're so smart. And he's buying it! The body language is intolerable. The bitch swinging her titties for him and him flexing his muscles for her. Make me sick. I'm getting out of this fucking place. Now.

To add to the frustration, on the way out of the VIP Lounge Kyle finds the creepy guy still standing there at the entrance trying to get in. And he has the unbelievable nerve to say: "Hi again. Bet you didn't think you'd find me here." The loser is chuckling like he actually thinks he's being humorous. He looks like a hog when he laughs and white gook is hanging off his chapped lips. All Kyle can do is scream at him: "Get away from me!" But the slobbering idiot is unfazed, not the least bit afraid of rejection, almost seems to be getting into it. The bouncer asks Kyle: "You know this guy?" and Kyle screams at the bouncer: "No, I don't know this guy!" and the bouncer doesn't care but wants the creepy guy out of his hair and calls after Kyle as he storms away: "Why don't you take your friend with you," and Kyle can't let it go and turns around and screams back: *"He's not my friend!"* Some people waiting there start laughing at the strange scene and the creepy guy is laughing with them, actually enjoying the attention however derogatory. At this point the frustration is beyond words. All Kyle can do is let out a curt shriek and dash away.

Kyle spends an interminable time waiting for his jacket at the coat check, looking around to see if he's being followed, feeling like a fugitive on the run. It takes him fifteen minutes to finally get his jacket. The whole time he's forced to listen to the most banal conversation. Two nellies discussing where they should go next. "Well I dunno like you said you wanted to go to Sound Factory." "No I didn't I never said I wanted to go to Sound Factory." "Yes you did I asked you where you wanted to go after you said this place sucks and you said you wanted to go to Sound Factory." "I did not." "You did too." And so on. Until Kyle is ready to tweak their already tweaked eyebrows. He tries to tune them out. The beat is pounding through his head. He finds himself constantly looking over his shoulder to see if the creepy guy is following him, then realizes he's being paranoid. He thinks he sees Dan the man, perks up – but no, it's some other muscle moron.

Out on the street he relaxes, even laughs off the whole thing. How ridiculous. That stud is probably an elevator man. I don't need him. I could get any guy I want. He puts the creepy guy out of his mind too. But on second thought thinks it would make a good story. I'll have to tell that one to Ken. (He did indeed.) The night is still young, although the sun will be making its way up soon enough. Kyle decides to head straight for the jerkoff club.

The sex clubs are close enough. Just down a few blocks in the meat district. What a funky part of town. Meat housed and slaughtered there by day, and another kind of meat pounded in the clubs late at night into the next morning just when the trucks are coming back with more meat. You can see the blood on the concrete. And then every kind of freak hangs out on the streets there. Maybe dangerous.

But mostly just whores. Strange ones. Kyle is practically accosted by a giant drag queen who follows him for half a block telling him that she has what he wants: "I got it baby. I got me a pair of breastisez like you ain't never stuck yo face in befaw and I got a big black dick like you ain't never had stuck up yo ass." No thanks. Really. No thanks. "Dat's okay, baby. I know it's difficult for you to accept yawself for what you is. You just take yo time. When yo ready I'll be right here waiting fawya." He speeds up his pace and she brings her six-inch heels to a halt. He turns the corner feeling like a man on the run. What is it about this night? Why are these people following me?

The coast is clear inside the sex club. It's been a while since the last time he came here. How do they manage to call this a club? And charge ten bucks to get in! It's no more than a little dark seedy room with an even smaller, darker and seedier room downstairs in the basement. The air is unbreatheable. The smell pungent, rancid, and foul. He holds his nose as he yawns. He realizes how tired he is from the long week even though he slept all day. Better get this over with and go home. He heads straight for the basement.

The smell of mold, sweat and poppers. A few guys standing in the one room. More in the back. The usual assortment of creatures. That one guy you see everywhere, the hideous monster with the nipple clips and the leather straps. Kyle is about to give up on this scene when he sees one hot muscle guy in the corner. A few young skinny guys standing around him. Ladies in waiting. They're everywhere. The guy is definitely hot. You can tell, even in the dark lighting. Big beefy guy. His jacket open. Torn teeshirt. Hairy chest. Great pecs. Definitely a hunk.

Kyle struts up to the hunk with the confident stride of someone who knows that there are only two hunks there and he himself is one of them. Some other okay guys. But it's clear to everyone who's who. There's an order to this anarchy. The pairing is based on a rigid code. Kyle only has to walk past the guy and look at him for the guy to ever so slightly nod, just enough to say the unspoken, and the two are following each other into the one semi-private cove. It's in reality not private at all. Just a removed nook. If the mortals want to watch the gods do it, let them. The gods are not opposed to being worshipped from afar. The A-list allowing for the adulation of some B students.

The ritual has all the trappings of a religious ceremony. The hierarchy is clearly established. As soon as Kyle and the hunk start making out, the others take their places, the more prominent worshippers on the inside. Kyle forgets everything around. The hunk holds him tight and close while they kiss. He shoves his tongue in Kyle's mouth and, gripping him by the butt, presses their groins together. Shirts up. Pants down. Cocks in hand. You jerk mine and I jerk yours and the circle jerk follows suit, whacking around the altar. It's the darkest corner in the room. You can barely see your own dick but you can smell the sweat and you can feel the body heat on all sides. Nobody reaches out to touch the gods. Too intimidating. Zeus towers over them enough to keep them at bay by his sheer presence. With Apollo, his son, in his mighty embrace.

Then the guy pushes his head down. Worship it, commands Zeus and Apollo cannot resist the command. The god of gods has a lightning bolt, fierce, powerful. Son pays homage to father in godly fellatio. And the mortal men gather around. The gods piss on earth and call it rain while their subjects prepare to bathe in it with a raindance.

But as we all know, even gods make mistakes. It's dark in paradise. The gods are fucking. Apollo is getting the full power of Zeus thrust up into him from behind, his own holy godrod jutting out so that some of the mortals can partake of his might. Hands and mouths in the crowded void, feeling around in the dark. Apollo would not have known the difference, so taken by Zeus' power, if it hadn't happened that as he shot his wad some mortal who had been stroking him with one hand and stroking his own mortal staff with the other, did something no man should do. He shot his earthly juices on his awesome god and as the heavens opened up and the rain poured and gods and mortals alike reveled in the ecstasy of heaven on earth the mortal spoke unto his god and said: "Well hi there. Bet you never thought you'd see me here."

## Man and His Toys

Harry is the original accessory queen. He can't do it, can't do anything, without his toys. Cockrings, buttplugs, and all kinds of rings and plugs, clips, cuffs, whips and chains. Never mind the pharmaceutical accessories. One time he forgot his poppers and had to leave the sex club a few minutes after arriving. He went all the way home to get them when they sell them right there in Times Square because they don't have his favorite mail-order brand. So he went all the way to

Staten Island and back, an hour each way, and had to pay a second admission because they're such assholes at the door and because Harry... is a bit of a geek. A monster actually, but unashamed. He would be the first one to call himself a monster. A self-proclaimed creature of the dark. Lurking. Waiting for someone, just about anyone, to pull his nippleclips.

You've seen him. That's right. *That* guy. The one in the corner. Stark naked except for his Florsheim shoes. Kind of fat, but kind of skinny, depending on where you look. I know, you try not to. But it's difficult when he manages to always be there wherever you go, spread out in his full glory, waiting for you. You've wondered if the guy sleeps there. You've wondered whether the guy has a life outside of there. But you prefer not to think about it. You don't really care. Just a bit curious. But you would never talk to him anymore than you would pull his nippleclips. Though you might watch someone else pull them.

Well I'm the one who will actually talk to him. No, I have never touched him. But I did follow him out one night because I can't help it, psycho journalist that I am, I love to hear about people's weird fucking lives. The nasty shit. New York is great that way. There's an endless supply of crazy people who will tell you their life story without your even asking. I ask. I want to know. The lives of the rich and famous are humdrum compared to this. Who cares why the Queen of England's daughter-in-law bared her breasts when Harry of Staten Island is hanging in a sling with his tits in pliers? For that matter, who wants to hear the monochromatic ramblings of the so-called normal people? Who cares how much money they make or what tacky shit they buy with it? Or politics and current events and how you think you can change the world and make it a better place. Go ahead, but I don't want to hear about it anymore than I want to sit around in cafes with artsy-fartsy wannabes and hear about their search for the lost chord, the perfect phrase that will make them enough money so that they too can buy a lot of tacky shit. No thanks. I prefer to hear about Harry's ridiculous life. I wanna know the details of his vomitous sexual escapades, his search for the lost dildo.

And so begins our story. Call it *Harry and the Lost Dildo.* Because it's all about how one day Harry lost his dildo and had to make do. No joke. It's a good story. Some of the funkiest people tell the best stories. They should be the writers of the world. I even suggested to him to write a book about his cockamamie life. He laughed. "Ya kiddin' me. You're a real kidder. Me? Write?" Well he does have a computer. But just to play with. He sends trashy messages through the Internet.

Along the lines of toilet graffiti. "Butt seeks plug. Your plunger fits my hole. Drop me a line if you wanna plug into my socket. No one denied." That kind of thing. Harry has a nonstop fetish for buttplugs. The accessory for all occasions. A classic. Every other word out of his filthy mouth is buttplug. No surprise, his story is about the sort of things a man might stick up their butt. If you're finding this gross and rather silly, I suggest you skip a few pages.

We sat in the window of a coffee shop in the Village. Harry hollering away in that loony voice of his. Only in New York can you sit in a place where people are quietly eating and have a guy like Harry yell out the most disgusting shit without anyone blinking an eye, never mind the management throwing him out. Harry doesn't give a shit. The only shit he gives is the shit coming out of his mouth. "Um not squeamish, ya understand. I don't care if there's shit on the dildo long as they don't stick it in my mouth." That's a beautiful thought, Harry. Thank you for sharing that with us.

Harry lives with his mother in Staten Island. She's blind and deaf and I gather somewhat crippled. In other words, she hasn't the faintest idea what strange things Harry is up to in his room. The same room he grew up in. He loves his mother to death, takes care of her, making a measly living working in a hardware store (he gets a discount). Harry's pious tale starts out innocently enough. One night he's putting his sweet old mom to bed, tucking her in, making sure her painkillers are in easy reach. She didn't look well that night and he was worried about her. Maybe that's why he was absent-minded enough to forget one of his toys, a vital accessory that cannot be replaced so easily. Later he would swear that he packed everything in his bag. The poppers, the clips, the rings, the plugs, the cuffs, whips and chains and all the leather gear, and the pièce de résistance – the dildo. And let's not forget the one thing you should never leave home without. The spare dildo. In fact Harry has a whole set of dildos. All sizes, colors, shapes and textures. But Harry has these certain methodical procedures. He has his routine. He always brings one main dildo with him, and a smaller spare one just in case.

In case of what? (I told you I'm curious.)

"Ya know. Just in case." It's part of the routine to pick out the lucky dildo for the evening. Sort of like a bowler who has a bunch of bowling balls and picks one lucky ball for the night. Variety is the spice of life. He'd bring them all if he could. But dildos can be cumbersome, though not as heavy as bowling balls. He has to fit all the accessories in his little party bag. The dildos are too long. He carries them separately in his jacket. He can bring only one main dildo and a smaller spare. It adds to the pre-party thrill to decide beforehand which one to take along. That night he brought his favorite, old trusty, the biggest and the best. Not one of the specialty items, the crooked one or the textured one. Just your basic giant rubber penis.

When he got to the party he realized that somewhere along the way he'd lost the fucking thing. Must have slipped right out of his jacket. Maybe in the subway. Or imagine it might have fallen off the ferry from Staten Island. "All I could think about was my fuckin' dildo floatin' around in the water. I mean, it's rubber. It floats. It does in the bathtub, anyways. So like I figure it'll probably wash up on shore somewheres. In front of the Statue of Liberty. Them Japanese tourists will be lookin' at it tryin' to figure out what the hell it is."

The party was a special invitation private affair for an elite clique of super kinky men organized by some fistfucker who has long since died but back when used to throw the hottest weirdest get-togethers. All the fetishists would be there showing off their fetishes and their accessories. Harry was most definitely not invited. He managed to get an invitation from a friend in exchange for tickets to the ball game. Harry had been looking forward to this event for a long time. When he realized that he was in fact without his trusty dildo he was almost tempted to go back home. Afraid he wouldn't get back in if he left now, he decided to stay put. Stick it through, as they say. There's always the spare.

"And whatta ya know, I stick my hand in the other pocket, the one I keep the spare in, and instead I pull out a fuckin' vibrator!" He's screaming this to the whole coffee shop. "A fuckin' vibrator! Can ya believe?"

What bad luck. First losing his best dildo on the way, and then realizing that he brought a vibrator for a spare. He attributed his absent-mindedness to the excitement of the event and to his concern for his poor dear mother who had not been herself that night.

"But look, I hadda make the most of it. This was a once-in-a-lifetime event. You don't get invitations like that every day. So I figure man has always hadda make do with what he's got, even if it ain't perfect. Right? So like Columbus lost a few ships on the way. But he still hadda go on."

Columbus checked his clothes, threw the little vibrator in the party bag and took off to explore the various rooms of the party. At least he hadn't forgotten his poppers. He took a good deep hit from the little bottle and staggered into the darkest corner of the fistfucking room. Naked and hideous he stood there getting ready for Prince Charming to come along and shove a fist up his asshole.

He began to unpack the party bag. Attaching the clips. Stuffing his balls and cock into the steel ring (his favorite one with his initials engraved). Leather wristbands. Cuffs in easy reach. And last but not least the all-purpose plug. The vibrator he kept in the ready, not quite sure what he'd do with it, but keeping it near by just in case.

In case?

"Ya never know."

Plenty of hot guys milling around. At one side of the room they stuck a skinny guy in a sling and took turns fisting him. Big brutes in tight leather. As usual Harry spent half the night waiting. Those who wait long enough sometimes actually get what they want. And more. When Prince Charming finally came his way he turned out to be something of a toad. A puny guy with a giant cock who wanted to shit on someone's face. Any face will do.

"I'll say it once. I'll say it again. I ain't squeamish. But I don't eat shit." Hard to believe.

The puny guy settled for a few tugs on Harry's nipples and took off in search of a more willing face. Finally Harry, in desperation, wanting this night to be a truly special night, goes for broke and pulls out the emergency accessory. The one added element that almost always insures a hot encounter. The leather mask.

If it's so hot, why don't you use it all the time?

"I got my pride, honey." Even harder to believe. "So then this guy comes by and stares at me tryin' to see what's goin' on. A big guy with a little thing. Not that little. But if it's not like really big, it looks little. If ya know what I mean."

You've seen too many dildos.

"And um thinkin', why is this guy starin' at me? Cause he's like really starin' at me."

Harry really is something to look at. I've had that pleasure. I can just imagine the added allure with the leather mask. This misshapen body fixed with all sorts of glittery attachments. The big guy with the little thing wants to see that body writhe in pain. He yanks on the nipple clips. Pulls on the balls. He wants to fuck Harry's hairy asshole up to the gut. But with a little pecker like that, he'll be lucky if Harry feels a thing. The buttplug is bigger.

"I hadda have this operation to tighten it up, ya know, cause the shit was dribblin' out. But still, it's gotta be substantial or I don't know um gettin' fucked. If ya know what I mean."

I'm in awe. I thought that was just rumor that if you get fucked too much you have to sew it up.

"Personally I think it was all the gerbilling I did in the 70's."

I let that one go. I want to get to the end of this horrendous story. Get to the punch line.

"So whatta ya know, the guy wants to fuck me with a dildo since he got such a little thing. And silly me, my dildo's floatin' around in the East River and I forgot the spare. So I figure, what the hell, he can stick the vibrator up there. It's not like I never used a vibrator before. But honestly I find them too electronic and all. Ya know, in a way um a natural girl. I don't even dye my hair."

I look at his hair. A greasy blend of muddy brown strands. I look at the hair in my plate, floating in the grease. Do I really want to hear the end of this story?

"The problem is, it's just a little bitty small vibrator. I keep it in the bottom of the bag for the hell of it. I never use it. It's still bigger than the guy's thing. So I pull out the plug and he sticks the vibrator in and like it feels okay at first but like I can hardly feel the difference between the plug and the vibrator except for the vibrations. Ya know how those things are, they kinda rumble around like one of them electric toothbrushes."

Get to the punch line.

"Um gettin' to it. So whatta ya know, the stupid shmuck sticks it in too far and it gets stuck and he can't get the fuckin' thing out!"

No!

"Yes! Cause ya know how dem dildos got the flat part at the end so they don't get stuck. But this fuckin' vibrator is just a little shlong with batteries in it. And the next thing I know um vibratin'. I mean um really vibratin'. Inside. My shit's vibratin'. I feel like um gonna start doin' the jig or somepin'."

Got ants in my pants and I need to dance.

"It was terrible. I was runnin' around that fuckin' party screamin' about this fuckin' vibrator up my fuckin' ass and like nobody could give a fuckin' shit and like you wouldn't believe – "

I don't.

" – but I hadda go to the hospital to get that fuckin' thing outa there."

Really. What did you tell them in the emergency room?

"Whatta ya think I said? I said I got a vibrator stuck up my ass and if they don't do somepin' pretty quick the fuckin' thing is gonna turn my insides inta mashed potatoes before it comes out my mouth!!!"

Harry is really screaming at this point. I look around. The coffee shop seems to have cleared out. The Greek machos who work there are flipping their worry beads. Harry is a sideshow. But I think he needs the right venue for his particular brand of entertainment. He certainly is full of a lot of whatever. At this point I'm not sure if any of it is true. I ask anyway: Did they get it out?

"Of course they got it out! Whatta ya think um walkin' around New Yawk with some gizmo stuck up my ass?"

I look out the window. So maybe they don't stick them up their assholes, but it seems like everybody walking by has some gizmo with them, some accessory to assist them in their daily activities. There's a man with a cellular phone. Another with a calculator. Another with a beeper. Another with a walkman, the headphones stuck in his ears.

"Lemme tell ya, I wasn't the first guy to walk in with somepin' stuck up his asshole. I know this for a fact. Years ago I worked in a hospital and I saw stranger shit than that. We saw it all. Those straight-laced types who look like they get kinky watchin' the Miss America Beauty Pageant. Guess again. I remember dis one guy come in with his dick all mangled. Straightest character you ever seen. Musta worked in a bank or somepin'. He *said* he was vacuuming his apartment in his robe when he bent over to disconnect the attachments... "

Out on the street each one has some attachment. Rollerskates, bicycles. A man looks at his watch. What would man be without his accessories?

"I think since the beginning of time man has been tryin' to get off in new and interestin' ways. If ya know what I mean," he says philosophically. "And like dat's where technology comes in. Helpin' man to do the impossible. Helpin' people to realize their potential. I tell ya, the search continues for the ultimate sex toy. If ya know what I mean."

I think I know what he means. The man is disgusting but in his own way he makes sense.

"By the way, did I ever tell you about the time I forgot I had my buttplug in – it happens sometimes – and like I took a shit and hadda fish it out of the toilet?"

## Dream Body

Waking up from it, out of it, he is so startled by it that he throws the covers off his body to rid himself of his memory of it. He shudders, wipes his eyes. He runs his hands over his body to feel the powerful muscles of his chest, reassuring himself. It was only a dream.

But what a dream it was. The dark world of his subconscious left to its own mischief in sleep. Forget it. Doesn't mean a thing. Psychology and its analysis of the personality through the inner-personality of memory has always seemed to be nothing but a big scam to him. Dreams are a bunch of random connections made by the brain when the rational goes to sleep and the memories go joyriding. Any analysis is the projection of the awakened mind. If he dreams about a fire engine in a swimming pool, it means nothing more than that the fire engine he saw on the news got mixed up with the swimming pool he loved so much when he was ten years old. The fact that he's stuck in the fire engine and can't get out and ends up drowning in his dreams is nothing more than an expression of his lifelong fear of swimming. Yes, he loved that swimming pool, the one at his cousin's house that he spent hours sitting around, staring into its awesome depth. But never jumping in, because he couldn't swim. And because his body was so skinny back then that he was embarrassed to take his shirt off. You see? One needs no Madison Avenue charlatan to tell you what you already know. The fact that he never learned how to swim requires no analysis. No need to blame mommy or daddy for that. And look at what he has been able to do as a man to compensate (the psycho words are unavoidable). No problems taking his shirt off at the beach these days. His muscles bulging, hard as a rock. At forty he's in better shape than he ever was. So he still can't swim. Who cares. With a body like that you don't need to. It's enough to lie in the sun and pose. Grease up that bod and watch the boys, and the girls, swoon over it. Pretend not to notice through the shades. And if he gets hot, he sets that dream body down in the wet sand and lets the tide wash over it, exhibiting it for the envy of all but the lifeguards who will sometimes nod at him like he's one of them. So who needs psychology when one has the power to change their life? To erase memory. Become your dreams instead of moping over them and rationalizing the frustrations. Forget mind over matter. It's matter over mind.

Except, his nightmare was not about drowning in a fire engine in a swimming pool. Although he's had that one a few times. Usually he can't even remember his dreams. If he does he forgets them by the time he turns the alarm clock off. This time the dream stays with him, haunting him. He opens his eyes still seeing it clearly in his mind's eye. The alarm didn't go off. He woke from sheer panic. He tells himself over and over that it was just a dream. But it hangs there, taunting him. His memory of it won't quit. Yet the picture is so horrible he can't even speak the words in his thoughts. To voice the image would be admitting some truth to it. And nothing could be further from the truth. All his life all he ever dreamed about was masculine to the core of it. His adult life revolves around fulfilling this dream. Working out. Pumping up that body. Cruising men. Hanging out in manly places with other big masculine men like himself. All his desires have been focused on these same images of brute male strength, to the point of monotony. Even the mention of something feminine would ruin it. Immediately. His hardon would shrivel at the slightest suggestion of anything having to do with the female anatomy. Unisex gyms are out of the question. Women are to be avoided. Wimpy men, as well. Drag queens make him sick. He has no female friends and plans to keep it that way. He works for an all-male company specifically for that reason. The sight of women is for him so much not to his taste that he has managed to somehow block them out when he walks down the street, which, considering the population of New York, is no small task. The way they move, talk, think, is offensive. He has nothing against them personally. He just doesn't want to have to look at them. So why after all these years of happily living without them do they pop up in his dreams? And worse, leave him awake staring at his morning hardon wondering what it all means.

He makes it through the morning by keeping himself busy. Sitting there at his desk with computer and phone, his muscles flexing with the slightest movement, growing under his white shirt, the starched collar stiff as a brick, the tie fixed in place, the short hair on his head standing up so straight you could brush your teeth on it. Sitting there at his big hard oak desk, a solid mass of packed flesh, only one word comes to mind. Man. What a fucking man. If there were an audience there, as there so often is in TV land, they would be thinking: Wow!What a guy. What a hunk. And they would ask questions like: Were you always such a hunk? And he would tell his life story. How he was a wimp until he started getting into weight-training. How hard he worked to build his body into the body he is now. How he grew those phenomenal pectorals. How he became a man.

He has a meeting with a representative from a company they plan on doing business with. The meeting is a success. The handshakes are firm and deep. Not like those wimpy ones you sometimes get when they don't reach all the way into the palm and end up crushing the fingers. The handshake gets the ball rolling and in the end seals the deal. He can tell that the man wants to do business with him. Both of them big strong men who don't need to mince words. This is straightforward business. Lay it on the line. No feminine maneuvering around here. The meeting leaves him flexing his muscles, his confidence at a peak. But no sooner does he close the door to his office than the memory of that dream creeps back into his thoughts. The horrendous unmanly picture exhibited. He sucks down his breath and vows to really push it when he does his training after work. The only remedy is the one thing that holds his life together like mortar holds brick. A good solid workout. His daily regimen at the gym will do it. Now that's therapy. He'll pump those thoughts right out of his brain. He'll pump so hard the blood'll shoot straight out his ears.

But that's not what happens. He finds himself feeling tired during the workout. He seems not to have his usual power. Of course from day to day working out has its good days and bad days. Sleep, food, and stress all affect it. After such a traumatic night's sleep it's to be expected. He thought he could work through it as he sometimes does. One can push through it and energize. But hard as he tries to push his strength and endurance, his soul is mush. He feels weak inside. He sees that horrendous image looming over him, laughing at his seriousness during the workout. He feels almost embarrassed as though the others can see what he sees. Are they smiling at him? No. His paranoia is getting the best of him. There is a dry aloofness about the weight room that he loves. The way each one is competing with himself in his own game of self-betterment. Each in his own arena. His eyes are focused on a black spot ahead as he pumps. No one else exists except the man and his machine. Not the time for socializing. It's disturbing when people start chatting. Usually no one does. The room with the free-weights and the big bars is off to the side so that people don't wander through while the big men are concentrating on their routines. The big men all keep the cool atmosphere with each other. With only grunts to be heard. But today of all days he hears soft giggles in the background and he knows that some wimps have wandered in. He pretends not to notice. But the giggling continues and it infects his muscles so that he's forced to drop the bar on the stands. A small earthquake is created. Followed by an unseemly giggle. One of the other big men asks if he's okay. Does he need a spot? No, man. Just one of those days. Yeah, man. I hearya. The brotherly talk reassures him. Through the line of curt conversation he sees the two little giggling queens eyeing him suggestively. Make me sick. They shouldn't let those bitches in. This side is for men only. Why don't they join the women's gym?

He's so disgusted he heads straight for the showers thinking about how he likes being gay but he doesn't think of himself in any way as being in any sense, even the slightest bit... womanly. He's found himself, his identity through body-building, and through being gay. But he hates that side of the gay scene – which admittedly seems at times to be the majority – that side that acts like women, emulates them. The whole campy draggy thing. Mary this and Mary that. *Those* gays have no respect for themselves. At least the ones who wear a dress and falsies are honest about it. But so many wear the butch outfits, work out, drink beer and still act like little misses. Who do they think they're fooling?

That last thought sticks in his gut. He remembers the image in the dream and the inevitable question smacks him in the face: Who do you think *you're* fooling?

But he manages somehow to put it out of his mind. At his locker the sight of other muscle-bound bodies centers him. Just as quickly he loses it. On the way to the shower some fat little faggot snarls at him provocatively. He takes a detour to escape, but the appalling flabby femmy image follows after him. Damn it! They won't let you be. They want to bring you down. To wallow with them in their mud. He vows to maintain his goals. To keep positive. That's the key. Forget all this psycho stuff. Positive thinking is what's needed.

In the shower his confidence is restored. At first. The water gently pounding his tight neck clears the mind. He's alone in the last stall. Just him and his muscles. He waits a long time before reaching for the soap. The water is hot cool relief. Finally he reaches for the soap, squirts it on his hands and rubs it in his chest, breathing deeply, enjoying the sensual power of his body. Nothing feminine about that. Men can be soft too. As long as their bodies are rock hard. His chest is immense. Like two giant boulders locked together in a grassy canyon. He rubs the soap into his hard body thinking: Superman. That's what I am. Able to leap tall buildings in a single bound. But the images of boulders and buildings are just as quickly transformed into balloons and waterbeds as the memory of the dream overtakes him again and he gasps and opens his eyes in order not to see what's in his head.

He sees something else entirely. Standing at the next shower is a guy he's seen around. A guy like him. The word *guy* turns him on to no end. Cause guys are guys. He looks at the other guy. Even bigger than himself. He watches the guy massaging his own muscles. The soapy hands move down to the groin. With one manly grab the penis gets soaped too. And it's half hard. The man is not embarrassed about it. Why should he be? Nothing embarrassing about guys, real men, with hardons. Penis in hand is like a good handshake when it's done right. No limp wrists. Pure man-handling. The man tugs at it, letting the soap foam around it. Looks down at it knowing full well that the other eyes are on it too. Then the eyes meet. The whole thing is right out of some porn fiction you skim over in those magazines. Anonymous sex so often is. Makes you wonder. Life imitating art?

The connection is made without a word. They could do it there. It's late and they're alone in the last stall. It occurs to both of them. The one turns off the water, and the other does too. They move towards each other. They're having sex with their eyes. Staring each other down like hungry wolves. Serious expressions. No fruity smiles around here. This guy is damn serious. He means business. The nightmare is totally forgotten as the mind drifts into a real-life daydream. His dick salutes the general. Addeez. They could do it right there. He usually goes home with the guys he does it with. Anonymous sex is not his thing. Too many distractions. The presence of some other bodies, wimpy ones, would ruin it. But just now it seems right. They're alone. He looks down the rows of stalls. Water somewhere, but no one in sight. It's a rational decision that precedes a passionate act. This is just what he needs after the shit of this day. The spontaneity takes him out of his worries and he gives in to it. And the next thing he knows he's having anonymous sex. No names. Just muscles. Anonymous muscles. And the guy's giving it to him. Fucking him brutally. Like bulls locking horns. Like rape. But it's good. And he feels like a man. Cause it's all manly. Two big muscular men. He feels like a *real* man. A big guy getting fucked by another even bigger guy. And it's okay. Cause there's nothing womanly about that. Nothing unmanly. Getting fucked doesn't make you a woman. Those are straight people's hangups. Society's problem. Here in the sanctity of the gym shower it's all man-to-man. Cause they're both guys. Real men. The guy giving it to him is a real man. And he's a real man.

Until the guy starts rubbing his chest from behind, holding those great big boulders like they're titties. And the dream comes back to him. And before he can put it out of his mind he's shooting his load and the guy is too (and without a condom cause real men don't need condoms) and the guy's fucking him so fucking hard, both of them shooting the shit from deep inside, the guy shoving it in as far as it'll go, just like in those porn flicks he watches on lonely nights when it's too cold to go to the bar. But then the image of the dream mixes with the porn flick happening right there and his subconscious is ready to burst from confusion while that man fucks him deep and grabs those boulders like he's trying to kill him, trying to break his back as he rapes him up the ass and it's all man-to-man muscle-to-muscle hard man sex but then why the hell is he screaming whispers in my ear telling me to take his dick good... *bitch!!!*

Lying in bed a few hours later he feels his muscles trembling in fear of the nightmare recurring, trying desperately to forget the image of the man grabbing his chest and calling him a bitch while his cum went splat on the wall. The cum lingers as evidence. Like the dream. It's undeniable. It happened. Even after you wash it away. It was. Therefore its meaning persists. He felt like a bitch. He feels like a bitch now. And the dream, like a nasty virus, has infected him to the point that nothing is the same.

Things mellow as the week progresses. He takes on an extra load of work. He's busy enough to skip the gym the next three days, something he never does. A few hundred situps and pushups on the floor next to his bed are enough to maintain the status quo. Then the weekend comes and he finds himself lying in bed not wanting to get out but not quite able to sleep. Finally out of sheer desperation he does something he vowed he would never do. He calls a shrink. A friend had once given him the number of his therapist recommending the man with such acclamations of praise, insisting that even if he didn't think there was anything wrong with him or his life he could still use a few sessions with the man because it would be so uplifting. The guy is a no-nonsense shrink. He gets right to the point. One session would do wonders. He only took the number to be polite. But on second thought, maybe he suspected then that there was in fact something wrong. And now there is.

The office is at Christopher and Gay. Wasn't the street named after some Admiral Gay in the Revolutionary War? Still the corner leaves him with the uneasy feeling that he's going to gay confession with the gay shrink. A second coming out. The therapist is an older gay man but fortunately not womanly. Not exactly. There's something a bit motherly about him. Compassionate. Caring. But he doesn't look like one of those little old aunties you see in the bars. You know, the ones who won't quit. Ever. Bad enough being a queen. But the old queens are fucking high comedy. Low comedy. At twenty they were dandies. At sixty, they're little old ladies. This guy is old, but burly enough to be okay, even if the burl is fat. He feels like he can talk to this guy. The handshake is firm and deep. He can be trusted.

But the subject matter proves to be so embarrassing that the words refuse to come out. He finds himself talking about everything but what he came to talk about. The words are the same ones he uses when he meets some guy in a bar. Cool bragging about his successful life, his job, his fitness goals. Going on and on about nothing, blabbing away in an uncontrollable frenzy of manly chatter for what seems to be a very long time. The therapist stares at him with an almost imperceptible smile on his face like he's seeing through it. The no-nonsense shrink?

Silence. He can't look up because he knows the guy is looking straight at him.

"Why don't you tell me what's bothering you."

Shaking his head. "Nothing's bothering me."

It sounds ridiculous. The obvious response: "Then why are you here?"

It occurs to him that probably every other patient sits there denying that they have a problem and each time the therapist gives that same response. Damn it. He tries to say what he means to say but what comes out is something else and it sounds worse because he doesn't mean what it sounds like he's really saying even though that isn't what he's really saying and he realizes that this is what he hates about psychology, this reading into things so that one can't be straightforward. What he says is: "It's not that I have any problem with being gay, you understand." And it sounds the minute he says it like he does have a problem with being gay. That slight smile on the shrink's face is obnoxious. Damn it! He knows that everything he's going to say will be analyzed and misconstrued the second he says it but he blunders on anyway. Uncontrollably. "No really. I like being gay. I hate that word though. Sounds so fruity. Let's say it like it is." Right. "I like being homo... sexual. I didn't when I was a kid. But that was before I started working out and like I was so embarrassed about my body and all." Silence. Unbearable silence. Because he can hear his words as an echo and he can tell what the shrink is thinking, how ridiculous it sounds. "I mean I actually didn't come out till really late. I was a definite virgin until... whenever that was but the point is that I really couldn't have sex with another man until I could make myself into the image of the man I wanted to be. I lacked the self-confidence. I was a wimp. Plain and simple. Being a *man* was only a dream."

The silence lingers with the last words to hang in the air demanding an explanation. Like someone is constantly asking: What do you mean by that? "I mean... how can I explain... my whole confidence is in being a man. A real man." Each sentence sounding more ridiculous than the last. "That's how I relate to other men. In a business deal. Or when I'm having sex. It has nothing to do with women. Do you understand? Nothing whatsoever to do with women!" He realizes his voice is getting loud.

"Then what's the problem? Why are you here?"

The no-nonsense shrink is getting annoying. "I'm here because... well I don't know why I'm here to tell you the truth." Right. "I mean I know why I'm here. Like I told you on the phone, this friend recommended you highly. He said it would be enlightening just to speak to you. Even if I didn't think I had any problems. And I mean, I'm always looking to improve myself. Make myself a better man. That's what body-building is all about. Self-improvement. So maybe this is *mind*-building."

"I see."

What an annoying thing to say. What does he see? The silence threatens to blow his mind and spill his guts on the floor and there's no escaping it. Say it. "I guess there is something that's been sort of bothering me lately and... "

"Uh-huh?"

"And I guess I sort of wanted to talk about it, but I guess it's sort of personal so like I didn't want to tell it to a friend so... "

"Uh-huh?"

"I mean like society has it all wrong, right? They act like being gay is somehow being womanly, especially if you get... ya know, fucked. Even the gays believe it. And the thing is, so many of the gays do act like women. But like that's not the whole scene. Not by far. The faggy ones are just the ones you notice because they stick out. And like on TV you only see the faggy ones representing the gay world because they're the only ones who will admit it publicly but there are so many more guys out there and there are so many really macho guys who are gay. And like you'd think the straight world would wake up!" His voice explodes suddenly. "I mean... didn't Rock Hudson prove the point finally that being gay has nothing to do with being womanly??"

No response. Not a word. The silence goes on for such a long time until it's clear that he's trapped. Imprisoned by his own fears. The world around him is closing in on him after all these years of building himself up to defend himself against their mockery. And now there's no escape anymore. He's trapped. He looks across at the other man for help but all he gets is a blank stare. So he looks away, out the window, and starts to speak, softly, as if someone else were speaking now. "I don't know where to begin."

"What started it?"

No way out now. "It started with a dream." He still hasn't voiced it. But once you dream it it's just a matter of time before the dream becomes a reality in one form or another. "I don't know how to say it." Looking desperately at the other for some kind of help. He sees the man, his judge, clearly now. The smile is gone, if it were ever really there. This is serious business. Truth or dare.

"Just say it."

"I wish I could."

"Why not?"

"Because. I don't even know you. You might tell someone." That sounded more ridiculous than anything else (though it has turned out to be right on target). "I mean... " sighs upon sighs, "I don't know what I mean. I mean I don't know how to say it but... " and more sighs, "I mean it was just a dream. Right? It doesn't mean anything except what you want to read into it? I'm the same guy with or without the dream, right?"

"Okay."

The muscle man puts his heavy head in the cradle of his brute hands and finally he's breaking down. Losing it. Like a little blubbery baby. Tears coming to his eyes. He tries to swallow them down, but he can't take it anymore. It has to come out. The tears, the words, screams, the truth. Something's gotta give. Yes, the truth. His own truth. In spite of Rock Hudson. Or Liberace. Either one. Hard as it is to confess, what happened happened. To him. And it has nothing to do with anyone else except his parents, his friends, his colleagues and the rest of the whole fucking world that won't just let him be. He puts his hands in his lap and stares up at the ceiling as though about to recite a memorized lesson. "I was naked in the dream."

"Okay." Nothing strange about that.

"I... I felt the muscles on my chest... "

"Yes?" Leaning forward, squinting, wanting to hear more.

"I don't know how to explain it. But I felt my pecs... quivering."

"Okay."

"Quivering. That sounds silly but that happens sometimes when you pump weights a lot. It's almost like the muscles are growing in your dreams. They do, in your sleep. I must have been lying on my front in bed and ya know how you can kinda feel the muscles hard against the hard bed. Cause like I sleep on a pretty hard futon so like you can really feel the hardness at the pressure points." He looks down. At his hands. Guilt, embarrassment written all over his face before he even says it. "You see, in the dream they weren't muscles anymore. My pecs, I mean. I looked down and I saw what they really were and I like freaked. They weren't just quivering. They were loose and bouncing. My pecs were tits!"

A great sigh. Said and done. But now that he started he can't stop. His face contorts in disgust as he unloads his disgust for himself. "I mean they were really tits. Woman's breasts. And like I was sort of into it. No I wasn't into it, but like suddenly I was wearing some kind of woman's lingerie and it was draped over my pecs, I mean my tits, and like it was so gross but suddenly I felt just like a woman and like I was proud of my tits, my fucking pecs were titties and they were swinging up and down and I was like getting off on it and... "

He can't go on. He closes his eyes. Too horrible to continue.

Time's up anyway. The therapist stands up. "That's very interesting. I'd like to get more into this but the session is over. Can you see me next week at the same time?"

He's dumbfounded. That the man can be so casual, so businesslike about it after he just spilled his guts on the floor. "Uh, yeah. Sure. But can't you like tell me something now? My friend said you're a no-nonsense shrink."

"I see. I do want to get into this in more detail because I do think there's more to it than meets the eye. But for right now we're out of time."

"What am I supposed to do until next week?"

"It's okay to be feeling somewhat vulnerable after these sessions. You'll find that that does happen. But you'll also find that life goes on, though you may start seeing things in a new light as a result of feelings you bring up in these sessions. Allow yourself these feelings. But try not to punish yourself for feeling them."

The beast soothed by the gentle words. He stands up. All six feet of solid manly muscle. He feels reassured. Relieved to have spoken the unspoken. And to have it received so mildly. "Yeah, I guess it was just a dream. After all. Just a dream. Right?"

"Right. Just a dream."

"I do feel better. Thanks, man."

"You're welcome."

They shake hands, manly as ever, and on the way to the door he says what after all sheds the most light because it's meaningless, ridiculous. A bad joke, but unintentional, so they both have a good laugh.

"I feel better already. I guess I just needed to like get it off my chest."

ↂↂↂↂ

## I Can't Get Enough

Sometimes there is no satisfaction. On certain nights, depending on the moon, I find myself wanting nothing else but sex. Sex is all I can think about and I will not rest until I get what I want. I go out on a man hunt. And I know I'll get what I want. I'm unstoppable. The problem is that when I get it, I just want more, and the only way to stop is to go home and sleep. The next day I wake up feeling as though I must have been possessed the night before. I cannot imagine that I did what I did and that it was so important to me. Sex is a diversion. It's just sex. Right?

The other night I had a seven-course meal and still went to bed hungry. I started out at a bar uptown, a seedy place that I like because it appeals to my chronic case of Latin Fever. There's always a crew of brown boys there. I know this sounds like the usual reverse racism. But fuck it. I got Latin Fever. Sure I like red, white, and blue guys too. But the minute I see brown I'm reminded of my incurable Latin Fever. It comes and it goes but living in New York it never really goes away. Too many macho Latinos everywhere. On the streets and in the bars. I make a special trip uptown or to the boroughs just to cruise the authentic culture. That's the thing about New York. A small place really. But take a subway ride and you're in another country. My posh friends wouldn't be caught dead in those parts of town precisely because they fear being found dead in those parts of town. Me, I'm not afraid. And even if I were, it wouldn't matter. Because I want what I want. It's a disease more potent than even the chronic fever. A state of mind that knows no racial bounds, no national borders. Call it sex addiction, if you like. I prefer to think of it as simply what it is: I want what I want and I can't get enough.

This bar uptown is a Latino candy store and it's obvious as you walk through the door that the other white guys had the same idea. It's a strange place. A certain confusion in the ambiance. That gay mix of masculine and feminine symbols. A dirty hardwood bar to put your pink lady on. Ornaments from Texas and Queens. The place has a manly smell in spite of the 70's decor. The guys don't swish and they don't vogue even with the old disco playing in the background. The kind of stuff they used to play at the Garage. (Remember the Garage?) And whatta ya know, they're playing my theme song. *I Can't Get Enough.* The bass line is a rumble. Dumadumadumaduma Thump Thump Dumadumadumaduma Thump Thump. Then the sexy syncopated voice: "I can't get enough." I'm standing there, gyrating against my will, thinking: how true, how true. I really can't get enough. Mostly I can. Mostly I put it out of my mind. But as soon as it pops into my little head, pulls into my harbor and drops an anchor, all I wanna do is satisfy it. And there really is no satisfaction cause I really just can't get enough.

That night I almost did. Five minutes after I get there I'm harassed by some Latino queen wanting to go cruising with me, mainly because he doesn't have any money. I don't have much either, but more than him. We go from Latin bar to Latin bar, "straight" ones too, me checking out the butch Latin guys and him checking out the feverish white guys.

My new friend has a queeny way of calling everything *cute.* Not only are the guys cute, but the bar is cute. The drinks are cute. The music also is cute. I leave him to his cute fetish and try to talk to a guy standing in the corner. The strong silent type. Could be Latino. Dark brown skin. A handsome rugged face to go with the strong body. I ask him if he has a name. He mumbles something like Ralph. He barely talks. I offer to buy him a drink. No response so I buy him a beer. He drinks it. This is not the guy you question about his career aims. Neither do you ask him to come home with you to fuck. You have to be subtle. Drugs are the answer (in spite of Nancy Reagan who never had to coax strange men back to the White House). I tell the guy I have some killer pot in my place (that's not a drug, is it?) and if he wants to we could go back there and smoke it. That sounds lame. So I tell him I have a little coke too. He barely responds, but he does follow me out and into a cab.

At my apartment he still isn't saying anything. I go in the bathroom and grind up an aspirin and sprinkle it on a mirror. When I come out he's still sitting there on the couch but now with his shirt unbuttoned. Act One. The whole thing seems ridiculous but it's turning me on anyway. The guy is so butch he doesn't have to say a word. His chest is brown and hairless. His muscles look like he got them without joining the Chelsea Gym. He is the object of my Latin Fever. I put the aspirin on the table, turn on the TV and the stereo, light up a joint and lie down with my head in his crotch (demure).

He doesn't object. He doesn't respond in any way except in his groin. His dick gets hard. What else is there to say? I pass him the joint so that I can sniff his crotch good. Fresh laundry and sweaty man. I undo his jeans with my teeth. He's got a big one. Excuse the cliché. But what the hell, it's true. And each time I unveil one of these magnificent specimens I am again awakened to the splendor of the male anatomy. As he sucks on the joint I suck on his joint. He pushes my head down. I am his receptacle. I feel reborn. All the stress of the day goes flying out the window. I get high on his dick. The rich smell, the feeling of being his cocksucker, whatever that means. He groans and pulls out so that he can come in my face (polite). In spite of my doctor's warnings I can't help but lick my lips. After a moment's hesitation I can't help but suck his cummy dick.

Okay, so I broke the rules. Crucify me. If I die I'll go to heaven and suck off Jesus. (I like Jewish guys too.)

He takes the aspirin and leaves. I stay to clean up the mess in my pants. Still hard because it was so hot. My mind is short-circuiting on endomorphines. What more do I want? Enough is enough. I'm satisfied. I got exactly what I wanted.

But I'm hornier than I was when I first went out that night. *I Can't Get Enough* is still running through my head and the beat is thumping in my groin. I want more. I decide the only rational thing to do is to go for a nice walk, maybe stop at the Korean store and get something sweet to eat. That should take my mind off of sex.

In the street I find myself staring at every other crotch that goes by, making a mental note. I'd blow him, I say to myself each time a suitable specimen walks by. I'd blow him. I'd blow him. Actually I had such a great time blowing the guy in my apartment and I certainly would blow all those other guys but now my mind switches gear and I wanna get fucked. My body opens up suddenly and I'm ready. I haven't been fucked in a while. Maybe that's just what I need. There is truly nothing as physically satisfying as getting good and plowed. The oral stuff is a mental turnon, a very potent one, but it always leaves you wanting more. I decide that the cure for my sexual dementia this evening is to get fucked deep. Standing at the corner I look up and the full moon shines over me. I knew it. The full moon always brings out the full lunacy of my libido. I head for the park.

I'm not the only moonchild in this city. The park is crowded. The moonlight adds an alluring glow turning the landscape and the men into a silvery fantasy. I walk up the little hill on the West Side where orgies often get going. When I get to the top I see a few guys, all different types, standing or milling around. I walk further on and there two guys are in the process of cruising each other. Both of them tall. I like getting fucked by tall guys because I'm tall myself and I don't like to feel like a big woman like I do when some little guy fucks me. Nothing against the little fellows. Just not up my ass.

These two are right out of a salt 'n pepper video. Both big and brawny, one white and one black. I'm an equal opportunity slut. I walk right in between them as though to say: Okay boys, I'm here, you can stop stalling. On closer inspection I realize that neither of them is very good-looking. But I don't give a shit. They're manly enough. And glamorboys are not my thing. So I kneel down and stick out my tongue and whatta ya know they both whip it out and take turns sticking it in my mouth. They're obviously into each other. But I'm the excuse. They suck each other's face while I suck their dicks. I know I've said it before. But here we go again. They both have big ones. Yes indeed.

But now I wanna get fucked. And good. I bend over a rock, pull down my pants and show them my tight ass. Mooning the moon, so to speak. The men take turns fucking me. I *do* insist that they put on a condom because I *am* planning on my retirement, early as it may be. Maybe I won't suck on a condom, but I won't get fucked without one. I get the gold star for best boy. Those two studs fuck me one after the other, taking turns like in some relay race, as soon as the one pulls out the other sticks it in and I'm lovin' it so much I don't even notice the audience until I come on the rock screaming my little head off. No applause this time, but lots of wanking from the balcony. They seem to have come from miles around, drawn by the scent. Perched on a rock. Or standing over my head. I should take a bow, but all I can do is pull up my pants and hobble down the hill and out of the park.

Okay, I've had enough. Two orgasms and three guys in one night. I'm walking home trying not to stare at the crotches. I cross Central Park West and I'm sure I've had enough for one night but on the other side of the street coming towards me is the cutest little guy. I'm really bisexual: I like men *and* boys. Something puckish about this one reminds me of a guy I knew in high school and fell in love with and almost committed suicide over. We pass each other now here in the middle of the street. It's not that boy anymore than I'm still sixteen, but strike me dead I can't help myself. I turn around. I bet he's headed for the park. I curse myself. There's no jism left in me but I follow him anyway and sure enough he walks straight down the hill towards the bridge and up the hill into the thick of it and when I stand there on the hill watching him some of the others are staring at me like they're thinking to themselves: "God, she's back. What a slut." That's right, honey. I can't get enough cause too much of a good thing ain't never enough! I follow the boy down the hill down a long winding path. He realizes I'm following him. He turns into the woods. I follow. He stops by a trickling stream. I kiss him. I rip off his clothes. I want to hurt him, or just get rough. He sucks my dick. I suck his. Maybe it's the moonlight or coming down from the joint but the whole time I think this is Davy Hansen, the boy who teased me almost to death throughout my high school years, the boy who turned Social Studies class into nonsense next to the important study of masturbation, and boy did I study hard whacking off to my dreams of Davy Hansen and here he is after all these years and he hasn't changed a bit and I'm wanking him and he's wanking me and I barely press my juiceless hardon against his crack when he shoots his wad all over a tree, pulls up his pants and runs away leaving me fucking hornier than ever and rubbing my dick on the juicy tree and actually coming one last time but so few drops that I'm not sure it qualifies as an orgasm and in any case it doesn't offer any relief.

So even if I can't get enough I suppose I've had enough. Time to call it a night. Think about the mundane things you have to do in the morning. That'll take your mind off of Davy Hansen.

In the all-night deli they're playing that disco ballad from the 70's, that one about mending a broken heart. It makes me homesick and boysick and my mind is beyond sex, traveling down memory lane to a place where I left my broken heart, lost it to become an adult and do adult things like going to bars and picking up men or getting fucked in the park. So maybe my heart is still broken, but I get some momentary relief even if the urge never really goes away. It seems I've had one of each flavor tonight, but I could eat a whole other box. I settle with a box of assorted candies. Walking home I eat the whites and the blacks, the reds and the greens, the blues, the oranges, the big ones and the little ones, but I save the best for last. I'll eat the browns when I get home.

## Confessions of a Smoocher

"I confess," Bernie confesses. "I'm a smoocher."

Nothing to be ashamed of.

"Yeah but you don't know the worst of it. Smooching is all I like to do." Bernie's voice, his mannerisms and his accent remind me so much of my Aunt Ida that if I close my eyes I'm sure I'm standing there in this sleazy gay bar with that sweet little old dumpling of a woman. When I open my eyes I see her standing next to me, bearded and pumped, dressed in motorcycle jacket and fatigues. From head to toe, the semi-mohawk to the Gestapo boots, Bernie's persona speaks aggression. But the pink heart-shaped brooch says it all. My Aunt Ida had the same one. She bought it in 1945 to celebrate the end of the war.

"People laugh. But it's not a laughing matter. I'm addicted to smooching."

The smoocher pervert. Sounds like safe sex to me.

"Yeah but it ain't so easy finding other smoochers."

Maybe you're looking for love in all the wrong places.

Bernie purses his lips. Just the way my Aunt Ida does. "I confess. I'm not looking for love."

Casual smooching?

"That's right. I can only smooch in anonymous situations. If they talk too much it ruins it."

Anonymous smooching. Wow.

Bernie goes on to recap all the hot smooching encounters of the last ten years. He doesn't like backrooms. Never goes to the park. Can't deal with the discretionary admission policy of some of the sex parties. "It really gets my goat." Aunt Ida uses the same expression. "These faggots act like it's some kind of popularity contest. The A-list! They should be ashamed of themselves. Weren't they persecuted enough as kids? You know these were the same ones who no one picked for the dodgeball team in elementary school. And now the sissy Maries think they're special just cause they pumped up their tits." Bernie likes to go where everyone is invited. There's no cover charge and the atmosphere is if nothing else... manly. "That's right. I smooch in the toilet."

Do people smooch in the toilet?

"Sure! You'd be amazed. I've had some of the hottest smooching action in the toilets of New York."

More smoochy stories. Enough to fill a book. Confessions of a smoocher. I listen with my lips pressed tight together. Here and there I take a breath and ask a pointed question. You can only take so many smoochy stories in one sitting. But Bernie's have an edge. One story in particular strikes me as odd.

He was using the library at one of this city's esteemed colleges, researching ancient weapons of the Mediterranean civilizations for a scholarly article he was ghost-writing. He'd heard about the men's room in the library building and this knowlege was getting in the way of his research. Hunched over his books, reading about stone picks and clubs, his mind was beginning to wander. Soft smoochy fantasies were beginning to cloud his concentration. "I'm an addict. I confess. When the urge comes, I just can't help myself. I *need* to smooch. And nothing will get in my way."

One more sex-addict in need of rehab. A few minutes later he finds himself cruising around the stalls. Not much going on, but there is one guy slowly brushing his teeth carefully at the sink. It's clear that he's biding time, trying to look like he's there to brush his teeth when it's quite obvious that he wants to screw around.

Bernie steps into a stall. He waits there for a bit, peeping out from time to time to see what's happening with the guy at the sink. His teeth must be awfully white by now. Bernie steps out and around and winds up in the stall directly behind the guy. He looks into the mirror. The guy looks into the mirror and their eyes meet. The guy finishes brushing his teeth, puts his toothbrush in his pocket and turns around as though he wants to follow Bernie into the stall, but perhaps he's too shy because instead he awkwardly turns and walks into the stall next door.

"So I'm waiting there thinking: What's up? Do you wanna smooch or what?"

Bernie exits the one stall and brashly enters the other. The two of them are hip-to-hip in the tiny stall but the guy is looking down at his feet, obviously embarrassed by the intimacy. The smoocher takes charge of the situation. He puckers up them luscious lips ready to plant a big wet smacker on the guy's face when the guy looks at him and says in a quick monotone hushed voice: "Do you like to get rimmed?"

Bernie looks at me as though I just asked him the question. "I just hate it when they talk too much, but this is really out of the blue. What kind of a question is this, do you like to get rimmed? Even if I liked to get rimmed, you don't ask. You wait for the right opportunity and then do it."

What did you tell him?

"I didn't say anything. I just pointed my smoocher in his direction, aimed and fired."

The guy turns his head. The smooch lands on his cheek. "What did you do that for?" He looks at Bernie like he just hit him. "If you don't wanna get rimmed you can come in my face."

Bernie purses his lips and looks at me with Aunt Ida's eyes as though to say: Nu? He can't answer the guy. That would ruin it. He can only wait until the guy stops talking and then try to maneuver him into another smooch.

Why didn't you just leave? Find someone else.

"The guy was very handsome. Just my type. Tall, a little bit chubby, and balding. You can keep your pin-up boys. I don't like skinny boys, with or without the muscles. I like men. Mature men with some meat on them. I think the thinning hair looks distinguished. I don't understand why all these fags want to be young forever."

Not only fags want to be young forever. But in any case why go to a college men's room if you're into older men?

"I'm not into older men particularly. Just not boys. And you find all types in every men's room. That's what I like. A mixed crowd. In any case, when I get the urge, I gotta go. I told you I'm an addict."

But the guy obviously doesn't want to smooch.

Bernie looks ashamed. "I confess. It turns me on even more when they don't like it."

So in spite of the guy's obvious distaste for smooching, Bernie plants a big wet one on his mouth. The guy backs up against the partition and says: "You wanna piss in my face?"

No comment.

"Listen, if you want to, you can take a dump on me."

I look at Bernie. This is incredible. Never were two people more mismatched. Aunt Ida purses her lips and exclaims: "What is it with these men? What kind of strange things they do? I never heard of this. I'm supposed to drop a turd on his head and this turns him on?"

What did you do?

"Nothing. I tried to kiss the man. He made a face like you would imagine someone would make if you did drop a turd on their head, like my kiss was the most disgusting thing imaginable, and then he looks me in the eye and in all seriousness says, and I quote: Fart on me."

Seems easy enough. Did you?

"Of course not! How do you fart on someone, anyway?"

Hm. I try to imagine that.

"So then I'm just about to kiss him again, to violate his face with my lovely lips, when he says: Okay, so you don't like to get rimmed, you don't wanna come in my face, piss on me or take a shit. You don't even like to fart. What *do* you do?"

What did you say?

"I told him the truth. I said: I like to smooch. That's it. But to be honest, I don't like to talk about it. It ruins the spontaneity. I'll see you later."

And that was it?

Bernie looks down at his necklace. Yet another confession?

"I'm ashamed to admit it, but we actually struck a bargain. As I'm leaving he says: Wait, don't go. I'll kiss if you let me rim you."

Desperate.

"It's amazing what a man will do to get what he wants."

Did you agree? But wait, how does that work? I mean the holes are on opposite sides of the anatomy. You can't stick your tongue in his mouth while he sticks his tongue in your ass. That would be quite a feat.

"Obviously we would do it one after the other."

I hope you kissed him first.

"I did. I did. But not much. The truth is I'm a selfish lover. I couldn't go through with it. We barely smooched when I pulled out my tongue and ran out of there."

You hate getting rimmed that much?

"No, no. The man had the worst case of bad breath."

## Alcoholics Anonymous

New York can be a dangerous place. I knew a guy who was stabbed seven times on a subway platform and then thrown in front of an oncoming train. Most of the time it's just a matter of being in the wrong place at the wrong time. But for some, their life itself is so dangerous it would seem just a matter of time before they get what's coming to them. I have a friend who's like that. The man is looking for trouble. He blindly walks into the most dangerous situations, inviting whatever's lurking in the shadows to come out and slit his throat. It's like he's on a suicide mission. He's asking for it. Yet as fortune would have it, he's never even been mugged.

I've decided that it's because he drinks so much. My friend the lush is literally walking through life on a sloshy cloud so that everything floats right by him. He staggers through the streets of New York like he's in Disneyland and all the seediest spots are fun rides and the seediest people your favorite cartoon characters. His penchant is for young heroin addicts. I would say that he only has sex with heroin addicts. Partly because he can only have sex by paying for it. My friend is a father figure of sorts. In fact he looks twenty years older than his age. Too much drink has pickled his face. The swollen belly has turned him into one of those skinny Santa Clauses with the pillow stuffed under the jacket. Worn-out as Santa is he likes his elfs young and pretty. The waif look. Whiteboys who dropped out of prep school to shoot heroin and live on the streets. These boys will only do it for money, of course. Which is no problem because my friend the lush is loaded (in more ways than one). He was quite brilliant as a young man. Discovered some plastic that he patented and retired on. You would never know looking at him now that he ever had such a mind, though he maintains the air of deranged professor. Running a dead poets society. A class full of heroin addicts. The boys flock to him. And he flocks to them. A marriage made in hell. A formula for dangerous dealings which surely should have landed him in the hospital or the grave by now. Yet the man has never been to the hospital since the day he was born. Never robbed. Never even punched in the face. And his liver shows no signs of faltering. Not yet. To his credit, he has no regrets. He accepts his fate as he does his dissipated life as something appropriate. He's quite the sober realist, making no plans for old age, actually inviting an early demise. "Best to die young," he will tell me in a slur. So it would seem.

It was his fiftieth birthday when he last called me up and somehow convinced me to come over. The man has fewer than few friends. He lives an anonymous existence. He reads all morning and drinks the rest of the day. He always has at least one heroin boy staying with him. They don't make for very good company, nodding off half the time. I suppose he called me up because it was his birthday and he sentimentally craved some more human company. Not that I'm the most fun person. But I do speak. And I like to listen.

When you first enter his apartment you realize immediately why his yuppy neighbors are trying to get him out of the building. The place is a wreck. Shit everywhere. Old books, last week's garbage, endless unidentifiable junk extending out into the hall. A large apartment, four or five rooms, it's absolutely overflowing with the worthless junk he finds on the street and brings back with the junked-up boys. Old magazines, broken furniture, an old porcelain toilet bowl. I think he fancies himself the historian, maintaining the archives for future historians. I'm sure he has every Sunday's *Times* from the last thirty years somewhere in that apartment. Along with every worthless old bottle. A liquor store of empty bottles. Plus coke bottles. Milk bottles, orange juice bottles. Old Heinz ketchup bottles. Shampoo bottles. All strewn among the countless empty beer bottles. A maze for the roaches. And let's not forget the piss bottles. I know by now to be very careful when you put your beer down to make sure that you pick the right one up. It better be cold. I made that mistake once. I'll never make it again.

When I get to the birthday party I find the front door propped open (a truly bizarre concept in New York) to make way for the mess spilling out into the hall. I climb over an assortment of junk until I get to the living room. The birthday boy is sitting in his easy chair, surrounded by the morning's books. If I ever pick one up it is always of the most esoteric nature. How does he do it? Scientific journals. Literary criticism. Ancient poetry. Heavy stuff. Read too much and you get a hangover. No problem for his fermented brain. Until he takes that first drink and then he can't so much as read the first line. The TV goes on and he and the heroin boy settle down to some daytime viewing. Today it's an old black-and-white sitcom. Maybe it reminds him of his childhood in the 50's. My friend is wide awake but lost in his drunken thoughts, barely looking at the TV. The boy is nodding off, but his eyes are most definitely glued to the tube. In fact he laughs along with the laugh track which tells me that he must be somehow concentrating on the show, seeing the images in spite of his droopy eyes. I walk into the room. I bid my birthday condolences to the wall and without invitation, practically unnoticed, I take a seat on the couch right next to the heroin addict who in spite of his dissipated condition is stunningly gorgeous. A bit skinny. In torn jeans and teeshirt he still looks like a young god and I get a glimpse of why my friend is so content with his decadent life.

The scene is typical. No talking. Just the laugh track coming out of the TV. The reception is so bad – my friend considers cable TV the death of Western Civilization – that I can barely make out the figures. The set is as old as the show. The antenna has a hanger stuck in it. The knob to change the channel has long since been replaced by pliers. I squint to see what we're watching. Oh my god, it's *Father Knows Best.* He sure does. I look over at all-knowing dad in his birthday outfit, a stained dress shirt and the widest boxer shorts I've ever seen. He's scratching his balls and playing with the saliva in his mouth, rolling it around with his tongue. His beautiful son seems to be in a coma. This scene would be comical if it weren't tragic. I feel alienated from humanity as one can feel more acutely in the naked city than anywhere else in the world. What's the point, I want to ask. Entropy, seems to be the answer. I realize why I never visit the guy anymore. I think about getting up and leaving. Would they notice? Instead, I get up and offer to get myself a beer from the kitchen.

When I come back the channel is switched to cartoons. The modern computer-generated ones full of superheroes and stilted explosions. My friend comes out of his trance: "The old cartoons were so much better." Ah, the good old days. The new generation doesn't seem to mind. The heroin addict is absolutely speechless, motionless, expressionless. I stare at his beautiful empty face. In spite of the absurdity of it, I decide to strike up conversation.

Hi. I'm Ken. Who are you? I chime, not at all expecting an answer.

"Scoop," he mutters, strangely right on cue. Like a horse who counts with his hoof. He seems to be in there, somewhere, taking it all in, but outwardly gone. Somewhere else.

That's an interesting name, I say in my most cheery voice. I feel like I'm talking to a small child. On drugs.

My friend fills in the blanks. "Scoop has been living here for about two months now. We're very happy to have him around."

I look around, wondering who else might be living here. My friend has this strange habit of referring to himself in the plural, some sort of old-fashioned politeness. His accent is pure Ivy League British-American and his phrasing of the language brings to mind something from *Little Women.* "We're so very happy to have Scoop with us. You know we found him in the street and dreadful to say had we not brought him home he might very well have come to no good."

He must be kidding. I can never tell if he's being serious. Is he making fun of the decadence or does he imagine he's running an orphanage? Nice of you to take such an interest, I add. It seems like the thing to say.

"Well you know, we do try to do our best."

We certainly do. This scene goes on for about an hour, mostly in druggy silence. For a long time we watch a show about fire safety. I'm ready to get up and leave finally – I can't take the excitement anymore – when the birthday boy pulls himself out of his chair and stumbles over to the couch to suggest that we should go out. He plops down on the other side of the boy, puts his arm around him and starts kissing his pale cheeks. The boy seems to be somewhere else entirely. I'm struck by this image of my friend kissing a corpse. My friend goes to the other room to dress and when I speak to the corpse he again gives these strangely cogent answers. I ask him how long he's been an addict, a tacky question when you think about it, but the boy has no problem answering me, doesn't even pause to recall what I asked. "Five years," is the deadpan response, like he's talking in his sleep. "I quit a few times. It never works."

Have you tried methadone, or one of those drug therapies? I don't know anything about the subject.

"Methadone sucks. You can't even get a hardon."

I get a hardon. I think about the fact that I could borrow the boy for a few days. My friend mentioned that on the phone. It's not the money. He just likes to give someone else the burden now and then to relieve himself of that burden. Housing him, feeding him and keeping him high is a job of sorts. I could handle the job but I decide that I couldn't make love to someone who wasn't in the room. I would feel like I was kissing a doll. As we talk I feel some connection. Almost like communicating through radio signals to a distant planet. I feel chummy. Probably just my hardon talking. I light up a joint. That's always an icebreaker. At least for the first few minutes. But when I pass the joint he shakes his head with only the slightest movement. "No thanks, man. I don't smoke that shit. It's bad for you. Fucks up the mind totally."

My friend comes back dressed in an old three-piece suit complete with pink bow tie. The raincoat covers most of it, which is good. Less conspicuous on the streets. I like to attract as little attention as possible walking the streets of New York. Best to be underdressed. My friend puts on his rubber boots. He stuffs his wallet and fills up his flask (for the long journey to the bar). We leave without saying goodbye to the boy. I feel a sadness come over me, from the joint or the scene or both. I take a shot from my friend's flask before we leave.

In the elevator I ask him why he goes out cruising with such a hot number sitting at home.

"Oh, yes. We're very happy to have Scoop around... but you know one has to get them at just the right moment or they're quite useless." I'm not sure what he means. "Before they shoot up is when they can get it up. We time it just so each day. We finish our work for the morning. We put down our books. We have our first drink and we get him stimulated. Dear oh dear, such an exhilaration to be performing fellatio on that boy's noble and substantial phallus. No doubt his juice is concocted from a divine potion." My friend's words are a demented combination of the poetic and the gutter. "As soon as it's over we eat a little something and the party begins. He takes his medicine and we open a bottle of wine and sit down to our main meal of the day. He doesn't drink anything and honestly he barely eats. We do worry about that boy. His lifestyle is extremely taxing on the body. But at least we've got it down to a routine. You know regularity is the secret to a long and healthy life."

He never quite answered my question. I answer it myself. It's clear that my friend has an appetite for boys bottomless as his thirst for liquor. And he knows how to get what he wants. He'll show me all his favorite spots. We take the subway straight to the East Village. He never takes cabs. "They're unsafe. The way those men drive." I think he enjoys the scene in the subway anyway. I know that he has picked up more than a few heroin addicts there. Standing on the platform he spots a group of boys panhandling at the turnstiles. He has a little conversation with them, gives them some change and then returns to me. "Crackheads. We never associate with crackheads."

In the train we are audience to an endless stream of beggars. One by one they exhibit themselves. The subway is their gallery, their stage. And the range is wide. From the lighthearted comedy of a man claiming to be from outer space to the endless array of tragedy. Every handicap is exploited in this show. Most of them have dark skins. Their presence makes an inadvertent sociological statement if anyone cared to notice it. My friend watches as everyone does, with cynical amusement, or in the worst cases a sort of detached horror where one looks away pretending not to see it. Not much is donated to the cause. If you gave a dollar to each one the subway ride would cost you twenty dollars. Those who give at all, use it as an opportunity to get rid of their loose change. A few coins here and there. I prefer to pick one tragedy and concentrate my donations. I give a man with no legs two bucks. One for each leg? I feel ridiculous paying him for his misery, but it seems like the thing to do.

We get out at 14th Street and walk east leaving a trail of misery. Stepping over the bodies or just walking by a million hard-luck stories. Maybe I want to see the misery. But I can't help it. It's there staring me in the face, blocking out the tacky displays in the windows.

We're walking down second avenue and my friend the erudite lush takes a swig from his flask. The party is happening right here and now. The streets are full of an excitement that you find nowhere else in the world quite like this. Frantic. Some of it bizarre. The lights, the cars screeching by, the people walking fast and slow and every which way. Everything is moving faster than you can take it in. The smells from the Indian restaurants wafting off of 6th Street mixed with the fumes of the gutter, a hearty blend of food, dirt and exhaust. A car goes by with the beat pumping like the whole car is one big speaker. Someone screams at the top of their lungs. People hanging out on the sidewalk. Selling things. Begging. Or just hanging out. We head towards Tompkin Square Park. The police stand guard protecting the park from the poor. Protecting the trees from becoming homes to the homeless. And protecting themselves from a riot. Someone screams out of a car: "Oink, oink." The pigs look the other way but keep their clubs close at hand.

My friend is oblivious to everything but his quest for heroin boys. We head straight for the hot spot. The park is full. It's a warm cool wet night. But the people are out. Smoking, drinking, hanging out around the congas. Dancing to a bohemian vibe left over from another generation. A bunch of punks sit around sniffing glue out of a mustard jar. One of them strokes a pet rat. My friend on the lookout. He can spot a drug addict a mile away. "Ahhh." He sighs. "There. Come. We shall procure some entertainment."

A gang of bruised whiteboys standing outside of the men's room. One indistinguishable from the other. Same dirty clothes. Skinny bodies, sulky eyes. Right out of the latest Calvin Klein ad. My friend approaches. He doesn't waste words. "Wanna make forty bucks?" He speaks their language. The boys look around nervously like their mothers might be watching. Some of them giggle. The others look more serious like in the middle of a business deal. They want to up the price. But my friend is a professional at this. Not only is the price fixed but there are stipulations. "You boys can get it up?" Sure they can get it up. "You don't get a dime if you can't get it up." Two of them go into the toilet with him. I'm not sure what to do. I follow them in. He takes the two boys into a stall. He sits down on the toilet seat and unzips their flies and blows them. I'm watching from outside. I don't know if I would get involved with these boys even if I were willing to throw away eighty bucks. But that doesn't stop me from watching. The door is broken on the stall, leaving me to fill in the gap. The boys put there arms around each other's shoulders forming a wall around my friend. Their necks are scruffy and their clothes in tatters and their bodies are awfully skinny but there is something hot about them. I begin to understand my friend's obsession. I picture him as a science nerd in high school privately drooling over the bad boys who called him a sissy. Those naughty boys who drank and smoked and did drugs while he was working late in the chemistry lab. And now decades later his chemistry dreams have turned into a lot of money but the dream has long since faded as creation gave way to business and all that's left is the same old pain, the longing for those bad bad boys. A new generation offers him an endless replay of getting what he always wanted over and over again. He never really gets it. Like an endless taste test. A wine taster who spits it out so that he can taste a hundred bottles of wine. Except of course, my friend, the man who can't resist courting danger, the lush, the "child molester," the hopelessly jaded existentialist, my friend the cocksucker... does indeed swallow.

It doesn't take long for the boys to shoot their loads. The virtuosity of youth. I try to peek over their shoulders to watch. I'm a tireless voyeur besides being the roving reporter. One of the boys shoots it into my friend's mouth while the other wanks off on his bald head. My friend seems thrilled and absolutely oblivious to anything else. To any danger. The police or the boys themselves. He's in his own drunken world and he wants what he wants and he doesn't give a fuck what happens as long as he gets it. They could slit his throat and he wouldn't notice. As soon as they shoot their cream, the one says: "C'mon man, give us the money," in a slightly threatening way. My friend pulls a wad of bills and they swipe it out of his hand and run out of the toilet stuffing their hardons back in their pants. My friend is left a cummy mess, wiping it off his head. I wait outside.

Leaving the park I have to ask if he's ever run into problems doing this. Never. He always has the money ready to go so he doesn't have to fish in his wallet. They just want the money so they can get the drugs. Junkies are easy to deal with, he tells me as a chemist knowledgeable about the effects of chemical substances. Stay away from the crackheads, he warns, and you won't have problems. Seems like sound advice. A few feet from a squad of fat-assed cops, my friend pulls out his flask and takes a long swig. Ah, that's better. Now why is it that all I have to do is drink a beer out of a paper bag and a cop will come out of nowhere and take it away from me? It seems my friend is untouchable by either side of the law.

We head for the bars. My friend is wobbling in his shoes. I have to ask. Has he ever considered quitting drinking? Maybe go back to work as a scientist. Discover something new. He answers my ridiculous question with the flat cynical certainty of experience. "The last and only discovery of mine was turned into toxic household items. Not very interesting."

Hasn't it improved the quality of people's lives?

"Yes, but only at the expense of other lives and only for the greed of mindless barbarians who think nothing of destroying an undeniably fragile planet."

I had no idea my friend was ecologically inclined. I approach him from a more personal perspective. Wouldn't it be nice to sober up for yourself, just to be sober?

"We quite enjoy our drunkenness. It runs in the family. For generations."

It would seem that alcoholism is yet another chemical matter. But one could fight the chemicals with the power of the mind. With professional support. What about psychotherapy?

"A quasi-science."

What about Alcoholics Anonymous?

"Dreadful Jesus slaves. We quite enjoy our debauchery. Something intangible in a tangible world. The soul sings where there would be only the noise of traffic."

His metaphors are slurred but sonorous. All around taxis are honking away in a traffic jam as he saunters across the street between the bumpers without looking either way. Bicycles zip by cursing him. I dart around trying to avoid getting run over, trying to save myself. For what, I can't say. My friend seems to have discovered that there is nothing to save yourself for. He wobbles through it all. His life is a near-death experience.

In the bar I try to drink the poison he orders for me. Don't get me wrong. I'm no teetotaler. But I prefer my poison disguised as something tasty and refreshing. A bit of lime if nothing else. My friend insists that it's a mixed drink. Two kinds of rum. He has the bartender pour it straight, no ice, and with the understanding that as soon as he puts his glass down they should fill it up. The money on the bar is used up in no time. It's clear that the birthday boy is trying to make this his last. He's guzzling the stuff, poisoning himself. I'm wondering how to get him home safe, trite as the concept might be. The bartender could help me put him in a cab. I hope my friend doesn't make a fuss about the dangers of riding in taxis, because it's bit of a walk to the train and at this point it will be difficult enough getting out the door. I watch him ease himself onto a barstool. He manages to balance his load, but just barely. His body is swaying unintentionally to the music. No one seems to notice or care. The anonymous city is oblivious to anonymous alcoholics and visa versa. I'm about to suggest that we get a cab when my friend points to the other side of the bar and says: "First we have a few more birthday presents to open." He staggers away. This bar is no bigger than some apartments. In the back is the tiniest backroom in town. More of a closet than a room. There's a druggy boy standing in the back of the bar. Yet another anonymous addict? My friend approaches him and in a minute they're wandering into the back area where the backroom and the toilets are. I don't want to watch this time but I feel responsible for my friend. I bum a cigarette and walk towards the toilet. I don't smoke cigarettes, except on occasions when life seems particularly hopeless. So when I do smoke them, I get really high. It's a quick high and I'm reminded why the tobacco industry beat the hemp industry. An instant satisfaction more fleeting than crack. And cheaper.

They are the only ones in the dark little room. Again my friend kneeling at the altar of youth. This time he's slumped on the floor in the corner. The boy is fucking his mouth because the man is practically comatose. I wonder how he has the energy to keep his mouth open and head in place. Why does he bother at this point? He can't be feeling much. And he's had plenty already. For the day. For the half-century. I guess the point is to drown yourself in it. Too much of a good thing is still never enough. I smoke my cigarette watching the rhythm of the boy's naked butt. Creamy white and smooth and showing none of the scars that street life has inflicted on his face. My friend gets what he wants. And in so doing makes his apocalyptic point. We can't change the world for better or worse. We can only get our rocks off. And even then, we won't ever really get satisfaction, as much as we get. It's all temporal. The chemist who gave up mixing chemicals for mixed drinks seems to imply that the latter gives some solace at least, fleeting as it is, whereas the other has done nothing but destroy. The spirit soars where the ego would invade. I stand there watching genius at work, numbing his creativity in pursuit of lower aims. Life is simple down there. You pay for what you get. And you get it. As much as you can pay for. Isn't that what all addictions are about? Control. At one point the boy pulls out, probably figuring he can get his money without shooting his load because the man on the floor is barely conscious. But the man on the floor is clear in mind and resolute in his aims and still in control in spite of his slumping body. He grabs the boy by the cheeks of his ass and pulls the weight of him down on his face. No juice, no money. My friend knows exactly what he wants. And maybe that's the key to the method to his madness. That's what keeps him going, surviving against all odds. Mindless orgasms give him something vital, and he knows it. Something to live for. He survives his precarious life by the conviction of his purpose, like a soldier in a "just" war. He once told me that all of math and science is merely self-obsessed man's lame attempt at defining his inexplicable existence, that the number ten is an arbitrary point based on the happenstance of ten-fingered creatures. So maybe my friend keeps on going and will never give up because he knows from experience that whatever the consequences, a mouthful of boy jism is still worth a million times more than a million-dollar formula.

## Old Love

I'm going to have that midlife crisis, he says at 55. It's now or never. To think that those rock stars from my youth are even older than me! The ones who are still alive. How ridiculous they look with the long girlish hair hanging down over their wrinkles, shaking those geriatric hips. The hair is a wig and the hips are implants. Not me. I'm going to accept my age. No more jeans. No more lovebeads. I'm going to shop at Macy's if it kills me. In the men's department. I'm going to wear a tie to work even though I work out of my living room. I'm going to grow up, goddamit. Act my age.

But what about the boyfriend, he asks the mirror, standing in front of it stretching back the wrinkles around his mouth. Always young guys for boyfriends, and when they grew up a little it was on to the next. This one has lasted the longest. Long enough that I could say he's an old boyfriend. An old love. He was just a boy when I found him. Now he's getting to be middle-aged. Maybe this is what's bringing on my own midlife crisis. I have to admit it. When I look at him sometimes, when the lighting isn't flattering, I can see where he's aged and I can imagine how in a few years those details will continue to age until he's old. Just plain old. Not youthful but aging. Old. And then what? I'll have an old man for a boyfriend! No. Never. I'd rather be dead before that happens. Or maybe I'll dump him.

I can't dump him, he tells the mirror. I love him to death. He's still my baby. When the light is flattering, or when he's had a good night's rest and the wrinkles aren't so pronounced, then I look at him as I hold him and I feel the love I felt for him when I first met him and it's as strong if not stronger than ever. I cry inside with this love for him, my boy, my baby. I may grit my teeth when I fuck him with my passion and hate for all those cute boys of my long life embodied in his puppy face and tight body, but when after he falls asleep and I hold him in my arms, I can feel his heart beating against my palm and I know I can never stop loving this person.

It's clear, he tells himself closing the mirror door of the cabinet, I'm going to go on as I have and nothing will change. Because... I've already had that midlife crisis.

Across town two old men sit around the TV arm in arm holding on for dear life while watching the latest episode of their favorite hospital drama. The slightly older one is watching without watching it. Seeing the life-threatening images without digesting them. His mind is somewhere else. Everything's hunky-dory in paradise, he silently tells the TV as he and his friend and the rest of America watch America's top-rated show. What more could I want? We've both had successful lives. No one starving around here. Plenty of insurance to stave off catastrophe, or at least pay for it when it happens. And we have each other. We are the living breathing gay success story. A love story about two young guys who fall in love and live happily ever after, or at least long enough together that they actually grow old together. Nothing kinky. Just the simple pleasures of marital bliss, without the license. A privileged life cherished together, not thrown away through excess. No drugs. No wild fucking around. Pure family entertainment. No need for cable fetishes.

Of course I had that one brief affair with that young but aging guy, he mentions to the TV. Love intrigue comes to the emergency room and the old man on the couch remembers a hot affair. It didn't last long and there seemed to be no reason to bring it out into the open so there was no reason to say anything. The young but aging guy has an old boyfriend who's been going through a midlife crisis for the last hundred years and the disclosure of this one bit of indiscretion would certainly have pushed him over the edge. Better to tell a few lies and save hurt feelings.

But now at this point, shouldn't I finally come clean? he asks the TV with his old lover still tucked in his arm. Lies are confessed in the emergency room and his old lover is so taken out of himself that he moves to the edge of his seat and pulls his arm out of the love lock to bring his hand to his mouth. Because this isn't just a meaningless affair we're talking about, he tells his old lover's bald spot. This is something vital. Call it a change of life. Maybe I'm having a midlife crisis myself, though I'm passed the age, passed any approximation of a midpoint. The problem is, suddenly I know what I want. It's not all I want. But I want it nonetheless. And I want it before it's too late. I want to explore my hot S&M fantasies like I did in that affair with the young but aging guy. I want to explore all my fantasies before I'm too old to make the fantasies come true. I don't want to give up this cozy life here. But I want to know what I'm missing before it's too late. Just to know. I want to really live, do all the things I ever wanted to do and still haven't done before it's really too late.

An old man is dying in his hospital bed. The actor is thinking that he won't be able to collect unemployment benefits because he hasn't been on the show long enough. And the man watching it all happen from the security of his couch without a clue to what anyone else is thinking but himself pours himself another glass of wine. It seems lately that he's been drinking more and more of the stuff. He always drank wine with dinner. His Italian background. But at the eleventh hour the drinking has become more anxious. Like he knows the party will soon be over so he has to get his fill in quick. He lifts his glass and drinks to the health of the TV and to the health of his old love kneeling down before the TV, bald head shining in the colored lights. He drinks to his own precarious health. He drinks to the good life and decides to leave his fantasies dead and buried. Because he realizes with some comfort that... it's already too late.

Far away, just barely within the confines of New York City, a young but aging man stares out at the polluted sea and contemplates his next move. Let's admit it, he tells the Atlantic. My whole life I've been a baby abused by aging babies. And now I'm one of them. Except I still feel like that baby. I certainly don't want to abuse any babies, real or otherwise. I like to be the one abused. I need to be abused. Some things haven't changed. But it's becoming harder and harder for me to see myself as that babyface I once was.

Okay, they didn't really abuse me, he tells the waves. Not in acts, but in spirit. How they all looked at me. How my parents showed me off like some prize poodle to the relatives and friends and all the leering adults who can't get enough of smiling at the cute little ones. At my confirmation party the way they all smiled at me like I was such a cute little boy and asked me if I liked girls. At my high school graduation the way they all smiled at me like I was such a cute boy and asked me if I had a girlfriend. At my college graduation they smiled at me and openly flirted. At the family reunion last year, they looked at me and said: Look at you, I didn't recognize you!

Look at me, he tells a bottle floating in the water, searching for his reflection in the waves. I'm getting old and I'm not even middle-aged. My whole life I've been a child. It's all I know. And if I can't be that, what else can I be? My whole life I've been a piece of meat. Young, fresh meat. Fucked every which way. But I'm not young anymore. Not really. I can see it in his eyes. My old love. He sees how I've aged and his love is –

He stares out at the long timeless sea. There's nothing left to say. He stops thinking and walks straight ahead slowly but surely until he becomes part of that long sea once and for all time.

↘↖↗↙

## Don't Drink the Water

The last decade has seen the end of an era. And nothing expresses that better than the disintegration of the piers. What else can you call it? Bits of them drifting off to sea. Each year they disintegrate more and more and the city fences them up and the anonymous men cut holes in the fences and the city patches them up and the anonymous men cut more holes and now the police come around patrolling and the anonymous men stay away... more or less. Like roaches. You never really get rid of them. In the 70's this was where it all happened. This was where gay liberation did its thing. If you walked all the way down Christopher Street you inevitably ended up on the piers. The era has come and gone but something of the spirit remains. There's a hole at the end of one of the piers with the words: QUEER LOVE FOREVER.

It had been a tradition on Gay Pride Day that while the crowds pumped away at the officially sanctioned disco on the big concrete pier, a free alternative party carried on, a latenight sex party on the worst of the piers, the one near the garbage dump. After everyone left the disco, the party was still going on this broken-down wooden ruin, to say nothing for the garbage dump. Actually the garbage dump had its own flavor. Not as smelly as you'd think, and more private than the piers. I was once taken there by a hustler. I blew him in the middle of piles of garbage. A trashy moment for even me.

The concrete piers are still in use. Mostly during the day because it's considered dangerous at night in spite of the repressive police presence. On a sunny day there's always a mix of rollerbladers and bohemians. The usual time-wasters, yours truly leading the pack. People sunbathe, some of them nude, which is a controversial act in the naked city, Catholic at its core. Sometimes you'll even find a lone fisherman out there. I asked one if he actually ate the fish. He said he does it for sport and gives the fish to his mother to cook. She can cook out the bacteria, but I wonder if she glows in the dark. The water in the Hudson is brownish green. I guess if the fish can drink it, it can't be all that toxic. And even if it looks toxic, the smell and the feeling of the place is fresh. I remember many cool warm nights sucking in the wet breeze, standing over the vast expanse of the great Hudson, the Twin Towers shining but small in the scope of clouds and sky. I remember the expressions on the faces I cruised by, full of the same joy I felt breathing deeply the sweet air. There was a common vibration of brotherly vigor. We were the daring ones who climbed through fences and jumped over giant holes to walk the treacherous planks. I remember men stretching out under the blue night, bathing in their freedom, masturbating to their reflection in the heavens. I remember passionate encounters, one-on-one with another who shared my exhilaration in being out there, as close to nature as you can get below Central Park. I remember the era like I remember the sex and the roll of the water. And I remember the guy who fell in.

He was clowning around with his catty friends laughing at the lonely men and making catty remarks when anyone walked by. I was there with a "straight" drinking buddy. I think he was sort of curious about what went on. Do men really get it on here? They do, but not every second. I explained to him that it's a bit furtive. A lot of circling around on the less disintegrated areas. There are always those veteran wankers, exhibitionists who will wank wherever they are, turned on by being seen and probably just by the feeling of their dick swinging in the breeze. The wind was swirling that night and it should have come as no surprise when the queen making the catty comments slipped off the edge and plunged into the sea.

We were standing nearby. I must admit it looked funny, but it wasn't funny because the idiot couldn't swim to save his life. His *friends* were laughing in spite of this. Maybe they thought he wasn't being serious. But I heard him clearly yell: "I can't swim!" They must have heard him too. He probably deserved to drown for being such a catty bitch. One of his catty friends yelled back to him: "Don't drink the water!" I began to think that if someone didn't do something quick he would drown, when my buddy, the drunken macho true to form, saved the day by stripping down to his jockeys and diving in after him. This brought more laughter from the bitches on the pier and all sorts of sexy whistling from the small crowd that had gathered. The brave man dragged the gasping sissy by the neck and swam him to safety at the base of the pier. We had some difficulty helping them up but in the end we managed without anyone else falling in and the deed was given a round of applause and a few swoons over the lifeguard in his wet jockey shorts. New Yorkers can't seem to get enough of applauding for whatever titillates them out of their jaded ennui. We made our exit from this broken stage, leaving the poor nelly sprawled out on the pier, drenched through and through, water pouring out of every orifice, his mouth open as though expecting some mouth-to-mouth resuscitation. All he got were more catty remarks. I whisked my wet friend away and slipped him into the first cab I could hail. Better get home as soon as possible and shower off the typhoid.

Later that night over Bloody Marys I asked him what it was like in the Hudson. It must be gross, stinky, oily. No, it was actually quite nice. Refreshing even. A bit oily, but nothing like you would expect. Since then I've been informed by an elderly gentlemen I know who used to swim in the Hudson as a boy that people swam there up until the 30's. The old man swam there as a young boy. There are always those diehards who refuse to believe that something is dangerous to their health even when it's common knowlege. Over the years it became known for sure that the river was toxic. Yet my friend survived his short swim with not even a rash.

This event was never reported in the papers or on TV. My friend was given no commendation from the American Legion. Just another anonymous story.

↘↖↗↙

## Something for Nothing

I have this friend who is without a doubt the stingiest person I have ever met. He's got plenty of money. But wherever he goes, for whatever he has to spend money on to get, he will always try to get it for less, or for free. Like so many people, he really wants something for nothing. And he expects people to give him what he wants. Like the world owes him a free ride. Who knows? Maybe they do. But I don't want to be standing next to him when the subject comes up. In the store he has to price every item, with no intention of buying a single thing, just to let the underpaid salesman know that it's all too expensive. In the restaurant he will endlessly complain to the waiter about the prices on the menu as though they could lower them specially for him. The tip he leaves is so embarrassing I will always attempt to add to it and he will always stop me from doing that. "With these kind of prices I refuse to leave 15 per cent!" he says just as the waiter comes around to offer a brandy on the house which my friend of course accepts but not without complaining about it being cheap stuff. My friend wants cheap food, cheap drink, but all of the best quality. He also wants cheap sex.

I must explain that my friend is unusually ugly. Physically ugly. It's not his body. Something in the face is truly appalling. He wears an ugly expression all the time. Age has added its bit of mockery, and there you have it: my friend, his homeliness so extreme and his personality so cumbersome that it's surprising he has even one friend (I often question why I don't refuse the honor). In any case a fat wallet goes a long way when it comes to getting sex if not friendship. It shouldn't be a problem because, like I say, my friend has enough. But of course he won't pay for sex. He wants something for nothing. Or for so little that it might as well be free.

We shall call him John. My friend John has become an expert at getting cheap sex. Literally. Not such a difficult thing to do if you think about it. In New York, like in a lot of places, there would seem to be more young men out of work than in work. They live with their family, or live off of friends. Or just hang out on the streets. Here and there they can shack up with a working man. "You got a nice apartment? You got cable TV? Plants?" they will ask. My friend John avoids all those questions. They never never, absolutely never get invited back to his apartment. No matter how much he wants them. He tells them he lives with his elderly mother. The truth is he lives alone in a splendid apartment, furnished sparsely, but with an incredible view. And of course he rents it for a pittance because he got the lease long before the neighborhood became chic and because he sued his landlord which lowered the rent still further. If he took one of those homeless boys home he would be too nervous about them moving in. There wouldn't be anything for them to steal, but he's probably afraid of them stealing something anyway. The main thing is the lack of control. John must always be in control. That's why he buys sex. Or finagles it. Anything mutual would leave him in the uncomfortable position of selling himself. And his winning personality. John only buys. At bottom price if he pays a dime at all. He redefines the phrase *cheap sex*. The man has no shame. He's the cheapest date in town. He won't even buy them a drink. Forget bars. Restaurants and clubs are out of the question. You may be wondering how he cons them into giving him something for nothing. The key is their desperation. When you have nothing, the littlest bit is in fact something. The lure of the possibility of something is something.

I remember one night wandering around the piers at the end of Christopher Street with John giving me tips on how to get cheap sex. Always poor boys hanging around the piers. Some of them dangerous, especially the crackheads. You can tell when they're skinny and mean-looking, hungry. They want money and if you so much as give them the time of day you will have to give them money too if you don't want them to follow you around. Mostly it's just a nuisance. But on a dark corner they could pull out a knife or just hit you in the face. I had a close call once. The boy followed me around through the little winding streets of the West Village. Call me stupid, but believe it or not I was actually just being friendly. As soon as I realized that he was going to mug me – the thought popped into my brain – he tried to mug me. On a lonely street he grabbed my arm insisting that I had agreed to give him fifty bucks and if I changed my mind he would hit me. A group of partygoers passed by dressed in urban armor, leather, big tough outfits. Well they were so scared they practically quaked in their army boots. I begged them to help me. They quickened their pace, frightened to death. They wouldn't even look at me to see what was going on. I couldn't believe it. Six of them together wouldn't stand up to one guy. Finally I told him I would give him the money – which I didn't have – if he let go of my arm. He did and I ran. I ran faster than I thought it was possible to run. He chased me and at one point was able to touch my back, but I pushed myself on and managed to outrun him. At the corner of Seventh Avenue a whole squadron of cops standing around chatting away. I told them, out of breath, that I was almost mugged walking in those streets in there. The one looked at me with faggot on his lips and said: "You shouldn't walk in those streets in there."

But my friend John can handle himself. He grew up in the ghetto. He knows the streets like he knows the boys. He calls the shots and in all these years he hasn't once been mugged. Meanwhile the French tourist gets off the plane and gets his throat slit on his first night out. John knows his way around. He knows how to get what he wants, whatever it takes. And he usually gets it.

But this night he wasn't doing too well. I stood by and with some embarrassment observed his window-shopping. One by one they come by selling their wares. Tall skinny ones, or short skinny ones. Thirty bucks buys a tray of crack. Too much money! The price comes down. Twenty bucks. Highway robbery! Fifteen. John walks from one to the next trying to get the best price. A scrawny kid says he'll do it for five bucks. No way. Believe it or not John feels that discussing money when it comes to sex cheapens the whole thing. The romance. The skinny one threatens to kill him if he doesn't give him the five bucks. John lunges towards him. "You wanna kill me, huh?" he shouts at him. "You twerpy little piece a shit! Don't you be threatenin' me, Miss Thing. I'll stick my fist up your asshole so far you'll be shittin' your nose." Now why can't I do that! The kid flies off like some flea. And you know that I would have been terrified of the little runt. He would have seen it in my eyes and followed me around until I gave him the money. Often enough I have given them the money. Not when they threaten me, but rather when they touch my heart with their pathetic life stories. The puppy eyes and the torch song about living on the streets after their family threw them out. Maybe it's true. Maybe not. In either case their lot is worse than mine. So they spend the money on crack. I smoke and drink. Who am I to preach to anyone about the straight life.

After an hour of haggling with drug addicts we venture back towards Christopher Street to buy some beer. John always saves money by buying his beer in the deli instead of the bar. I don't mind because it's a warm night and I prefer being outside. John gets into an argument with the deli man over the exorbitant price of the beer. We walk out onto the street with our beers in paper bags. Typical New York. You can die in the gutter. But you're not supposed to drink beer on the street. I use a straw to make it look like soda. It's an awesome night. People on the streets. Cars whizzing by on the West Side highway. Some of them, sound systems on wheels, pumping a beat so earth-shattering you can feel it in your chest as they go by. People everywhere. Urban warriors looking to get laid. Clubkids in packs. Black queens dancing in the street. On nights like this New York is literally throbbing with the pulse. One feels like anything can happen.

We walk down to the highway and cross the street. Always a little gathering around the public telephones. Some swishy guy pretending to be talking on the phone. You can tell. It seems staged. As soon as a man walks by his gestures to the phone become more emphatic. My friend snickers pointing to the little tart: "Mary calling long distance to Queens." I turn around to watch the view in the distance. The Twin Towers. The reddish blue night. And then I see him standing there. This young guy. Just standing there waiting. He's hot. Big brown boy. Twenty-something. Strong and sensual. Shy, though. He looks a bit lost. Waiting for someone?

I nudge my friend. He agrees. A stud. What is it about the combination of the boyish face and the manly body that has come to represent gay desire? From Adonis to Marky Mark.

John wastes no time. He calls out: "Hey, c'mere." The boy smiles. But too shy to walk over.

"C'mere. Don't be shy." My friend knows how to command people. The boy responds, slowly at first, and manages to shuffle his way over.

John, half his size, looking up at the boygod: "You Spanish?"

"Yeah."

His teeth are rotten. Oh well. So he doesn't have Clark Kent's smile. But the body is pure Superman. From Puerto Rico instead of Krypton. John, whose father is Latino, strikes up conversation in New York street Spanish, a funky blend with more than a few English phrases thrown in. Occasionally he translates for me. The boy is fresh-off-the-boat. Lives in Brooklyn with his cousin. Doesn't know anybody. Looking to make some money. I would like to warn him at this point that John is going to con him, but of course I keep it to myself. They go on and on in Spanish. Then out of nowhere John says in English, looking the boy straight in the eye, almost threatening: "You like to get your dick sucked." I try not to laugh. The boy smiles.

We end up wandering through those little streets where I almost got mugged that time, John searching for a suitable nook to use to blow the boy. I don't understand why he won't take the boy home. Much more comfortable. But there's no telling John what to do. And the boy is easy. He does whatever he's told. He's inexperienced enough to assume that there's money in it for him. I'm not looking forward to the surprise. Personally I want to go home and leave them but my friend has convinced me to stand by as a lookout.

Finally John picks a stoop in front of a small brick townhouse. I roll a joint and we have a little party there with the beers and the joint. I feel bad because no one bought the boy a beer. I offer him mine and he greedily accepts.

The boy sits between John and myself, a few steps higher His crotch level with my mouth. I breathe in deeply. The smell of the pot mixed with the boy's crotch is thoroughly intoxicating. Sweet and musty. Rich and masculine. The dope makes me feel sorry for myself. After all I'm just the lookout. John has a way of getting people to do what he wants without any consideration for their own feelings.

The two of them go down a few steps into the cove that leads to the basement. I stand guard, but after hearing the first slurpy sounds I can't help but desert my post. I peek over the rail and watch John, the ugliest man alive, suck off this great specimen of youth and beauty. In the shadowy light the boy really looks like a young god. He stares down at the head bobbing up and down on his cock. As for John, he seems to be in heaven, sucking and sniffing away. I can tell that his mind is exploding with orgasmic sensations. His mind is being fed so that his body can turn on. I can't see that far but I know he's wanking himself. I'm glad I can't see that far. My eyes are focused on the boy.

Here and there, people pass by glancing over in the direction of the slurps. Nothing worth stopping for. They sense that something is going on. Seem to be almost afraid of me. Or just afraid. A man with a big dog strolls by. The dog sniffing around wants to join in the fun. The man tugs at the leash. Poor dogs. Denied the simple pleasures. Locked in tiny apartments. Isolated from the rest of their species except for a few sniffs in the park. If they're lucky. In some respects worth the compromise. They don't have to fend for themselves in the wild. Civilization has something to offer the tamed animal. I look over the railing at the dogs in heat down below getting it on next to the garbage. Get it while you can. This is your bit of release. John looks like he's enjoying it for all it's worth. The boy looks like he's trying to do a good job.

When he comes he looks up, groans and starts fucking the head, the head gasping for air. When John stumbles up the steps wiping the cum off his lips his head looks purple. It has certainly been an exhilarating experience. He looks disembodied. His soul is floating over the grime of the street.

Back on earth he completely ignores this boy who has given him so much, for nothing. He literally acts like he doesn't know him. In a way he doesn't. But this is weird. To be so intimate one moment and the next so utterly cold. We walk along with the boy tagging behind. I feel embarrassed. I mumble that this is ridiculous. You can't turn your back on the guy after he gave you such pleasure.

"I gave *him* pleasure," he blurts out. His face has become rigid with smug stinginess. I look at him like he must be insane. The young man is a stud. You are not. He fucked your face silly with the understanding that you would pay him something for his efforts. Something.

"I never said I'd give him a dime."

The boy is tagging along, shuffling his feet, too shy to ask for money. I feel embarrassed. I'll pay him myself.

"Don't you dare." John grabs my arm. "Don't go spoiling him. That's how they turn into these money-hungry sluts."

Okay. But then let me take us all out for some pizza. I'm hungry and the kid deserves something for his troubles.

John looks at me, hard. "Nobody deserves nothin'." Each word spit out with the force of experience. I know that my friend did not have an easy start in this world himself.

We stop at a bar near the pizza place to take a piss. In the entrance to the bar it says for customers only. A few guys shooting pool. Otherwise the place is dead. We stroll through to the back of the bar without looking at the bartender. My friend takes the urinal. I take the stall. The kid waits outside the door like an idiot. The stall is broken as usual. There's shit in the toilet and piss all around. I try not to look down, peeing freely. I read the graffiti. Phone numbers everywhere begging to be called. One large red arrow pointing to the toilet with the words: *Tanya the shebitch lives here.*

The pizza place on Christopher Street is a pit stop for whatever comes by. Everyone in costume. Half the costumes the same. The usual leather jackets and baseball caps. Some black queens dressed right out of a Gucci catalog are laughing and screaming. My friend says he knows them. Only too well. Under his breath he calls them "low-life Marys." The greasy machos behind the counter watch them without expression, but you have the feeling on their night off they'd like nothing better than to beat them over the head with baseball bats, for being queens or for being black or for being black queens. I order a round of slices and cokes. The kid is standing behind me looking around, lost.

I always like to sit at the table in the window. People-watcher's paradise. They go this way and that way. On the move. Some stop by to pick up a pie taking the smell of pizza down the street with them. The boy joins us hesitating. I have to pull out a chair for him. I decide his mother gave him a lot of love.

Meanwhile John ignores the kid completely and complains about the grease. Too much grease. That must be why they charge 25 cents more than the place on Seventh Avenue. I remind him that it's the choice location that ups the price. He holds the pizza up so that the grease can drip off. The cheese wants to slide off with it. I look around at the greasy walls. The pizza certainly is greasy. Everything is greasy. I remember a place on 73rd Street where they had a picture of Jesus (a photograph!) hanging lopsided on the wall and you could see the different shades of grease by the line where the picture used to hang.

The boy eats quickly but self-consciously. I want to kiss his sad face, play mommy for a minute. She never told him that the world is a shitty place where nobody gives a fuck. That's probably why he's such a sweetheart. I start to think my friend is right. Nobody deserves nothin'. I turn to watch him fuss over his greasy slice. An asshole, a brute, a stingy selfish New York creation who would bury his own mother in an unmarked grave to save the money. I can't help but think that he is justified in wanting something for nothing even if he contradicts himself. The world owes him but he doesn't owe anyone. Because that's how you get by.

There they are. A slice of life. The anonymous hustler and the anonymous john. They sure make a funny couple. Strangers brought together by necessity. They get by. There they sit together eating their pizza, the poor and rich of America, the newly-arrived and long-since-settled. One searching for his American dream and the other living it in all its greedy glory. There they are breaking bread at the same greasy table. Both of them living proof that you can indeed get something for nothing because in spite of everything there's still plenty to go around.

↘↖↗↙

## Foreign Films

Forget all those gay cinemas of yesteryear. Forget all those contrived scenarios that spilled out into the audience and left them hungry for more. Here's a true story of love and hate that's sure to warm the cockles of your cold heart. And remember, even if they close down every last gay cinema in the world, there would still be all the straight ones.

Divaldo watches the movie, but his mind drifts. He sees the images, hears the music, but the bits of dialogue are incomprehensible. Difficult enough for him to understand Americans when they speak directly to him. Coming from the speakers in the theater the words are garbled waves of sound. It doesn't matter because the plot is in the action. The words don't matter. Divaldo carries on his own dialogue in his head.

He's thinking about the party last night and how much he enjoyed it. He should make more friends here. The last year has been filled with too much loneliness. Back home never a day goes by that he doesn't see twenty friends and relatives, say hello to a hundred more on the beach, on the street, in the shops. Here in New York things are different. American people are strange. Sort of friendly. But without warning the friendliness changes. You ask for a favor and suddenly they don't pick up the phone. You leave messages on the answering machine and no one calls you back. You invite them over. They stay for one drink and then look at their watch and say they have to be going, after you prepared a feast. That party last night was wonderful. The Italian girl is nice. All the people were fun to be with, even the few Americans, though they couldn't get enough of laughing at his name. The party reminded him of being home again. He brought casseroles of food. No one laughed at him for that like the time he brought food to an American party. This time everyone brought food and they ate and drank the whole night. Divaldo will have a party in a few weeks and invite all of them, and all the other people from his new job. The waiters, waitresses, bus boys, dishwashers, the hostesses and coat check girls and even the petty managers, though they probably won't come. The Americans won't show up, but that won't stop him from inviting them. In any case he can count on those Mexican guys to come. And the Italian girl and her friends. Those black gay guys. The Haitians, the Dominicans, the two Pakistanis, and don't forget the Korean girls. They're sweet even if they never talk to anyone else. And of course Divaldo will invite all the Brazilians he knows. Even the ones who snooted him when he first came to New York. They thought they were better than him because they'd been here a long time. Now he can show them that he made it in America too. He'll spend every penny he has on this party. Only the best. Sea food, prime ribs, the best French wine. He'll show them.

The movie is getting into full swing now. A white woman with pink skin and a blonde wig and the biggest tits this side of the Grand Canyon is kneeling down with her ass in the air, her red lips poised to blow the two giant cocks dangling in front of her face. The one is black. The other brown. What is the name of this movie anyway? Divaldo tries to remember the strange coupling of words. *Jungle Fever?* Maybe that was the other movie. *White Ass?* Divaldo likes ass. He thinks to himself how Brazilian people love ass. Americans are prissy about their bodies. Don't touch me there. You can do this, but don't do that. Or worse: Stand here. Like this. Sit like this while I'm here. This way, not that way. Like they're directing a movie. Divaldo never made this kind of love until he came to America. He feels like a prop. Like a fuck machine. And then when it's over... leave. Get outa here. Like a minute ago they weren't screaming for you to fuck them, like you didn't have your dick inside them. Now suddenly, after *their* orgasm, it's: Leave me alone. Don't touch me. Or: You can't stay over. I gotta get up early tomorrow. Like he's some gigolo. Some sex slave. The white people treat you like you're a nigger. He never felt like that in Brazil. Everybody has a dark black tan. Black is really beautiful. Not just a slogan. And everyone is Brazilian first. In America it's different. When you're not American you're considered weird. And when you're not white you're considered a nigger.

The movie is making him horny. He forgets his loneliness sitting in the filthy broken-down theater, in the silent company of other lonely men. Only a few men evenly dispersed in the rows of seats. The film reflected on their serious faces. Mostly Latino, black. Older and fat. Divaldo vows to keep his trim Brazilian waist and to pump up his upper body which is pumped enough but Divaldo wants to look like Arnold. Wants to be a famous muscle man, become an actor, move to Hollywood and go to parties with Madonna when he's in New York on business. His dream has faded over the last year but it hasn't left him entirely, in spite of the setbacks. The worst was when he married that crazy Jewish lady shortly after he arrived. The breakup was a real slap in the face. He thought they were a happy couple, Lucy and Ricky. He thought she really loved him like he worshipped her. It turned out she just wanted him to fuck her when she wanted to get fucked. She went on trips by herself, locking up her expensive things when she left like he was some kind of thief. She did buy him some stuff, but as soon as she was tired of him and threw him out she took all the presents back. They were divorced not long after they were married, fortunately after he got his working papers. His status is confused. In a way he's legal and in a way he's not. Typical America. They want you here (to do the shit work) but they don't want you here. In spite of being treated like some Mexican maid, Divaldo manages to keep his Brazilian arrogance. And through it all his American dream still leads him on.

With the white woman sucking the black dick on the screen Divaldo gets going in the seat. He pulls out his dick and strokes it, whispering English obscenities to the white woman on the screen. "Suck my dick, bitch. You know you want to suck that black dick. You know it, bitch." Hard aggressive clichés he read in some American porn mag. Violent utterances of hate to suit that hard language which he finds so difficult to pronounce. Then the white woman shows her ass, spreading her cheeks, pressing her painted fingernails into the white cushions. Divaldo's heart beats faster. "Oh, yeah baby. Show me your ass... I *eat* you." A translation of fucking in Portuguese. His dick is as hard as it gets. He strokes it slowly to get the most from his pleasure. In his mind he's doing it with the white woman. And she loves it. Every man in the theater is lost in his own relationship with her or with whatever turns him on. He loses himself in the colored lights, indulging his private fantasy in the comfort of his isolated seat. No one crosses the invisible boundaries.

No one except Billy. Little Billy with his soft blond hair and rosy cheeks still wearing his tie because he couldn't wait to stop off at home to change his clothes after work so horny he was. Little lilywhite Billy whose greatest passion in life (besides singing church music on the weekends) is to crawl around the sticky floors of the theaters in the Bronx with his tongue hanging out like a little doggy wanting nothing more than to run after the bone. Little Billy who would never go to a *gay* theater, although he would be the first one to admit that he's a slutty little gay boy (at least when he confesses to me). Little Billy who gets so turned on when he walks on the streets of New York by the threatening looks he gets from tough Latinos and homeboys that he has to run to the nearest men's room to whack off and manages to whack off four or five times a day in between work and his singing career. Little Billy who's got a lot of balls for a little guy like that to crawl around the filthy floor with his tongue hanging out, risking a punch in the face at the very least. Little Billy who has never been hit or hurt by anyone because he's so sweet and little and harmless and because most of the guys in the theaters don't mind when he blows them and if they do they just push him out of the way. Little Billy, the theater mascot.

And when little lilywhite Billy crawls over to Divaldo's big brown black dick, Divaldo of course lets him suck on it all he wants – "Suck it, baby, suck it," he whispers – because Divaldo is looking up at that white woman's ass on the screen and because Divaldo is lonely and even though he could always pick up some cheap white woman at a bar she would certainly throw him out after he fucked her and he would be even lonelier then and here in the theater he can dream his American dreams and because it feels good to have his dick in a warm wet place and because Billy sucks it with more love than all of America has for Divaldo, sucks it like no white woman ever would and because when the black guy and the brown guy in the movie both come in the white woman's face and Divaldo rams his dick into the warm wet mouth and shoots his own sticky milk, little Billy swallows it like a baby drinking from a bottle and when it's over rests his head on Divaldo's lap with the dick still in his mouth feeling Divaldo stroke his blonde hair and whisper in the darkness words of soft love in that language that is so hard to pronounce: "Baby, my baby, my sweet baby."

↘↖↗↙

## Bottoms Up

I have certainly been to my share of swanky parties. For a while I supported myself playing piano at cocktail parties for the rich and very rich. It's a particularly New York thing to have a pianist play while you entertain. Andy Warhol took my picture at a party where he spent the whole time hiding behind his camera snapping away. No doubt my drunken pose is catalogued in the archives. Titled *The Bored Pianist.* These soirées are usually as boring for the guests as they are for the servants. If I learned anything from the experience it is that people are people, from top to bottom, hard as they try to set themselves apart from the common lot. Full of the same anguish, the same nonsense. Crude in different ways. Bitchy crude when they're rich and plain old crude when they're poor. But crude either way. And I learned that in all cases wealth is a relative thing. Sitting there searching for the lost chord I would look around and think that there are those who are so endowed with material possesion that there should definitely be a law against it. The next night I play another party and realize that those people were impoverished compared to these. There's money, and then there's money. In neither case related to taste. What does taste really come down to anyway? I know a vulgar Jewish lady who even on a warm spring day will wear her mink to the bargain stores just to demonstrate her vast wealth to the hungry masses. I know a tasteful German lady who even on a warm spring day will wear her mink – which is actually a plain drab raincoat with the mink sewn on the inside – to the bargain stores to demonstrate her vast wealth, I suppose, to herself. To know she's fabulously wealthy without anyone else suspecting it. To know that she has good taste. Either way it comes down to the same thing. Clubbing that poor little furry animal to death.

Personally, I prefer to see the ostentation as it is. Purely vulgar. From the pianist's view, the most fun parties are not the tasteful ones where everything is so understated and quiet and precariously held together that you spend the whole time imaginging there's a piece of snot hanging from your nose. The fun parties are the ones where the people have absolutely no taste at all but enough money to rule the world. The slobs who aren't afraid to show off their incredible wealth no matter how disgusting it makes them look. The decadent privileged who are so bored with all that money that they stop buying things and start buying people. Who can be much more lively than inanimate objects, and are, if you have the cash, just as easily bought. Quite often for less.

I remember a party in a penthouse in midtown. To this day I have never met such rich vulgar people. The host – let's call him Caligula – is a gay man in his fifties, a coked-up moron who seems to take thrills in making other people suffer. The way he ordered around the staff made you realize that he really thought himself to be emperor, and them his paid slaves. In front of the arriving guests he would mock the servants. "Look at her run. She's my bunny. She hops." This a reference to a scrurrying maid. "Hop, hop." And so she did. At one point in the evening he started throwing twenty dollar bills at me, exhorting me to play faster. "Faster. Lemme see those fingers roll. Play faster." And so I did. I needed the money, as they all did. And this man paid more per hour than anyone I ever worked for. He could afford to throw it away. He obviously had enough of it to wipe his ass with and indeed he treated it like toilet paper, and us like his ass. The worst treatment was reserved for the *slave boys*, a squadron of half-naked boys hired as waiters. They endured the most humiliating mischief of host and guests. Seltzer spritzed on their hairless chests, food thrown at them, and endless pinching and goosing. Poor boys. They were making three times the going rate. They smiled through it.

The conversation was equally idiotic. And loud, much louder than my tinkling. The cultured voice of the nouveau riche. A man with too much plastic surgery and caviar droppings on his tie discussing the price of good caviar. "Ya can't get good caviah around heah." The local accent in full color. Then the witty response: "Whatta ya tawkin' about. Ya can get anything ya want at Zabar's." Meeting of two minds.

The highlight of the evening is near the end. Most of the guests have left. Only a handful of Caligula's closest and most despised friends are standing around the piano drinking and drinking but still not feeling it because they're so coked up. All gay middle-aged men, fixed up to be young again. Primped surgically and otherwise just like the queen, but cheaply done. The maids-in-waiting. These guests are not the rich ones, who left early for their other plans for the evening. These leeches who never leave are the court mooches. The ones who knew the host back when and hang around to collect the interest. You can tell by the way they follow him around like sniffing dogs every time he pulls out his phial. These are clearly the only loyal friends he has.

The view around us is awesome. Sky and skyscrapers on all sides making the penthouse seem lowly. I'm the only one noticing it, as I continue to improvise my variations on a theme by Liberace to an audience of deceased. The fun starts when a rather bitchy man comes out of another room with a pair of pricey binoculars. "Look what I found." He peers around at the other penthouses. More of the same. Then he slides open a window and stares down at the truly lowly street. It's far down, a long way off. Dirty and common down there. But it's obviously more interesting than the scene up here. He makes an arc in the air with the binoculars, slowly taking in the view from side to side, sniffing all the way. They're all sniffing. But the bitch with the binoculars looks like he's done too much sniffing. Too much plastic surgery to reconstruct his sniffer. A nosejob that's turned his weary shnoz into a beak. It's so thin and delicate and long it seems perfect for sticking into a phial, like the surgeon had that in mind. It seems capable of smelling long distance, because just then he stops the binoculars, sniffs loudly and says: "Look at those dirty men down there."

One of the others sniffs, yawns and ventures to see what all the commotion is about. "Lemme see, bitch." He grabs the binoculars and has a look for himself. Sniff, sniff. "Oh my, they are dirty. They're bums." The power of suggestion is undeniable. One by one they join in the peep show. How the other half lives. Down there in the dirty stinking gutter. Clearly of more interest than life in the shimmering penthouse. At first glance anyway. "Why don't we invite them up."

Caligula immediately objects. "If you want some sexy boys I'll call up the service." More high-priced slaves.

The bitchy one grabs back the binoculars and intones the mood of the night. "Boring."

"Boring."

"Boring."

"Those glamorboys are so boring. Same old tired numbers. Actors-slash-singers-slash-sluts. Why don't we get those dirty street bums to come up here and entertain us with their dirty bums." Sniff, sniff. "How thrilling."

"Thrilling."

"Thrilling."

The senate rules. Caligula seems peeved, as always. He'll get them back. I just know it. The man is evil. But first he'll give them what they want. "Okay. Let's invite your dirty bums up." That word said with a vicious overtone, so much that I stop playing for a moment. I know the bastard is up to something. Without turning: "Play it again, Sam, or I'll cut off your fingers." Then loudly: "Drew!"

The head slave comes running. "Yessir?"

"Take a look in those binoculars. Then go downstairs and invite those dirty bums to the party."

The slave, always ready for some new prank, looks about him unsure of what exactly they're up to. He's handed the binoculars. He points them straight out and tries awkwardly to focus them.

"Drew, Drew, you dreary cunt. Look down. All the way down. On the street, idiot."

"Yessir." The slave looks down. "You mean those homeless men?" Unfathomable. "Up here?"

One of the callous crew with a ready repartee: "They're not homeless. They have homes. In the sewer. They live in our shit." Charming.

Another: "Don't you just hate calling them homeless. So clinical. They're bums. Always were and always will be. Bums sound nice and soft and squeezable."

Caligula is impatient and irritable, as always. "Go, Drew. Get them. Now."

"Yessir." And he runs off, leaving the room to simmer in its ennui with anticipation. Only one thing left to do.

"Why don't we have some more goodies," suggests the bitch with the pointy nose. "Just a few more lines to get spirited."

"Spirited."

"Spirited."

Sniff, sniff.

"No." Caligula is unwavering. "Let's save it for the new guests. Let's share what we have with those less fortunate."

Right. Now I know he's really up to something, the monster. The effect of his remark already shows. The bitchy one sucks her teeth. The rest bite their lips. They're greedy addicts. They can't get enough, and now it's being dangled in front of them. They will have to wait. And suffer. Five whole minutes. It makes them nasty. They take it out on me.

"Can't you play anything else." Finally they noticed.

What would you like to hear?

Caligula smirking: "How 'bout *I Get A Kick Out Of You.*"

I fake it. They sing along. I get no kick from champagne... When the last kick comes Caligula kicks the bitch in the ass.

"Ouch!"

"There's always pain before pleasure, dear."

I want to add that for these addicts there is no pleasure without their drugs. I'm quite sure that they cannot enjoy a single moment of their lives without being high or at least the anticipation of getting high the next moment. Until they finally sleep it off, three days later and the cycle starts all over. In fact, when the homeless men come sheepishly creeping into the sprawling room – three dirty men with their mouths hanging open in awe – the guests have forgotten that this is what they were so keen on just five minutes ago. Their brains have switched channels. Back to the same old show. And all they care about is the popcorn. "Now do we get the goodies?"

"Oo, goodies."

"Oo."

Sniff, sniff.

"No." Enough said. Caligula grinning. "Didn't I say that we were going to share with those less fortunate?"

"Well there they are. So let's share it already." More bitchy by the minute.

"No. Not just yet. We haven't even offered them a drink. We haven't made the introductions."

A round of teeth sucking. We look over at the three wretched men. Two of them are black, and the third is brown or just very dirty white. They're big men. Butch in a vanquished way. In the prime of their life but looking close to death. Adult visages with childish expressions. They look like scared kids at the zoo. Or else, the scared animals in the cages. I get the feeling that they were more appetizing through the binoculars. Up close the fantasy is lost. This is the real thing. Depressing. Seeing them, I feel sorry for the whole world. It's a sobering sight. We could all use a drink. No doubt the three of them are drunks. Well they came to the right place.

"Drew, get them some whiskey."

The fiercest one has a mean scar on his left cheek. Almost apologetically he grunts something that sounds like: "Hi, um Mike."

But no one responds. No one cares who the fuck he is. He's a bum. Plain and simple. A no-name stinking bum. Smelly entertainment for the evening. One of the queens gives a good loud sniff, then holds her nose and whispers delicately: "Pee-you."

Sniff, sniff.

"Smells like garbage."

"I told you they live in the sewer."

Drew bustles in with a tray of three elegant whiskey glasses and an aged orange-brown bottle. The three dark kings grunt in unison and Scarface grabs the bottle. They take turns chugging from it while Drew stands by like a stiff British butler with tray and glasses and the rest of us watch them in silence. I pause in the middle of my fifteenth chorus of kicks without the champage, cocaine or refrain or whatever the hell those tedious rhymnes are. A round of burps fills the gap. Caligula says smugly: "Bottoms up."

"Now do we get the goodies?"

Sniff, sniff.

Ignoring it: "Let's get to know our friends from the gutter. You gentlemen *do* live in the gutter, don't you?"

Scarface does the talking in a voice at once timid and brutal: "Sleep in the subway when we can. It's safer."

"My, my. The pot calling the kettle black."

Chuckles and sniffs.

Caligula intrigued. "But you look like you can handle yourself."

"Ask him where he got the scar."

The man touches his cheek and laughs in an animal way. "It's nothin'. I got into a fight."

"I'm sure you did." Caligula smiling.

"They look dangerous. Especially the one with the scar."

"Dangerous."

"Dangerous."

They look pathetic more than anything else. The three wretches swallow as much of that bottle as they can. If they looked like drunks before, now they look drunk. Wobbling from side to side.

"Well, well. I think the entertainment is ready." Caligula has the most awful look in his eyes. Hateful. Mean. Cruel and cold. His voice is steady, giving nothing away. "Shall we begin?"

"What d'ya have in mind?" Scarface does the dealing. "Ya gonna take a video or somethin'? I been in a few videos." Proud of his achievements. "This guy on the East Side, he pay fifty bucks if ya jerk off in front of his camera. It's cool cause no one touches ya."

A man of scruples. I want to warn him not to mention money. That always makes Caligula pay less. I have the feeling he'll get exactly fifty bucks for his trouble when he might have walked away with five hundred if he would have shut up about it.

"No video this evening, but I'll pay you that fifty each if you turn around and drop your pants and show us your dirty bums." The pun is growing tiresome. But Caligula is serious. Seriously demented.

The three men stare out at us through pie eyes wondering what kind of crazy rich people we are. Scarface shakes his head. "No way, man. I tole ya I don't let no one touch me. You ain't gonna fuck my black ass."

"I don't want to fuck your black ass. I just want to see it. Then I want to see my friends here get down on their hands and knees and stick their posh noses up your black ass."

Sniff, sniff. At this point no one but me has a clue as to what he's got in mind. They're all too coke-crazed. I am definitely getting the picture. But the guests are dumbfounded and squawking. Nervous pigeons. The bitch with the beak: "What makes you think I'm going to get down on my hands and knees – "

"Shut up, bitch," Caligula orders quietly. "Well, gentlemen? Do we have a deal?"

The three look at each other. Duh. They're thinking about it. Scarface plays hard to get. "Do we get some more whiskey?"

"As much as you like." Teasing them: "It's 16-year, you know. Not the greatest, but drinkable. Drew, get the gentlemen a fresh bottle."

Drew runs off. I play. The drunks lick their lips and the guests sniff. The bitch getting pushy: "Listen, I think we should have some of the goodies now before the show starts." He seems to have no idea that he will be part of the show.

"Don't worry, darling. You'll get as much as you like."

The fresh bottle brought, opened and swigged. A round of fresh burps. The guests hold their sniffy noses. The most horrendous smells come with those burps. These three desperate men are not only dirty but sickly as well. Their bodies and clothing are saturated with a rotted odor.

"Bottoms up, gentlemen."

They take another swig.

"Forget the goddam whiskey. Bottoms up." He's damn serious, aggressive, staring at them with icy eyes. "I mean, turn around and drop your pants. Now."

They stumble around like drunken ballerinas. A quick undo and the pants fall down. No underwear.

"Bend over, so we can get a good look."

"But don't you try nothin', or I'll bust ya mouth." Scarface looking over his shoulder as he bends over.

The scene is revolting to say the least. The bitch with the nosejob doesn't get it. "This is ridiculous."

"Ridiculous."

"Ridiculous."

Sniff, sniff.

"I bet you wouldn't find it so ridiculous if you got a good buzz going."

Sniff, sniff. "Finally. It's time for the goodies. We barely had any all evening." Poor little bitch. Starved. Caligula is usually pretty stingy with it, to keep them at his mercy. Which they are now.

"You want it? Come and get it." The gracious host pulls out a large phial of white powder and opens it. He steps up to those smelly butts and holds the phial over the biggest blackest one, Scarface's. "Come and get it. As much as you want. I've got plenty more where this came from and I promise you, you shall all have as much as your little piggy hearts desire."

The piglettes are not amused. The bitch, hands on hips. In shock. "You don't really think I'm going to..." Sniff, sniff.

In the end, he did. It took a bit of coaxing. Enough spilled powder to glaze a cake. That night I must have played a hundred choruses of *I Get A Kick Out Of You* (a song I always hated but have since come to appreciate). But then people will do the strangest things for money. Or drugs. The bitch certainly looked ridiculous aiming her pointy white nose at that black ass with Caligula holding the phial, shouting: "Stick it in!" The problem was when it did go in. Scarface, feeling that sharp beak piercing his asshole, completely forgot the agreement, yelled, "I tole ya not ta touch me, man," and turned around and socked the host in the face, thereby saving his manly pride and ruining Caligula's fabulous nosejob. And with that the three wise men pulled up their pants, grabbed the whiskey and headed out knocking over everything in their way leaving the bitch on all fours, as bitches will often be, sniffing around the floor for the spilled goodies. Sniff, sniff.

↘↖↗↙

## One Bitch's Story

Here's one about a woman. Not a queen. Just a woman, though some of the experience might reflect. In fact, it could explain something of the lives of anonymous men as well, of all persuasions. One woman, like many women. Not so exceptional, but not the usual. A particular story about one individual fitting into a mold.

My friend Sandra was brought up to be a nice girl. She did her homework, got top grades, did gymnastics, and played the viola. Her viola playing got her a scholarship to study at Juilliard. It was during her first semester there that she realized that her viola playing was only part of the reason for her scholarship, that you get things in life not only by being a nice girl and doing your homework and practicing. That things are not always as they seem.

She was playing her arpeggios correctly, or so she thought, when her aged teacher stopped her saying sweetly, "My dear, my darling. You must use more bow. Play through the phrase. Like this." He then proceeded to wrap his arm around her to help her bow properly. Each time his hand managed to brush against her breast, and by the end of the phrase he was massaging her breast with sensuous, loving, legato strokes. At this lesson she learned, among other things, not to pay too much attention to the little inconsistencies, that if you play through the phrase the little inconsistencies will pass unnoticed and the performance will project.

Sandra has a radiant smile and enormous breasts. She had even bigger breasts back then, but after that first semester she went home for Christmas vacation and had an operation to reduce them. Like many large-breasted women she opted for a cosmetic surgery which removes some of the breast in order to relieve the back muscles from the strain of having to hold them up. It is certainly a questionable operation. Though Sandra will tell you that it was the right thing to do because it improved her posture, physically and mentally.

Her breasts are still big enough. Some things haven't changed. Even with reduced breasts she can't walk down the street without attracting attention unless she buries herself in an enormous winter coat. Every vile male creature, every pig young and old, seems to consider her breasts his property and to assume that she in turn would want him to mount her because of course she must be equally obsessed with his penis. He demonstrates this by whistling and yelling after her while grabbing his crotch. Since the operation she continues to endure this but at least now her back suffers less of a strain. So it was worth it, even if it left scars that never quite healed and required many more operations in order to reduce the scars. These scars are a crude reminder of what she has had to do to herself for health reasons and for other reasons. On her way to the shower Sandra will not walk by the mirror without noticing the small but noticeable scars and feeling somehow mutilated. Still she insists the operation was a success. And with time she has grown accustomed to the scars as she has to the pigs whistling at her and to many things in life in the big city and the real world. She takes it as it comes.

After four years of fending off her teacher and getting straight A's, Sandra went out into that real world with her mutilated breasts and her Juilliard diploma. For a while she played in little pick-up orchestras. The money wasn't good, but she was able to retain some sense of propriety. She could send home the programs from the concerts and her parents could take pride in knowing that their daughter was making a living in the service of great art. Then she joined an all-girl string quartet and started playing weddings and parties and Sunday brunches and all sorts of *gigs*. The money was better, but more and more she was fending off drunken men intoxicated with her breasts or with their fantasy of her breasts. She dropped out of the little pick-up orchestras. She was making much more money now playing gigs. She became cynical about the viola and serious music. Were they really listening to her playing, anyway? She remembered that time playing in an orchestra when a man jumped up on stage during the applause and handed her a bouquet of flowers, singling her out of all the rest as she sat in the back of the viola section. Or she remembered that conductor who kept hitting on her, telling her that she had the talent to make it to first-chair viola if only she would let him become her mentor and guide her. Better to play weddings and have the groom hit on her. Less pretensions and more money.

Sandra spent the money on better clothes, better food and drink, and eventually on drugs. At first the drugs were for after the gig. The emptiness that stole her soul after each wedding was so deep and numbing that she needed something to restore her humanity. Drugs seemed to do that as they numbed this feeling of having been raped by the commonplace. They helped her to forget the tackiness of it all: the first families marching awkwardly to profound Bach, the pompous holy man saying pompous holy things about love and God, the empty vows parroted, the never-ending excess of food and drink, the kitsch clothing, the kitsch music, all the kitsch trimmings and general ostentation... every last bit of it videotaped for posterity, all except the best man grabbing his crotch when he made eyes at the violist with the big tits. The drugs help Sandra to forget. They bring her back to the purer world of her childhood. One hit and music comes back into the veins. The heart is filled with romantic longing for a place that does not exist except in the realm of inspiration, a far-off place where sincerity matters because the music will not stand on ceremony, will not sing on histrionics.

After a gig, Sandra could barely wait to put her viola down before lighting up. Soon one hit turned into two hits. After a while the hits were no longer reserved for after the wedding. She was working more and more, making more money than ever but needing even more money and more work to keep up her extravagant indulgences. She seemed to be reflecting some of the spirit of the weddings in her private life, spending lonely afternoons shopping, buying useless items to pacify herself before putting on her black dress (cut for cleavage), taking a few hits, and running out the door with her viola, off to her job. The viola now had all the significance of a plumber's wrench, never used except at the job. The routine turned her mood sour and her behavior at the gigs became nothing short of outrageous. She started taking up the best men on their offers. Suddenly it was all a game. She sucked off the brother of the bride, the photographer, the bartender, and the DJ. She adopted the role of the bad girl. It felt more sincere than the role of the nice girl. Or at least it was the role she was finding easier to play. Blowing some stranger in the bathroom at a formal wedding was her way of mocking the falsity of the ceremony. Pulling down his tuxedo pants and sucking his stiff dick added that bit of irony that was needed to turn the oppressive melancholy of so much stifling kitsch into light humor. And when they shot their pent-up loads in her mouth she felt some power, control over her masters, and in that way felt less a servant in her own eyes. More the artist.

Sandra was never a prude and could be quite a hedonist. She always had boyfriends, although they never lasted very long. She lost her virginity to a percussionist back in the Juilliard days, who proudly recounted to all the other percussionists how he had conquered those giant mounds and how disgusting they looked untamed by a bra, dripping off the sides of her chest. Incurable romantic that she was, she maintained a blurry fantasy of someday meeting the right man, some noble character from a novel who would appreciate her for herself and take her away from the real world of the big city, sweep her off her feet and fly her off to paradise. A few times she actually thought she met him. But with each the truth behind the lies revealed itself. They were men, human like herself. They could no more sweep her off her feet than she could them. She gave up on true love. Swore it off and dug up her old love, music. A passion you can always have. By the time she played her hundredth wedding and had her first abortion she'd lost her passion for music as well. One night alone in bed she couldn't stop crying. For no reason, it seemed. She cried and cried, took a big gulp of vodka and cried some more. She smoked a few hits, putting out the match with her tears. But as much as she smoked that night she couldn't for the life of her get high. She felt positively brain-dead. No more crying. Numb. Just as melancholy as ever, but no longer caring. Apathetic. She lay in bed staring at the ceiling with the TV on blasting the static between channels, thinking she's put it off too long. It's time. Finally. She's gotta get cable TV.

Sandra became a wild girl, outdoing herself as the opportunities arose, reaching new heights of debauchery and brazenness. Drinking so much she could barely hold the viola. One time blowing an entire crew of the groom's buddies. Another time puking on a tray of mini-quiches and convincing the wedding party it was a case of food-poisoning. One time telling the priest he was a screaming faggot. Another time blowing the rabbi. One time not realizing she'd gotten her period and leaving a trail of blood around the catering hall. Another time dropping mescaline with the DJ before the gig and going on to play the whole ceremony without the bow once touching the strings. A sort of viola lip-sync. What's amazing is that so much went unnoticed, or at least unmentioned, lost in the sauce of pomp and circumstance. Until one drunken reception where two handsome young men got into a brawl over her and knocked over the wedding cake. Word got around and the other girls in the string quartet started gossiping about her, saying some very bitchy things. The second violinist, a skinny flat-chested bitch, convinced the rest that besides being a slut, Sandra was a lousy violist. Her legato was faulty. And that dress... They decided to get another violist. It was just as well. Sandra had had enough of music and the pretense of art. It was time to get a real job.

So she became a waitress and joined all the other aspiring or jaded performing artists in New York who parade themselves between tables carrying trays of inflated cuisine, dutifully serving with a smile. Of course the manager of the restaurant hit on her, and the cook chased her around the kitchen and the customers inflated their tips with endless innuendoes and occasional gratuitous feels. But she could deal with it. Just another real world lesson. She became good at serving with a smile. She always had that radiant smile. Now it was becoming fluorescent. She learned to turn it on and off. To smile to one and all until she got back to her apartment, locked the door and became herself again, greedily counting her tips while greedily sucking hits into her lungs. The days and nights settled into a groove. Working a real job structured life. The money wasn't quite as good as from gigging but more steady and less taxing in a way. More of a routine. The people she worked with were less pretentious than those musicians, easier to be with, more real. And if the cook pinched her ass now and then at least all the waiters were gay.

As a waitress Sandra learned things they didn't teach you in viola lessons. She got to see what the real world is really about. Domination. Humans exist together under the unspoken understanding that some are better than others. The determining factor: money. I'm better than you, therefore you serve me. You get me my food and drink. You carry my dirty dishes away. For that I pay you. And tip you if you're nice. And maybe squeeze your buns if they're nice. With this knowlege comes the realization that what her parents taught her back when she was a nice girl was complete bullshit. All that nice pious talk about how in the eyes of God the Father we're all equal. Mommy, Daddy, the kids, and the black maid who cleans our toilets. A wholesome setup. One she never questioned as a child. It made complete sense that the black maid *should* clean their toilets. Because that's what she was paid to do. Now for the first time in her privileged life Sandra knows a tiny bit of what it is to be that maid. And with that knowlege comes the end of Sandra's life as a nice girl.

At this point Sandra realized that she was no longer a nice girl. Not even slightly. Ironically, in spite of all the bad girl antics, she'd become asexual. But she drank and drugged and even without much of any sex life she felt like a bad girl. It wasn't a game anymore. It was her. If you play a role long enough, you may turn into the character. It didn't matter though, because she didn't care anymore. Nothing left to cry about. She got real along the way. Nice girls, like brave men, wedding vows and serious music, all seemed to be one big atrocious lie. There are truths within the lies but first you have to find them, if you can. She stopped trying to find them. Usually they are so covered up with romantic illusions of gallant knights rescuing innocent virgins to a symphonic score, of true love and great art sanctified in heaven, that one would be embarrassed by the truth. One prefers not to think of

Beethoven practicing his scales or Romeo farting during sex. It ruins the fantasy. Sandra had lost her illusions along with her youth and naiveté. Her heart felt cold. Her soul dead. And it didn't fucking matter because Sandra had become a bitch, just the thing she was so often treated as. And now she was. A real New York bitch who could deal with just about anything because she didn't care about anything except getting hers. Maybe her illusions, her soulful lusts, were still there, somewhere buried inside. But at this point she needed more than one more hit to find them.

She must have taken one hit too many that day she went to the restaurant because she ended up dumping a chef's salad on the customer's leering face as he stared up at her tits with his tongue hanging out. Her only regret was that she was fired before she had the chance to quit. Otherwise, no regrets. She enjoyed doing it too much. The staff had something to laugh about for the rest of the week while Sandra stayed home and smoked it up. She decided she liked being unemployed. The freedom of doing what you want when you want. She got cable TV. Finally. She started going out drinking with a bunch of waiter friends, got to know all the gay bars. Stuck dollar bills down the crotches of muscled go-go boys. Let someone serve *me* now. Suddenly she had a lot of free time. She got lonely and horny. She went out one night to a straight bar and picked up a young guy and brought him back to her place. He seemed nice in the bar, but in her apartment when she opened his fly he threw her against the wall like he was going to beat her up and she was going to enjoy it. She kicked him in the balls and threw his ass out the door. See what bitches can do? To think that only a decade before she would have thought that any girl who picked up a strange man in a bar was not only out of her mind but deserved whatever she got. Now, look at her. She got a job waitressing in a sleazy bar. Appropriate enough. She could drink for free and pick up men right there at the end of the night. She feels mature. She's grown up, doesn't have to play the wild girl. She gets hers. And she can handle her liquor like she can handle her men. She can take care of herself. Or so she thinks until one night a rather mature man buys her a drink after work and slips something in it and she wakes up on his couch stark naked. The bitch debitched. He chases her around his duplex. She runs stark naked out the door and down twenty-six flights of stairs (she's not going to take the elevator) to the lobby where the doorman is falling asleep and is barely awakened by the sight of yet another naked lady telling him to call the police. She stands there in the lobby wrapped in the doorman's jacket feeling raped by the world wondering if she really was raped by the man in 2602 who when the police knock on his door and ask blandly: "Did you rape this girl?" says blandly: "No. She's a drunken slut. She picked me up, passed out on my couch and then got hysterical." So the nice girl who became a bad girl who became a wild girl who became a bitch became in the end a drunken slut. But life goes on.

Unemployed again Sandra went through her savings, working hard at doing nothing. But drugs. She experimented with different drugs. A new high could bring you to a new place. Until it got old. The downers especially. Lost in space, passing out in front of the TV. The uppers made you nervous and edgy but at least they got you going. She started going out dancing with her gang of gay waiters and learned the true meaning of libidinous asexuality. Dancing all night long in a drugged void alone in a vogued pose among the multitude of poses became the answer to her romantic frustrations. Surrounded by gay men she could let those titties fly and nobody blinked an eye. And she could express some of that creative energy she once had but thought she lost. The disco was a far cry from the concert hall and surely pronounced the end of Western Civilization but so what. It was fun to dance and those little hits of E were really quite ecstatic after all. You could forget everything and lose yourself to the movement of your body. The only thing that mattered was the beat. All fucking night long. A sort of marathon gig. With breaks, full of meaningless chitter chatter with her entourage of druggy faggots who treated her like their bitch, but lovingly, in a way. At least when they pinched her ass she knew they didn't mean it. It made a joke out of all the abuse she'd taken over the years. Their very being was a parody on the sex roles and their campy banter something between ludicrous and pathetic, cynical and romantic. Always searching for that elusive real man, but willing to settle for a dildo in the meantime. They played bitch and she played mommy. The hag. If you can't be one of the boys you can always be one of the bitches. If nothing else, they made her laugh. Yes, bitches laugh. Laugh like she hadn't laughed in years. Laugh, laugh, and laugh until there are tears in your eyes. Laugh, bitch, laugh!

When the money ran out Sandra halfheartedly called around about waitress jobs. She needed a job, but she didn't want to work anymore. Ever again. She felt that she couldn't go through with it, not again. It was so nice not to work that she couldn't bring herself to find a job. She thought of asking her parents for money but couldn't think of how to break it to them that she'd long ago stopped playing in that string quartet. (Never mind that she'd sold her viola to buy drugs.) Then a singer/actress friend told her about a place in New Jersey, a go-go bar where she danced from time to time when not singing or acting. The pay was quite good, the work minimal, and if it seemed slutty, well so was a lot of singing and acting and so was waitressing and at least with go-go dancing the patrons are not permitted to touch. The bouncers make sure of that.

Sandra thought about it. She really liked to dance. It had become her emotional outlet, almost her reason for being, along with the drugs. She needed money desperately. What the hell. She rationalized that everything she had done for a living had essentially come down to the same thing. Even walking down the street she was performing and it wasn't her bowing arm they were looking at. Maybe it was time to face facts. She was a go-go dancer whether she liked it or not. Might as well get paid for it.

I ran into her one day on the street. She joined me for a cup of coffee. We hadn't seen each other for a while. She told me she was still go-go dancing. She was beginning to feel too old for the profession, though she wasn't the oldest by far. You'd be surprised how many aging single moms are out there stripping nights to keep the kids in running shoes. Sandra's skin had become sort of droopy, and her smile still fluorescent but too false to even pretend to be a smile anymore. Resigned. The flippant way she tossed off her sentences sounded too chirpy, her words too choppy and staccato for the underlying lack of expression. She'd lost her legato for real. The smoothness was somewhere in the eyes.

We laughed about the old days. About the stranger than strange gigs. She filled me in on the rest. One woman's story. Strange enough, but not so unusual. She kept referring to herself and other women as bitches. Gay men too. Straight men as dicks or fuckwads. In the middle of all the campy cynicism I asked her if she ever missed the music. Not at all. Her fantasies for the future are in a family way. She showed me her ring. Engaged to a bartender at the go-go bar where she works. They're saving their money to leave the city, buy a house and have kids. Then she told me a wonderfully ironic story. A story within the story that resonated with the absurd posturing of men and women performing in their roles, in place filling preconceived niches, fitting into the molds assigned to them, doing what they have to do to survive. Doing what they're taught.

One afternoon she's dancing as usual. It's not really dancing. More like gyrating. She long since lost her enthusiasm for dancing too, and now that she's a real-life go-go girl it's strictly shakin' it for bucks. Her outfit, supplied by the bar, is an elaborate but extremely skimpy nightie. The lace that covers her breasts and genitalia is more camouflage than anything else. You can see everything. If you wanted to, you could see the little scars made where her breasts were reduced. You could see the folds in her vagina. But no one looks that close. It's not even a topless bar or any kind of sex bar. The businessmen who go there for lunch are served steaks with their drinks and go-go girls with their steaks. It's a classy place.

She's right in the middle of her routine when suddenly her nightie comes undone. The one snap between her legs which keeps the whole thing together and tight around her form unsnaps in the shake of the performance and the nightie comes loose. You can see her pubic hair just below the dangling snap. And the skimpy shoulder straps loosen enough to expose in the hot lights her scarred breasts from under the see-through lace. Staring up at her from their steaks, the two men in the front row are so embarrassed – yes, embarrassed – that they turn away. They furtively look back, but somehow they've lost their appetite. The manager aggressively signals to her that she'd better fix her nightie, immediately, and she does. She would have fixed it as soon as it happened, except that at the moment it happened she unconsciously remembered what her viola teacher had taught her long ago, what had become second nature with her as a performer ever since. When performing, one must not pay too much attention to the little inconsistencies. Play through the phrase and no one will notice the little mistakes. She learned her lesson well. But perhaps the mistake is just too noticeable. And perhaps the audience doesn't want to see what is right in front of their eyes for fear of seeing the truth behind the lies.

↘↖↗↙

## The Man in the Toilet

His life is divided into work and play. In between he finds time to eat and shit and sleep seven hours a night. But most of every day is divided into just two activities, equally time-consuming, equally monotonous in their different ways. Other people might find it startling that a man could live such a reduced life. He would say his life is full.

In spite of the fact that he is at all times physically surrounded by millions and millions of people he spends most of his time alone.

New York is like that. They say that for every roach you see crawling around your apartment there are 70,000 crawling behind the walls. The one you saw was just the overflow. Roaches, like men, can function with a minimum of space. But when it gets too crowded some will spill over. Some will roam around outside their confines. Cruise around outside the walls.

He lives alone. He works alone. Hours go by, staring into his computer, sitting at his desk in a row of desks with other workers staring into their computers all together but separate in a room the size of a studio apartment. Partitions divide the desks into cubicles. For privacy. Stalls, to pretend you're alone. There isn't much air, or elbow room. Who needs elbow room when both arms are locked in place so that the fingers can do their soft work. The only noises in the room created by a symphony of fingers lightly tapping, a counterpoint of very fast typing over a steady hum, really a mix of all the hums of all the computers, printers and copy machines blended together into a quietly deafening drone.

Each day at five o'clock the anonymous man stops in the middle of whatever he's typing, hits the SAVE button and makes for the door. He punches out the clock and the workday is over. All thoughts of work are left behind in the memory of the computer. Nothing much to think about anyway. Although highly skilled, he deals with subject matter that he has no knowledge of and would not be able to speak at any length about anything that he's working on. His knowledge is solely in the computer rendering of the subject matter. The man who screws the first bolt on a missile has no idea of the destruction his work may lead to. In this case the man who typesets complex documents can't spell half the words he types. Why should he? There's a spellcheck. He knows nothing more about his work than about the sex lives of his fellow workers. In fact he barely knows their names. The partitions prohibit socializing. He recognizes them when they walk by in the hall, and will even say hello. But that's it. On his lunch break he eats alone at a restaurant around the corner. He likes the toilet there.

Which brings us to rest of his life. When not working at the office the anonymous man works at his one and only pastime, his play, his obsession, his duty, his reason for being. It's an arduous pastime, time-consuming and enervating. A tough job which most people would not have the stomach for. And it's strictly on a volunteer basis. No money, but the man deserves to get paid for all the effort he puts in. As with many an artist, he gets paid to do work he has no passion for. The stuff that makes his life worth living is strictly for the love of doing it.

Five o'clock is tea-time. The tea is of a special brew. For some a men's room is no more than a men's room. For others it's a gay bar without the bar. A wall-length urinal to stand in front of with your drink in hand. Toilets instead of barstools. No music. No video. No cover charge. Best to leave your wallet at home. For some the sounds of defecation are something to tune out. For others music to their ears. Some masturbate alone. Some together. Some linger at the urinals. Some squat in the stalls. One man's piss is another man's lemonade. You can't generalize about a thing like that. What one man wouldn't enter even if his bladder were bursting... a homeless man calls home.

As unflinching as the routine may seem, change is always just a matter of time. Life by the nature of it is about change. Mostly gradual, but also sudden. And when the routine of half a lifetime is broken it can happen in a single moment and then nothing is ever the same.

He left work that day like every other day. On the way to the toilet he grabs a 16-ounce beer at the deli. One beer a day is the limit. You'll never become a drunk that way. Chugging it as he walks down the avenue, he feels his blood surge with expectation. The thrill lies dormant throughout the workday ready to burst out as soon as he makes his way to the toilet. Today he's going to his favorite, which means a short subway ride. Well worth the effort. A lot of action there, and spacious. The stalls are actually larger than the stalls at the office. It doesn't matter. Physical space is not what he seeks. Impossible to satisfy in this city. His freedom is in anonymity. Among other anonymous men. From the lack of inhibition comes free expression. The bodies come together here like nowhere else in the compressed city. In the street, the subway, the elevator, or the office, people are close enough to smell each other, yet no contact is made. Brushing into someone is enough to cause a fight. In the men's room hardly a word is spoken, but the most basic connections are made. And if someone pisses in your face it can be cause for celebration. Or at least an orgasm.

Out of the crowd in the street down into the crowd in the subway the anonymous man moves unrecognized, a shadow on a dark wall. People, so many people of every description going someplace as if they know where they're going. Crowds of nameless faces of people who definitely have names and histories worth telling if anyone cared to listen. All of them coming together but only for brief moments, long enough to go their separate ways, traveling to unknown destinations, unrecognized, forgotten before they can be remembered. The only ones who offer their life stories are the homeless, at the mercy of an apathetic crowd but not shy about opening up. Everywhere men, women and children beg for money, with placards announcing their pitch or just mumbled phrases unheard in the roar of the crowd. They persist because they have nothing to hide and no place to go and all the time in the world to kill waiting for someone to give them money. These are the street poets. Real-life verse spewing from their chapped lips. Their life is their art, a self-portrait in progress, and it's for sale if anyone wants to buy it. If anyone gives a shit. In the background a band plays fast bebop. The commuters seem to be racing with the beat, trying to keep up with the frantic music. A hectic crowd of mute people racing through the underground caverns. Through a whirl of echoes. The trains louder than the drums. A black man beating them as hard as he can to be heard. Sweating out his anger. Hard work for the unemployed.

Out of all of this the anonymous man seeks his refuge, a place where he can feel at home without being solitary, a shelter from the cold world where he can make that connection that can never be made any place else without losing his anonymity. To be alone together, together alone. His own apartment cannot offer him the sanctity of the public men's room. His one room is where he sleeps, alone, or eats in the company of his TV friends, listening now and then to see if he can hear the neighbors and their TVs. On all sides. The men's room is where he really lives. He comes alive. A place where he can be himself. The public toilet is his social life. It goes beyond sex. On those nights when he stays home he'll often watch some porn on video. It relieves him. But there's no comparison with the real thing. With the feeling of being there, with the other men. Their bodies humanly imperfect. No match for the video images. But then, those muscle guys are just two-dimensional fantasy. Just more staring into a screen, like at work. In the men's room you can touch it. Smell it. Taste it. It's real. Alive. You can be a part of it. In it. Better than anything Virtual Reality will ever be able to come up with.

Out of the subway and into the bus terminal through waves of people going this way and that way. Everyone with a destination and none more anxious to reach his than the anonymous man. He sighs with relief when he gets there. His whole body comes to life as soon as he walks through the open door and the smell of shit and piss overtakes him. He stands there for a moment recovering from the journey, checking out the day's offerings. A man is washing his face at the sink. Another man stands in front of a urinal but in a way that suggests that he's not in any hurry to leave. The light is broken (on purpose?) so that one can see but not too clearly. In the dim gray soft shadows cover the dirt. Grimy fantasies lurking in every corner.

Strolling by the stalls he peeks into each one. The first one empty. The second closed. The third, a fat man sitting on the toilet with his pants down. His penis hanging over the rim of the stained porcelain. The eyes search out the passerby, but upon recognition avert as though to say: "Next." In the next stall an old black man is moving around packages, removing this and that, preparing for something. He seems to be making himself at home. Often homeless men will take refuge in a men's room. It's a sobering sight. When their eyes meet, the anonymous man looks away and the homeless man says in a quite friendly voice: "How ya doin'? Nice seein' ya. You have a nice day, hear?" There is so much bizarre misery in New York, comical if it weren't so tragic, that the only response the New Yorker can come up with is to simply look the other way. Tune it out. He says nothing. He keeps going. He hears the words, sees the picture, but in no way reacts. The anonymous man walks on to the last stalls, but they are either out of order or locked. So he turns around and makes his way back, by the homeless man, then the fat man on the toilet seat. The stall is like a booth at the freak show. You just can't help but look, even if you've seen it already. The next stall is still closed. He steps back to see how many feet are in there and can only make out three. He turns around again and walks to the end, by the fat man who averts his eyes again, by the homeless man who wishes him a nice day and on and on, checking each locked door in a quasi-panic. Finally he opens one that seems locked, but isn't. There's an out-of-order sign taped to the back wall pointing down to the toilet bowl. The bowl is full with brown water. He puts the lid down. He can barely control his excitement. He turns around and squats right next to the bowl with his head peeping up over the rim. He waits. The man in the toilet. Like the man who works in the toilet at a swanky hotel and spends his life listening to the sounds of piss and shit. Waiting.

He hears a toilet flush. A door is opened and someone leaves. He hears the sound of farting somewhere in the distance echoing off the stone walls. He hears moaning. Heavy breathing. The homeless man wishes someone a nice day.

Then he hears footsteps walking down the corridor. They seem to be heading his way. The excitement builds with each footstep. It sounds like boots. The steps slow down as the open door is recognized and in a moment the man is walking by. He turns to the side. Eyes meet. For only a split second, but long enough to decide. No way, his glance suggests. It would be hard to say who averted his eyes first. It all happens so quickly. And then the man is off, down the corridor to the very last stall. His footsteps stop. He seems to be waiting there. A few minutes go by. Again the homeless man wishes someone a nice day. The boots make their way back. When the man passes his stall he doesn't look in but from the rim of the toilet bowl the eyes follow him. The anonymous man sucks his teeth. He tells him off silently. Trashy queen. You're not all that. His thoughts ring out. And the homeless man wishes someone a nice day.

More waiting. He waits for what seems like a very long time. More and more footsteps. They must be coming in. But where are they? Here and there a man walks by. More furtive glances. More looking away. He reminds himself how often after the initial excitement upon arrival he finds himself sulking in the back of a stall and no sooner does he give up than he finds himself embroiled in an orgy.

His knees are beginning to ache and he hasn't even sucked his first cock. He sighs and places his hands on the toilet to prop himself up. But before he can bring himself to accept failure he listens carefully for any more footsteps that might be coming his way. And there they are. Always more footsteps. A symphony of walking men. This time it sounds like a whole bunch of men have entered the sacred chambers. Footsteps scatter, some of them aggressive and loud. These are coming closer and before he knows it a man has pushed open the locked door of the stall next to his and is locking it behind him.

He hears a zipper go down. His ears are straining to hear something else when all of a sudden his body is shocked out of its stillness by someone touching the back of his neck. He turns around, startled, and realizes it wasn't a hand on the back of his neck. A long penis is staring him in the face. Right, this is the stall with the glory hole.

It looks strange all by itself. Some slithery creature. A giant sludge. He usually avoids the glory hole because he likes to see the man attached to the penis. Not that he's picky, but he prefers to see that the man attached to the penis is at least a man if nothing else, and in decent shape. At this moment his desperation gets the best of him, as it so often does, and he goes for it anyway, sight unseen.

The anonymous man mindlessly sucks on the anonymous penis for a long while as it grows in his mouth, wilts and grows again. He's taken back to some dreamy infantile place where thought processes are non-specific. He's in a pacified blur when awakened from his trance by a man entering the stall. The rule of the cruisy spot is that as soon as you begin to do it with one many more will want to join in. Suddenly they come out of the woodwork. The first to arrive whips out his cock and displays a much bigger harder one than the droopy one peeping through the hole. So the mouth is removed, replaced by a hand, and still open wide makes its way over to the penis of the man there in the stall and dives down on it.

The stall is filled with groans and slurpy noises as more men come by to watch through the open door. One of them enters the stall and whips out his cock which is even bigger. The mouth removes itself and goes on to the next, leaving the last dangling in midair. So the man turns around and pulls down his pants and sticks his ass in the face of the mouth. The nose finds itself up that ass and then the mouth is off and running again to join the nose, the tongue moving in, working its way up the ass. The other man takes the cue and competes by turning around and baring his asshole. The anonymous man, squatting on the floor, takes a deep breath, his face sandwiched between two assholes. Once again he finds himself appearing in his own pornography. Starring in his very own fantasy flick. The men seem to be acting. Complete with sighs and groans. Someone says: "Suck my dick, man." Just like in the movies, but said like you never heard that one before. Someone starts pissing somewhere close by. Hard to tell in the thick of it. Meanwhile the penis in the hole shoots its stuff and is removed so that the dangling dick from the other side can shove its way in. From somewhere else yet another man has joined in the stall orgy, pushing his way in and standing over the toilet to try to get in on it ahead of the other latecomers waiting their turn at the open door. One just can't wait and wastes no time in kneeling down in front of the stall to blow a leftover penis. With so many mouths to feed, nothing goes to waste at this table.

By the end of it the anonymous man is bathed in enough bodily fluids that his face is beginning to resemble the toilet and after a hard day's boring work at the computer his soul is replenished from the discharge of his libido. He's high as a kite. His mind is still orgasming long after the last drops are drained from his sack. His soul is elevated. He picks himself off the floor and tries to steady himself on numbed knees. He wipes his dripping face with the back of his hand. All around the sounds of wiping. Pants pulled up. The show's over. Instantly the stall is cleared without a single word spoken. Business as usual. And it would have been no different from so many encounters just like it if not for one curious thing. One of the men as he turns to go studies his face, and he in turn studies the man's face. Their eyes meet for a long second, long enough to realize that they both work in the same office.

The man is gone just as quickly and the recognition is left hanging in the air. He tries to remember which one that was in the stall. Which dangling dick. Which smelly asshole. And more importantly which face in the office. Out on the street he can think of nothing else. Eating his dinner in front of TV he can think of nothing else. That face sticks in his thoughts. Could it be?

The change comes over time, but sparked by that one single moment of recognition. An unwanted connection made. Anonymity lost forever. In the life of the anonymous man, that means something has to give. The next day he walks into the office with a cloud hanging over him. The embarrassment would be too much to take. He goes about his work as mindlessly as ever. He feels almost safe hiding in between the partitions. At lunch he scurries out the door without looking around him. He doesn't spot the familiar face at any time during the day, but the memory of the recognition sticks in his craw enough that he avoids the toilets later in the day and goes straight home.

For the rest of the week he tries to keep a low profile at the office. He's tempted to stroll around the stalls to see if that was actually a man from the office. The face was not of someone who works there every day. That leaves a large selection of part-timers and temps. Might have been one of them.

Weeks go by. He almost manages to put it out of his thoughts when one day in the hall he sees the man. Unmistakable. And before he can avert his eyes the man says hello to him. Actually smiles at him. He stands there, dumbfounded, cannot bring himself to respond. All he can do is avert his eyes. But it's too late. He drops his papers and rushes out of the building.

He never went back to that office. He was unable to find another job, lost his confidence, his will to go out there and pound the pavement. He stayed at home, watching TV. Watching his porn collection to relieve himself. Staring into the screen at the empty, bland images. Missing the real thing, but incapable of getting over his embarrassment. He started drinking beer all day and night, sleeping in between, rarely eating. Eventually he lost his apartment.

He's homeless now. You may run into him if you happen to visit a certain toilet downtown. He bathes there at the sink. I had a conversation with him, one day, right there in the men's room. He'd lost his shyness a long time ago. He told me this strange story in an unabashed way that only a man who has lost everything can. It created such an eerie effect in the men's room that in a few minutes the whole place cleared out. The ones who came there to relieve their bladders, and the ones who came there to relieve their souls. His story, too personal for the public toilet, ruined their sense of anonymity, whatever they were there for. Nobody wanted to hear it. Except me. But as much as he said, and as graphic as his story got, never once did the man look me in the eye or even glance at my face. His head stared down at the busted sink and the filthy floor or to the side at the urinals and the toilets in their broken stalls. A weary host surveying the damage after the party. In spite of my journalistic curiosity, I soon lost interest in his never-ending story. I felt he was speaking to me but as if not to me at all. He seemed to be talking to everyone else there even though no one else was there. I became skeptical over some of the details, trying to remember if there really were glory holes in the toilet in the bus terminal. It's a story from the 80's. You remember, back when men were men and toilets were tearooms. Before virtual reality made jerking off with your laptop a sexy thing. Was the man just extemporizing? It made for an interesting story anyway. To be embellished as true stories inevitably are in the telling. Perception makes fiction out of all reality. Maybe there used to be glory holes there. Does it matter? Either way, here's this man living in the toilet telling me a story about how that came to be, and all I can do is ponder something I've always wondered about: who makes those glory holes anyway? Does some guy sneak in at night and start drilling away?

In the end I couldn't take the smell of shit and piss any longer. I'd long since relieved my bladder. I wanted nothing except to get out of there and away from him. He wouldn't stop talking. Finally a man walked in and stood in front of a urinal. One more anonymous man in the men's room. This one looked like he really just came there to piss. I used the opportunity to escape. The homeless man was still talking. A long story if ever there was. A toilet epic. I had to interrupt him if I ever wanted to leave. I blurted out: See ya around. Take it easy, guy. I walked away in the middle of his sentence. I figured it didn't matter to him. His life so rude, what could politeness mean to a guy like that. Sorry. I couldn't hear it anymore. Another sad New York story. I'd stopped listening. More city noise to tune out. But I couldn't help hearing his last words to me echoing in the almost empty room, bouncing off the stained tile. He wished me a nice day.

## Love Will Keep Us Together

You can't expect to get lucky every night you go out. Even the piggiest ones who are absolutely indiscriminate in their pigginess come up empty-handed now and then. The gods have a funny way of sometimes giving you everything you want and other times denying the smallest bit of pleasure. I'm feeling more cynical than usual one morning after a long night of cruising with nothing to show for it but my cynicism. What a waste. All those hours standing around like a zombie. The worst was when a guy started puking. Two guys were standing near me. The one had his paws all over the other. For a second I thought they were lovers because the one was being so tender and affectionate like he really loved the guy. That was until the guy slumped down and puked. His date fled the scene without so much as an RUOK? Maybe a silly question, but you could do something. Show you care. Not a chance. He was off and cruising by the time the guy hit the floor and passed out. I was about to reach down and try to help in some way, or at least I was thinking about it, when the Pakistanis who run the door came by and dragged the obstruction out to the street leaving me standing there alone to stew in my unbearable cynicism.

I spent the rest of the night running into the same shit. On the train home a woman was sleeping on the bench, sprawled out like the living dead. A cop came by and banged his club on the seat near her face. "You can't sleep here." Why not? There's plenty of room in the car. Why does the man with the club have to be so heartless? And you just know that he spent Sunday with his wife and ten kids sitting in church in humble worship of the Lord and the Lord's son and the priest and the bishop and the pope and all the king's men. It's a beautiful world.

I find myself the next night at a dinner party. Maybe the sincere warmth of old friends is just what I need to overcome my suffocating misanthropy. The host is introducing his new lover, young lover, to his old friends. Most of the clique are into theater. Show music faggots. Big smiles. Big teeth. Big voices. Big mouths. They look like any minute they could break into song. Sure enough the one sits down at the piano and the rest start singing. Full of that woman-against-the-world attitude. The show must go on even if the set caves in and the theater bursts in flames. Why? They don't bother to explain. They sing and that's enough. The theme for the evening is love, in celebration of the new couple. One song segues into the next. *The Man I Love. Love Is A Many- Splendored Thing. Love Walked In.* And finally just because it's sitting on the music stand, *Stop The World I Wanna Get Off.* I like that one. Then on to the modern stuff. Pop songs, rock musicals. *What's Love Got to Do With It. I Don't Know How To Love Him. Sex Machine.* Cynicism seems to have come with the era. But romanticism will never go out of fashion. *Love So Right. Love Me Tender* with the host doing an Elvis imitation. And *Love Grows Where My Rosemary Goes.* Are those really the words? You know you're getting old when the "modern" stuff is sounding old. *Theme from Love Story* is performed as a piano solo. On to *Endless Love* and I'm gagging already. Then some bluesy things, but I can't hear the words through the hillbilly accents. Finally, *Love Will Keep Us Together.* Sung by the oldest of the bunch, a black man who once made a failed attempt at a singing career, followed by a failed attempt at suicide, and now owns a successful business, a beauty parlor. He gives it his all. His voice is croaky and off-pitch but the sincerity is clear. A certain pathos in his ravaged old cords sets the tone and not a few tears are shed, the first coming from a man who just buried his lover of many years. There's some guilt mixed in with the salt of his melancholy because he dumped that lover of many years as soon as he got sick. Dumped him for a young healthy guy. My cynicism gets the best of me. Again. I can't cry, for myself or anybody. All I can think is what a shitty world it is that people profess endless love one day and then when the going gets tough and age or sickness takes its toll the tune changes and it's on with the show. A revival with a young cast. Stop! The cynicism is killing me. I wanna get off and if I can't stop the world I'll just get off. At the nearest toilet. While the friends console each other I make myself another drink and the pianist tries to lighten things up with *Let's Fall In Love.* Cole Porter reminds us how birds do it and bees do it and all of the animal kingdom does it, but he couldn't come out and say that we should do it too. That would have been too crass for the period. So he implies that humans fall in love, not just fuck. Well I understand that some of the animals fall in love too.

I talk for a bit with the young lover of the host. He's young enough to be his son and can't relate to the scene. He doesn't sing, doesn't know those old songs, doesn't understand why they started crying. He likes going to clubs. He likes techno. He likes to dance, have a good time. He doesn't say any of this. He's barely verbal but I can just tell by the way he seems bored and out of place. I ask him where he met the host. At a club. Which one? He mentions a club I know but it's not a disco. Rather, a sex club. Well isn't that special.

They met in a backroom. Something to tell the grandchildren. The host strolls by with that showbiz smile to hide his possessiveness. I'm not interested in his little tart but it's obvious that he's not going to take any chances. He puts his arm around the little fella and pulls him close, still smiling away. I remark about how interesting it is that they met in a backroom. Do they have an open relationship? The smile turns into a monstrous grin. He clarifies. They met outside the backroom, at the bar. And they didn't fuck until the second date. Well isn't that special. He confesses that he doesn't like those places. And of course now that they're a couple they don't have to go to those places. We're strictly monogamous, he says like it was a religious observance.

A week later I'm standing in one of those places when I run into the little tart. If you go often enough to anonymous sex spots you'll find yourself feeling less and less anonymous as you run into too too many people you know. There are only so many men out there and confined to their ghetto. It's not surprising to see a familiar face at the local haunt. You see the same faces all over town even if you don't know the names. You bump into each other in the dark and run to opposite corners. You try to avoid each other but inevitably walk by without saying a word pretending you've never seen each other before. After the ninety-ninth time you suck your teeth in disgust at having to endure that gay face one more time, both acting like the other is invading their turf. It's a beautiful world. I'm no better than the rest. I don't say hello to the kid when I walk by his corner. But I think about calling my friend and letting him know what his strictly monogamous boyfriend is up to. Yeah and I'm strictly kosher. I don't eat pork on the Sabbath. On second thought I decide to keep my mouth shut. Who am I benefiting with this information? Who besides my own gossipy cynical self?

Some more cynical weeks go by. My cynicism seems to come in waves. Maybe it's the weather. The winter becomes dreadfully cold, colder than I can remember. People freeze to death sleeping in the streets. I turn up the heat in my apartment as high as it will go. I get sick. Very sick. I'm sure it's the beginning of the end. I spend most of the winter inside, warming up by the TV. I become well-informed in a trashy way. War, famine, ecological catastrophe, poverty, economic disaster. Racism, sexism, religious extremism. Communism loses, capitalism wins. The world forum as football game. Or worse, as B-movie. All of it turned into sensationalism. Tune in at six for the gory details. They make it sound lurid, salacious. Stay tuned for more on the plane crash. I can't stop watching. The more horrible, the more hopeless, the more I watch. They tempt you with the pictures. A few glimpses before the commercial to keep you watching. Coming up after the break... The bodies, mangled and maimed. Or the bodies, sexy and taboo. Dangling the naughty bits in front of your eyes telling you how you better not because it's naughty. The world seems to be coming to an end and they're preaching abstinence. The young are too busy partying and fucking to give a shit. Drugs are big business, like war. Just say no. To love. Don't do it. Save yourself. God loves you. That word God said with such pomposity. Is it any wonder people say it instead of shit and can't get enough of saying it? God! How the godly go on and on about family values and the evils of men loving each other while cheering the football game and praising the war on the other side of the world. In the name of God. But it's a just war. In someone else's backyard. The president goes to church to pray for the war. For our brave boys who fly high in the air to save the world by dropping bombs. Meanwhile the queers are demonstrating because they want to serve their country with pride? I decide that as soon as I get better I'm going to join some radical queer group dedicated to overthrowing the government and bombing churches. In the meantime I watch the talk shows. America, the family of families parades its dysfunction through TV-land right into my bedroom. Now I really can't stop watching. World news is boring compared to this. Politics a big yawn. Even celebrities stale compared to the average folk. Love and hate, sex and lies, every strange fantasy, every freak, every story outside the norm exhibited for the studio audience. For the righteous to throw stones at. The shrinks save the day. There's hope at the end of the tunnel. Psychology takes over where religion left off. The masses are opiated but still they want blood. They hurl abuse at the guests. Pass the microphone and let's hear what America has to say. "You're nothing but a fat whore." "You're gonna get AIDS and die." "I don't want you in my neighborhood." "You deserve whatever you got." "You need to find God." GOD!

When I get better I vow to change the world. I look for that radical queer group that wants to overthrow the government and bomb churches. I can't find it so I join a group of AIDS activists. I go to a meeting. Seems more like a fashion show than a political movement. I'm snubbed before I can get a word in. I decide to stick with what I know best... cruising. Love will keep us together. Stuck together, fucking.

Months later I'm standing in that same sex club where the last time I ran into my friend's young lover and there he is again standing in the same spot wearing the same trendy outfit smoking the same cigarette like he's been there the whole fucking winter. Does my friend have any idea? He must, or he's stupid. Or just plain fool enough to be in love. This time I decide to seduce the little tart, just to make a point, although I'm not sure what point I'm making. I go over to him, say hey, and without three words of conversation we're pulling at each other's dicks. He's got a nice one and a tight little bod besides. His youth says it all. In a few years he might look like some old queen but right now he's a young prince and I have my way with him. He's no innocent lamb. He has his way with me too. He takes whatever I can give and gives it right back. He seems to enjoy his orgasm with no holds barred. He lets it fly without the slightest repression, not even the suggestion of a guilty conscience. He's proud of his sexuality. His liberation. The guy gets his satisfaction and it has nothing to do with love.

When it's over I awkwardly stuff my shame back where it belongs. I want to get out of there quick because I feel pretty shitty about the whole thing in spite of my cynicism for the world. I feel like a traitor to my friend. I'm feeling guilty and thoroughly embarrassed. But the boy looks like he wants to talk. "Can I ask you something?"

"Sure."

Hesitating: "Do you think he really loves me?"

Who? You mean... I can't believe this. Is he kidding? Here we are in this place after what we just did and he's questioning my friend's commitment to *him*? Hello? But he actually looks serious about it. Almost teary. Not out of guilt, out of love. Or at least possessiveness. Though he didn't ask me whether my friend sluts around. That doesn't seem to matter. No, it's not possessiveness. Just love. I'm too cynical for that. Let's call it need. In any case he's acting as though the sex we had or the sex he had with a million other guys is completely irrelevant. All he wants to know is whether my friend really loves him or is only using him for his youth like I just used him. I don't know what to say. So I tell him sure, he loves you to death. It's all he can talk about when we talk (we haven't spoken since the party). I'm touched by the sincerity of youth. I tell him what he wants to hear. My cynicism is fading fast. Sometimes a lie is less cynical than the truth. The boy kisses me and hurries away. He says he'll be late for his early morning volunteer work. He goes around helping sick lonely people. For the moment I snap out of my pessimistic view of the world. Maybe I should do some volunteer work. Better than TV.

So maybe love won't keep us together, but the next generation will.

↘↖↗↙

## What's In a Name?

Think of all the words generally used to describe people in one word. Sometimes used in groups but even alone enough to sum up everything you need to know about a complex individual. Think about it. Young. Old. Rich. Poor. Gay. Straight. Black. White. All the races. All the ethnicities. Each soul stamped and labeled. Tagged pedigrees, as though half the world weren't mutts (like me). When most of us are in fact ethnic and racial cocktails, mixed drinks forced to pledge allegiance to one or the other bottle. Then on to the types. Often in adjectives. Fat. Thin. Cute. Ugly. Cool. Uncool. Or nouns. Jock. Nerd. Clubby. Yuppy. The professions. Accountant. Salesman. Waiter. Actor. Actor/waiter. On and on the list goes of words and phrases that pretend to say so much about a person but actually just pigeonhole them. But try avoiding them. I dare you. You won't last long in a conversation. And why should you avoid these words if the *New York Times* uses them on every page. Two black men arrested for holding up a Korean store. Gay man arrested for propositioning teenage boy. We could just use our names. First names to protect the anonymity. (I understand the phone books in Iceland are in first names because the last names are just first names of the fathers with a suffix.) Joe and Bob arrested for holding up Don's store. Ted arrested for propositioning Pete. Somehow that wouldn't do it. If we need to call a rose by its name, then we should. But let's not forget that it can be more than just sweet.

I remember one night wanting to go out cruising after a particularly awful day and due to my state of stress and confusion and the confusing weather that came with the evening – an Indian summer well into the fall – I could not for the life of me pick out what to wear. I'm not that vain, and I have few enough clothes. But I like to be neither hot nor cold when flying away from my nest. And I do recognize that when you walk out the door you enter the stage of life in costume, play an appropriate role, and are treated accordingly. This one confused night I couldn't decide whether to dress for summer or fall or whether to disguise myself as up-and-coming yuppie or down-and-out waif. So I dressed like a nerd. Sneakers and jeans with a sports jacket. A fashion statement once and now the height of dorkiness. Seeing myself in the mirror I felt positively goofy. Same person as always, but the clothes do make the man. Along with the hairdo. I had shaved my head recently and was first realizing that without hair the head gets awfully cold even in mild weather. So I added a baseball cap to the costume, and turned it backwards just to make it gay. More name-calling. Okay. Let them laugh.

When I walk in the bar they don't laugh, but they certainly snicker. Actually each time the door opens and someone walks in, they snicker. I shouldn't take it personally. As soon as I sit down at a table with a bunch of "friends" I begin to snicker too. It's the thing to do. Our victims give us something to talk about. It never ceases to amuse me how people can endlessly talk about and laugh at other people and then be surprised if not put off to learn that other people are actually talking about and laughing at them. The group has its power over the individual. No place for a conscience. I sit among them and join in the name-calling feeling safe in the snickering mob.

This bar is a strange mix of everything. Sleazy hustlers and jaded intellectuals and everything in between. At one end of the table the conversation is about who's who in the bar. There go those words again: Queen. Butch. Puerto Rican. Banker. Hot. Black. Old. Ugly. Cute. Stupid. At the other end of the table the conversation is philosophical. Deep. More words to say everything and mean nothing. Except these guys think they're on to something. They think they're intellectual. What they are is pseudo. Pseudo-morons.

"Spiritu*al*ity." That's Al feeling the spirits. "It's a matter of spiritu*al*ity."

"Whatta ya tawkin' about? God is queer!" Said with conviction. At least this guy has some freaky ideas.

"Shame on you, blasphemer. We don't say things like that. God is god. Look, I'm as queer as they come. But one thing I'm not going to do is sit here and claim that what I do is normal or natural."

Too of the silliest words. Normal is what most people do, or say they do. Natural is what no one does. Except animals. Real ones. You know, being naked and eating dinner raw right off the carcass. No steak knives. Just your teeth and nails.

"Natural is what's spiritual. As in spiritu*al*ity." There goes Al again. "Let's face it, honey. Smell the coffee. God did not make Adam and Steve."

"Ah. Now I gotcha. The point is... that God made Adam. He didn't make Eve. He made Adam. He made a hunky butch guy. A straight guy. And Adam, because he was straight, needed a bitch to fuck. So God made Eve, out of Adam, and sat back on his cloud and watched them fuck. Now if that ain't a queer idea of making the world I'll eat my umbilical cord."

Tasty. And natural, I add. Just had to put my two cents in.

Not appreciated. "Why is everything such a joke with you, Ken. Can't you take anything seriously? Go out and play with the other children. We're having an adult conversation."

I slide over to the other side of the table. They're discussing belts.

"Belts are cool, but only if they're like cool belts."

"That's a cool belt. There. On that black guy. He's cool."

"I like his belt. But I think he's a sleaze."

I look at the guy with the belt as he starts making his way over to the table, perhaps sensing that he's just been reduced to an article of clothing. A complexion. And an aspersion. It takes nerve to walk up to a table of snickering bitches and be friendly. I like this guy with the belt already. Notice, I didn't call him this black guy, or this sleazy black guy. I used the belt to signify him until I know his name.

"Don't I know you?" he asks me, of all people. "My name is Adam." Apropos. I decide he probably came over because he heard the spiritualists mention his name.

I don't think we've met, but here, have a seat. My name is... Steve.

What the hell. At least I introduced myself. The others make no effort at in any way recognizing the new arrival. They look annoyed that I invited this stranger to sit and interrupt their appraisal of his belt. You'd think they would like to take a closer look at it. Instead they look away on to their next victim. "See that cute hunk over there. Young. The white guy with the tank top."

"He's cute. But he's a sleaze."

So who's not? The guy with the belt – I mean Adam – gets up and takes his leave. "See ya later, man."

See ya. I give him a curt wave feeling bad that we snubbed him. You bitches scared him away.

The bitches suck their teeth. "Oh, please. He only came over here because you look like such a sucker in that outfit. He left because you didn't buy him a drink. They're all hustling in this dump."

I watch the black guy and his belt go to the other side of the bar. I look at the young white guy with the tank top. In a moment he's walking towards us.

I'm scolded. "You sucker, stop looking at them or they're all gonna come over here."

We wouldn't want that. Preferable to dissect them from a distance, ever-so-tactfully seeming not to actually look at them as it's done. I'm amazed at this dexterity in being cruel. As the guy with the tank top comes within ten feet of our table one of the bitches mutters inaudibly to anyone but us her words of reduction: "White trash. New Jersey."

Enough said. Our unsuspecting victim comes over with an ingratiating smile and flexes his muscles for us. The bitches snicker.

I invite him to join us. Wanna beer?

They turn and look at me like I'm an idiot. Well why not buy him a beer? I can afford it. I don't care if he takes me for a beer. Really. What's the big deal?

They turn away as soon as the boy sits down. I signal the waiter to bring us two beers. I might have even bought a round for the table if they hadn't been so bitchy about it. I snub them, turn to my new friend and smile. Okay, maybe I'm a sucker. It suits the outfit. My role for the night.

We sit in silence. The beers come. I pay. We drink. And now that I've bought myself a little conversation with a young hunk, I proceed. What's your name? I ask and the others grunt.

"Mario." Mario has a cute smile. Little teeth to go with the big muscles.

Really? You're Italian. So am I. My name's Carlo, I say with a lilt. Two of the bitches get up and leave without saying a word, banging into the table and almost knocking over the beers. Mario and I laugh it off. We're in love. At least that's the fantasy. He's so strong and handsome and sweet and friendly it must be love. The way he's smiling at me. You can't fake a smile like that. Does he really just want money?

The only thing to do is kiss him this minute and fall madly in love the next. I lean over. I can smell his young manly scent. I'm ready to go fly off to paradise with him when along comes... the Jinx. A strange character I see in the bars sometimes. A guy who must have a name but I don't remember it and I've only ever known him as the Jinx because he has this irrational fear of jinxing himself and those around him. Every other word out of his mouth relates to that. Ripley's law gone berserk. You know, you take your umbrella everyday that week and it doesn't rain. Then the one day you don't take it, it rains. Well maybe this happens, but it's nothing to base your existence on. Compared to this, a belief in God seems scientific. When the Jinx sits down next to me just as I'm ready to kiss my young prince on the lips, he says just the wrong thing at the wrong time. "I'm not disturbing you?"

And whatta ya know, he is. My prince gets up and excuses himself to the bathroom and I'm left to explore the realm of the negative with my aquaintance from beyond.

"See that. I jinxed you. I said, I'm not disturbing you? And then it turns out I did." He's serious. "Whatever I say, the opposite happens. I should have said, I *am* disturbing you. Then he would have stayed."

Do you spend your whole life trying to say the opposite of what you want in order to get what you want?

"I try. But the problem is that if you know that you're saying the opposite on purpose, then it can backfire on you by making the opposite of the opposite happen. A double jinx."

And then you're right back where you started.

"Listen, I'm really sorry I jinxed you. Your friend was real hot. Too bad he ain't comin' back."

How can you say? He just went to the bathroom.

"Then why did he take his beer with him? He ain't comin' back. Anyway, he just wanted you to buy him a beer. He knows you're not gonna buy him for the night. In that outfit you look like a sucker, but not a john."

The Jinx is not only negative, but smug. Awfully confident in his judgments for someone who walks around in perpetual fear of the polar opposites. An eerie mix. I drink my beer comforting my feelings of loss with my confidence in the rational. The boy got his beer and used the Jinx as the opportunity to make his exit. I can live with that. It's clear. It makes sense. No morality. No hocus-pocus. I look around the bar. It's all a game anyway. The black guy with the belt is laughing a bit too hysterically with some ugly old pink-faced businessman. His employer for the evening. There I go. These words again. One is so sure they know what's what just from a superficial glance. Doesn't leave much room for the unexpected.

The Jinx continues to talk in cosmic opposites, jinxing himself and everyone around him, trying to minimize the risk by discussing the weather. "We sure are having strange weather, huh? It's gonna be like this for the rest of the week." Sensing the jinx. "I mean, it might be, but you never know with the weather. Like last week I bought a winter coat cause it was starting to get cold. See and I jinxed myself cause now it's warm."

Enough. I inch down the bench towards the intellectuals. Anything is better than the Jinx. A third deep thinker has joined the roundtable discussion. A black opera singer. There I go again. But what am I supposed to say? I don't remember his name if I ever knew it. The diva is big and black and sings opera for a living. She speaks seven languages and makes a point of dropping foreign words in conversation in order to demonstrate her utter fabulousness and leave the rest in awe. At least a well-educated pseudo-intellectual. The two spiritualists are duly belittled by the diva's multilingual eloquence, but understanding a bit of German I'm only left in awe of the sheer breadth of her voice.

"It's a matter of the Zeitgeist. The Sinnlosigkeit of the last generation has been replaced by a new Spiritismus." Turning towards the bar she calls out to the waiter in his mother tongue. "Joven! Un cerveza, por favor." That voice. Like a great bellows the diaphragm sucks in quantities of air and out comes this stupendous tone. A fog horn at open sea.

The Jinx adds the negative. "The waiter just finished for the night, diva. You gotta get your beer at the bar."

And of course, the waiter comes right over with a beer. A benevolent jinx. But I'm too much the realist for this magic stuff. It's Friday night. The waiter gets off an hour later.

Confident in his powers, the Jinx rubs it in my face. "I told you your friend wasn't comin' back."

Don't be so sure of yourself. I look around the bar and spot the white trash with the tank top. He sees me and comes walking right back to the table. Ha! So much for all these theories. I hear in back of me the diva voice the motif. "Look at that hunky whiteboy."

That hunky whiteboy comes right up to me and says: "I was lookin' for ya."

Right.

"I got some weed. You feel like takin' a walk?"

So there. Now it's my turn to show off my powers. Nothing like a little eye contact to make a wish come true. I get up and give the Jinx the evil eye. In turn he winks at me, as sure as ever of his philosophy of opposites. "I told ya. It's a double jinx."

He jinxed him to leave and then jinxed him to come back? I think about it, but not for long. My dreamboy is heading for the door, with me at his heels.

On the street the Indians play havoc with the seasons. Almost 70 degrees in November. A slight chill in the breeze but my sports jacket keeps me warm. My dreamboy needs no protection from the elements. The tank top is there just to show off his muscles. A frame. For a picture that can't be reduced to words. Young. Hustler. Italian. Macho. Muscles. Mario. The name says it all. But I'd call it, simply, too good to be true.

His line is that we're going back to his friend's apartment to get high. His friend? There's plenty to smoke there because Mario's mother deals. She just got out of prison. She needs the money.

Okay. Sounds kosher. We're going back to his friend's apartment to smoke pot with his ex-con mom who sells pot for a living. So what is he selling? His body? I'm not interested in buying, much as I'm sold on the product. I tell him I'm from New Jersey, here for the night, looking for some fun but low on cash. It goes with the outfit. I play dumb. In turn, he tells me that he's unemployed at the moment but fortunate to be able to live with his friend. Good for mom too.

The building is posh. The doorman lets us in with no problem. His friend is posh. The apartment is high up (for the Village) with a river view. Where's the friend? I ask. Oh, he lives in one of his other apartments. His friend is very posh.

Inside it looks just like what you'd expect of an apartment that some rich older man would use as a spare apartment to keep his live-in hustler et al. Posh but run-down. Soiled carpeting. Eccentric modern furniture, some of it broken. African sculpture. And there she is surrounded by it, not quite as posh as the surroundings but certainly run-down. Mom. Just out of prison, sitting around the TV with another ex-con. A Latino man with tattoos. There I go again. Ex-con. Latino. The tattoos are the only thing I can say with certainty, but in any case I don't know anything about the man. He could be an Argentine harpsichordist buying weed for his chamber ensemble. Or he could be the rich man who owns the apartment. Mario murmurs to me that that's his mother's boyfriend. A real dick, he says.

Mom calls out in a sloppy voice from around the TV. "That you, Joey?"

"Yeah ma."

Well whatta ya know. He keeps an alias around the house. No excuses offered. To me, or his dear mother. Joey takes me straight to the bedroom. The master bedroom.

"My friend's room."

Nice room. The central air-conditioning humming quietly. King-size bed. African masks hanging on the rose walls. Antique highboy. The gay man's bedroom. The view is nice. Bits of the Hudson peeking out between the other roofs. My adventures continue to afford me splendiferous vistas. I peer out the window until it gets boring. Then on to the more exquisite view inside. My dreamboy standing there in his friend's decor making the sculpture look silly. Does he know you take guys back to his place?

"Yeah, he's cool. He lets my mom and her boyfriend live here too. She needs a place to deal, but he don't know about that."

The extended family. It's all so wholesome. They're not the Brady Bunch. But maybe this is the real American family, sticking together in hard times. We lie on the bed. His body stretched out before me. A sculpture of the young male form. Symmetrical. Each muscle chiseled to perfection. I'm ready to dive into him. Bury my head in those brown armpits. He jumps up. "I'll roll a joint." He gets a big bag out of the highboy, turns on the stereo, and jumps back in bed. What does he want from me. I know what I want from him. Does he want a nerdy friend? Does he want me to buy him for the night? Then why is he so up and about, and why didn't he talk prices? And does he really want to do it while his mother's in the other room?

She comes in. She's fat, aging and fake-blond. There I go again. Summing up the complex individual in three words. How about two. White trash. I see where he gets it from. She gives me a dirty look, turns down the stereo and opens the window. "If ya gonna smoke, open the fuckin' window." Then, without warning she snatches my baseball cap off my head and tosses it on the bed. "We got manners in this house. I don't let nobody wear no hat inside, ya hear?"

See? One cannot so easily pigeonhole people. The slob fresh out of gaol knows her etiquette. Meanwhile my head is cold. The AC is chilly enough for my shaved head. The open window adds a draft.

The slob stares at me. "Whatta you lookin' at?"

Nothing. Absolutely nothing.

"I wouldn't be actin' all high 'n mighty in that outfit, kiddo." She waddles out of the room.

Your mother's real nice. (And I thought mine was weird.)

"Yeah, ain't she a trip?" He rolls the joint. Déja vu. Another joint. Another beer. Another strange encounter with some guy you sort of know, but don't know any more than some guy in a backroom. Not anonymous, but still sex with a stranger. I've had enough joints and enough beers and enough strangers. What I want, here, now, with him is – silly as it always sounds – love. I want to give my love to this, my dreamboy. And I want him to give me his love. Forget the joint. I'm tired of all the hors d'oeuvres. I want the entrée already.

What I get is a smoke and a free show. He takes a hit, hands me the rest, pops out of bed, whips off that tank top and starts flexing his muscles. He does pushups with one hand. He performs his karate exercises. I eat it up, ready to burst with jism, shower him with my applause. His torso is a work of art. A Michelangelo in progress. A young marble god. The sculpture developing before my very eyes, growing into full manhood. It's painful to be so thoroughly teased. He smiles at me while standing on his head. Such cute teeth, even upside down. Ouch. My love for him is a pain throbbing down deep in my stomach down to my groin and all the way back up to my broken heart. Stop. Don't hurt me like this. Slit my throat but don't torture me with your sexiness.

He comes back over to the bed. I can smell his sweet salty sweat. The joint goes to my head and I'm incapacitated by it and my desire for my dreamboy, spreading his legs in front of my face, showing me how limber he is when he does his stretches. It's time I made my move. But it would seem out of place. Like it's against the house etiquette. His dear mother might barge in and tell us to take our shoes off. For now, I could scream. He's near, yet so far away. An exhibit in a museum, not to be touched, appreciated only with the eyes. He rolls another joint. Enough with the stimulants. I'm stimulated enough. I would like to tell him to stop smoking dope. You'll ruin your health. Choke the lungs, dry the silky skin. We must preserve the great works for as long as they will last before time takes its toll. Stop. Don't smoke that. Kiss me. Let me kiss you.

He smokes. I smoke. I'll soon be unconscious, the dreamer lost in his unreachable dreams. Pity me. I live in a state of the undeniable denied. I'm lifted on a cloud and I drift off to the heavens where the Lord, Adam and Steve, and Al too, all of them stand around wanking with King David sitting on the throne and me, Michelangelo, lying at his feet kissing his toes, worshipping the Lord's creation out of undeniable Catholic lust. Love so deep it's lust. It hurts until you can't feel it anymore. Thank god the pain is gone now. All that's left is the smell.

I open my eyes. He's standing over me, his chest glistening with that aromatic sweat. His full lips part. "You okay. Ya like passed out or somethin'."

He stands up. I sit up. There's a man in the room with us. The Lord? A dark-skinned majestic older man sitting in the corner in the Eames chair. Latino? Mom's boyfriend? But no tattoos. This man is well-dressed. Refined. An arrogant face. This could be the Argentine harpsichordist.

"Hello. You have perhaps smoke too much and go to sleep. Almost one hour you sleep."

It felt like a minute.

"You very tired."

Or very drugged.

"You feel better now since you sleep." The accent is South American. With a slight lisp.

Apologies seem in order. Sorry for... sorry for passing out on your bed.

"You must not feel embarrassment. I like when Mario brings home friends."

We're back to the other name.

"He tells me you are just visiting this wonderful city I love. Where do you come from and what do you do there?"

Nosy. I come from... Alabama. I play the banjo. On my knee.

"Oh, a musician. I play myself violin and piano. I study many years the repertoire when I was young man. But I could not reach, how to say, I could not reach my dream of playing as I want to play. Perfection for the artiste is only the goal, but he have to get close."

Must be an artist. A painter or something.

"Now I am sculptor. These pieces," pointing to the African masks, "are by me."

Scary. The whole scene is kinda creepy. I want to take my throbbing head out the door and home to bed. What was that shit we smoked anyway? One is always too quick to take the passed joint, having no idea what might be in it.

"Maybe, you like to lie down. Get more comfortable. When you like, take your clothes off. Mario, help him get comfortable." My dreamboy pulls down the covers for me. I can't resist the invitation. I squirm in under the covers and Mario gets in next to me. So it seems the Lord likes to watch while his creations get it on. I guess I'm Steve after all.

Meanwhile Adam is back to his evil apple, rolling another of those horrible joints. I thought I'm supposed to be the one to court the serpent. When he lights it up I actually tell myself I'm not going to partake. Throughout biblical history people have been sure they could resist temptation. In the end, they succumb. Why? Because they're alive. And they want to taste life's pleasures even when experience has taught them that the sweet fruit is not always what it seems. That a mushroom can be poisonous. Oh well. He tells me this is some *other* stuff. Different. Better. Probably laced with the better dust. When he hands me that dusty fruit I know that it's not what I want. I want the serpent. But I take the fruit for now and taste it. Just a taste. From behind, the Lord Almighty hands me a foamy drink. I take it passively and drink the sweet liquid asking myself how I came to find myself in the middle of this religious ceremony, wondering if I am to be the sacrifice.

I can only piece the rest together. The segments of the puzzle falling through my memory in a soon forgotten dream as I woke up on the street the next day. The images are clear but disconnected. My head lying on his strong chest, smelling his armpits. His arm around my neck. His hand on my face. In the distance, words of passion. Spanish poetry, the rhythm exhorting us to play out the poet's fantasy. I can remember my dreamboy ramming his manhood into my passive mouth, his fist hitting my lips. And each time that incredible smell of salt and earth, sea and trees and the sweat of youth, of blooming flowers and pollen and the funk that grows in the thick of the forest, rich and essential to my being alive. I can remember, I think, getting fucked. How could I forget a thing like that? But maybe it was just the poet's fantasy, his hot words playing tricks on my hallucination. Words, like images, get muddled. They last only as long as you don't forget them. Whereas a rose by any other name has a precise smell that stays with you long after you rub it in your lapel.

When I did finally pick myself up off the curb and stagger this way and that way on a street I swear I have never seen before, I could not for the life of me remember my name. Or anyone else's. But the smell of cummy sex all over my ravaged body brought back pieces of images, broken icons of unknown heroes, my savior found and lost. I blinked my eyes, shrugged and stared out into the bliss of morning light hovering over a too too red traffic light, straining to remember something more tangible to sober me up, to bring me back to earth. For the moment, walking through that haze of Indian Summer, I would be awakened by the smell still lingering on my lips.

## The Smelliest Man Alive

Too often love demands compromise. Especially if the ideals are too high. A man I know is forever compromising his deific standards, willing to overlook certain mortal flaws in order to get what he wants, which is what he ordinarily wouldn't be able to get. I dub him the compromise queen. Allowing for a few blemishes in the fantasy, he pursues his impossible dream, ignoring the reality, skipping the person in favor of their body. I suppose we are all guilty at times of this sort of superficiality. But then not everyone has such high standards. And not everyone is as accepting of such exceptional flaws.

I don't know the man well, but I know all about his sex life. He's an acquaintance. A familiar face I see around. I don't remember his name, if it was ever mentioned. The scene is like that. You run into certain people over and over without ever really getting to know them. But each time you see them you chat as though the closest of friends. Anonymous friends? Close strangers? The conversation is often too intimate to deny that this person is a friend, but then one would never trade phone numbers or arrange to get together. Who's going to trade phone numbers when you never traded names? A friendship must start with the introductions. If over the years you continue to run into each other when no introductions have been made, then it's too late. It would be awkward to start now. The relationship is doomed to remain anonymous, however candid the talk may get.

Each time I run into the compromise queen, always at some sleazy bar downtown, he tells me the intimate details of his fascinating sex life, filling me in on his latest conquest. The object of his desire is always none other than Adonis himself. A new one each time. He follows them around until he manages to seduce them. I don't know how he does it, and I don't much care. I'm never sure how much is true for that matter. What is incredible, and interesting in a truly perverse way, is what he must settle for in pursuit of his fantasy, the eerie compromises he makes in order to get what he wants. On the one hand he's a dreamer, chasing his vision of physical beauty. But on the other hand he's quite practical. He realizes that he won't be able to get Adonis into bed. So he settles for Achilles. And overlooks the heel. He will tell me about some gorgeous guy he had sex with. Stunning good looks. Long blonde hair. Tall Olympian body. Just one thing. The guy has no arms. Another is tall, dark and handsome, but has a deformed foot. Another has all the body parts, is perfect in every way, right out of a magazine ad... except for that bluish blotch on the side of the face which continues down the back, a scar from a fire. The first time he told me one of these grisly sex tales I thought it was a bit strange but figured that sort of thing can happen. You meet someone, you like them. So it turns out they have a large mole on their penis, or a club foot. You don't throw them out of bed. You allow for human imperfection as you allow for yourself. You like the person, not just the body. Right? But after hearing the same scenario each time we met, I soon began to form a picture of his warped sensibilities. He obviously is only interested in the most physically beautiful of men but considers himself unworthy of them and as a result must settle for these few unfortunate details. I think the details are a big part of the picture. I think he relishes them. The compromise gives him back his pride, makes him feel like he's doing charity and in that way balances the charity done to him. Strange what one will go through to adore their fantasy. I must admit I find it all a bit much, even for my jaded ears, but that doesn't stop me from listening. Though I may cringe.

The last time I saw him I was sitting on a barstool at the end of a long bar, watching music videos, lazily sipping my last drink for the night, thinking how incredibly stupid music videos are, wondering why I was sitting there drinking in this room with these men at this bar when nobody was talking and everybody was glumly watching the videos. Might as well stay home. What an alienating experience to be so alone among the many. With Michael Jackson singing *You Are Not Alone* in the background. All eyes on the King of Pop with his shirt open and blowing in the breeze, exhibiting his extra-terrestrial body for all the world to see. I'm sitting there wondering whether he did actually have some skin-whitening therapy or if as Latoya claims it's just a lot of makeup when I hear a familiar voice, turn around, and recognize the compromise queen. Hey, he says. Hey, I say. That's what you say when you know someone but you don't know their name. He sits down next to me on the stool I have been reserving for Prince Charming. Oh well. At least I'll get some titillating conversation. I'm drunk enough that I'm actually looking forward to hearing about the latest chilling deformity. What is it this time? Some gorgeous guy with three nipples? Two penises? A missing eye? No asshole, but a nice hole where the colostomy bag hooks on?

"Do you see him?"

Who?

"I can't believe he's here."

I look around. No obvious deformities in sight. It could be something not especially noticeable. The compromise queen has had his share of deaf-mutes and mental retards. I remember one blind guy he pointed out to me. Except for the frozen eyes the guy was in every way a dreamboy. Personally I prefer my fantasies not too pretty. I uphold my fantasy of the common man – strong and rough around the edges. But one can admit an attraction to what is clearly beautiful. A stunning flower. An exquisite vase. Even with a crack in it.

"I can't believe he's here. I can't look at him. I'll pretend I don't see him. Let's pretend we're talking."

I thought we were. My curiosity tickled, I ask him to point him out.

"I can't look. It's too too embarrassing. He's over there," nodding ever-so-slightly, "in front of the cigarette machine."

There's a whole crowd in front of the cigarette machine, all of them staring up at yet another Michael Jackson video. This one with Michael showing off that extraterrestrial body in the slums of Rio with a backdrop of little brown drummerboys while he sings all about how *they* don't care about *us*. Poor, poor Michael. If he really just wants to be one of the boys, maybe he should give away his millions and get a tan.

I look around at the transfixed faces in front of the cigarette machine trying to spot some missing limb when I realize which one he's talking about. The one with the glamorboy profile. The one with the Hollywood good looks. The one who Michael Jackson was trying to look like when he bought all that plastic surgery. The guy looks perfect in every way. Sparking my interest. What am I not seeing?

"That boy is so hot. He has the most incredible body. Pure perfection. Blessed. The gods were in a good mood the day he was born." A dreamy look comes over his countenance. He's seeing something far off and untouchable.

Why don't you go over and talk to him if he's the man of your dreams?

"I can't. Not after what happened."

As usual, there is something amiss. That bit of imperfection that brought them together, without which the compromise queen would not have had a chance. As always, that bit of imperfection pulled them apart after the first and only encounter.

"I wish I could. I wish I were a better person. I wish I could overlook the man's flaws. But I can't. As beautiful as he is, as hot as the sex was, I can't. I just can't. It's too gross for words."

Listen, deary, I think you should take what you can get. You overlooked his deformity, whatever it is, enough to have sex with him once and you admit it was hot sex, so why not go on for the second round?

"What deformity do you speak of?" Pray tell. Her eyes wide in wonder.

I look over at the specimen, studying his blank face. The features are godly, no doubt. And the manner is too cool for words. But it doesn't seem to be doing him much good. He's being ignored, like the rest, in favor of the King of Pop.

"Well in a way it is a deformity. Mental deformity."

He's psycho.

"In a way."

I love this guessing game. Don't tell me he's into whips and chains?

"No. Nothing like that."

I notice a smirk on her silly face, suggesting that she's had her share of whips and chains.

"That's one thing I would never put up with."

Right. Michael Jackson likes girls.

"Once was enough. There was this one man I used to be into who was absolutely incredibly gorgeous, but he wanted to do the most dreadful things to me. Gag me. Beat me. Poke me. Rip me. The man couldn't get enough of yanking on me. He yanked at anything he could yank. My dick, my balls, nipples, arms, my head. Even my teeth. Couldn't deal with it. What a shame, because the guy was an absolute dream. Absolutely perfect, except for those two missing fingers on his right hand."

Ouch.

"No, I can put up with a lot. But not that. I'm really very vanilla. I like to do the most normal things. No pain, piss or shit for me, thank you. I like to kiss, touch, rub, and suck, and if it's love I fuck too. But nothing abnormal."

A lot of people would consider all of the above abnormal when it's between two men.

"Let them. I know what's right for me. Funny, because I had no idea about this one at the cigarette machine until we got down to it."

You must have known something was off or you wouldn't have seduced him.

"Excuse me?" She's in shock. "Don't assume things. I didn't seduce him. This one seduced me."

I look again at the man in front of the cigarette machine. And then at my lady friend. No way. Unless...

"The man has a fetish. A very particular one."

Hm. A fetish for silly queens? The silly queen sitting next to me is average-looking, but rather unkempt. So many of the queens are impeccably neat, everything freshly washed and tucked, each hair in the nostril in its proper place. This one has hair growing out of her ears. Her clothes are sloppy and dirty. On a macho it would all pass as part of the butch attire. But on a queen it's just gross. I can't possibly imagine that handsome man in front of the cigarette machine seducing *her*. Until she blushes bright red and says,

"That gorgeous man has a fetish for smells."

What kind of smells?

"Man smells."

You mean woman smells.

"No, man smells."

Nothing wrong with that, as long as they're good smells. Some manly mustiness can be thoroughly erotic.

"There are smells... and then there are *smells*. Let's just say that in the subway on the way back to my apartment I thought I smelled something really terrible but I figured it was just the leftover residue of the garbage in the street following me around. I kept looking at the bottoms of my shoes like maybe I stepped in something. I got up to my apartment, took off my shoes, and I was still smelling it."

You must have noticed it when you first met him.

"It was smoky in the bar."

Should have lit some cigs in your apartment.

"I don't smoke.."

Should have sprayed him with Lysol.

"So there I am with this beautiful man in my bed and I'm trying to hold my nose closed without being obvious about it and like I'm starting to think maybe it really is me. I didn't get a chance to shower that day and like... but no, couldn't be. You can't smell yourself."

You can try.

"And besides, I never smelled that smell before in my whole life. The worst grungey smell you can imagine. Like blue cheese and shit."

I sniff the air. All I can smell is the smoke. Thick. Odorless in a way. Pure, bland exhaust.

"Anyway, there I am trying not to breathe. I get up, turn on the TV just to get away from him, and before I can suggest we take a shower – separately – he jumps on me, throws me on the bed and starts ravaging me... with his nose."

Nose-fucking?

"He's sniffing *me!* All over like a mad dog, a mad smelly dog that just rolled in shit and I can hardly speak the smell is so bad. I'm retching as I push him off of me and suggest all quiet and ladylike that I might want to take a shower because it's been a long sweaty day and maybe, perhaps, by chance, he might want a shower too."

Demure. Difficult as it is for humans to smell themselves, one must be tactful in letting them know when they stink.

"And you wouldn't believe. Not only does he refuse to shower, but he insists that I don't shower either. He tells me that he's into it. Body odor. All fucking kinds of odor. He purposely doesn't wash too often and when he does he doesn't use soap, doesn't soap his dick or armpits. He uses alcohol to disinfect his smelly asshole without destroying the authentic fragrance. He rinses his mouth with warm water but never brushes his teeth and he actually keeps his used socks and underwear in plastic bags overnight to intensify the stench."

I'm gagging just thinking about it. I stare across at the smelly guy in front of the cigarette machine. In the thick cloud of smoke one couldn't smell it if someone took a shit right there on the floor. Even so, I notice a man standing next to him look around, stick his nose out, and walk away. Maybe it's just my imagination. Often when they try to subtly cruise they look like they're smelling the air. The smug nose pointing up. Insecurity coming off as disdain.

"I must say, when the guy confessed his incredible fetish for putrid smells I was absolutely speechless. I didn't know what to say. I sat there on the bed with my mouth open and my nose closed staring into those gorgeous eyes and before I could think of what to say or do he stripped naked."

I can't believe you actually had sex with him.

"Hard to admit. But the man was too perfect to resist. Flawless. From head to toe a dream. You can see for yourself the face and the hair. Absolutely perfect features. And what a body to go with that face. Perfect chest. Smooth, with just a tuft of sexy hair down the middle. Perfect abs. Perfect arms. Sensational armpits. Muscular, connected perfectly to the pecs. The hottest butt. Perfect. Every part of him absolutely perfect."

The body dissected into parts and inspected for flaws.

"And oh my god... what a dick."

Lemme guess. Big?

"Incredibly big. And incredibly smelly. I never in my whole life smelled a dick that smelled like that. I mean, I like smelly dicks, when they're just a trifle smelly. You know, manly?"

Yes, I know.

"But this thing of his smelled so awful, it even looked horrible. Like some green stuff was growing on it."

Plant your dick. Grow mushrooms.

"I thought I might get used to the smell after a while. Smells are like that. But not this smell. I smelled it to the end. Till the next day after he finally left and three days later."

Why on earth did you go through with?

"I went through with it because the man is that gorgeous."

How she suffers. I'm thinking that the whole story is a lot of nonsense when the smelly guy starts making his way towards us. Uh-oh. Fortunately, he doesn't stop. But he does say hi to the compromise queen on his way to the men's room. The hi is suggestive, almost pleading, but it's met with a bitchy mumble. The queen looks away, snubbing him. It seems ludicrous, in spite of what I know. The ugly duckling snubbing the swan? By the looks of things he should be snubbing her. She should fall begging at his feet. And smell them. Such are the laws of the jungle where what you see is all that matters. I'm impressed, in a way. This girl can handle herself. She has her pride. Smelly as the smelly guy might be he certainly is stunningly handsome. A stud. I'm tempted enough that I think about following him to the men's room, just to see if his dick is really green. I find myself sniffing the air. And then coughing.

"You won't get a whiff in this smoke," she coos.

Enough smelly conversation. Enough fantasizing about the perfect mangod. We join the ranks and content ourselves to abandon all sense to the video screen and the *herstory* of the Queen of Pop, now saving the animal kingdom from extinction by turning the tape backwards. A little fantasy goes a long way in this world.

A few minutes later the smelly guy walks by us again. He almost pauses to say something but finally just offers his puppy eyes. The bitch keeps her eyes on the video, pretending not to see him, so he heads straight for the door, rushing out as only the lonely will to pretend they have more important places to go. Alone. I look at the grungey queen sitting next to me. She's untouched. A defiant sneer written across her face. Staring up at the video, ignoring the pleas of hungry men. Hard as nails to the plight of gorgeous, albeit smelly, guys. I remind her that she broke his heart.

"Sorry, but I ain't no charity. And I ain't easy. Besides, I'm spoken for."

I don't quite understand. Without turning her head she thrusts her hand in my face to exhibit the prize of every woman's dream. The ring. It looks like a toy, big as it is. Like something you get in a candy machine. Who's the lucky fella?

"We just started going out, but it's already serious." Turning finally, full of trashy etiquette. Composed, serious, but swooning a little bit. "It's awfully soon to be getting serious. We only met last week. But he's just too wonderful to let him slip through my fingers. He's really and truly that gorgeous. Handsomer than handsome. One really and truly handsome man."

Except?

"Absolutely perfect. A godly specimen of manhood. Big and brawny. No mere pretty boy. This one's all man. Tall, dark, and handsome. A big brute. A lion, with a monstrous tail."

But?

"But nothing. He's perfect as perfect can be. Chiseled body, gorgeous face, luscious mane. Lean, mean, stately stride. Legs of steel. A real thoroughbred."

What is he, a horse?

"Built like one. But no, he's pure hundred per cent superman. A girl couldn't ask for more."

So what's the catch?

The mischievous grin says it all. The compromise queen enjoys her compromises, as long as they're not too smelly. Part of the fun in ordinary life is the out-of-the-ordinary, even the downright odd. "These men do have their quirks, don't they?"

He likes to get saddled up?

"No, darling. Nothing like that. It's just that sometimes the most beastly ones have their – how can I put it – even the most ferocious beasts have their tender side. My man is a bit of a baby at heart. No diapers, mind you. But he does like it when I tickle him and call him my little sweety-poo."

Does he call you mommy?

"Not exactly. But sometimes when he gets all cuddly and googoo gaga, he likes to suck on my nipple. Not my most erogenous zone, mind you, but for a hunk like that – I can deal with it."

↘↖↗↙

## The Chicken and the Egg

David is a nice Jewish boy. He lives less than ten blocks away from his mother, but manages to see her at the most once a month. His excuse? He's just too busy of course. Which he is. In a way.

You'd think they might run into each other in the street. Never. Imagine living in the same neighborhood, near the same stores, the same park, and never running into each other. That's New York. If you don't hang out in the same seedy spots you can keep your anonymity for all it's worth.

His mother lives alone. She's one of those old Manhattan ladies that you see dragging their shopping bags back to their apartments. Three inches of makeup caked on the wrinkles. The fur coat from back when. You see them getting on the elevator when it stops on the 2nd floor going down. You see them getting on the bus, their heads peeping out to see where they're going because their spines have long since hunched over. Tall young women will look the other way. Osteoporosis does not make for a pretty picture. Poor little old ladies. Their husbands long dead. Most of their friends dead or living in Florida. Why do they stay in the delirious city? Why do they put up with it? The city whizzes by them. Cars, buses, trains, bicycles, skateboards and rollerblades. Even the most basic pedestrians whiz by, cursing them under their breath because they dare to move so slowly when everybody is in such a rush. Why do they persist? Poor little old ladies are not so poor to be living in chic neighborhoods, inhabiting valuable real estate. Why do they hold on to their cheap rents? Why do they cut out coupons and make everybody wait in line so that they can save five cents on a can of cat food? Because their late husband's money is tied up in the stock market and when you live off the interest it's not that much especially when you're saving for the future. Of course there are also the many who are really poor, living off of social security, alone in their poverty with only pussy for company. Many couldn't leave the city even if they wanted to. The landlord won't buy them out because it's cheaper to wait for them to die. Our hearts go out to them when they count out the coupons for a shopping cart full of cat food. Only cat food. Poor grannies, really poor, ignored and forgotten by their grandchildren.

Not David's mother. She'll never be a grandmother. That's for sure. And she's got more money than she knows what to do with. David's father set up a small fortune for her before he had his massive heart attack and died in the middle of a phone call. That was years ago and she could have at least bought a second place in Miami just as a winter getaway. No such luck. David's mother is a *real* Manhattan lady. New York is the world. Cross the Hudson River and you're in dangerous territory. The boroughs are the outer limit. Florida is pioneer country. New York is all there is, and by New York she means Manhattan. What would she do without Fifth Avenue? Where would she shop? Where would she buy her food without Zabar's? They don't have bagels in Miami. They don't have bagels in New Jersey. Not like New *Yawk* bagels. She's as happy as a wad of cream cheese stuffed in her bagel, closed in on all sides but with that nice hole in the middle to squeeze out a breath here and there. "I love Manhattan, the night life, the culture," she says twice a day. What would she do without Broadway, without the theater? The fact is she hasn't been to a show in twenty years and spends most of her time watching TV. "The thing about living in the city," the one and only city, "is that when you want it... it's there," she'll tell her one and only child, David. "Whatever you want... they got it. And whenever you want it... it's there." And that, for both of them, is precisely the point.

David is not quite as happy. He's told me often enough how frustrated he is with his life. He would like to leave New York, hates the place, but his work keeps him here, he claims. Seems like he could make those phone calls from anywhere. Must be something he likes about New York. He grew up in the city. Knows it all and hates it just as much. Hates the congestion, hates the noise, the grind, the money mania, the cars, the trains, the buses, the people, too many people, the food, the phony restaurants, the phony people in the phony restaurants. He hates everything about the place. Especially the theater. Broadway gives him heartburn. Hasn't been to a show since his mother's sixtieth birthday. If he ever has to go through midtown on an errand it makes him sick to see all that nonsense, the tourists, the kitsch shows. If they dropped a bomb on New York he wouldn't cry a minute, as long as he got out in time. And he hates the fact that his mother lives in his neighborhood and refuses to go join the relatives in Florida and get on with dying already. He's convinced that she stays to torture him. As if he doesn't do a good enough job himself.

There is one thing David likes about the city. Something he needs as much as he needs his work, though he hates his work. David is yet another sex addict worming around the big apple nibbling where he can, addicted to dick, out of control, incapable of stopping himself even if he wanted to. He tried. Five years of psychotherapy made him finally realize that he wanted to have sex with his shrink. The dangers of promiscuous sex have not stopped him either. He won't get tested. Too much of a hypochondriac. With a death wish. He tells me that the sooner he dies the sooner he can get away from his mother. His ambivalence haunts him. He hates New York, but won't leave. His mother tortures him with her sheer presence, and yet when she invites him over for dinner – "David, you never visit your mother" – he cannot refuse. I've decided that David is his own worst enemy, no matter who his therapist blamed. The last time he threatened to kill himself, which he does every time we speak, I told him to go ahead and do it already. Put yourself out of your misery. He said he wouldn't give *her* the satisfaction.

He called me the other day right after he got home from one of these evenings with mom. He was supposed to go there straight from work but it had been such a tough day of screaming on the phone that as soon as it was over he needed to get out and loosen up before submitting to the quiet subtle torture from his dear mother. It's a question for the psychotherapists: Does David's mother torture him or is David tortured by his feelings about his mother? For all I care, the chicken can eat its own egg. Who cares which came first. In an endless cycle of laying the only important thing is that the egg gets fertilized. Before the nice Jewish boy could deal with an evening of his mother's unbearable warmth he was going to get good and fertilized so he could feel like a man.

He starts out at the cinema. The usual afterwork crowd. He sucks three cocks and takes another two up the ass, for the latter feeling around in the dark to make sure they're plastic-coated. At one point he has it coming from all sides. Getting it and giving it. One guy fucking him, another sucking him while he jerks yet another, who as well is getting fucked and all around more bodies in a free-for-all huddle, hands groping in the dark, reaching for a body or for a way out of the bodies. These cramped cruising spots can get as overcrowded as the subway. Bodies pressed up against each other so that you haven't the faintest idea whose leg is cramming up your ass. David starts to feel like he's in a football game and he's the one with the ball. There are penises everywhere and he can't figure out whose is whose after a while. Then all the other body parts. Legs, thighs, assholes. Chests, necks, nipples, shoulders, fingers here, fingers there. Get me out of here. Too late. He's stuck all right. Stuck in the middle of a pile of anonymous anatomy. He gets off, comes on someone's pants and then has to dig his way out, the others pushing in to take his place. Stumbling out the door he's as horny as ever and heads straight for the park.

He joins in a circle jerk under a big old tree. He and five guys wank like a bunch of pubescent boys. At one point he drops down to his knees in the middle of the circle to shower in their spud. David has a cum obsession. Nothing turns him on more than the sight, the smell, the taste of it. Kneeling in the mud with penises on all sides he's beside himself in ecstasy over the thought of those penises squirting him. Penises are circling around his head like swarming insects. Penises are all he dreams about anymore. Dicks without bodies. Just dicks. Especially the uncircumcised ones, which seem otherworldly. His life has turned into a cheap sci-fi movie: *Invasion of the Penises from Outer Space*. They invade earth by turning earthlings into crazed cocksuckers. When David looks around at those giant penises in his face he's seeing creatures from another planet. I surrender. Take me to your leader.

He leaves the park cleaning jism out of his ear with a tissue. David always carries tissues. When he was a boy his mother would stick a tissue in his pocket "because you never know when you'll need one." Ain't it the truth. David goes back in the park, cursing his mother for having made him into a faggot. You made me into a cocksucker, Ma, and now I'm going to kill myself with it and I hope you're happy when I get AIDS! He stops off at the toilet in the park. Nobody usually cruises there. David needs to sit and think a little while. He sits on a toilet and puts on his thinking cap.

He isn't there long before a man in a jogging suit walks into the stall, closes the door and pulls out his hunk of flesh. David sticks his tongue out while the guy smacks him in the face with it. The dick almost hurts his face. It's heavy and each time it hits his cheek his jaw seems to rattle. After the guy shoots his load David is left there alone on the toilet trying desperately to get a last drop of juice flowing from his own dick. Something comes out, but he can't be sure what it is. Venereal discharge? Oh my god! He goes straight to his mother's apartment, still cursing her, the men in the park, the City of New York and life itself. He plans a morning visit to the doctor, then decides against it. The last time, the man told him he needed a psychiatrist not a doctor. God in heaven! There is absolutely no satisfaction in this life. Might as well be dead.

His mother always cooks the same thing. She calls it stew. It wouldn't be so bad if she could somehow resist throwing everything in it. It's not a chicken stew. There's chicken in it. But so are there meatballs, hot dogs (kosher), and some kind of fishy lumps, along with every last vegetable in the market and a variety of starches. You feel like you're eating everything on the menu in one dish. This is what ends up in the garbage pail outside the restaurant. The pea soup joins the chicken fricasee and the salmon mousse with the salad bar thrown in for good measure. "I made a stew," she says as he walks in the door. She always says that. "You want some egg salad before the chicken stew?" That's when it occurs to him that maybe it doesn't make a difference which comes first, the chicken or the egg or the soup or dessert for that matter. It all goes to the same place. He picks at the chocolate cake and she yells from the kitchen that he'll lose his appetite if he eats dessert before the meal. Have some egg salad on a piece of bagel if you can't wait for the stew. He picks at the egg salad but discovers tuna and raisins in it and could it be that there are little bits of chicken too? Or are those tuna bits? She serves the stew with a plate of pickles on the side. "I was going to add the pickles in the stew but I thought some people don't like pickles. Can you believe it? Some people don't like pickles." Who is she talking about? It's just the two of them. But he's glad she didn't add the pickles although he likes pickles well enough. At least the pickles are just pickles. Or are they? Little bits of something are sprinkled on top. What's this? Herring? Herring sprinkles. Skip the side dishes and dive into the stew already. But once in, he finds himself fishing around, picking through it, pulling out all sorts of strange bones.

"Ma, what kinda bones are these?"

"Whatta ya mean? A bone's a bone."

Maybe he's been sucking too much dick lately. Too many nameless body parts. He pulls out an anonymous bone from the stew. He wants to know whose bone it is. Lamb, chicken, beef? What is this shit? Thigh, breast, leg, ankle, finger? Forking around he finds all kinds of food of undetermined origin. An assortment of gizzards, some of them looking truly extraterrestrial. The whole thing comes together as such a brown slop that it's impossible to tell what anything is without tasting it. Even then. And what's this? More raisins? Flour drops? Tofu? Looks like bird turds. The chicken took a dump in its own stew. And what the hell is that? An eel??? No. It's a hot dog. Relax, it's only a hot dog. David contents himself with the hot dogs. At least he knows what he's eating.

Her apartment is overheated. The TV is always going. She watches the most inane shows. The weather channel for an hour. Or pay-per-view previews. She talks all through dinner with the TV on in the background. He doesn't say a word. Tries not to get angry at the idiocy of her innocuous remarks, her in-depth commentary on the shows. "I like this newscaster. I think he's very good. He does a wonderful job." Does she hear the news or just watch the newscaster. "He's very handsome, too. David, don't you think he's handsome?" David sucks on a bone, against his better judgment, sure that his mother turned him into a cocksucker. What kind of question is that! You don't ask your son if he thinks the newscaster is handsome unless you want him to be queer. Right?

She serves sour cream and bananas with the chocolate cake. Are those raisins or herring sprinkles in the sour cream? He shoves the creamy bananas down his throat, force-feeding himself. My god, she's feeding me cummy cocks. And what's that brown stuff? Peanut butter?

When he gets home he calls me to tell me about his night of sex, his mother's stew, the chicken, the egg, the hot dogs, the sprinkles and even the creamy bananas dipped in shit and asks me what it all means.

David, a bone is a bone. (I'm starting to sound like his mother.) A pickle is a pickle. Until you shove it up your ass. Then it's a pickle with shit on it. So what. Don't make yourself crazy over what is after all nothing more than a bunch of molecules stuck together. I can't deal with these neurotic connections between different compartments in the brain. Don't think about sex when you're eating a hot dog, for godsake. Compartmentalize.

He asks me why he can't be straight. Normal. Moral. I answer his question with a question. Who wants to be moral when it's so much fun being immoral? He says he's ready to jump off the Brooklyn Bridge. So what are you waiting for? He wants to know if I think he was queer at birth or if I think his mother made him queer. Neither. I don't believe in all these genetic theories. But I don't believe in this psycho nonsense either. I tell him the truth. David, you're not gay. You just like dicks.

He starts shouting at me. The man is clearly under a lot of pressure. I hold the phone away from my ear. When he settles down I try to give him some calming advice. Why do people tell me their problems? Why me? Why do they want to tell me their darkest, dirtiest fantasies? What do they want me to say? David, life is short. Don't waste your time kvetching. Stop analyzing. It won't change anything. That shrink took a small fortune from you and made you weirder than you already were. Change what you can to make your life better, but don't beat yourself up. (I'm starting to sound like a shrink.) If you're sick of your job, get another one. If you're sick of your mother and New York, go somewhere else. It's a big world. Not everyone is Jewish. Not everyone eats bagels. Not everyone loves New York. There's a whole world out there. So many different people. So many men pulling their dicks out. And you'd be surprised – a hell of a lot of them have never heard of Christopher Street. They're just getting off. I've traveled half the world. Europe, Asia, Africa, South America. The human mind is just a bunch of cells. There's no one way to think. The only thing you can be sure of is that every physically healthy man in the world has a physical need to shoot his stuff. Some more than others. But they all do it, one way of another. So stop driving yourself crazy about it! You're making *me* crazy.

The anxiety is contagious. Proof that any egg can get scrambled. With or without a chicken around. At least I calmed him down. Or did I? There's a long pause after my speech. Full of heavy breathing. I'm thinking that I gave him his long-awaited heart attack when I hear that whiny voice of mother and son speaking as the desperate soul of the anonymous man in need of some wide-open spaces, the voice of earthly lust whispering in my ear: "Do they have cruisy parks in Africa?"

I can only answer such a question with such a question. David, David. Answer this, but first think about it. Do they have wildlife in Manhattan?

↘↖↗↙

## The Anonymous Crab

It appears one morning. Out of the blue. He's sitting on the toilet, peeing, barely conscious after just waking up. He happens to look down and spots something in his underwear. Something very tiny, and could it be – it's crawling? He wouldn't have even noticed it, but at the same time he saw the tiny spot in his underwear he felt an itch in his groin and in a second he was wide awake thinking one and only thought, one and only word. In the plural. *Crabs!*

I'm the first to get the news. "I can't believe it. I got crabs and I swear I haven't had sex with anybody in a long, long time." My friend, an old friend, insists he has no idea how he got them. He hasn't had sex in almost a year. After fifteen years of continuously slutting around he couldn't take it anymore and got into Jesus and Yoga and swears he has no idea how he could possibly get crabs now after all these abstinent months of piety and spine-flexing.

Maybe the eggs were hiding out in his suit pants. Can they survive a year? I suggest maybe he's forgotten some brief encounter. No, he remembers every encounter he ever had. And proceeds to tell me about them. After a half hour of that he goes on to tell me about all the celebrities he's had sex with, all in anonymous situations.

But a celebrity could hardly be called anonymous.

"I had sex with Keith Haring and I didn't even know who he was. It was before he became, you know, *Keith Haring.* He was just some guy at the baths. After I fucked his white ass he said to me: I'm gonna be the most famous graffiti artist that ever was. And I'm like: Yeah, right. And then I like saw him on TV."

Wow.

"I also fucked Nureyev and Bon Jovi."

Bon Jovi? Yeah, right.

"Well, I almost fucked Bon Jovi."

Almost doesn't count.

"It was in the men's room at *Tavern on the Green* last month. He was there for this party for the rainforest and like I was working as an extra bartender and like he was coming out of the stall and like I was going in and like he like stared at me hard and like I knew he wanted it because he was like watching me the whole time at the party but of course nothing happened."

Maybe you got crabs from the toilet seat after Bon Jovi used it.

"Can you get crabs from a toilet seat?"

Probably not. If you could, half the world would be scratching away. Maybe it's a new super-strain. The beginning of a new epidemic.

My friend sighs. The sigh of a life of too much anonymous sex. "The whole thing is creepy."

Sure is.

"Like a whodunit. Who done laid a crab in my pubes?"

The possibilities are endless. I start to think about the endless transference of crabs from groin to groin all over this crabby city. I get itchy just thinking about it. My old friend – who's actually still young enough but tired and weary beyond his years – is going on about all the whodunits he's ever read. I pull the phone away from my ear. I tell him I gotta go. Maybe the butler did it.

"Did I ever tell you about the time I like did it with this butler?"

He proceeds to tell me about the butler and all the servants, maids (male maids), waiters, bartenders, cooks, doormen and gardeners he did it with. An impressive collection, monotonous as the tales unfold. Same old sex story. The phrases out of the same old porn: big dick... so hard... come in my face... take that dick good... he came and I came and our cum came coming all over... An endless epic on leaky faucets. What's the point? Seems to be to get off. To come. Finally. But there is no end to this epic until illness, death, or just boredom end it all –

Or the will steps in and says, enough is enough. My friend was saved and has been pure ever since in spite of what's crawling around in his underwear. On a pious note he wraps up his syphoning soliloquy with some good old-fashioned preaching. The Christian kind, about abstinence and self-respect. My body the temple (in ruins). Except he skims over Christ (too sensual) in favor of a potpourri of mind-cleansing techniques. He has buried his ravaged libido in new-age soul-searching and TV psychology. Yoga, Buddhism, and self-help. (To say nothing of Prozac.) The point is the same. Denial. A timeless cause. And non-denominational. Starve the senses, feed the soul. There has always been a new generation to take up that banner. Purity and cleanliness will bring salvation. If not in this life, then in the next. No shortage of humans attempting to negate their humanity. Their infested animal bodies. And their mortality. A tireless refrain. I've heard it before. And I don't want to hear it again. He tells me anyway.

At first he tried to learn to play the flute. Seemed like an obvious phallic substitute. But he lacked the discipline to practice hours and hours. The truth is, learning to play an instrument does not require as much discipline as it does a sincere love of music and a steadfast devotion to the instrument. My friend had no trouble applying himself to hours and hours of cocksucking. He insists that he loves music but that his soul was starved and that what he really needed was not to substitute the sexual urge by feeding alternate senses, but to feed his starved soul – "to get like spiritual."

Wow. Here we go again. Another new-age convert jumping on the transcendental bandwagon. Chanting. It's better than thinking, he says. Meditation. Positive energy. Nothing as empty as a drugged-out sexed-out generation replacing the drugs and sex with superstition after having already replaced their parents' materialism with drugs and sex. I want to tell him that, clichéd as it sounds, he needs to find himself, a life-long struggle for us all, and accept what he finds along the way. But it occurs to me that he may already have found himself – in a toilet – and after too many years of finding himself realized he just didn't like what he found. That's the problem. Often there is no answer. No path other than the inevitable. No advice worth giving, doctor. So I just let him talk. Hard as it is to listen.

Then he tells me something interesting. About the very last time he had sex.

It starts out like too many sex stories. Too much drink, too much drugs. Numb and inebriated the anonymous man finds himself kneeling on a dirty sticky floor somewhere, drowning himself in his desire, past the point of enjoying it. And isn't that precisely the problem? Isn't it just a matter of basic moderation, some Hellenic ideal to keep wine-tasting from turning into round-the-clock drunkenness? I suppose they had their share of drunks and drunkenness back then, but it would seem by comparison that modern society has lost its ability to taste, numbed by its own capitalist excesses. The masses drowned in opiates. Two-for-one. Twice as much because it's half the price. I give my advice. But cheap philosophy is not what my friend needs. He knows himself. Too late to learn moderation. It's all or nothing at all. That last time was a perfect example. He started out with good intentions. A drink at a bar. A nightcap and some friendly conversation. But as always the one leads to the many and eventually to the same old scene, the same position on the floor surrounded by more dicks than one mouth could handle, gagging on cum and piss, getting fucked without knowing it, or at least not remembering it, with only the mess in his pants as evidence.

So if that night was like so many other nights, what made the difference?

He sighs. "Nothing really. Except that I couldn't get off. Hard as I tried, hard as my dick got, I just couldn't come."

No wonder, after all the booze. But he claims he never had that problem before. Always drunk, and always able to get off. The problem was something else. Suddenly all he felt was the discontent. Disgust perhaps, but that can be a turnon. Maybe he just finally had had enough, and that made it all seem pointless. Unsexual. Gross. Not disgusting, just gross. And absurd. Down there in the muck, in the thick of it, he felt strangely ridiculous pulling on his limp dick, surrounded by dicks hard and soft, all trying to get to that point of ecstacy. In an instant it occurred to him that the point is just too pointless. The fantasy left him and he was left with nothing but the shit of life in all its ludicrous splendor. The filth. The stench. The penises and the assholes. The sighs and moans in the darkness and the reality of a dozen grown men acting like schoolboys in heat and as quickly as the thought occurred to him he was up off his knees and out the door and hasn't returned to that dark world ever since. He's saved! The only time he gets on his knees these days is at church. So how in the hell did he get crabs?

A clear case of immaculate conception. Proof of the divine power. Or proof that the little buggers lay some pretty sturdy eggs. The physical realities of this universe are such that cleansing the mind or soul is not enough to cleanse the body. I tell my friend not to worry. Do the laundry. Put some of that DDT shampoo on your pubes. Take an aspirin and call me in the morning. And don't let the little buggers get you down. Remember, at all times tiny microbes are living and crawling all over our bodies. The physical realities are not always noticeable to the naked eye.

He sighs that weary sigh again. The sigh of burnout, of too much of a good thing. The sigh of growing older. "It's natural, anyway."

I'm not sure what he's referring to, the crabs or his ascension to purity, but he uses it as a segue into a discussion of what's natural and what's not and his quest to be natural and to at all costs avoid the unnatural. Fruits and vegetables, Jesus and Yoga are part of the natural. Pesticides and processed foods, drink and drugs are not. I inform him: Natural is when an animal shits on its leg. So who needs toilets? Crabs are natural. Why not live with them?

He doesn't hear it. His mind is set on a course. He's as immovable as a fundamentalist. And as vague and contradictory. It seems to suit this indecipherable life. Who needs the impossible pursuit of truth when catchphrases are so readily available. Forget Hellenic ideals. Forget Christian metaphors. Forget history altogether. Leave the past right where it is, dead and buried. Check your brains at the door. Onward new-age soldiers. My old friend needs a new battle cry. Instead he continues his monologue with a rundown of what's hot and what's not. His latest cure... Stairmaster. Already getting passé. Personally I can't imagine stepping up on a stair in a room full of people with stairs, all stepping to the latest machine music. And paying money for the privilege? You could just run up and down in the stairwell of your building and skip the long wait for the elevator. But my passé friend would insist that Stairmaster, the latest version, has changed his life. Which only goes to prove that all any aging and fearful person on this planet needs is a good master to keep them walking a straight line.

I tell him that I really gotta go and he tells me we should really get together sometime but he thinks I need to lighten up. His guru says cynicism is just fear in disguise. I couldn't agree more. Still better than Stairmaster. Lighten up, Ken. Don't worry, be happy. My fearless and giddy friend has just the thing for me. And it has nothing to do with sex. He'll show me some new massage techniques. I decide that if he truly hasn't had sex in a year, then considering what's crawling around his penis he should probably be wearing rubber gloves when he massages his slutty friends. I don't say it. I offer one last bit of advice. I suggest that maybe, just maybe, he got crabs from the phone. He thinks about it. He's silent, for a moment. Finally.

↘↖↗↙

## Strange Shadows

I'm at a party. Another party. This one has a theme. To each their own. The host says that a hundred times, each time he introduces one guest to another. I'm not sure what he means by that. Maybe it relates to the decor. The apartment has a theme too. Yesteryear mod. Shag rugs. Beanbags. Where does he get the stuff. Shag bedspreads. His shirt is shag. Some kind of braided threads dangling from his pumped bod. His hair is shag. Short red Rasta braids. Shag hair. What else do you call it?

As we all know, taste is a sense subjective beyond the powers of the mouth. What one person loves, another hates. Others simply don't have an opinion and just go along with the general consensus. Sometimes it's a matter of mood. Probably with enough drugs in my system I could get into the shag. And it goes according to association. In a way I like the man's shag because it reminds me of growing up in the 70's. I hate it because it's ugly and tacky and because when I sit on it I can't help thinking that bugs are crawling around in it. Another guy at the party can't stop running his hands through it and making sensuous noises. "Shag turns me on," he tells me. I move away from him and hurl myself into the vacated beanbag. Pop! I am instantly turned into a beanbag, a spineless blob sprawled out on the floor. Something rattles around me. It sounds like loose beans. I mush around to see the beans dropping out of a hole in the side and bouncing around the shaggy corners of the rug.

The host is standing over me, scolding me. I busted his beanbag. The others stop talking. All eyes on the perpetrator. I try to get up out of the thing. No one will give me a hand. The host interrogates me from up there. Why did you do that? he asks. Why? I don't know. To each their own.

I am told to leave. I think it would be best if you left, he says. So I roll over onto the shag and make it to my feet. They're all looking at me like I'm an idiot. A childish fool who comes to a party where he doesn't know anyone and then goes and wrecks the furniture. No one's friend, and an enemy to beanbags everywhere. Okay, I can take the hint. I search for my jacket in the pile on the shag bed. The host is watching me like I might steal something. He follows me to the door.

I walk out and he slams it behind me. It's a shaggy world. To each their own.

I decide to walk home. It's a nice night. A long walk down Broadway is more fun than any snooty party anyway. That's the thing about living in the delirious city. Forget the bars, the theaters, the soirées and drug orgies. The action is right there on the streets. A million one-act plays whizzing by on every corner. Plenty of lonely people of all types to connect with. If you can break the barrier of anonymity. If you can somehow make contact with a passing stranger. With rows of streetlights and storelights on both sides, Broadway casts its shadow on all those who pound its pavement. And when the shadows cross anything can happen.

As I mindlessly strut down the boulevard my attention is drawn to the men and boys I find desirable. I'm not the only one playing that game. You can tell that everyone is checking out everyone on the street, for whatever reason. The TV is on. You watch. It's channel surfing as they drift by. I check out every last persona. Man, woman, and beast. When something cute and butch goes by I stare into his eyes and look down at his crotch. It's a fun game.

Along the way I realize that right there next to me, walking parallel in the same direction, is something very cute and butch. I wonder that I hadn't noticed him before. He's tall, dark and handsome and he seems to be brooding about something, walking with hands in pockets, kicking a can. My heart goes out to him. Let me make it better. I follow him. Though we are independently going the same way. But as soon as I notice him and begin to follow he seems to be aware of the fact and stops kicking the can. He becomes self-conscious. He looks over. I look away. Force of habit. I look back. He looks away.

We walk side by side for many blocks. Our stride is in sync. Does he have the same thing in mind? I look over again. He turns slightly and raises his eyebrows at me but there isn't enough body language to entitle me to speak to him unless I just blurt out something. What would I say? We follow each other in silence, our shadows extending behind us at an angle. Parallel. Not once crossing. Could he be thinking what I'm thinking? Our movements are as one. Our stride. We notice the same things. The argument on the corner. The ambulance whirling by. The graffiti on the wall. Unintelligible scribble. But we both study it. Because it attracts our attention. Only the artist knows what he's really trying to say, if even he does. But that doesn't stop us from looking.

I have in the past met men simply walking down the street. The right eye contact and a few minutes later you're off doing it in some alley. One turned into a lover for a while, though we never got along. I think sometimes of calling him out of the blue. What would I say now? I think about all the old lovers who came and went and maybe never really were lovers or boyfriends or whatever we called ourselves. In the end we returned to being strangers. I forget all the strangers from the past and focus in on this new one who will take me away to the intimate world of his passion and love. We'll be together at last if only we can connect – soon. But how? If he turns a corner will I turn the corner and in that way signal him that I am actually following him? Blocks and blocks go by and still he doesn't change direction. Maybe he's just taking a long stroll down Broadway with no destination in mind. Sooner or later he has to stop or he'll walk into the water. Where I would dutifully follow.

I get aggressive. With my eyes. I stare at his crotch. That swell in his jeans is rugged and easygoing. The crotch next door. I'd like to bury my face in his warm strength. My stare gets a response. He grabs it and tugs. Could have been nothing more than a reflex. To an itch. I continue to stare. Once or twice he tugs. This is going nowhere. But far away from where I live.

I decide to smoke a joint. That'll get his attention. Then I can offer it and make contact. I have a freshly-rolled joystick weighing down my shirt pocket. It was planned for the shaggy party. My contribution to the ceremonies. I pull it out and light it and make sure to blow that pungent smoke across my shadow to his.

He notices. He turns, still walking. He smiles at me and nods his head in recognition. Works every time. It's a cheap trick. But then, I'm cheap. I gesture with the joint. Want some? He looks around. No one could care less. We're still walking. I extend my hand with the joint. He takes it. Instant friendship. Our shadows cross.

We walk on. He smokes. He passes it back. Nods a thanks. Maybe he doesn't speak English. Not a word exchanged so far. I take a toke and pass it right back. I'm not in the mood for the joint. I want him. He's so sweet. The friendly eyes and the strong body. I'm in love. He's everything I've waited for in my dreams. I'm this close to making it come true. But now that we've passed the peace pipe, how do I get to the next step? So much easier in the park. You know why they're there. You know what they want. But a stranger on Broadway could have something else in mind. Or nothing at all. To each their own. It's a shaggy world.

He passes me the roach. I gesture that he can keep it. Smoke it.

Throw it away. I love you. Let's do it. Nothing said. Minimal gestures. We walk on. Our shadows no longer crossing.

I'm speechless. It's awkward now after the initial contact not to say anything. I have to say something. I'll ask him something. Something stupid. Where are you going? I ask, and he smiles. And nods. I knew he didn't speak the language. I sigh. We walk. On and on we walk. It's a nice night. But not that nice. My legs are getting tired.

After a few more blocks I become desperate. I'm far from home. I can't stop now. I have to have him. I need him. To love me with his body. His strong hardon in me. To let me love him. I have to touch him. But I can't. Not here on Broadway. Not just like that. I'll signal him so that we can take a detour. Give him a sign that I love him desperately. It *is* love. Call it what you want. Desperation. Lust. I had passionate sex just the night before. This is love. A coincidence in time when two shadows come together on a lonely street. If only they could.

I could turn the corner and hope that he follows. I could gesture with my head that he should follow. I could stick out my tongue. Too lewd. I could propose. Let's leave this fucking city. Go someplace really nice. Not just the illusion of nice. Let's live in the country and farm all day and fuck all night, one with nature and each other.

Okay, I'm ready. I'll get it across to him somehow. The language of our eyes will speak love. I'll make him see. Somehow. I open my mouth. Hey. Universally understood. Hey, he answers. Our eyes connect with watery passion. This is it. It's going to happen. He stops. He waves goodbye and turns to go in a doorway. I stop dead. He doesn't look back. He walks through the hall, turns, pulls out a key and lets himself into an apartment. He slams the door shut.

I stand there feeling the pain of that unspoken love, the slammed door reverberating through my stoned head. My longing for him rips right through my chest. His shadow is gone. Forever. I stand there like an idiot. Nothing else to do but walk away. I turn around and walk back up Broadway to where I live, casting a lonely shadow like the incredible fool for love that I am. I walk on and on past all the scenes I noticed coming the other way. They look different this time. Less vibrant. More poignant. The graffiti means something. I'm not sure what. But it speaks to me. I wander through all the strange lonely shadows on Broadway and it isn't long before I find myself following one.

## Nasty

Like so much of life, nasty is a relative thing. For some, a yellow shower is beyond the limits of decency. For some, licking the shit off a dick with a gerbil up your ass is too too nasty, but tasty nonetheless. For others, licking your fingers after chowing down on a chicken leg is rude behavior at the dinner table and simply not to be done. For yet others, eating a dead bird, even cooked, is inconceivable.

Rhona... the drag queen from hell. Now there's a walking bit of nastiness. Nasty as they come and proud of it. I remember when I first met her (though I would later realize that I had known her before when she was a he). I was at a lesbian party on a rooftop in the East Village. The whole evening I kept glancing over at some cuter than cute muscle boy only to realize on closer inspection that I had in fact been lusting after a girl. With short hair and muscles. How embarrassing. Then I saw Rhona. Confusion may be a way of life for some, but with Rhona there's no mistaking her for anything but what she is. A filthy nasty drag monster, fresh from the clinic with a stopover in the toilet to massage her surgically bloated lips with some antiseptic piss. Standing next to the buffet table on the roof at the party that night she was a vision to behold. The epitome of nasty. Redefining the word. The whore's outfit. The plumber's etiquette. That night I spotted her and it was love at first puke. There she is. Miss America. Brown goo smeared in with the red lipstick. Even if it is just chocolate cake, it's disgusting.

Rhona is the trashiest nastiest thing the Good Lord saw fit to create and have recreated again and again by some of the worst surgeons in New York. I mean if you're gonna have plastic surgery, for godsake don't shop around for the bottom price. Splurge. Live a little. No point in having balloons for tits if they don't bounce. Rumor has it that Rhona had floor wax injected in there. Just like those drag pioneers from way back when. Her nosejob looks like a Groucho Marx mask, like the nose was stuck on. Scars on all sides. And what you can't see you can only imagine. Deep down there, somewhere hiding in her panties, must be a specimen worthy of sci-fi. There in the folds of her thighs lies the unexpected, the otherworldly. The truly nasty. Something I would eventually come to understand through her own description of that, her proudest possession, the one piece of the puzzle she spent the most money on because it took the most attempts to create and recreate to get it just right.

Curiously enough, she hangs out with a lesbian crowd. The gay boys won't have her, except maybe on a stage where they can laugh at her. She's too nasty for the prisses. And those really nasty men who like to have fists rammed through their exploding sphincters - well they don't want anything that looks remotely like a woman around. I have a theory that the lesbians have taken her on as a sort of poster child for the cause. The drag queen, the transsexual, or any man as impostor woman, is the ultimate sexist statement to the diehard feminist. It's not enough that men dehumanize women in all aspects of life, but now they want to be one too. And in some horrific burlesque caricature. I think that Rhona is such a botchjob on the whole concept that the lesbians have taken pity on her, embraced her as the club mascot. There she is in the corner of the party, a hunk of brie in one hand, a cigarette in the other. Nice combination. Especially with some of both dangling on her pleather pocketbook. The only woman with a pocketbook at the party. Little miss the six-foot-two drag monster posing for the catalogues. Each accessory in place. The heels. The stockings. The oh-so-short floral dress from K-Mart showing nice cleavage, scars too. Isn't she talented. She does her own tailoring. And what a subtle hand with the makeup. Sort of like those impressionist painters using the palette knife instead of the brush. Thick globs of bright colors to cover up the pink complexion. The carrot red wig crooked and loose. Or is it sewn on? There she is, my dream girl. The one who brings out all my deep-seated hate of mother, allowing me to relish my homosexuality as an escape from having ever to touch anything that even slightly resembles that thing sticking her greasy fingers in every platter on the table so that the dykes have dubbed her Helen Keller.

But whatever you say about Rhona, whatever names you call her, she is and will always be one of the nicest people I know. She rarely gossips about others (not like some people). In fact she mostly talks about herself. Endlessly. Nonstop nastiness. But nasty as she is, she's a sweetheart. When we first spoke I saw through it all to the warm needy soul and I knew that she could give a lot of love as much as she takes a lot of shit. I stepped up to this bride of Frankenstein, watching her maul the buffet, and I had to ask: "Which did you like the best?"

Scratching her groin, egg in the mouth, she says it like she means it: "I like it all."

Specifically?

"I like it all cause it's all nasty. Nasty shit."

She says this a lot. Rhona is the nastiest drag queen around if for no other reason than she uses the word obsessively. Nasty this and nasty that. "That guacamole is some nasty shit."

It certainly is. Oozing between her teeth.

"Nasty like I like it." A growl. Nothing ladylike about the voice. Eventually she would have that voicejob to raise the pitch. Again she opted for the budget surgeon and nowadays she's got the voice of a boy in puberty constantly shifting from low to high. It suits the chronic acne which you can actually see popping out through the makeup. This reminds me of a story I heard about her from back when she was a he. Like I say, I had known her or known of her when she was a he because back then he was a pianist like myself. Through conversation I came to realize that she was that pimply student at the master class with the famed Mozartian nicknamed by her admiring students as Madame Crass for her subtle wit. After performing a rather sloppy rendition of a Mozart sonata, Rhona – then Ronald – was given a cheery smile by the master of crassness herself who offered before a room full of his peers this infamous critique: "Dear," it always starts with dear, "if you can't clean up your face at least clean up your Mozart."

Is it any wonder the shy pimply-faced boy grew up to walk around in drag armor, dressed like the Mozartian having her period on acid. I have tried to get him to talk about his days as a pianist, something we have in common, and her days as a he, but it seems clear that she'd rather forget all that. She sometimes makes her living as a phonesex operator though she gets fired a lot for the quirks in the voice. Honestly I think she hasn't done that work for a while, supporting herself instead with her old standby profession, yes, the oldest profession of them all. I understand that prostitution is the career alternative for the largest percent of DQs or TVs or TSs or GWs or whatever they like to differentiate themselves as. It's understandable. Only a very few can really *pass*. Difficult to get a steady job as a creation of the night unless you turn back into Mr Normal by day. Maybe the GWs can pull it off because they really are women. Almost. For the uninitiated, that stands for Genetic Woman, something a man becomes when the surgery is so good that his own mother wouldn't recognize him.

But now for the story. This most nasty of nasty stories. Rhona may be a nasty sloppy drag freak, but she tells a good story. This one she told me when I ran into her at yet another lesbian party. Once again I find her in full costume posing by the buffet, stuffing her face with all of it, cause she likes it all. Cause it's all so nasty, I suppose. How's tricks, I ask.

"Same old nasty shit."

Getting by, huh?

"The only way I know how. On my hands and knees."

Gotta do what ya gotta do.

"Gotta eat. And you won't find me eating out of the garbage. Done that. Been there. Hated it." Her dialect as fake as the jewelry. A bawdy mix of high and low.

And then it begins. A long soliloquy on the nasty. Rhona has what is clinically known as *diarrhea mouth.* At first it seems clogged. Pull out the plug, and once it starts coming out it comes pouring out in mudslides and waterfalls.

"It's been tough lately. It's like the older I get you'd think it'd get easier but it doesn't. It gets harder. And nastier."

How about going back to making an honest living. As waitress. Receptionist. Phonesex operator.

"The more honest the more shit ya gotta eat. Least now, when I eat it, I know what I'm eating. It's up front. They hand you the toothpick and say: Dig in, bitch."

I suppose there's an honesty about that.

"Um just sayin' it's tough, that's all. Still better than some of the legit shit I usta to do. No way I'm going back to all that smiling and brown nosing and phony shit, the do's and dont's of the working poor. They got your soul. It's paid slavery. With a clock to punch in and punch out. It ain't me. Much better this way. Still, it's tough bein' self-employed. Freelancing ain't as easy as it sounds."

When the going gets tough –

"The tough get nasty. This last gig I be down on my knees doing something I never in my whole life thought I'd ever do."

Lemme guess.

"That's right. Scrubbing the kitchen floor. I got a gig with this psycho-sadist, this crazy fuck who wanted me to clean his apartment in the nude. With a fucking toothbrush! Which is tough enough. But imagine, the guy's trying to stick his dick in me the whole time."

How distracting.

"I'm trying to scrub the fucking toilet with the fucking toothbrush, so okay I play along but like the whole time he's trying to stick his fat pecker in me. Finally I tell him to like wait until I'm finished cleaning the toilet and he slaps me in my face, shoves my head in the toilet bowl and flushes, screaming like a maniac: You dirty whore, that'll teach you not to disrespect me! Like I mean who the fuck's disin' who, huh?"

Life's a bitch.

"And people say I'm a bitch. I am not a bitch. Life is the bitch. I'm just doin' what I gotta do to survive, honey. Plain and simple. If I'm a bitch, life taught me everything I know."

Couldn't you do something a bit more conformist? Less stressful.

"Nothing as stressful as waking up early in the morning with the rest of them zombies, crawling out of bed and into the subway, packed and shipped off like sardines, off to the grueling job only to come home at the end of one of those endless days and stuff your face in front of the TV only to do it all over again the next day. And those jobs are so boring, so tedious, you gotta be brain dead to do that year in and year out with two weeks vacation, Christmas and Easter off. All these mindless tasks and everything you do is wrong. Hard as you try it's never good enough. Just like working for them sadists. Might as well work for the real sadists. The money's better. You can keep your nine-to-five job. Done that. Been there. Hated it. Making money makes whores of us all. Least I ain't bullshittin' nobody. I'm a whore. Plain and simple. Least I pick my own hours."

No complaints?

"I ain't complainin'. Um just sayin' it's nasty. Sometimes it's real nasty. Nasty shit."

One of the lesbians, a trombonist, puts on a CD of Strauss and Wagner excerpts. Heroic German music with lots of brass. Rhona's eyes light up at the moment of recognition. Nostrils flaring. The face contorted in legato pain. "This part is so terribly beautiful, isn't it? Must be Karajan conducting." Her dialect switching gears midsentence as she starts conducting with a Swedish meatball. "I shoulda been a conductor. Why I wasted all those years trying to play the fucking piano."

It wasn't a waste. You'll always have it.

"Right. The closest I've been to a piano is last year when this old man paid me to bend over the ivories and fart in his face while he practiced his scales. And he had the nerve to complain that I wasn't with the metronome."

I hope it was a slow movement.

"My musical days are dead and buried. You know, when you're a kid and you play the piano, and you're a pianist not just some kid playing the piano, your imagination opens up to the great music and you're taken away by it, out of Mommy's living room to some far-off fantasy place with princes and princesses and ladies of the court." She pauses to stare at a spot on the ceiling, a distant vision. "Look at the size of that fucking roach up there." I look. She grabs another Swedish meatball. "The point is when you grow up you find out that the world's a nasty place full of greedy roaches and big feet ready to squash 'em at every turn. And you learn that those worlds you were dreaming about were even nastier. People living like animals while the ladies of the court played the virginal with lice crawling around under their chastity belts. I don't want any part of that fantasy anymore. I'm here now in the real world. And nasty as it gets, it's real. And here I am in it, being myself. Moi. Before your very eyes. Just as I am. Nothing more. Nothing less. Real as the shit in the toilet."

It's hard to say what she really is. But then that goes for us all. Hard as people try to typecast themselves, there's always more than meets the eye. Real or fake. In a curious way, in spite of the surgery and the costume, Rhona *is* real.

"Speaking of fantasies, did I tell you I met a man?"

Congratulations. When's the wedding?

"No plans yet. We've only been living together for a few weeks. It was rough at first but now we kinda settled in for a smooth ride."

Sounds charming. Who's the lucky man, and where d'ya find him?

"I met him on the street."

Where else.

"He's real cute. His name is Victor and he's had a lotta shit go down in his life."

I hate that expression.

"It's true. Nasty, nasty shit. For one thing he grew up in a fucking jail. You know, reformed school, or whatever they call it. It's jail for kids."

What did he do?

"He killed someone. I don't know how it happened. He doesn't like to talk about it. It brings back bad memories. He still gets nightmares."

Poor baby.

"He had a difficult childhood and I think it was affecting our sex life."

How so?

"I don't know, it seemed like he was afraid of me. Or my body," she says sticking her tongue out at me. "To be frank... "

Let's.

Purring: "I think he was kinda scared of my pussy."

I can't imagine why.

"It's a very sensitive instrument. Finely tuned. Not just your run-of-the-mill gash, you know."

We wouldn't want one of those.

"I mean these bitches think they're so special just cause they were born with the fucking thing. Well mine is a manmade creation. The work of more than a few craftsmen."

How so?

"Partly because they didn't get it right the first time."

The budget clinic. Dial 1-800-444-CUNT.

"And because I changed my mind a few times. I mean when I first got it, it was just not the one I wanted. They worked on it, botched it and hadda fix it up so many times that I finally decided I wanted what I had in the first place. I didn't want to be a TS. I liked being a drag queen. Lotsa hormones and surgery, but still a man down there where it counts. It paid off with the johns cause a lotta the ambivalent ones want a chick with a dick. But then something inside of me still really wanted that pussy where it belongs, smack between my luscious thighs. So I had it done again. This time I did it right. No cutting corners, if ya get my drift. I had the good doctor give me something really extraordinaire. The man was a real artist. Ahead of his time."

Avant-garde.

"I know it sounds confusing, all this switching around, but now I really know who I am even if it don't fit in a nice slot with all the other apples and oranges."

What are you? Help us to understand.

"I... am a dragsexual." Her voice jumps registers. The forever changing anatomy. A lifelong puberty. "Yes, I'm a DS. It's something nouveau. Something really nasty. An undecided caught between the two-party system."

Why not simply call yourself a TS like the rest.

"Because I ain't one. I don't feel like this born-again woman. Those bitches think they *are* women. I don't want to be a woman. Fuck a duck, I like bein' a drag. It's so campy. I like bein' a scream. I don't wanna pass, like them wonderwomen. And my cunt is something so special, almost a dick. It protrudes. It's something in between. A pegina, if you like."

A dunt.

"It's nasty, whatever you call it. Nasty shit."

You can say that again.

"Nasty nasty nasty nasty nasty nasty nasty nasty just like I like it."

But back to the subject. The new boyfriend coming to terms with his woman and her pegina.

"Ah, Victor." She sighs. "He's soooo cute. Strong and mean and tough. Like a wolf. Sniffing around me like a hungry animal. I don't blame him for bein' a little put off at first. He'd never seen a twat like that. It was a new experience. I said to myself, give him time. He'll come around."

And he has?

"Finally he has. But first we went through problems of another kind."

He's gay.

"No, not really. I mean he fucks gayboys for money, but he's not really into it."

I bet they are.

"The problem was, as it always is in this bitchy world, a financial one."

But with both of you working, the money must be coming in.

"It comes, and it goes. The problem is to hold on to it."

Cut down on eating out.

"I do. I do." She grabs another dripping meatball and slurps it up. "I even learned to cook. Tried some of those recipes on the Velveta package. But you can only save so much money when there's three mouths to feed and the third one is a bottomless pit."

Crack?

"It's nasty shit. Victor is not a thief. It's not him stealin' the money. It's the drugs. Got a mind of its own. Makes him do it. Do anything for it. It's not him. He's a sweetheart underneath. It's the drugs that makes him so nasty. It was tough in the beginning. I had to hide my money."

Where did you hide it?

"First I tried the flower pot. It's an old trick. You stick it in the dirt. The next thing I know my peonies are ruined."

Poor peonies.

"It's just terrible. What a waste. My nicest flowers. I was pissed. I decided to let him have it. I'd had a few too many that night waiting for him to come home. He was seeing this old man who liked to have Victor piss in his face. I knew he'd be pissed when he got back. Hustling makes him even edgier than he already is. But hell, I was even more pissed."

Sounds like a lot of piss to me.

"Well the shit hit the fan as soon as he walked in the door. I held up the dead flowers and the flower pot and I told him I was sick of this shit and he better stop smoking crack and he better stop stealing my hard-earned money and ruining my beautiful peonies or else."

Or else?

"Or else I was really gonna get nasty."

What did he say?

"He didn't say shit. He hit me. Punched me in the mouth. Threw me against the wall, took the flower pot and dumped it on my head. And after I'd just done my hair." Adding a little primp to demonstrate her rare beauty. I look at the hairdo. Always the same one. It looks like something that should be in a flower pot. A bunch of weeds tangled in hairspray. Still the question: does she take it off before sleeping or is it sewn on?

"Let me tell you, I decided right then and there that I wasn't gonna take this shit. I wasn't gonna let him steal my money that I busted my balls for. I'm gonna hide that money so he'll never get it. I'm gonna stick it somewhere nasty. I looked around. I thought about the toilet. But you could flush it by accident. The garbage you might throw out. I had a friend, this slut hid her jewelry in the garbage and threw it out by accident one day. She threw her own fucking jewelry in the trash without realizing it! Trashy whore. So I decided right then and there to hide my precious greenbacks in the kitty litter where my prize pussy could keep an eye on it."

But you could just as well throw the kitty litter out.

"I never clean pussy's little home. She cleans it herself."

Sounds smelly to me.

"Well if it's smelly in there then maybe it'll keep out unwanted guests."

Did it?

"No, of course not. When a crackhead knows there's money somewhere, he'll find it. And he don't care what he's gotta do to get it. I heard of one guy who punched a hole through the wall to his neighbor's apartment. Like they weren't gonna know who did it. These crackheads are totally without any sense of anything but getting what they want. A few times already Victor tore up some gayboy's apartment in a crack-crazed fit and couldn't go back. Tore up a few gayboys too."

Ouch.

"So one night I see my deranged honeybunch sitting on the couch smoking his deathpipes and I notice his arm is all scratched. Well I put two and two together and went straight to the kitty litter where pussy was growling in a dither, her sacred home sacked by thieves!"

Thieves with smelly fingers.

"That's it, I thought. Enough is enough. I went back to that nasty pussyrobber and yanked that fucking pipe right out of his mouth. You piece of shit, gimme my money! I said."

And what did he do?

"The lousy crapwad laughed in my face and told me he spent every last penny of it. So I said well then that makes the crack mine since he bought it with my money and I'll just have to keep it. And I snatched the stuff and walked away."

Bad move. I can just imagine, but tell me, what did he do then?

"You wouldn't believe."

Try me.

"The fucking slob ran after me. Hit me. Punched me in the mouth again. Threw me against the wall. I hit my head on a nail and got a nasty nasty cut, bleeding and all and does the piece of shit feel the least bit sympathy? The creep couldn't care less. Finished bullying me – and I can take it – he goes right after poor pussy. Picks up her home in his grubby hands and hurls the thing across the room. Kitty goes flying and all her little mounds of kitty litter go flying with her all over the apartment. Everything covered in the shit. What a mess. I haven't even gotten around to cleaning it up I been so busy trying to make money to keep us going."

To keep him cracked up.

"That's right. I accept him for who he is."

A deranged crackhead.

"Like I say things have smoothed out. He still smokes his crack but least he ain't stealin' the money from me no more."

You give it to him?

"In a way." She becomes more ladylike than usual. "Let's just say...he comes and gets it."

He punches you out and snatches it out of your pocketbook.

"In a metaphorical sense."

I'm confused.

"You see, after that catastrophe with the kitty litter I decided that I was going to have to hide my money somewhere really nasty. So nasty that he really wouldn't stick his grubby paws in there. And I figured it had to be somewhere on my person. So I could keep an eye on it."

Hm.

"I thought to myself, what is the nastiest thing I can think of."

I don't want to know.

"Don't be squeamish. Everyone has one. It's natural."

My favorite word. Looking at Ms Thing the dragsexual, the word sounds more ridiculous than ever.

"Everyone on the whole pretty planet has one. If they're normal."

My other favorite word.

"Think about it. Every last one of God's children has a body. Their body is their temple. And in the temple is God's own creation. The shithole."

Somehow I knew we were leading up to this.

"So I figured, what better place to hide my wad of cash than right up there with the shit in my fabulous all-natural shithole."

Talk about dirty money.

"Ain't that nasty? The nastiest shit you ever heard?"

Probably. But how do you avoid shitting your life savings down the toilet?

"Easy. *My* piggybank can be opened and closed at will. I just stick it in when I need to and pull it out when I need to make room for more."

Clean out the account. Start an IRA. You're telling me that every time you go to buy a newspaper or a soda you –

"No silly. It's just like a bank. You don't use it as a purse. You keep some in your purse and the rest in the bank."

Fascinating. Horrendous. I study her flatulent pose wondering if there's anything on the account now.

"It really worked for a while. But I knew it was just a matter of time before Victor caught on. One day I'm in the bathroom making a deposit when the sonofabitch comes barging in screaming bloody murder that he wants that money and if I don't hand the shit over he's gonna pull it right outa my shithole. I dared him to do it and it didn't take long for that lunatic to take me up on it, He shoved his fist up there till I was singin' high Cs and yanked out every last dollar."

A large withdrawal.

"I call it what it is. Bank robbery."

Then did he hit you?

"No. But he smeared the shitty money in my face, called me a fucking shitface, grabbed me by the head and threw me down on the floor and fucked my shitty asshole and made me bleed."

Love hurts.

"And you know something? It got me thinking. Maybe I should

use the situation to my advantage. Turn on some of that feminine manipulation that comes with the hormones. There's a way to give him what he wants and get mine too. So ever since I've been stashing the loot in my very own private purse, that black hole where no man has gone before. And sure, maybe my man is still a crack-crazed fiend but at least he ain't afraid of my pegina no more."

You stash the money up your... dunt?

"You got it. The first time he reached in there he nearly broke it. It's quite tender, you know. The scars never heal."

Calluses?

"After the last operation the doctor said it'll always hurt a little and I said I didn't mind."

Obviously.

"And Victor ain't known for his gentility. That first time it felt like having another operation. Without the anesthesia."

Call it surgery and maybe your insurance will pay for it.

"But lemme tell ya, nasty as it sounds, in truth it's pure pleasure. Cause now my man loves all of me. Every nasty piece of the puzzle. That first time he was really intrigued. He was like: Wow, this is cool! All these little nooks and crannies."

Cavities.

"You shoulda seen how he calmed down. He'd just finished strangling me and spitting in my face he was so mad, screaming bloody murder. You bitch! Gimme that fuckin' money or I'll rip your fuckin' ugly fuckin' head off and stick it up your ass! Well I told the fucking animal where to go. Through my bush. Up my gash. And soon as he stuck his grubby finger in there the big bad old grizzly bear turned into a sweet little teddy bear."

Hard to imagine.

"And now every time he needs money, which is often, he just comes barging through the door, punches me in the mouth, throws me on the floor, rips open my dress, practically bites off my panties he's so edgy when he needs that money, and sticks his fist up into my pleasure purse to get what he wants and in turn gives me just what I always wanted."

What's that?

"A man, a strong man, to love me, to want me. To love me for what I am and want me for what I got."

↘↖↗↙

## More Love That Sucks

• When he kisses you, tells you that he loves you, and then wipes his mouth.

• Making passionate all-out love, no holds barred, fucking like wild animals, sucking each other from head to toe, licking, biting and doing each other to death until the cum hits the roof and the ceiling caves in and you both immediately jump out of bed, clean up, say goodbye and never see each other again.

• Any time someone loves money more than people.

• All forms of footsucking.

• This friend of mine had a passionate love for Chinese food. He spent a lot of time in Chinatown, knew all the restaurants, even learned a bit of the language. He took me out to dinner there one night and taught me how to suck noodles off a set of chopsticks. We sucked plate after plate of a variety of the most succulent saucy cuisine. The spiciest too, because he liked the Szechwan stuff. He would have the cook make it as spicy as possible, returning the dish if it didn't completely blow him away, telling the waiter to tell the cook it's still not hot enough. God only knows how they obliged. To complete his Chinatown fantasy he got to know a cook at one of the restaurants, a cook who made it like he liked it (the hottest cook around) and promptly fell in love. A cute little Chinese boy with an incredibly subservient personality and a deadly spice rack, who lived with his family and was looking to move out. So they took an apartment in Chinatown where he kept the boy as his little Chinese suckbuddy, sucking him as much as he could with plenty of time left over for the plates and plates of the boy's succulent saucy cuisine spiced to nuclear proportions.

• When every time he comes near, the penis waves hello.

• Don't you just love these tribal mating rituals. All tribes have them. You know, the male approaches the female, lets out a birdcall, performs an age-old courtship dance, offers sweetbreads and honey wine and after a few hours of cooing hits her over the head and drags her off. Or the more modern version. He says hey baby, shakes his booty, offers to buy her a drink and to turn her on with his coke and E and within minutes sweeps her right off her feet. Love. It wouldn't be the same without the courtship. Well males have their rules for courting other males too. Especially in the late twentieth century. They walk around in circles. For hours and hours. Staring at each other. Without saying a single word. Fortunately or unfortunately there are always those nonconformists who simply refuse to go with the flow and abide by the rules. They skip the birdcalls. They don't bother with the honey wine. I know a guy like that. I dread seeing him. Because when I do, it's always in one of the more traditional mating sites where males are walking around in circles without saying anything. And along he comes with his mouth wide open. Hey Ken, he says. Loud. Just as I am in the middle of an age-old custom where the male signals that he is ready to receive the other male's penis by kneeling on the ground and sticking his tongue out. I gotta hand to him. He's not shy. When he's not harassing me he goes from one to the other shouting: Hey cutey-pie, wanna come home with me and fuck? I understand (from the horse's mouth) that only once has anyone taken him up on the offer. It certainly seemed like his lucky day. Sex at last for free. He told me later that the guy did indeed come home with him. Handcuffed him to the bed, taped his mouth, and beat the crap out of him.

• Castration done in the name of love.

• I have a friend who claims he isn't gay. He's a human watering hole. He doesn't like sex with men any more than with women. He just likes to get piss shot up his asshole. For whatever reason, that's what he likes. Loves. And if a woman could, or would, do that to him, he'd be more than happy to be her drain. He could even love her. Get married and settle down and live a normal life. So long as she did what a surprisingly fair number of men are more than willing and able to do. Piss up his ass.

• When you haven't the faintest desire to piss up someone's ass but you do it anyway.

• A red rose in the garbage.

• "Ken, I met my love yesterday. The man of my dreams. And this time I know it's love." How do you know? "Oh, you'll know it when you find it. When it walks right up to you. Yesterday this man stopped me on the street and asked me which way is 52nd and Third. We were standing on West End and 78th Street. He was obviously from out of town. He had an accent. It was so cute the way he asked me all innocently which way is 52nd and Third, like you could just walk there." You could if you wanted to take a long walk. "I tried to explain that but his English wasn't so good. I would have walked him there myself but I had an appointment I couldn't break and now I wish I had walked him there because now it's too late. He's walked right out of my life, forever." Why not try one of those ads in the back of the *Village Voice*. Something like: You asked me which way is 52nd and Third. Meet me there ASAP. Well he actually took my advice and spent a few days after the ad came out waiting at the corner of 52nd and Third for the man of his dreams, who of course never showed up. But another out-of-towner walked up to him and asked where 51st and Third is and he wasted no time in taking him there. They've been a couple ever since, though it's a difficult relationship because of the long distance between them. The man lives in Hungary.

• When your heart feels actually broken from the pain of love. Like an arrow stuck through your chest.

• Getting a knife stuck through your chest by an old lover.

• Dinner for two by candlelight complete with wine and Rachmaninoff and all the trimmings, two of each. Two candles. Two glasses. The arms intertwined for each loving sip. Two cushions in front of the fireplace. Two pillows on the waterbed, and a two-sided dildo tucked under the covers.

• I met a guy once who told me that there is in fact no such thing as romantic love, that he had never experienced such a thing. He loved his cat, his apartment. He loved at least one of his parents and some of his friends. He knew love in his life, but never romantic love. He liked very much to have sex with men, but to love another in a sexual way seemed pure contradiction to him because the whole point of sex was to express your passionate hate for this object of your lust. I must have given him the surliest look when he said that but I'll admit he made some bizarre sense out of his philosophy when he went on to give examples. You fuck someone by thrusting your hard dick into them while they hopefully scream for more. As foreplay you might thrust it into their mouth. You might now and then come or even piss in their face when you're both feeling kinky. An awful lot of people call that making love. Having a lover. But it's really just sex. A rather hateful expression of dominance. If ever someone tries to kiss him during these mad proceedings he immediately pushes them away. Even when his cat brushes against him he is repulsed. Yes, he loves his cat. But he wouldn't kiss it.

• Kissing each other deep in the mouth staring open-eyed into each other's eyes and not remembering each other's name.

• Any time someone eats shit and loves the taste.

• When a drug addict is given the choice of either going into rehab or having her baby taken away and doesn't have to think about it.

• Happily married men cruising the park. I remember one of

those in particular (there are so many). This Puerto Rican guy lived the perfect double life. He claimed it was no problem for him. He had the wife and baby at home, and when he felt like having some hard mansex he just took a stroll through the park. He wouldn't want to live without either one because they both satisfied different needs in him and as long as he kept them absolutely separate it wouldn't be a problem. This went on for some years and he became quite the popular guy in the park (where I got to know him). A friendly sort, he wasn't afraid to say hi to friends and strangers alike. Everybody seemed to know him. He told me that only once did his two worlds come close to colliding when one Sunday he went for a stroll through the park with wife and baby and for a change his wife wanted to check out some other areas of the park rather than their usual family strolling ground. He went along with her and when they were getting too close for comfort he tried to lead her away. She said: "What's down there?" Where? "Over there where that bridge is?" What bridge? "That bridge, silly. Let's check it out." And so they did. It was during daylight so he felt almost safe, but just being on those same paths where at night he did his dirty deeds made his heart beat and his dick throb and his ears turn green. He calmed down when he saw the birdwatchers tweeting to the twees. Then he heard a whistle, turned around and saw in the light of day an old flame, a flaming muscleman he'd sucked off once or twice. A Brazilian queen with feathers and a foot-long cock. "Hey! Yoo-hoo!" The two worlds were colliding as he reached down to pick up baby's bottle and stick it in her little mouth with his sweet innocent wife by his side and his suck buddy screaming after him. "That person is calling you," his wife said. He bent over and nervously squeezing the bottle too hard squirt it on baby's mouth. Don't turn around, he said. Pretend you don't notice. There are a lot of strange birds flying around the park.

• "What's a Puerto Rican?" our Puerto Rican friend asks us. He's been standing there watching with disgust while me and another feverish white guy lust for the Puerto Ricans at the bar. Me feverish for the tall slender ones. Him feverish for the short fat ones. The rest we ignore. "What's a Puerto Rican? Explain." Our Puerto Rican friend is insistent. We look at each other with guilty expressions. How to answer his question. Aprez vous. I step back and let them battle it out. "*You're* a Puerto Rican," pink tells tan. "You're dark, you speak Spanish, and your father is Puerto Rican. What more is there to say?" "But my mother is Italian and I was born in Miami. Why don't you think of me as Italian? Or Miamian? Or just plain American?" "You don't look

Italian. Sorry. You look Puerto Rican." "Then if you're so hot on Puerto Ricans why don't you come home with me and suck my spic dick, you pink piglette?" "Sorry. You're not my type."

• Unhappily married men cruising the park. I had sex with a very handsome young man in the park, had sex with him a few times until I sort of got to know him. Our conversations always got around to the same subject. His boyfriend. That's why he cruised the park, he said. Because his boyfriend was so critical of him that they barely ever had sex. What doesn't he like? Oh, he says I'm too skinny, my clothes are all wrong, I'm too hairy, my head is lopsided, and he hates my dimples. I look at the guy. He's really very handsome. The clothes are out of style and a size too small, but who gives a shit. I couldn't care less. His body is really sexy. The hair on his chest is virile. He's got the face of a farm boy. The dimples are cute as cute can be. I try to see if his head is somehow lopsided. Maybe a little bit bigger on one side but if he hadn't mentioned it, it would have never occurred to me. And who cares? This boyfriend must be a *GQ* model. Honestly I prefer men who aren't too perfect and I detest style queens. It's the imperfections that add a touch of vulnerability to the perfections and it's the lack of style that signifies the real man. I did finally meet that boyfriend at a bar where he and his lopsided lover were standing in a corner making out for all to see. I walked up to them, interrupted the free show, and asked: So, is this the boyfriend I've heard so much about? Introductions were made. I shook hands with the little man. The ugliest hairiest troll this side of the Seven Dwarfs.

• Perfect couples everywhere.

• When the one-room apartment is in such bad condition, the ceiling leaks, the roaches run amuck, you have to pour buckets of water down the toilet to get the shit down and you're as happy as can be because you can share this misery with the one you love.

• When you live alone in that misery and don't complain to the landlord until the TV antenna on the roof breaks.

• Soap operas.

• Passionate love stories involving children. Except *Romeo and Juliet.*

• Fathers having sex with their sons (to say nothing of fathers having sex with their daughters). A friend tells me he finally met that manboy of his dreams. Fell desperately in love. A perfect match made. They share the same interests. Classical music and fucking. My friend is monstrously proportioned, well over six feet tall and built like a bear, and the manboy little and skinny, Peter Pan at thirty. My friend only fucks. The boy only gets fucked. They fit like a glove. But the next time we speak he tells me they broke up. So what more do you want? He tells me they had sexual problems. The boy passed out during sex. The first time it happened he thought he killed him, crushed him, fucked him to death, literally. His monstrous bod was just too much for the little thing. Then he realized the boy was still breathing. Sleeping in fact. Each time they fucked the boy went into this dream state. You would think he would ask him about it. But it was such a strange situation that he felt positively tongue-tied the next day. Their sex life continued but in a state of awkward denial. It got to the point where he couldn't go through with it. The boy noticed his reticence and confessed. He knows that he passes out during sex. Don't worry. You're not the only one. It's a psycho-traumatic condition stemming from the sexual abuse he suffered as a little boy. His father, good upstanding Catholic man that he was, fucked his own son from the earliest age until puberty made him no longer desirable. My friend is shocked by the revelation. It puts a damper on the relationship. Though they have both enjoyed their fucking sessions, each in their own way, it seems too bizarre for my friend to continue fucking this sleeping child, especially now with the knowledge that he would be sitting in for the demented Catholic father. Too much to handle. He tells the boy that he still loves him but it would never work. They can remain friends, but as a friend he strongly advises him to seek psychiatric help. The boy, who has been in therapy for the longest time, cries his eyes out. I don't blame him. I told my friend he was being stuffy about it. What's wrong with each getting off in their own way? As long as you get off. And I thought this was love. Real love. At least stick by your man. Your manboy. Instead he not only broke off the relationship but the friendship as well and got himself a live-in hustler who may be all of twenty years old but looks not a day over thirteen. Years later my friend gets a Christmas card from the narcoleptic with best wishes from him and his new lover. The card is a company card from the new lover's firm. A mortuary.

- Kissing and making up at least once a week.
- Mothers having sex with their sons (to say nothing of mothers having sex with their daughters). The truth is this friend did not actually have sex with his mother. But their relationship was so — how shall I say — so orally intimate it qualifies as a case of child molestation if not legally such. The fact is that his mother, an immigrant from the old country, was an extremely oral woman. She licked her fingers obsessively. Cleaned the house with a good deal of her own saliva and cleaned it thoroughly enough that you could lick the floor, if you

wanted to. She had a way of constantly sticking things in her mouth and wetting them. Or wetting those around her. If she saw a speck of dirt on her husband's face as he left for work she would stick her finger in her mouth and dab him clean. Or just lick it off. It seemed quite natural at the time because this was a woman from the old country and that seemed to be what women from the old country did because clearly the other mothers in the neighborhood didn't behave like this. For her only child whom she loved more than anything in the world she would even chew the food and regurgitate it into his mouth. A vomitous old-world tradition that she may have carried on past the appropriate age. But mostly, for her baby boy she could come up with buckets and buckets of motherly saliva. Constantly dabbing him with her wet fingers. Licking him. Sucking his flesh. Not his penis. His flesh. Especially as an infant. He heard about this from the relatives, how because he was such a cute baby his salivating mother couldn't get enough of sucking his arms and legs, even biting his thighs. Now there's no law against this sort of thing. It's actually considered earthy. Maternal and loving. But my friend suffers strange neuroses to this day. For one thing, he keeps his body fanatically dry at all times. His hands are as dry as sandpaper. All wetness, grease as well, are kept at a distance. Which makes life difficult. I had dinner at his apartment once. No he didn't regurgitate the food in my mouth. Quite the contrary. It took him ages to prepare the spartan meal because everything in the kitchen throughout the preparation had to be kept perfectly dry and greaseless. The food tasted perfectly dry and greaseless. He chewed very carefully, mouth closed, as he divulged the nitty gritty of his sex life like a horny ventriloquist. And I thought I'd heard it all. The man doesn't kiss. Never. Won't suck or get sucked. Won't open his mouth. Won't do anything that will get him wet. One day he meets his match. A fuck buddy who doesn't fuck. Doesn't kiss or suck. They have totally dry sex. They stand next to each other over the sink and wank in unison. Get down! You've heard of vanilla sex? This is diet ice milk. Recently though, they've been getting kinky, experimenting in what he calls S&M. While wanking over the sink, they threaten, but only threaten, to come on each other. With their mouths open.

- All bodily functions done in the name of love.
- Eating disorders. Who doesn't love to eat? Too many people have a love/hate relationship with their sustenance. I know a guy who's fat as a cow and has absolutely no qualms about eating as much as he can stuff in his mouth. He's the first to admit that it has replaced sex in his life. But he would phrase it differently. Who needs sex when you

can have so much fun eating. Once at a dinner party I watched him put away mounds of food. Not in a neurotic frantic way. He chewed his food well, seemed to relish the various tastes. He ate slowly, but continuously over a long period of time. Another man at the table was barely eating and couldn't keep his eyes off my fat friend. It turned out that this man was a psychologist. With a problem. He quietly informed us of his life-long bulimia while we noisily munched away. The bulimic shrink ate only the tiniest portion, something like four tablespoons of food after which he sat back and gave us the complete history of his eating disorder and just for good merit warned us of the dangers associated with the food we were eating, morsel for morsel as we stuck it in our mouths. Fat, cholesterol, preservatives, an array of toxins, chemical reactions, hormones, pesticides and antibiotics. At the end of the meal we burped and cleared the table and retired to the living room to digest the pesticides. All except my fat friend who went on for seconds and thirds, and the bulimic shrink who snuck into the kitchen and without realizing I was spying on him shoved a few fistfuls of leftovers down his throat quicker than I thought humanly possible. It was then decided that before dessert we would take a breather and have a little concert. My fat friend sat at the piano and accompanied an opera singer with a particularly shrill voice in some particularly shrill excerpts from *Turandot*. Throughout the performance I thought I heard strange percussion coming from the audience, but decided it was just my ears ringing. As soon as it was over the bulimic shrink excused himself to the toilet bowl wherein he promptly stuck his head and puked his guts out. From the piano my fat friend suggested that food, like music, should never be over-analyzed and that as passionate as one may feel about it one should never let it get the best of him. The difference between falling in love with a singer's voice and falling for the singer. With that bit of wisdom shed, the singer embarked on her next encore. And her next encore. And her next until I felt like throwing up too but instead pondered with abandon the difference between hating a singer's voice and just plain hating the singer.

- Burping during fellatio.
- Farting while getting fucked.
- Geriatrics cruising the park. I met an old man in the park one night. He must have been seventy-something. My curiosity got the best of me as usual and I got to talking with him after seeing him earlier in the evening with his cock out, an enormous healthy erect specimen that seemed entirely out of place jutting out of his decrepit weasel body. It made me think of my late grandfather as a porn star.

The image was haunting. Maybe that explains my need to talk to this man. His presence certainly got me thinking about my own questionable future as an anonymous man. But his conversation reassured me that sex after seventy can be quite as fulfilling as it ever was, if it ever was. First of all, there are enough gerontophiles out there whose greatest passion is to do it with grandpa, the dear old guy who was so much nicer than those cruel, strict parents who beat them. Sure it's playing a role, but what else is new. Then there is the phenomenon of flattering lighting. You'd be amazed at what you can get away with in a dark corner. Though he admits, his ego is such that he prefers to be seen for who he is. A little help from the lighting is okay, but he wants to be loved for himself, not some pitch-dark fantasy. In fact he's very competitive about the whole game, as so many are in these places. He wants the cutest boy, not just because he finds the cutest boy the cutest but because everyone else does and he wants all those snickering fags to see him have sex with that cute boy that they chased all night. Remember, he has a few things going for him. He's the image of grandpa with a killer cock. And he's had years and years of hard-earned experience in the finer techniques of the chase. He knows how to get his man. He usually has eyes for that one who prances around like little Miss Fabulous and half the time he succeeds in fucking little Miss Fabulous and teaching her and them all a lesson, a bit of aged wisdom. The other half of the time he goes home frustrated, but then the frustrations abound for everyone in these places. Even when you get it, it can be frustrating. Just the other day, he told me, he had a relieving but frustrating experience. He snared the cutest little clubkid. Fucked him for all to see. And you can just imagine how they stood around and watched the spectacle. The cute boy getting it. And the old fart with the huge dick and the huge grin on his face proud of the fact that he got the cutest boy in the park because that boy thinks that he is the hottest man around. So what's the frustration? When it was over the boy asked which way out of the park. Sorry, he tells grandpa, but I'm totally night blind.

• Growing old in body but not in mind and wanting, needing to be loved for the child you once were.

• Teenagers full of youth and beauty who commit suicide over love.

• Baby talk coming out of anything but the mouths of babes.

• One last ageist story. I'm with a friend in a bar. I point out the cutest guy in the place. Perfectly young and beautiful, showing off his tight bod in a tight green shirt. My friend smiles. "He's really hot. I had sex with him." Yeah, right. "I did. The guy next to the guy in the tight green shirt," he says licking his lips. I look. A human corpse hanging off the barstool drooling over the pretzels.

• Going to confession, confessing your sins, saying your Hail Marys and licking your lips.

• Having sex in church, or any bodily functions in the house of the Lord. I've got a few stories about that. One is from an organist I knew who clearly abused his privilege of having keys to the church. Late night he would bring his cheap hustler boys up in the organ loft and suck them and fuck them right there before the glassy eyes of Holy Jesus wilting on his cross. Once or twice he even got kinky and did it on the altar table, a rite of sacrilege if ever there was one. He never got caught but one of the boys stole some candle holders and a gold-plated crucifix. Another friend confessed that as a teenager he crept into the chapel and took a dump in the pew. (No pun intended.) A steamy confession, but hardly qualifying as sex in church. Was it sexually motivated or just spiritually depraved? A bit of both, he says. While taking that hot shit he jerked off and prayed for forgiveness.

• All forms of unrequited love.

• Being lovesick with no remedy except falling in love again.

• Grandfathers who fuck their grandsons. Believe it or not I've got a story for that too and it just goes to show how much of this sort of thing is out there and kept quiet until it comes spilling out into my ears and onto my typewriter and into your bedroom. In this case the "victim" tells me that I am the first he ever told which just goes to show how much blind faith people have in my discretion. He told me a truly disturbing story of how at five he was fucked up the ass by his own grandfather until the parents put a stop to it, sent the old bugger away, and then never even mentioned it ever again. What's remarkable is the way the victim remembers it. With fondness. His grandfather was a funny-looking bald man with hair on the sides like a clown. A clown who sucked big dildos and little infantile penises with the same relish. To this day the victim, who has grown into a handsome young virile man with a strangely childlike aura about him, has only bald boyfriends, funny-looking ones. For as long as he can remember he's had a special feeling for clowns. If he so much as sees a clown on TV he gets tingly all over with anticipation. He tells me that though the molestation has clearly affected him he doesn't feel bad about it. He remembers enjoying the sex, strange as that sounds, actually looking forward to it. He loved his grandpa. Would ask him over and over: "Are we gonna play now, are we gonna play now." Fortunately grandpa had a rather small weener. Fortunately babies are flexible. Still it hurt going in the first few times. My friend remembers it as turning him on though incapable of reacting with an erection or any kind of ejaculation. The nerves were stimulated. And there was plenty of love and affection going both ways. Sick as it is to say, the old psycho-clown didn't have to force it on him and as a result he doesn't consider himself to have been abused. I tell him that any shrink or talk-show host would disagree and bring him around eventually to seeing that he was in fact abused and scarred for life by the abuse. He tells me that he doesn't believe in psychotherapy and that if anyone abused him it was his mother who force-fed him giant liver steaks until he gagged.

• All forms of self-analysis.

• Being passionately in love with no one but yourself.

• Having an enormous cock but no love. So with no date for Saturday night you stay home and blow yourself.

• Throwing kisses.

• Saying that you've absolutely fallen in love with oysters on the halfshell but only when they're really fresh as you swallow one down with a chilly white wine ten feet away from a bag lady sifting through the garbage for a rotten chicken wing.

• Mixing food and sex. I don't understand these people who squirt whipped cream on a penis or pour perfectly drinkable champagne on some dirty asshole. A guy once wanted to spread mustard on my dick. Talk about love that sucks... I zipped up and told him to get himself a hot dog.

• Here's one last story of racist hate and love that really sucks even if it can be reduced to merely a symptom of the ills of society. This black friend of mine only fucks white guys. He proudly describes how these little whiteboys love getting raped by his big black dick. And how much his big black dick loves raping them. You've heard this one before. He fucks them and they scream for more. One time he had a Jewish guy who loved it so much he lost control and in the heat of the moment screamed: "Fuck me with that big black dick, fuck me you big black nigger!" That word was a bit too much to the point and pushed my friend over the edge. Though he's proudly told me time and again with a smile on his face how much he loves raping whiteboys and how much they love getting raped, the utterance of that single word during the rape triggered something in him that turned his hot fantasy into the deepest resentment transforming this kinky black fag into an angry black man. He gritted his teeth and started slapping the guy in the face over and over again screaming: "Don't you call me a nigger, you little Jew bitch!" Well the bitch didn't skip a beat. He screamed back: "Oh yeah, slap me you big black nigger!" At that point the rage exploded into murderous violence. He grabbed the Jewish guy by the throat and began strangling him. Until the guy was turning blue and finally came in buckets. That's it. Never again, he said. My friend still enjoys fucking little white guys with his big black dick (and they still enjoy it as well) but he stays clear away from Jewish guys and for that matter only fucks the most repressed tight-lipped waspy Protestants he can find.

• Sucking dicks of all races, creeds, and colors, but only if they're circumcised.

• Quicker-than-quick quickies. I know a man whose whole life is timed so that not a loose minute is left. Everything he does is rushed through like he's finished before he ever got started. The five-minute lunch break. The walk around the block. The ten-minute visit. And the sex act as minute waltz. I once went cruising with him. He did it with a guy behind a tree in less time than it took me to finish my cigarette. What happened? I ask. "I got fucked." Boy that was quick. "I don't waste time with all that tiresome foreplay." Did you get off? "No, but the guy did. He said he only likes to fuck. He barely got it in when he came." He must really like to fuck. But where does that leave you? "On to the next quickie." You can sort of piece them all together at the end of the night and have one last monumental orgasm. "Listen I'd love to chat, but I gotta run," he says glancing at his watch. I saw him years later. Life in the fast lane seemed to have left him bitchier than ever and still in a rush. All he could say as he rushed by in the street looking like a speedwalker on speed was: "I see you're still alive." And without even waiting for my bitchy reply (And aren't you looking fresh... from the grave) he glanced at his watch and said, one more time, "Listen I'd love to chat, but I gotta run."

• When you say I'm leaving you and actually mean it.

• All crimes of passion.

• Any kind of love that hurts. S's & M's certainly deserve each other. I wouldn't want to get in their way. But it has always seemed to me that there is far too much pain already in this life. Call me chicken, but I don't like anything that makes me say ouch. At least not until I stop saying ouch.

• Killing someone, and regretting it.

• I'm sitting through a movie that I didn't want to go to but did because I want to have sex with the guy who invited me. We hardly know each other. We met at a party. This is a first date. When you meet some guy in the park and blow him, there's no standing on ceremony. But once you get to know someone a little, without blowing him first, it can be arduous to get to the next step. So much polite and careful waiting for the right moment. Here we are, sitting through this horrible movie in an over-crowded theater, trying desperately to avoid rubbing elbows when we both know we're going to fuck like maniacs as soon as the movie is over and we can maneuver each other back to one of our apartments. (We did indeed.) The movie is awful. It's one of those New York meanstreets things full of tough talk and lots and lots of bloody savage violence. Two Italian guys mercilessly beating the crap out of some guy who didn't play ball, beating him over the head with a baseball bat until the head starts to look like a purple watermelon. The special effects are awesome. I feel like vomiting. The audience is laughing. The dialogue throughout the film is nonstop fuckin' mothafuckin' this and fuckin' motha fuckin' that. Who the fuck do you fuckin' think you fuckin' are. I'll fuck you up you fuckin' mothafucka. And so on. The audience speaks the same language. Somewhere behind me a young woman shushes some guy. The guy doesn't like to get shushed. He says: "Who the fuck do you fuckin' think you fuckin' are. Don't you tell me to fuckin' shutup. *You* fuckin' shut the fuck up." And then he hits her. Or at least she claims he hit her. She says: "Who the fuck do *you* fuckin' think you fuckin' are. Don't you fuckin' hit me you fuckin' mothafucka." At this point all I wanna do is run out the nearest exit. But of course I don't because I'm on a date. And my date seems to be tuning out the crowd and thoroughly enjoying the movie, taking it very seriously. He loves the director. I must admit the direction is excellent. The way they hit that guy over the head with the baseball bat and at the same time kick him in the balls and the way he writhes in pain... it's so true to life it's spilling over into the theater. The people behind me are really going at it now and the audience in between peals of laughter is telling them to sit the fuck down and shut the fuck up. If only I could blow my date right there and then and get it over with already, but this is not that kind of theater. I would be afraid to even put my arm around him here. What one endures for a little bit of love. I decide the only thing to do is to tune it all out and focus in on the couple in front of me. A young macho Italian guy and his cheap girlfriend (dressed as his motha). The two of them, ignoring it all, have been passionately sucking face since the lights went out.

• Waiting until after the first date to blow him, blowing him, and then never seeing him again.

• Blowing him in the park and then seeing him every time you go to the park but never blowing him again.

• A straight man asks me in all sincerity why gay men are such sluts. Because straight men treat them like sluts. He thinks I'm kidding. I think he's smiling at me like he's picturing me prancing around in a skirt. Lifting it up each time I wiggle my tushy for him. Seriously, he says, I don't understand why you gay guys have to go hunting for meat every night. Craving it like some nympho. Ready at every turn to lift your legs like some cheap slut. I don't get it. What's with all this anonymous sex? I tell him to think of it as a sport. A team sport. He thinks about that. He's picturing me prancing around in a skirt with a basketball. Dribbling away with all my sissy friends chasing after the ball. Wiggling our tushies in unison each time someone shoots. Then he asks me in all sincerity why I don't try playing real sports instead of slutting around. Join a team. Be a man among men. Work those muscles and get smelly. It might be just the thing to cool the libido. Right. I tell him he should cool his own libido. Go hang out in the ladies' room.

• Belts that require instruction manuals to undo.

• I remember doing it with this guy in his dumpy apartment. A masculine young man with a moustache and an identity crisis. I swear, every last spot of every wall of his dumpy apartment was covered with pictures big and small of all the most fabulous divas who ever lived. Judy, Liza, Joan, Betty, Lucy and the list goes on and on. It was unsettling to say the least. Try sucking dick with a lifesize Liza open-mouthed and staring down at you. I got my revenge. When I peed in his toilet I made sure to draw a mustache on Marilyn.

• Diapers with pins.

• I remember this strange character I once knew who collected army knives but was so afraid of his own shadow that he could barely walk the streets of New York. He claimed to be shell-shocked from having had too many near-death experiences in his years in the delirious city. Muggings, street fights, barroom brawls, racial attacks, police harassment, subway fires, swerving taxis, bicycle terrorists, fallen gargoyles and vengeful pigeons. It all happened to him. Now every time someone looked at him or stopped near him or laughed in the background, every time someone called out or a car slowed down or someone shouted something from a passing car — all of which happens a lot in New York — every time a fellow pedestrian passed him in the street and in a rush seemed to be sneaking up behind him, this poor fellow would flinch in expectation of the unexpected, tremble with fear and recoil in dread. A pathetic existence. The only solution seemed to be to lock himself in his apartment and file his knives and spew on the four walls his paranoid hate of all ethnic groups including his own, all races, men, women, young and old, rich and poor, the mayor, the police, bicycles, gargoyles, the pigeons and the roaches. Maybe it's time to move. I asked more than once why he doesn't just leave the fucking city if it's come to this. He said he would never. He loves New York.

↘↖↗↙

## Sleaze City

I arrive in New York on Halloween. Standing in the airport I already see why I left. Gotta get outa New York, I said for ten years. Then I did. But kept coming back. Each time to recognize the subtle changes. New buildings raised to the sky in a few months. Old shops closed because they can't pay the rent as the neighborhood changes. Boutiques on every corner. Old sleazy bars closed. Replaced with coffee bars! Old druggy friends turned sober. On Prozac. The whole city has been cleaned up by the Republican mayor. At least that's what everyone is telling me. To woo me back. Or scare me away. I know why I came back this time. Because my landlord is trying to evict me. And maybe that colors my perception. In fact the city seems sleazier and dirtier than I remembered it the last time. In spite of the coffee bars. More hardcore. Maybe I've been away too long. I'm just not used to it. The beggars are still there, even if they're not allowed to beg at a cash machine. When I walk into my apartment I can't believe I ever lived like that. Piles of junk everywhere. I'll have to sort through it at some point. The Chinese woman who sublet fried my apartment in peanut oil. Apartment fried rice. All the junk fried in grease and soot. Friends tell me it wasn't so different before I left. The wood floors are as dirty as the streets. Soot city. When I get off at 72nd St there are a million people on that corner. And a traffic jam. The people walk faster than the cars. I almost get run over by a pedestrian. In my apartment I drop my bag and fall into the couch and listen to 72nd St exploding outside my window. I'm sticking to something. A layer of grease and soot covers everything. I'm sticking to the couch.

All the drawers of my desk are stuffed with bills, legal threats, and junk mail. Half of the legal threats are from my landlord. The case is clear. They want my apartment. They can get double the rent and they know I'm not there, another New Yorker living somewhere else. Fuck them. I lived here when the neighborhood sucked. I braved through the shit. Half my life breathing this soot. The neighborhood hasn't really changed. Add a few hundred thousand yuppies and line the streets with homeless people and you've got the Upper West Side after the 80's. Add some more and sweep the streets and you get the Upper White Side after the 90's. The ever-changing neighborhood. Same soot either way. I go pay my phone bill in a check-cashing store. A bit of the old neighborhood. The dark workers stuffed in an airless cell protected by a steel barricade from the dark out-of-workers waiting in line to cash their welfare checks. I hurry off to visit a dying friend. Not a day too early. I get a last glimpse of someone I used to know. The end of an era. And all I can think is... I gotta get outa New York.

Trick or treat? That's what the kids are supposed to say on Halloween. I walk by two kids in death costumes walking in front of the hospital. The one says something about some fucking asshole mother fucker. I step over the smashed eggs. It's Halloween in New York. What are you going to be? On the next block I walk around a man lying on the sidewalk. The people are unsure whether to call an ambulance or just let him sleep off whatever he needs to sleep off. Imagine calling an ambulance a block from the hospital. Nobody is going to carry that man over there. Nobody's business. You could get sued. In New York you have to do things the right way. It's not as lawless as it looks. In the hospital my friend waits to die. We say cheery things to cheer him up. I decide that the man lying on the sidewalk should stay where he is. My friend has a last request, whispered in my ear. Can I clean out his closet? Oh god, more piles of junk. No, just the dirty stuff so no one else runs across it. Dirty stuff? Porn, dildos. I promise to protect his good name. He asks me how the park is these days. Any action?

In court I wait for my name to be called from a long printout of tenants. Most of them suing their landlords. Most of them black and Latino. There's an interpreter. When my name is called I'm asked why I'm there since my lawyer has postponed the case. My cousin is handling the case. I guess. I can't get through his secretary. We slept in the same bed when we were kids and now I can't get through his secretary. We were close but always opposite. He played football. I played the piano. Now he's a lawyer and I'm a drug addict. I leave the court feeling like an idiot. I go straight home and order Chinese food.

I go back to the hospital the next day. The show is held over for one extra day. The man won't die on request. His few friends wait around. I say hello to a ditsy girl I haven't seen in years. My mistake. She talks nonstop about her career as a wannabe. She's still shopping her tape – tape #999 — but wants to go into the theater. Do I know anyone? I tell her she'll need to make a new tape. Then she fills me in on the gossip. Just as the dead man falls asleep we hope for the last time. What a relief that would be for us all. Especially him. In between last breaths I hear bits of such incredible gossip that I can't believe it but I know it's mostly true. This is New York. Anything can happen. Or maybe the same crazy shit happens here like everywhere where people live, but a lot more happens here because there are a lot more people. She tells me about an old friend who lost his business, left New York and is living somewhere in the Midwest hiding from the IRS. Spent the employee deductions on drugs and cosmetic surgery. Word is he has full-blown AIDS anyway. The IRS might find him in the Midwest but they'll never find him where he's going after that. We look at each other knowingly. But with these new wonder drugs he could live for a long time. In prison. The dead man takes one painful breath and we think that's it but it's not so the gossip goes on. She got a job in a new restaurant on Columbus Avenue. Turns out she knows the cook. He came into the kitchen drunk, screaming and yelling at the carrot-peeling Mexicans. She recognized him and remembered where she last saw him. He'd been working for some mega-wealthy producer she was sucking up to. One night they caught him drunk out of his mind sticking it to the dog in the kitchen. The dead man laughs. Or does he? I try to look out the window. The blinds are covering a spectacular view. I hadn't noticed it before. The view is from the fortieth floor. Wow. You can see the helicopters taking off over the East River. I want to tell my dying friend he's got a great view. But he can't see anything through the lesions devouring his face. There it is. The fucking irony of life and death. Here he has the best view he'll ever have in this city of views after years of staring at a brick wall and he can't even see it. I leave in the middle of another ditsy story. Same old story. Something about getting high with record producers and the next thing she knows she wakes up on some bed with five guys doing her but they said they would listen to her tape and like they're really big so maybe this could be the big break or something...

I leave the bedside watch to go cruising in the park. But sucking some guy's cock I'm reminded of the dead man and suddenly the cock tastes like AIDS bile. So I go home and jerk off to some porn tapes I find in my piles of junk. It doesn't really get me going and I get a stiff neck. I spend the rest of the night into the next day trying to organize my useless shit. I can't decide what to do with those piles and piles of greasy sooty junk. Everything I used or stopped using for twenty years in and out of that apartment. Most of it stuff that you can't throw out but you know you'll never use and you don't want to carry around wherever you go but you have to deal with somehow because in the end when you die someone is going to have to throw it in the garbage anyway. An old love letter. An unfinished symphony. Stuff that merely looking at would mean a trip down memory lane. I have to do something with it before I leave if I want to have the option of never returning. Right now I want to give it to them. The apartment and all the junk. You want it? Take it. This cell is not worth the fuss. But what to do with my life's possessions? I'll probably just leave it right where it is. Let someone else throw it out. My life's possessions recycled through the garbage.

I call the hospital. No one answers. I go to see my dying friend figuring this is it, finally. But when I get there he's flossing his teeth. Very slowly. Like he's getting ready for a long sleep. No one else is there. I want to tell him something. How he's been a good friend. How I love him. But I can't. Too sentimental. And too morbid. He's not dead yet and I don't want to imply that after all the party is over because it's not until it is. So I don't say anything. He doesn't say anything. He can barely move. I'm amazed he's so much better than the other day. He hunches forward in order to floss. Very slowly. Very carefully. Painfully. A dead man flossing his teeth. With incredible precision. Like he's got all the time in the world. Until I can't take it any more. Why is he flossing his teeth if he hasn't eaten in weeks? Did you have turkey for dinner? I ask not really expecting him to answer. He does. Pulling the floss out of his mouth ever-so-slowly he says: "If you don't floss, the taste gets bad." I'm feeling sick. He lies back. His eyes roll back in his head. I leave telling him to get some rest.

The next day he finally dies and I feel nothing but emptiness and sorrow. I'm glad it's over. He's through with his suffering. But I feel like I never got to say goodbye (not that I could have) and that his whole life ended so abruptly with no more meaning attached to it than anything else in this fucking city. Another lonely death in the loneliest city in the world. Another dead friend to remember. Who's next? The funeral is far out of town where the family lives. The Manhattan friends decide to have a memorial service, as he requested, in his apartment. They can kill two birds with one stone. Celebrate his death while they clean out his apartment. Fight over his CD's. I decide not to go. I go to the park instead.

This time the dicks don't taste like AIDS bile. In fact New York is starting to taste good. I meet a Mexican guy. His father is a super in a building two blocks from mine. I suck the super's son's dick deep sniffing deep into his groin every time he shoves my head down on it. He comes in my face and I start thinking about staying in New York for a while. Try to make a go of it yet one more time. Not until I get back to my apartment and the piles of junk, the evidence of my sleazy life in this sleazy city covered in a sticky layer of grease and soot, and all I can think about is my dead friend and how I forgot to clean out his closet of the porn and dildos before the party of mourners got there. Shit. You die, and then the embarrassment goes on.

I can't stand the smiling. Everyone is smiling at me. The doormen, the super, the guy who works in the shop next door. They say: You're back. They don't say: Not for long. My neighbor waiting with me for the elevator smiles at me from ear to ear. She wants my apartment. She could break down the wall and have two apartments. In one. You want it? Take it. Maybe the landlord will buy me out and everyone will get their share. I'll get my bribe. The landlord will get his rent increase. The neighbor will get her dream apartment. And the super and the doormen will get their revenge. They already got their bribe at Christmas.

I pay all my bills. I don't bother to sort through them, see what costs what, check for mistakes. I just call all the companies whether or not they sent threatening letters and pay them what they want. Take everything. There's nothing much to take. I want to live in a log cabin somewhere where there are no bills to pay. No phone to answer. Instead I sit in that apartment waiting for the phone to ring, for my cousin to call and release me from my prison. The phone rings constantly. Mostly wrong numbers or old friends down-and-out in New York looking for drugs or money. In between I'm besieged by telemarketers trying to sell me shit I don't want. I finally get a call from my parents. They heard from my cousin through my aunt that I'm back. Why didn't I call? Because I've had enough mental abuse for one lifetime. Because my parents are insane, vulgar, loud, insensitive, arrogant, obnoxious lunatics, New York specimens the likes of which Woody Allen made a fortune immortalizing. Nothing personal. They invite me to Thanksgiving at my sister's.

I take the train to Suburbia. They're all there. My family, the in-laws, the cousins I never see. All except the one cousin who matters.

My brother-in-law holds court. The dentist in his castle. Complete with wall-to-wall carpeting. Orange to match the orange walls. My mother gets drunk and insults my grandmother. The baby's crying. The kids are screaming. The cousins are arguing about politics. How to stop all immigration to America. The grandchildren of immigrants are proud of their nation. Meanwhile the turkey is over-cooked, dry and tasteless. Half the food is burnt. My sister comes out of the kitchen with a fresh-baked pumpkin pie and promptly drops it face down on the orange carpeting. Matching pie. Hysteria breaks loose. I leave with what little sanity I have left.

Back home with my piles of junk I realize I can't stay. So I go to the park for one last tour. I get it on with a rather hunky little guy with a big cock. We play with each other's cocks like babies with pacifiers. Silly as it is I can't get enough. I know I've said it before. Proof that enough is never enough. And when we shoot our stuff I feel a bond with this stranger. Our intimacy speaks for itself. Two souls coming together in a city of lost souls. So maybe we're gonna die but right now we're living. We shoot our seed on a tree holding on to each other's manhood feeling the warm pulse of the other in our grasp, holding on for dear life. He smiles at me, a cute brotherly smile and I know I'm alive.

I finally just leave. I catch the next plane out, leaving the apartment, the junk, the grease and the soot, everything just as it is.

## And May the Best Man Win

The three lobsters sit in the pot. Our host instructs us from an old French recipe. Lobster should be slow-cooked in cold sea water. The meat will be tender, not chewy but not watery either. The lobsters are to be slow-killed in a pot of their beloved ocean. They seem at home at first. Until our host turns on the flame.

Then the lobsters begin to die. Beads of sweat form on their shells. They turn redder and redder, almost orange, as though getting a sunburn. You and I make jokes about our host, all three hundred pounds of him, and his sinister recipe. Each tries desperately to be the funniest.

The laughter stops. The biggest of the three lobsters is pushing the others down trying desperately to raise himself to the top of the pot away from the heat. Our host reassures us that this age-old recipe is the best way to insure the succulence of the flesh. The water must be getting very hot for our oceanic friends. If they seemed to sweat at first, now they start to really cook. The big one manages to hang on to life by pushing the others down into their death brew until the heat is just too much for even him and he drops in a last great sigh and dies with them. His one claw manages to stay above water, hooked onto the rim of the pot, but is steamed to death anyway.

Our host breaks off the stray claw to test the meat. He breaks it in two. The meat juts out and he quickly sticks it hot in the mayonnaise (as though it weren't rich enough as is) and then in his mouth, sucking out the meat. It seems to quiver as it slides down his throat.

I, you, and he have been getting together over dinner since I can remember. It's always the same. You are instructed to pick up the groceries, and I cook them but only as instructed by the recipe. You basically live on the streets. I rent a small room from our host in exchange for doing the cooking and playing the piano.

The talk is always the same. You are trying to survive and I just wannabe famous. Our host more or less talks to himself, chattering away in a dither about his vast wealth, inherited, about his priceless heirlooms, about the history of his family and how the world has changed (for the worse). He claims to be descended from a long line of European nobility. If one were to look far enough back into history. I like to remind him that we all – I, you, and he – descend from a long line of monkeys and if we wanted to look far enough back we might find that we were in fact about to eat one of our distant relatives. One could say that he is at this very moment dipping his long lost ancestor in mayonnaise. But our host has no mind for science. He shows us his grandmother's china. You are impressed, but I find it rather kitsch. And I am annoyed because although he shows it to us, we are not allowed to eat on it. Typical.

You always bring the subject back to survival. I don't know how you do it. With what little money you are able to pick up on the streets you manage to buy our host his groceries. He reimburses you, partially, and you eat with us. Sometimes he even lets you sleep on the floor. But what about the rest of the week? Where do you sleep? What do you eat? Life is tough in the lower class.

For me the problem is not about food and shelter. I get by but that's not enough. I, like so many wannabes, wannabe famous. And like so many of the children of the middle class, I want to be an artist.

A great artist. I have tried poetry, music, painting, dance, drama. It always ends with the realization that I am stuck in old forms, that I have not embraced the new technologies. But I'm too unmechanical to operate these machines. When I do take the time to learn the synthesizer or the camera and make an attempt at expressing myself with them I am frustrated because the expression seems not to be mine, but rather the manufacturer's. I played a recital on the synthesizer. The audience applauded heartily. I ate up the applause but later became depressed. The performance was actually no performance at all. The sounds were pre-programmed. Even the pieces were just my own collage of pre-programmed sequences. They were applauding the manufacturer! I made a short film with the idea that music in our time is subordinate to the narrative as depicted by the camera. This is the media age. So I spent all my money on the film itself. It came out too dark. I took it around anyway, hoping that the important people would see past the dimness and recognize the great truth of my expression. They did not. They told me to bring it back when it looked like the films in the theaters. They told me I need a story line that speaks to the common man. Can you believe? I, the artist, am supposed to suppress my great personal vision in order to appeal to you, the lowest common denominator, because that's where the money is. I do write for you, as much as for him and for myself and for anyone who will listen. But I will not underestimate you. They actually think that you would prefer to watch mindless sex and violence, action thrillers and romantic comedies with happy-go-lucky endings instead of an abstract scenario based on the life and death of a depressed tree. I give you more credit than that.

You are frustrated too. You work your ass off and still barely survive. You raised a family in a desperate attempt to break the cycle and give your children a better life. Your one child works in a grocery store and the other is a drug addict (not including the ones in prison). But perhaps your grandchildren will go to college. You seem confident that the American dream is still worth fighting for. All you have to do is turn on the TV to see proof that a man can come from the ghetto and rise up to become a media star. Or even better, start a fastfood chain and hire the stars for the commercials.

The lobsters are quite tasty after all. It must be the slow-cooking. Over dinner we discuss the usual. You talk about your plans for striking it rich. All you need is a product to sell. Veggie burgers. Insomniac tapes. Hair replacement. Chocolate-covered Jesuses. Edible dildos. All you need is the start-up money. Our host snorts as he devours the biggest of the lobsters, washing it down with overpriced French wine. I ask him how his family made their money. Their American dream come true. He burps and garbles: Ant food.

Ant food?

Made it big during the Depression.

Selling ant food?

He clears the fatty flesh in his throat with a long chug of wine and softly enunciates: *Canned* food. Big business during the depression. Still is. The company long since sold. The money invested. Conservatively.

You are duly impressed. You really believe that the best man wins. I interrupt provocatively: Okay, so even if it *is* the best man who wins...what about the losers? What are they supposed to do?

They win at something else, you say. Everybody is best at something.

I would like to tell you that in that case you are best at living in the gutter, where capitalism and Catholicism meet. But I hold my tongue. Anyway, I find these utopian discussions boring. I'm not trying to change the world. This silly world is my inspiration, but creation is the only noble cause. I bring the subject around to art. Where is art going? What's really new, and how can I become a part of it?

You say provocatively that I am full of shit. I don't really care about art. I just wanna make money. Like you.

I enlighten you. Money is not the purpose. You can't take it with you to the grave. Our host burps. I insist that the objective is to create something truly great, beautiful, and essential. Something that will live on.

Bullshit, you say. It's just vanity. It's all about being a famous notable, better than the common lot, the talk of cocktail parties so Mom and Dad in Suburbia can say my son the playwright is on Broadway. It's easy to sneer at money when there's enough bread and wine and a roof over your head.

Ah! But I know what it's like to be poor, I say with pride. I know what it's like to be vulnerable. After all, I don't even have health insurance.

You laugh. Neither do you. But you don't have a rich family in Suburbia to fall back on when you need that operation.

Our host clutches his chest.

My family is not rich, I pronounce defensively. They're middle class. You know, the ones who pay the taxes to support your kids in prison.

You stand up. You are seething. You call me a... a racist!

Our host tries to settle us down. He puts on a recording of baroque organ music. The good old days of the king of instruments when kings were kings and paupers nervous. When great art flourished under church and monarchy. When everyone knew their place under God and poor boys would pump the king of instruments for a few crusts of bread and a prayer. Our host studied history in college. He has age-old solutions for everything. Bring back the monarchies and there will be no more unemployment. Abolish the minimum wage and the welfare problem is solved.

You and I have lost our appetite. We sit across from each other brooding over our wine while our host, having cleaned out his giant lobster, devours what's left of our smaller ones. The claws, he says, are the best part.

We end up in the living room with the TV on. At last, something we can all agree on. The evening news entertains us with images from around the globe. More of the same. The latest war. The latest earthquake. What's hot and what's not. The trial of the century and who's fucking who in Hollywood. During the diaper commercial I unglue my eyes and look around the room. You and he watch gaga like they were telling you about something that would make you live forever. Maybe it's the sound of synthetic music, a pre-programmed lullaby, or maybe it's the picture of us gathered around, mouths hanging open, but it suddenly occurs to me that we – I, you, and he – all of us are nothing more than a bunch of babies playing at being grown-up. You, a baby with a gun. Me, a baby with a pen. And him, our host, the biggest baby of them all, a baby with an inheritance. Here we are. The children of the classes. Seems like for as long as the monkeys have been wearing clothes and calling it civilization, we have been playing this grown-up game that each generation inherits from their parents, dressing the part and believing it. Our host, whose attention span is not quite up to the demands of the commercial, clutches the mayonnaisy remote control in his lap and flicks through the channels. More commercials. And more commercials. One commercial after another until he leaves it on a commercial about the need for advertising. He likes the music. He gets up and leaves the room. You and I stare at the remote, eyeing the little gadget that gives control. Power at last. One of us would grab it if it weren't so mayonnaisy.

Just as we're both about to lunge for it, our host comes back with dessert. Drugs. A small phial of cocaine and a large fruit bowl of marijuana. His stash, but all of it purchased by you through your connections – with his money. Our host invites me, the artist, to decorate the table.

I roll the joints and cut the lines. It is decorative, at least. This genre celebrates the sublime. Our modern deity.

As we consume we become friends again. The spirit of competition is lost in a haze of space and time. No one wins. We are all the best in our own little world.

Suddenly the music coming from the TV transcends. The three tones of the station identification sound like bells tolling in the universe. We are traveling into the future as we regress from the infantile into a fetal state. 2001, a drug odyssey.

You and I are no longer at war. We are thankful to our host for his generosity, for taking care of us. And there he sits in his throne, a great big fat monkey king. Picking and scratching. The meal is complete. The entertainment petering out. He suggests I play the piano. I oblige with a Beethoven sonata, but I can't seem to get past the first bar. Drugs have turned my artistic perfectionism into an obsessive disorder. Minds are wandering. Farts overheard. Beethoven and I lose our audience to the lowest common denominator. Bodily functions. And now, for the finale.

You are summoned to the bedroom. But not until you clean the dirty dishes. I go off to put the finishing touches on my hallucinogenic screenplay. You go off to the dirty dishes. And our host carries his enormous body off to the bed. He lies there stark naked in his plush white coffin waiting for you to give him his last rites. Sprinkle him with your holy water and cover him with embalming fluid.

You are tired. The wife kicked you out of her apartment last week for stealing her welfare check. She changed the locks on the door. You have been sleeping wherever you can. You would like to just go to sleep, alone, in a nice big bed, and forget. But duty calls. You will survive. Any way that you can. Whatever it takes. Only the strong survive in your world. And may the best man win.

Our host graciously leaves the money in an ashtray next to the bed. You think about taking it without performing your duties and leaving him for dead. But you have to think of the future. Your plans. With his money. Much smarter to give him his jollies, take the money, and then on the way out steal some of those nice silver spoons he wants you to polish. He won't notice if a few are missing. Take what you can get. But give him what he wants. And maybe you'll get yours in the end. For now, he's got the power. So you better play nice.

Our host seems asleep or half dead as you piss in his face. The only way you can tell he's alive is by his erection. Okay, so you're a prop in his theater of the absurd. Aren't we all? You wank off to mental images of strangling your wife and come in his face. It's all over before anyone can yell encore. At the moment he tries to secrete his own nasty juices, his flabby chest buckles, and he drops dead with only a single squirt to show for it.

You back away. He was certainly more dangerous alive, but now he incites your worst fears. A dead man. Long live the king!

Your fear is of the police and the white man's justice. Would they believe that you were an innocent bystander? You're not gonna hang around to find out. You take the money and run. I bump into you on your way out. You lie. You say that our host is not dead, just sound asleep, figuring that no one is going to believe that you didn't kill him for the money. But you are mistaken. Our host is not dead. Not yet.

It was a heart attack. But not enough to kill him. In the hospital we sit on opposite sides of his bed, staring across at each other, waiting for him to give up and die already. It's high time we got something for our trouble. We have been his loyal subjects, his friends. He certainly won't leave the money to his family. Not after the way they've shunned him since Mother died. They couldn't deal with a faggot for a brother. Mother never knew, although they tried to tell her. They wanted his share of her inheritance. But Mother could not understand what they were saying about her beloved, her favorite. *Gay* meant stylish when she was young. A flair for dancing. She left him the biggest share.

And now we wait to get it. But which one will he leave it to? To me, because I am the artist and the kings have always supported the bourgeoisie in their artistic endeavors. Or to you, because you gave him the only real joy in his unfulfilling life. You pissed in his face.

Our host lies there trying to breathe. Our nerves are on edge. The nurse won't even let us smoke. The doctor with a concerned grim expression tells us that the patient's arteries can simply take no more. A bypass will not be enough. The heart is severely damaged. A life of excess has finally taken its toll. Too much rich food. Too much of everything. You insist it was the lobster that killed him. I insist it was the mayonnaise. We can't both be right. Our voices get louder. You say how typical of the upper class to kill themselves with pure gluttony. It serves the fucker right to die gagging on lobster. I disagree. Lobster is all-natural even if it's full of cholesterol. It's the mayonnaise that's deadly. The hydrogenated soybean oil clogs the cardiovascular network (never mind what the carcinogenic preservatives do). The nurse tells us to lower our voices. The doctor reminds us that the man is not dead yet. There is still hope. The miracles of modern medicine are to be performed. For a price. Everything that can be done to him will be done to him to save his precious life. He's fully covered with mounds of insurance. He'll get the best of care. He's got a private room, the best in the house. Round-the-clock private nursing. The best specialists. I can't help but think about how awful it will be to have to share a room when I'm on my deathbed. You're thinking about the people lying on the floor in the emergency room. The doctor assures us, our revered friend is in safe hands. He'll be subjected to a battery of tests. Painful horrible tests. But the best money can buy.

The holy man is called in. He starts reciting some high-church shit, holier-than-thou Episcopalian well-connected whites go to heaven while the heathens may also go to heaven but are kept in servants' quarters. This infuriates you because you are a Catholic. On the ambiguous left wing of the denomination. God loves everybody the same no matter what complexion or class. Except of course if they don't repent for their sins or if they don't kiss the pope's jeweled ring or if they are not Catholic or if they're perverts or worse, atheists. Then they go to hell for sure. This infuriates me. I mention that it is quite typical of the lower classes to be mindlessly sucked in by the very patriarchy that enslaves them. Work yourselves to death for us in the here and now and you will be rewarded for eternity. Nice.

You stand defiant, ready to slug me in defense of your bloody Jesus. I cool you out with spiritual catchphrases that I picked up from some new-age cult. This reassures you that I am at least not an atheist. Actually I'm not really sure. I mean I guess I'm spiritual like the next guy. I mean like I did write that rock opera that ended with this very hallucinogenic godlike vision. It was vague, but I think I got the point across, postmodern and all that, ya know like we're not really so in control as we think cause like there are higher forces like call them supernatural or something so there's ya know like no real point to anything which is the whole point ya know like stop trying to make sense and all that. I tried to get the opera produced. The producers said it was like hip and all that but the music didn't sound like the musicals that were already out there. I said that's because it's an opera. But maybe they were right. Maybe I should finally rewrite it. Yeah. I think this whole death thing could be really current, relevant. Ya know like with all these people like dying and all –

You tell me to shut the fuck up. I tell you your mother's a whore. You slug me. I fall back. You fall forward. Your weight on our host's big fat belly is the straw that breaks the camel's back. That's right. *You* killed him! You with your lowlife mentality, with your common man brutality. He should have never let you in the house. You wanna act like an animal? Then stay in the fucking gutter where you belong! My face is damaged. Your mother's virginity is damaged. And our host looks up in terror with open eyes at something truly awful.

He burps and dies. The party's over.

At the funeral the electric organ plays our host's favorite. Some baroque thing with lots of ornaments. His family sits in their pews with proud stoic phony expressions plastered on their freshly-scrubbed pink faces. I recite a poem I composed especially for the occasion. Death is an endless source of inspiration, ain't it? Maybe I should write a whole book of death poems. Would it sell?

You sit in the back row. You weren't even invited. You seem out of place in your street clothes sitting among the formal attire. I'm surprised they let you in.

The moment of truth finally comes. It is just the two of us at the reading of the will. The family does not make an appearance, so we are reassured that they will not be getting the money. Hell, they don't need the money. You and I have big plans. I shall now be able to produce my own screenplay independent of the studios and create something really new, something really great, something really beautiful, but not necessarily beautiful because beauty is not necessarily relevant in our time. Either that or I'll give it all up, get married, settle down with a nice yuppy and live the suburban life. Buy an old house to renovate and decorate. Raise dogs. Be just like my parents except with better taste. And you? You'll sell everything that our host cherished so much, even the rare antiques, so that you can buy some hideous house and plenty of ostentatious furniture and showy cars and open some auto-body chain or a burger franchise or a small amusement park or whatever tacky schemes you've been brewing all these years. The question for the moment is still: Who gets the money? Our future depends on it.

You? I? Maybe our host realized in the end that it's time for a change. Time to divide the spoils equally among everyone because there's more than enough to go around.

He leaves it all to his nieces and nephews, every last penny and every last silver spoon. It is his last and greatest wish that they will maintain the legacy and pass it on to their sons and daughters.

## The Anonymous Ball

It happened so unexpectedly. Out of nowhere. Like it dropped out of the sky. They were walking along as they do every Sunday morning. Jonathan as usual a few paces ahead, nervously walking and then stopping to look at something, ignoring Tommy. As usual. They were half fighting. It's not really fighting. Often they get into these tiffs. Tommy feels ignored. Jonathan is more interested in the facades on the buildings then in Tommy and his silly cruisy stories. Tommy thinks that Jonathan is punishing him for slutting around the night before. Jonathan can be heartless sometimes. Scolding Tommy over breakfast he said: "Go ahead. Be a slut. All you want. Just don't come crying to me when you catch something." Tommy tends towards hypochondria. He carries a phial of hydrogen peroxide with him so he can gargle immediately after sucking cock. When he gets crabs he locks himself in his room for a month like a leper. Every time he gets a bruise he's sure it's KS. "Why do you slut around if it makes you so nervous?" Maybe because he doesn't have architecture to obsess over. He has nothing except his boring job and the boring TV when he comes home. Cruising around makes him feel alive. He sneaks off at night while Jonathan is working late at his drafting which is most every night. He puts on his cruisy jeans and his cruisy leather jacket, grabs the condoms and the phial of hydrogen peroxide and quietly sneaks out the door and usually ends up not far, just around the corner in the playground which gets hopping after midnight. Jonathan will endlessly warn him about the playground. "That's exactly where I would go if I were a fagbasher looking for some fag to bash." There have been a number of incidents, but not enough to keep the men away. Something about a playground. The men can't resist it after dark anymore than the boys can during the day.

It could have been just a coincidence. After all no one said anything. No one screamed *faggot die!* Just an innocent little baseball flying through the sky and landing on Tommy's head just as they were standing in front of the playground. Jonathan photographing an old doorframe across the street. Tommy standing there on the sidewalk behind him, complaining about being ignored. And then boom and the next thing he knew he was on the ground with Jonathan bending over him frantically stroking his face. "Tommy, Tommy! Speak to me! Tommy, Tommy!" He opened his eyes and for a second didn't know where he was or who the face was staring into his. "Tommy, Tommy!" He recognizes his name. His vision is blurry, but even before his eyes come together to focus on the face he knows the name and he speaks it. "Jonathan," he whispers with what feels like his last breath. And the man picks him up in his arms and kisses his face and rocks him like a baby. "Oh my boy, my love. I thought you were dead." No one is around and it seems for this one tender moment that no one else exists except Jonathan and Tommy. Like all the millions of people were wiped out by germ warfare and the two lovers are the last two people left on the planet. Two men, so there's no chance of continuing the species.

He picks him up and carries him home. The streets are silent. In a Latino neighborhood like this, Sunday morning is quiet. The people are either in church or sleeping off Saturday night or both. No one was even in the playground when the ball was thrown. If it hadn't happened right there in front of the playground they might not have called it fagbashing. No one said anything to that effect, but it felt like that. The ball hit him like someone threw it at him aiming to hit the faggot in the head. Maybe this is paranoid. But carrying him home Jonathan imagines he's running through the enemy lines with his wounded soldier buddy in his arms.

In their apartment Tommy spends the afternoon on the couch with an ice pack on his head. "I could have been killed," he tells me on the phone. Jonathan is in the other room working at his drafting table, but every few minutes he looks in on the invalid, strokes his face and coos at him. Tommy is mopey and grouchy as always, but perkier than usual. His heart is pumping in the warm embrace of knowing that he is loved. His man rescued him. His man loves him, cares about him. Couldn't live without him. Tommy tells the phone: "You don't know how much he loves you until the ball drops out of the sky. And then it could be too late." Jonathan comes in from the other room with some tea and chocolates. "I think we should call the doctor," Jonathan says in the background. "No doctors. Please, no doctors," Tommy whines. "I'm fine. Really, I'm fine." Doctors make him nervous. His whine is coquettish, like he can't get enough of being worried over. For a change he's not indulging his hypochondria. He's not kvetching over himself because he has someone else to do it for him.

The phone is held away as they kiss. Ken, your life is lived in third person. You are an incurable voyeur. I hear Jonathan promise not to ignore Tommy. And I hear Tommy promise to stay away from the playground. I call into the cold telephone: I'll let you two go. I can hear them kissing again.